THE WOODS

THE WOODS

Vanessa Savage

GRAND CENTRAL
PUBLISHING

NEW YORK   BOSTON

Copyright © 2020 by Vanessa Savage
Cover design by Faceout Studio. Cover copyright © 2020 by Hachette Book Group, Inc.

Grand Central Publishing
Hachette Book Group
1290 Avenue of the Americas, New York, NY 10104
grandcentralpublishing.com
twitter.com/grandcentralpub

Originally published in 2020 by Sphere in the United Kingdom.

First U.S. Edition: August 2020

Grand Central Publishing is a division of Hachette Book Group, Inc. The Grand Central Publishing name and logo is a trademark of Hachette Book Group, Inc.

The publisher is not responsible for websites (or their content) that are not owned by the publisher.

The Hachette Speakers Bureau provides a wide range of authors for speaking events. To find out more, go to www.hachettespeakersbureau.com or call (866) 376-6591.

Library of Congress Cataloging-in-Publication Data
Names: Savage, Vanessa, author.
Title: The woods / Vanessa Savage.
Description: First U.S. edition. | New York : Grand Central Publishing, 2020. | Summary: "There's a lot from Tess's childhood that she would rather forget. The family who moved next door and brought chaos to their quiet lives. The two girls who were murdered, their killer never found. But the only thing she can't remember is the one thing she wishes she could. Ten years ago, Tess's older sister died. Ruled a tragic accident, the only witness was Tess herself, but she has never been able to remember what happened that night in the woods. Now living in London, Tess has resolved to put the trauma behind her. But an emergency call from her father forces her back to the family home, back to where her sister's body was found, and to the memories she thought were lost forever."– Provided by publisher.
Identifiers: LCCN 2019050642 | ISBN 9781538730126 (trade pbk.) |
ISBN 9781538730119 (ebook)
Subjects: LCSH: Psychological fiction. | GSAFD: Suspense fiction.
Classification: LCC PR6119.A94 W665 2020 | DDC 823/.92–dc23
LC record available at https://lccn.loc.gov/2019050642

ISBNs: 978-1-5387-3012-6 (trade pbk.), 978-1-5387-3011-9 (ebook)

Printed in the United States of America

LSC-C

10 9 8 7 6 5 4 3 2 1

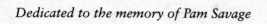

Dedicated to the memory of Pam Savage

"You have to be brutal, cut right back to the bone," he says to the girl.

She's hesitant, blades held close, but not making the cut. "Won't it kill it?"

His hand covers hers, forces her to cut. "No. It'll give it the chance to bloom."

"Once upon a time, two girls went into the woods and only one came out..."

"No. I don't like this story."

"You have to listen, Tess. You have to get to the end of the story."

THE WOODS

AUGUST 2008

"Can you take us through what happened after the wedding?"

There are two policemen in my room, one sitting by the bed in a crumpled shirt, one pacing the room, watching me. I'm in a private ward and there's a uniformed officer outside—I saw him when the other two came in; he was talking to Dad and Julia. Dad was still wearing his suit, his jacket draped around Julia's shoulders, white carnation drooping in the buttonhole. They both looked like they'd been crying and I wanted to call out that I was fine, but the pacing detective closed the door on them.

"I don't remember," I say, voice hoarse. My throat aches and my head is throbbing, the stitches tight and tender. It hurts to try to remember. It should have been such a happy day—for Dad and Julia, even if the rest of us weren't feeling it.

"You went into the woods..." the sitting detective says. I don't recall their names. They introduced themselves but I don't remember.

My foot is bandaged and feels hot and swollen. Just a sprain, though, from the fall: I was lucky, they said.

"I was at the wedding, I drank too much champagne, and I went to lie down for a bit. I don't remember anything after that."

They've cleaned me up and stitched my head but there's still dirt under my nails. Or is it dried blood? Oh God. Vomit rises, sour at the back of my throat. "Where's Dad? I want to see my dad." My voice breaks.

"He's right outside, Tess. He'll be in in a second. We're trying to understand what you and your sister were doing in the woods near Dean House, some distance from your home. There are at least two hours unaccounted for, after anyone at the wedding last saw you and Arabella."

Dean House: Bella and I were there, but that was last night—the night *before* the wedding. *That* night is all so clear. Not the wedding—pretty much everything about today is a blur, but last night...

Tess, wake up.

The voice makes me jump, but it's not a whisper from the corner of the room, it's an echo: Bella's voice, the night before the wedding, pulling me from a dream of sex and Norse gods. The night before the wedding that we'd all been dreading. I had been sweating, skin damp and clinging to the sheet, the heatwave still going on. I wasn't shivering like I am now. The storm didn't break until the night of the wedding.

Bella was dressed in shorts and a T-shirt and I twisted to look at the clock, thinking I'd overslept and should already be at the hall, trussed up in my mint lace bridesmaid's dress. But it was only four o'clock, still dark outside and hours from morning. I'd stayed up too late, trying to make inroads into the mountain of reading I had from school that had been gathering dust since the beginning of the summer holidays.

"Can't you sleep again?" I pushed the sheets off me and sat up. All this, I remember, the crisp cotton of the sheet brushing against my legs, the groggy disorientation as I was pulled from sleep.

She shook her head. "I need to tell you something."

"Go on then."

"No—not here," she said, pulling on my arm.

"Where are we going? We have to be up in four hours to get ready."

"This can't wait. Come on."

I was thinking I was still in that dream as we walked up the lane in the middle of the night—Bella in shorts, me in my pajamas and flip-flops. I was thinking it was still a dream and, any minute, some Norse god would appear with Max's face and sweep me off into the woods.

Max. Where is Max now?

The night air was thick and still. Hot, even at that hour. It felt wrong. Unusual for August: there should have been rain in the air, clouds to cover the stars and moon. The heat and dryness made it seem like I'd been transported somewhere else in my dreams, somewhere with warm seas, twisted olive trees, cicadas, and bright lizards swarming the walls.

Bella stopped by a crumbling, ivy-choked wall and turned back to look at me. She bent down, laced her hands together. "I'll boost you over," she whispered.

Dean House watched from behind the wall, windows black. My scalp prickled and I could feel the hairs rise as I figured out where we were. No way.

"Not scared, are you?" she said, a challenge in her voice.

I remember all this, I think, but I'm not sure I'm remembering it right. There's a woodenness to the memory that makes me think I'm missing something. The dream I had seems more real than this.

"What is it?" the detective says, leaning forward. His hair is thinning on top; I can see the light from the fluorescent bulb shining on his scalp. "Have you remembered something?"

I shake my head. He doesn't want to know about the day before the wedding. It's not relevant. It's not. Then why does my chest feel tight, full of fluttering fear? Why is the night at Dean House so vivid and the wedding a blank?

I look up at the detective. "I remember going upstairs and then I woke up in the ambulance."

I pick at my nails—is it my blood? My hands are shaking.

I was scared. I didn't want to go in there. Bella looked on the verge of tears and I wanted to be back in my bed.

The night grew quieter as we dropped into the garden. Even my breath, quick and panicked, sounded muffled. That house had always been the haunted house when we were little kids, daring each other to open the front gate and go up the path. I never did it. I've never been the brave kid. Then Julia and Greg Lewis bought it, and what was it then?

Bella marched away around the house and I hurried after her, tripping over tangled tree roots hidden in the weeds. I knew this garden well but it was the house I was afraid of. Bella didn't stay in the garden, she went right to the front door and opened it. It wasn't locked.

Wait, why wasn't it locked?

I'm wondering now if any of it was real, or if it was all part of a dream—haven't I had this dream before? The house, a rainy night...a scream hidden by the roar of a monsoon-like downpour?

"Bella, what are you doing?"

She glanced back at me and then stepped inside the house.

I can't tell the detectives any of this; I don't want to get my sister into trouble. I followed her up the dark hallway, hissing her name, flinching at every creak of the floorboards. What if someone was there? What if Greg came back and found us in his house? He could have had a heart attack.

Bella flitted like a ghost in front of me in her white T-shirt, disappearing through a door on the left. I glanced nervously up the stairs—what monster exactly did I think I'd find?—and followed my sister.

The room was like something out of Miss Havisham's house. Everything coated in dust, cobwebs hanging from the corners, lit up from the moonlight shining in the uncovered window. There was an empty mug on a side table, a book facedown on the arm of a chair, a pair of shoes lined up in front of the cold fireplace. That was fine, perfectly ordinary, but it was all covered in dust like no one had lived there for months. That seemed impossible, I remember. It shouldn't have been so dusty. Greg hadn't been gone that long. And despite everything, it made me feel *guilty*—that no one was looking out for Greg, that no one was helping him while his house crumbled around him.

The goose bumps rose on my arms again. Bella was standing in front of the back window, pressed right up against the glass, fogging it with her breath, looking out into the woods. I could see her footprints, a clean path through the dust on the floors. Too much evidence we'd been there.

My stomach lurches and I have the urge to jump out of my hospital bed and rush back to the house to clean everything we touched. Or have they already been there? Do they already know we trespassed there?

"I'm sorry," Bella whispered—whispers still from the shadows in the corner of my hospital room. Her shoulders were hunched and I think she was crying. "I'm so sorry, Tess, but you need to see. You need to *wake up*."

I can taste sour champagne in my mouth, and mud and dead leaves. I can feel them on my face still. I keep touching my cheeks, expecting to find them covered in leaves and dirt. I was found in the woods near Dean House, but I don't remember how I got there.

I should tell them we were in the house the night before the wedding. We didn't do anything wrong other than sneaking in. We didn't steal or break anything. It had nothing to do with what happened after the wedding. I should tell them. But...

"I'm sorry," I say.

wake up

"I really don't remember anything."

I remember the taste of mud and leaves, but I don't remember being in the woods in the storm. I do remember the ambulance, the paramedics wheeling me into the hospital on a stretcher. Dad and Julia were there, and Max. But...

I blink and see a flash—Bella in the woods, sprawled on the ground, facing away from me.

"Wait," I say as the detectives move toward the door.

Another flash. Me crawling toward her, reaching out my hand to touch her shoulder.

"Where's Bella? Is my sister okay?"

Clutching her shoulder, rolling her onto her back and...

wake up

NOW

CHAPTER 1

"Wake up, Tess." Sophie leans in closer to me. "Stealth approach, two o'clock."

I blink and pull myself back into the present, glancing over my shoulder to see two men approaching our table, creased shirts and red faces a sure sign they've been here a while. Not bad-looking, but neither does anything for me.

"Are you interested?"

Sophie pulls a face and shakes her head.

I grin. "Okay—so who am I?"

Sophie looks at me. "You're...Tanya Nibbington, a tree surgeon from Norfolk, here visiting a friend, celebrating graduating from tree surgeon college."

My smile widens. "There's a tree surgeon college? In Norfolk?"

She shrugs. "What am I?"

"Maeve Larson, undercover detective over from Sweden. Working on a case."

She drains her drink. "Nice."

"Or..." They're almost through the crowd to our table. "Or we could just tell them to buzz off and enjoy our girls' night."

"Is that what you want? If you want to go somewhere quieter and talk...?" She says it quietly and seriously and it makes me aware of how off I've been tonight.

I'm not being fair. We play this game a lot. We come to this pub a lot. It's full of city boys, looking for a pickup. I'm rarely interested, but since Sophie turned thirty she's become keener than ever to "meet the one" and we're here for her. But I don't think he's going to be here, in a sweaty shirt, five pints down on a Tuesday night.

I squeeze her hand. "Don't be daft. I'm fine, and we don't want to miss the chance of finding your Prince Charming, do we?"

"It's all right for you, Tess, you're twenty-six. Oceans of time before you're old and wrinkled and on the shelf like me."

I laugh at her. Sophie looks about twenty-two.

"But really?" I say, nodding toward the approaching sharks.

She sighs. "You're right, you're right. We should be going anyway—I've got twelfth graders first thing in the morning and I won't survive the class with a hangover."

"Ladies..." Creased shirt number one has reached the table. He crouches down, drapes his arms across our chairs. He smells of beer and sweat.

"Did you want our table?" I ask. "We're just leaving."

I stand up just as creased shirt number two arrives and manage to bump into him.

"Ah—don't go. We wanted to buy you a drink."

Creased shirt number one has said something to make Sophie laugh and I roll my eyes.

"Come on, Maeve Larson," I say, pulling on her arm. "We've got school in the morning."

"School?" This is from creased shirt number two, sounding alarmed. "You two are still in *school*?"

I swallow the urge to laugh. The lighting isn't that dim in here— how much have they had to drink?

"That's right," I say. "We're both fifteen. Still want to buy us that drink?"

"You are such a cow," Sophie says after they've fled, stumbling over chairs in their haste to get away from us. "He wasn't bad close up."

"Oh, please—you would have hated yourself in the morning. And he would never have called again."

"But I wanted to be Maeve Larson, top detective with fourteen brothers and sisters. And you—I would have called you Nibs as a nickname and you could have told them all about your charmed life as..."

"A single, broke woman. Living in a one-bedroom flat. Who has to be up for school in the morning to teach five classes of snarky teenagers."

"Ugh. The truth does not make for a sexy story. Although do I really want fourteen brothers and sisters? Sometimes I wish I was an only child. My brother is twenty-five going on twelve and a total pain in the ass most of the time."

I pause by the door to stare at a blond girl walking away from me. It's another game I play a lot—the pounding heart, the twist in my gut when I see a blond girl in skinny jeans, or hear a laugh that sounds familiar, the tilt of a head. Sometimes I make myself look away. Sometimes I follow her, just to check, just to see...

Of course it can't be her. Could never have been my sister.

"Shit," Sophie mutters, going pale and touching my arm. "Sorry, Tess. I didn't think—my crass remark about wanting to be an only child..."

I sometimes wish I'd never told Sophie about Bella—it's such a tragic mess. It's easier to be what I pretend to be to the rest of the world, my own permanent version of our games: an only child, a city girl with a nice flat and a good job.

"Oh God, I don't want to go to school tomorrow," Sophie says as we walk toward the bus stop.

I laugh and tuck my arm in hers. "A sentiment echoed by every kid we're teaching tomorrow."

"At least we get paid for it, I suppose. And I do love it most of the time."

"Do you? Really love teaching?"

"Of course." She sounds surprised. "Why on earth would I put myself through all the crap bits if I didn't love it for the good bits?"

Do I love it? Even the good bits? Have I ever *loved* teaching, like properly "it's-my-vocation" loved it? It's a question I've been asking myself too often lately.

"Do you want to stay at my place tonight?" I say as I see a bus heading toward us. "It's not late—we can be sensible and drink tea, but continue the evening."

I'm feeling...melancholy. Flat. None of the night-out buzz I felt earlier, getting ready for two-for-one happy hour with my best friend.

"Aw, Tess, I can't. I haven't got any of my stuff with me and I can't go to school tomorrow dressed like this." She gestures down at her sequined skirt.

I smile. I laughed when she turned up earlier in sequins and high heels. If it's over the top for a Tuesday night in town, it's *definitely* over the top for teaching. "That's fine. It was just a thought."

"Are you okay? You've been a bit down tonight."

"Things are...I've been having bad dreams. Bad thoughts that keep creeping in and..." Sophie frowns and I shake my head. "No, don't worry. I shouldn't have had gin-based cocktails, that's all. Gin makes me maudlin."

"But it's not only tonight..." Her voice trails off and she sighs. "No, sorry. Not the time. But let's catch up tomorrow, okay?"

She gets on her bus and I wave as it signals to pull away.

"Good night, Maeve Larson—I love you and your fourteen brothers and sisters!" I shout, and I see her laugh and blow a kiss through the window as the bus accelerates away.

My smile fades and I pull my coat closed as I wait at the empty shelter for my own bus and the bad thoughts crowd in around me to keep me company. I'm lucky, I tell myself. I have a good job— a great job. I have amazing friends. A flat of my own. My life is good. It is. All I need to do is believe it.

CHAPTER 2

I'm late. I'm bloody late. I took forever to fall asleep last night and when I did my slumber was filled with tangled fragments of dark dreams that kept jerking me awake.

My phone buzzes—a message from Sophie: *Where are u? Not still sleeping off the cocktails?????!*

I call her. "I overslept! Can you—shit!" I bang my leg on the table and lean down to rub my calf through my trousers. "Can you cover for me?"

"Again? Oh Christ, Tess . . . I'll try."

Eight forty. Shit. It's the third time this term I've been late and we're only five weeks in. Sophie's got her own class to teach—I can't expect her to keep this from the head of the department for me.

The anxious knot in my stomach grows as I wait at the bus stop and it passes nine o'clock. There are going to be twenty-three teenagers waiting at school for their English lesson and I'm still fifteen minutes away. I've already had one verbal warning; this time it's going to be a written one, a permanent warning on my record. I'm tempted to call in sick, pretend I was too ill to phone earlier, but I've already done that twice this term. Two missed days, three late days in less than half a term. I can't lose this job. I can't.

The bus comes and, despite my anxiety, I'm tempted to let it drive by. Same route to work, same walk at the other end. Every day, the same. I get this urge every so often to get on a different bus, ride it to the end of the route and see where I end up. Walk away from the school and the sick feeling I get in my gut when I sit in front of my first class, feeling like a fraud. What am I *doing*? That's what I think on those days.

On the bus, I close my eyes and feel myself drifting, jerking awake with a start as my phone starts ringing at the bottom of my bag, a harsh interruption that has my fellow passengers staring at me. I fumble for it, hunched over, pausing before answering when I see it's my dad.

"Tess?" His voice is faint, muffled.

"What's wrong, Dad?" I know he's not ringing for a casual chat. That's our Sunday-night routine, ten minutes of talking where we fill the silence but say nothing at all.

"It's . . . Julia. She's home."

There's too long a silence as my brain scrabbles to make sense of his words. "Home? She's better?"

His turn for silence. "No . . . there's nothing more they can do. She wants to die at home."

Breath gone, I lean back in the seat. It shouldn't be a shock. Julia has been slowly dying for the past year. I've seen it on my too-infrequent visits to see her in the hospital. Less Julia, more shadow each time. But still . . . had I thought she would go on fighting forever? Maybe I had—she's always been so bright and alive. All my most vivid memories of her from the beginning are of her bringing our house back to life—against our will at first. Well, mine and Bella's at least. The three of us, after my mother died, were drifting along living a half-life, then along came Julia, so vibrant, a whirl of glaring color impossible to ignore or freeze out and, God, Bella and I resented that. We were so horribly hostile toward her at the beginning, but she never gave up trying, our so very not-wicked stepmother.

"Will you come home?"

Home? My throat closes at the thought. Go back to the house, to the village, to that fishbowl where everyone knows me and everyone knows what happened to Bella? I can't be anonymous there, can't be safe and invisible like I am here. If I go back home, will they all be there—Sean and Jack and Max and Lena? I can't. Christ, what a reunion that would be. I can't do it—can't gather round Dad and Julia to watch Julia die when the last time we were all together was to watch them get married. The gap where Bella should be would be too huge and glaring. I just can't.

"I... I can't. I have work. It's midway through the term and..."

"Please, Tess, she has no one else. Come for a weekend, at least. You haven't been back here in so long. Jack and Sean... they won't return my calls. I even tried tracking Greg down but no one seems to have any idea where he is. I've left messages for Max and Lena—their parents can't get back from Spain until next month and that might be... I don't want her to die alone."

Jack and Sean—no, of course *they* wouldn't bother, not even with their mother dying.

"Dad, I..." My voice trails off. What excuse can I possibly give?

"The doctor says she has weeks at the most."

He doesn't need to say anything else. Last chance, last chance for all of us to say goodbye, to say anything. What would I give for a last chance with Bella? With my mother? A last chance to say all the things I never got to say because I thought I had forever to say them.

I glance up. We're approaching my stop. "Dad, I have to go. I'm already late."

"But Tess..."

"I'll call you later, okay?"

I end the call and drop the phone into my bag, getting up as the bus stops. God, I want to run back to my flat, climb into bed, still dressed, and pull the covers over my head. I force myself to take deep, slow breaths, pushing away the panic Dad's call has elicited. Stupid to be scared of a place. My fear is irrational, but it invades my dreams at night. Not the house, but the woods, that's where my dreams relentlessly take me. Back to West Dean, back to the woods, back to Bella's body.

*   *   *

I have a tenth-grade class first. By the time I get to school, the class is almost over. I rush in, apologizing to Sophie, who's struggling to make herself heard over the noise. Half the class are on their phones, the other half talking among themselves. Not a single one of them has their textbook open. *Sorry*, I mouth to Sophie, who raises her eyebrows and leans in toward me.

"You're lucky. I had twelfth graders first thing—I've left them with revision."

Lucky. Yes, that's me. I think of Dad's call and shake my head. I might have gotten away with it this time, but I can't ask for time off now, not when I'm sailing so close to the wind. Julia would understand.

Sophie comes over as I'm pouring a coffee in the staffroom at break time.

"What's going on, Tess? You look..."

A mess. I know I look a mess. Curls wild, eyes dark-circled, my shirt as creased as the ones those guys from last night were wearing. I stayed up way too late, putting off this morning and avoiding sleep.

"My stepmother's home. There's nothing more they can do."

"Oh God, I'm sorry."

I told Sophie about Julia's cancer on another melancholy gin night.

"Dad wants me to go home."

"Of course. Of course you should go home."

"How can I? I was late again this morning. Karen will be gunning for me if I ask for more time off."

"But it's Friday the day after tomorrow. You could go home for the weekend, couldn't you? It's not that far."

It is, though. Way too far. Not in physical distance. That's easy enough to travel.

Sophie doesn't understand. Because I haven't told her enough about Bella—how it happened, *what* happened. Or the wedding. Or Julia's family.

"I can't go back," I say, draining my coffee. "I have a mountain of marking to catch up on over the weekend. Lesson plans as well."

"But..."

The buzzer goes off, signaling the end of break. "Back to class," I say, walking away from Sophie.

She doesn't get it. I can't go back.

CHAPTER 3

wake up

That night I wake with a gasp, a shout echoing in my head. What was it? Was it the dream again—the abandoned house, Bella, the night before the wedding? I haven't had that dream in a while. Lately my dreams have been filled with Julia and school and...the woods. All my nightmares seem to end up there.

I've always slept so well here, in the city. In the stifling confines of the flat I live in, I've felt safe, the bad dreams held at bay. Boxed in, I can sleep, knowing there is no expanse of trees and emptiness outside, just more flats and houses, light and people everywhere. But recently...What's woken me again tonight? Is it worrying about work? About Julia?

It's two a.m. I came to bed after midnight, so I've slept for an hour or so. I think I slipped into a dream. It was the night before Dad and Julia's wedding again; Bella and I were in a garden...

I push the covers aside and get up. I have to distance myself from the dream before I can try to sleep again. The floorboards are cold. I curl my toes and grope under the bed for the slippers I kicked off only a couple of hours ago.

I make tea, taking comfort in the familiar steps: cup, milk, teabag. With my back to the window, sipping my tea, I can pretend it's day. That everyone around me is awake and I'm not alone.

When I turn, though, I spill it, my hand slipping as I see I'm not alone at all. Bella is there, silent and smiling. My breathing was too loud; the kettle boiling was too loud. I didn't hear her come in. Not awake then. This is still a dream. I look down at my wrist, stinging and red from the tea spill. A very vivid dream.

"Bella?" I whisper it, but in the dead of night it sounds as if I'm shouting.

She glances behind her at the dark window and then looks back at me. Her smile fades and I wonder if she sees it, the changes the years have wrought. When we were kids, Bella used to pinch my cheeks, laughing at how red they'd glow and stay glowing. Apple cheeks, wild curls, and freckles. That was me. She was the pale one, the skinny one, the one they always said should be a model with her blond hair and killer cheekbones. Now, ten years later, I know I look like a wild-haired imitation, a hollow, dried-up copy.

"God, I've missed you," I say, and my eyes burn.

"You're the one who left," Bella says, lifting a cigarette I didn't see her holding. She inhales, blows out a smoke ring. She's leaning against the windowsill, looking the same as she always did back then, skinny jeans and a tank top, bare feet, even though it's February and below zero. She grins and holds up the cigarette packet.

"Want one?"

I haven't smoked since I was sixteen but I can taste it. I want to. I want to stand in the kitchen of my flat at two in the morning smoking with my sister, pretend it was something we did together even though I never used to because I was the good girl.

"Couldn't you sleep?" she asks, and I shake my head, frowning.

This dream is too real. *Are you awake or asleep?* my mind whispers. Of course I'm asleep. How could Bella be here otherwise? All my dreams of Bella since the accident...they've always been about *after*, nightmares: I've never dreamed her alive, never talked to her. The longing to hold her again, not let her go, is fierce, a physical pang.

"Remember when we were kids?" she says, stubbing her cigarette out in a plant pot. I don't say anything—the plant's fake anyway. I don't like fake plants, don't see the point, but I inherited it with the flat. Here are your keys and a fake plant to welcome you. Like half of my day-to-day life, it's just there, existing unseen in the corner of my eye until now.

"Remember how you could never sleep until I came home?"

"I used to worry," I say. "I liked to stay awake until I heard you come in. Until I knew you were safe." I wipe a tear off my cheek as she sighs.

"Dad would go off to bed, trusting everything would be fine, but I'd stay awake and watch the minutes ticking away and wait. I'd imagine so many awful things happening as every minute past midnight ticked away."

"You always were an old woman for worrying," she says.

"I was right to worry, though, wasn't I?" I feel the heat rising in my cheeks. Funny, all these years I'd never realized how angry I am. I'm angry at how irresponsible she was.

"Are you still waiting?" she asks, and I frown.

"What do you mean?"

She leans in. I can smell cigarette smoke in her hair. I can hear her breathing, her breath overlapping mine. "Is that why you can't sleep now?"

I exhale, release it and reach out a hand, wishing I could touch her. It's Dad's phone call doing this. Calling me home. Making me remember.

I don't want to remember.

"You never came home," I say. "I waited and waited but you never came home. You know I can't sleep until you come home." Stupid tears won't stop now; they're filling my eyes so I can't see her properly. There are smudges on her tank top, dark mud on the knees of her torn jeans. They weren't there a minute ago. Her hair looks less smooth, it's tangled, leaves caught in it. A drop of blood trickles down her cheek. Wrong. I close my eyes and shake my head. I don't want to see her like this—I've spent years trying to erase that image. This is the way I last saw her, but I don't want to remember her like this. I open my eyes and she's bright, shining Bella again; beautiful, eighteen-year-old Bella.

"I'm sorry I died," she says. "I'm sorry I never came home."

I rub my eyes and press my hands to my aching head, touching the old scar on my forehead. She'll disappear again in a minute, fade away like she always does in dreams. "You never came home. How am I supposed to ever get to sleep again?"

"You can't," she says. "Not yet. Promises to keep, miles to go— like that poem, remember?" She steps closer and whispers her next words. "And Tess? Remember this as well. It wasn't an accident."

I wake with a gasp and sit bolt upright. My hand flies to my wrist, expecting the sting of a burn. I sniff the air and, for a second, swear I can smell cigarette smoke. I lurch out of bed, looking at the clock. It's two—same time as in the dream. There's no Bella in my flat, not even a sense of her. I shake myself. Of course there isn't.

I falter, though, when I go through to the kitchen to get a glass of water. There's a mug on the side, half-full of tea. When I touch it, it's warm and my wrist throbs with a remembered sting.

Not real, of course it wasn't real. But...it was so vivid. Was I sleepwalking? Talking out loud to a dream of my sister's ghost? I must have been.

I shiver, remembering her words. *It wasn't an accident.*

Why am I doing this to myself? Talking to Dad, thinking about the others, it's made me remember the aftermath of Bella's death, how I insisted something sinister must have happened, that it would take more than a stupid accident to kill my sister. Months of denial right up until the inquest findings. I've projected my own long-buried fears onto a figment of my imagination. Of course it was an accident. Of course it was.

CHAPTER 4

"Right—let's get straight on with it. Poetry today." I turn the pages in my poetry book to the page I've bookmarked. "This poem is called 'Sold,' by Paul Henry."

Someone in the front row actually yawns and I grip the book harder to resist the urge to chuck the damned thing at him. I barely slept after last night's dream, or hallucination, or whatever it was. And now I'm supposed to enthuse this eleventh-grade class about poetry?

I start reading the short poem and my throat gets tight halfway through. I've read this poem before, taught classes extracting every meaning and emotion from the poignant lines about a life embedded in the walls of a house, but today in my exhausted state the words stir up too many memories and thoughts of home, of Bella. My eyes are burning and I blink. When I look up, my voice trails off completely and I wonder if I'm so tired I've actually drifted into sleep, because for a split second the yawning boy turns into Bella sitting at the front of the class, leaves and twigs from the woods on the desk and an open poetry book in front of her. *Come home, Tess*, her voice whispers in my mind. *I'll wait for you in the woods.* I rub my eyes and shake my head but she won't stop. She won't shut up.

It wasn't an accident, she says. Over and over. The world spins and I lean forward, elbows on my desk, head in my hands.

"Um...Miss? Miss Cooper?"

I open my eyes and Bella's gone. Someone in the class giggles, someone else is on their feet.

"Are you okay, Miss?" It's Rebecca Martin asking, and there's laughter in her voice, a hint of glee as her teacher goes gaga. Don't they all long for this, some sign of weakness they can get their hooks into? Rebecca most of all.

I grit my teeth. "Sorry, I just...lost my train of thought for a second."

Rebecca laughs again, loud, derisive, joined by more of the class this time. *Gotcha*, her laughter says. "A second? You've been sitting with your head in your hands for, like, *ages*."

I stare at her, paralyzed. It would be Rebecca Martin, of course, with her sly smile, the whole class laughing now as she sets off again.

"Think you need a break, Miss—get yourself a Red Bull. Had a few too many last night, did you? Or was it this morning even?" Laugher rolls again through the classroom.

Suddenly, she's not Rebecca Martin and I'm not Miss Cooper, she's Lena and Nicole, she's every one of Bella's bitchy friends who'd laugh at me, make her embarrassed by me; all those girls who made my sister a stranger. I'm sixteen again, too fat in my school uniform, and there is Bella, dripping blood on her desk. I'm not going to let them do this to me again. I will not sit by quietly this time.

"Why don't you shut the fuck up?" I say to Rebecca/Lena/Nicole.

There's a gasp from someone.

"Excuse me?" Rebecca says half laughing, half shocked. I can only partly hear her through the buzzing in my head.

"Shut the fuck up, I said." I get up, my chair scraping across the floor. My head spins and I can feel Bella urging me on. *Go on, Tess, show them. Tell them.* "You have no idea what's going on in my life and you don't even care, do you? All I want is for you to give me a break and do your bloody work. And maybe, for once— just shut your damned mouth."

There's total silence now. I look down at the poetry book in my shaking hand but then Rebecca fucking Martin laughs again and my control snaps.

I march over to her desk and she gets up, as tall as me, taller than I was at sixteen. But her bravado is all fake as I grab hold of her stupid short tie and pull her forward until our foreheads are nearly touching.

"Seriously? You're still laughing? Will you still be laughing if I throw you through the fucking window?" I shove her backward and she falls, her chair clattering to the floor.

The silence is broken by someone shouting, "Miss has gone rabid!" It's a boy's voice, jubilant and scared all at once and it brings me back and Rebecca Martin isn't Lena or Nicole anymore, she's a scared-looking kid with tears in her eyes sprawled on the floor. Bella is gone from the desk next to her. Of course she is. She was never bloody there.

The door flies open and Sophie runs in, white-faced as she takes in the scene.

She puts her hand on my shoulder. "Tess?"

I reach out a hand to help Rebecca up, but she scrabbles away from me, fury and fear on her face, her cheeks burning red.

Sophie grips my shoulder harder and pulls me away. "What have you *done*, Tess?"

Oh God.

What have I *done*?

I go straight to Karen, my head of department, trying for damage limitation before the whole of the eleventh grade gets here with their own exaggerated versions, but I'm made to wait outside while Rebecca and Sophie are brought in before me.

"I'm so sorry...I didn't sleep well last night," I say as soon as I'm called in. "I had a call from my dad about my stepmother. She's...she's dying."

Karen stands behind the desk, her hands gripping the edge. The way she looks at me makes me aware of the shadows under my eyes I can't cover with makeup, my unwashed hair.

"I'm sorry," I say again.

Why did it have to be Rebecca Martin? She sits at the front of the class, all hostile eyes, challenging everything I say, criticizing me with a look every time I fumble over a lesson or forget where we are in a book. The sick feeling is back, rising higher until it's difficult to breathe. Rebecca Martin, whose parents come storming in here every time their precious daughter gets into trouble, always blaming someone else, insisting on an investigation into whoever was unfortunate enough to give her a detention this time.

Karen looks nearly as upset as I know I should be. "Tess, this goes beyond an apology. This is not you sleeping through your alarm or missing the bus or losing coursework. You assaulted a pupil in full view of the class. Jesus Christ—Sophie told me she heard you threatening to throw Rebecca through the window."

"That was just words. I never would have done it. She wasn't hurt. I—"

"And thank *God* she wasn't injured or the police would be here right now. As it is, I can't guarantee that her parents won't want to press charges. We've had to call them. They're on their way in. Jesus, Tess—why did it have to be Rebecca Martin?"

"You know she's had it in for me since..."

"Since what? Since you stole her phone last term?"

"I didn't steal it. She had it out in class—I saw the pictures she was flashing around. I was trying to help her."

"You took her phone out of her bag and called the damned police." Karen shakes her head. "You should have come to me. We could have had a word with her, spoken to her parents."

"She's a kid—a child."

"She's over sixteen; so is her boyfriend. What they get up to, what messages they send, has nothing to do with us. If you'd told us, we could have disciplined her for showing the photos in school, but you took the phone without her permission. You called the *police*."

"But—"

"But nothing."

"I thought—"

"You thought *wrong*. We talked her parents down that time.

But this? You can hardly claim you were trying to help her this time, can you?"

Oh, why did I have to be so stupid? When I saw the texts she was showing her friend, that damned porno close-up of someone's penis, I thought...

I really did think I was helping her.

"I'll do my best when Rebecca's parents come in—she was provoking you, you're under strain, there are mitigating circumstances. But I can't let you remain at the school. You're suspended as of now. And Tess...I'm sorry, but I don't think there's any way the board will let you back."

My eyes threaten to fill. What the hell have I done?

Karen steps back. "Go home, Tess. Get yourself sorted out. We'll be in touch soon."

Go home? I shiver. My flat isn't what I think of when she says go home. I think of Bella waiting for me in the woods.

Sophie calls as I'm leaving the school.

"What happened?"

"Suspended."

"Shit, Tess..."

"Karen was really good, but what else could she do?"

"Did you tell her about your stepmother?"

"Yeah, but..."

"Oh, why didn't you call in sick?"

I shake my head even though she can't see it. "It's not just a momentary meltdown, though. I mean, today was, but Soph—I don't think I want to do this anymore. I don't think I want to be a teacher."

"One hell of a way to tender your resignation, babe."

I let out a laugh that's half a sob. "I had this dream last night. It was...it was awful. I don't think I slept at all afterward."

"What was it about?"

"I'll tell you about it later. Can you come round?"

"Of course. Sure you don't want to go out? We could come up

with a new and improved life plan over some cheap cocktails and a late-night kebab."

I stop on the corner, waiting for a break in the traffic so I can cross the road. "I'm not sure going out and getting drunk would be a good idea. Come to my place, help me drown my sorrows in strong tea."

"I'll be there."

"Are you sure you'll still want to associate with me now? The disgraced ex-teacher up for assaulting her students?"

"You daft cow."

There's so much affection in her voice it makes my eyes fill with tears.

"You know everyone working here will back you up, don't you? We've all wanted to have a screaming fit at some of the kids we teach."

"But wanting to and actually doing it are two different things, aren't they?"

"At least you didn't go full-on Miss Trunchbull on her."

There is that. But what if Sophie hadn't come into the class-room? What if Rebecca had fought back? How far would I have gone?

THEN

CHAPTER 5

AUGUST 2006: TWO YEARS BEFORE THE WEDDING

"Come on, Tess!"

Bella's calling me from the other side of the stream. She jumped it in one flying leap, clearing the fast-flowing water by a foot. I'm dithering. I always do—never quite finding the guts to make the jump, my stupid brain imagining me fudging it and falling face-first in the dirty water. Wouldn't be so bad if we hadn't had such a wet summer. If it had been dry the last few weeks, the stream would be nothing but a dank, stinking trickle I could step across.

I could walk farther upstream—there's a fallen tree that acts as a bridge. But it's a five-minute walk away and I can see the impatience on Bella's face.

Just bloody do it, Tess. I take a few steps back, hold my breath, and go for it—a run and then a huge jump. My feet plant in the mud on the other side, water soaking into my sandals, and I can feel myself falling back. My arms fly out for balance but I know I'm going to fall—Tessie the Elephant splashing down—but then Bella's hand grabs mine and she hauls me up the bank.

"I got you," she says, laughing as I fall to my knees, muddying my jeans. She keeps hold of my hand as I clamber upright.

I'm sweating—that moment where I thought I was falling translated into great damp patches under my arms and down my back. I wipe my forehead with the back of my hand.

"It's so bloody hot, maybe we should have jumped in the water rather than over it," Bella says. She's still laughing, but it's not a cruel laugh. It's her indulgent laugh for the clumsy kid sister who couldn't tie her laces until she was ten and was forever falling over. I have a vivid memory of a smaller me, my big sister crouching down to tie my school shoes for me. It's bright, that memory.

I squeeze Bella's hand. "Thanks, big sis."

"Anytime, baby sis," she says, letting go of my hand to ruffle my curls. I push her hand away—isn't my hair bad enough in this humidity? An insane mass of frizz.

"What do you want to do now?" she asks, sinking onto a log, stretching out her legs, brushing off the tiniest speck of mud.

It squeezes my heart watching her as her hair falls over her face. I get this a lot—this huge wave of love for my perfect sister, almost a pang, almost a pain.

I shrug. Four weeks into the summer holidays, first dry day in ages, and we're in the woods. Adventuring, we used to call it when we were little kids. But Bella's sixteen now and I'm fourteen. Too old for adventuring. She is, anyway. A bit of me wouldn't mind playing the games we used to—intrepid explorers lost in the jungle. But Bella's bored of it, I can tell. She's restless, jumping back up and pacing about.

"God, I swear this place gets more boring every year," she says. "Nothing ever changes." She rummages in her bag and pulls out a pack of cigarettes and a lighter.

"Want one?"

I shake my head. The smoking is new. Her and her mates—saw them huddled round the back of school at the end of term, surrounded by boys, sharing cigarettes. I've tried it a couple of times, but I don't like it. I feel stupid with one in my hand.

"We could go to the beach?" I say. "Or the amusement park?"

I don't want to. I want to stay here in the woods where it's cool and dark and it's just me and Bella. Half the school will be down at the beach on a day like this, and Bella will be off with them. It's different when we're here. She's different when it's just the two of us.

She hesitates, then smiles and stubs the cigarette out. "Nah— I'll stay with you." She gets her camera out of the bag. "Let's go take some photos."

"Are you sure? I don't mind, honestly. It's been at least a week since you've seen any boys. You must be getting withdrawal symptoms."

She shoves me, but she's grinning. "Shut your face, bitch. At least I'm not a nun like you. Besides, there is not one single sexy boy in this entire village. When it comes down to it, you're actually better company."

"Oh, I'm so flattered."

"You should be. Most people would beg for this much time in my company."

She's joking but it's actually kind of true.

Her phone dings and she pulls it out of her pocket. "Oh—I spoke too soon."

"What is it?"

"Text from Nic. It seems a new family has been seen viewing Dean House and, apparently, there are two insanely hot boys."

Her restlessness is back. I can see I'm no longer better company.

"Go on then," I say, although it comes out all sulky. "Go find yourself some insanely hot boys."

She hesitates and looks at me. "Nah, it's okay. I'll meet Nic later." She sends a text and puts the phone back in her pocket. "Come on then."

Her phone dings again less than a minute later and I sigh as she looks at the message and laughs. "Nic says they're checking out the village and I will regret it for the rest of my life if I don't come right now." Another text comes through. "And she's not going to shut up until I go and meet her."

She looks at me, giving me her best puppy-dog eyes. "Please, Tess? Pretty, pretty please come with me to look at some pretty, pretty boys?"

I laugh unwillingly. "Oh go on, bugger off, you daft nympho."

"Aren't you coming?"

I look at her blond perfection and my own mud-streaked fat-jeans, hair a frizzy nightmare. "In this state? With you and Nicole? I don't think so. Go. I'll hang out here a bit."

She's wavering. "Go on," I say again. "Seriously—go and check them out and report back to me."

She doesn't look back as she lopes off, and it's only after she's out of sight that I realize I'm going to have to get back across the stream on my own.

SEPTEMBER 2006

The insanely hot boys and their family have bought Dean House. I kick the Sold sign as I pass it and go round to the side gate, swinging my carrier bag full of gardening stuff. I've been coming here since last year when Dad shouted at me for working in our own garden. Our garden was always Mum's thing and he hasn't touched it since she died.

Dad hardly ever shouts, but he had tears in his eyes and so I stopped and promised I wouldn't touch it anymore, even though it kills me to see all Mum's plants get strangled by weeds and brambles.

I never meant to break in. I never go in the house, though, just the garden, so maybe it's just trespassing? It's not like I'm the only one who comes here—the house has been empty for years, since the old man who owned it before actually went and died inside. Of course, it then became the local haunted house. Kids come here on dares and teenagers come here to drink and smoke and other stuff.

Me, I come here and plant flowers and pull up weeds. My very own secret garden, pretending I'm Mary Lennox, even though I'm way too old for games. Pretending my work will make some magic happen.

Bella heard that they're moving in next week, so this is the last time I'll be able to come here. A stupid part of me wants to rip out all the stuff I've planted. Why should I leave it for *them*? But what would I do with it? It's not like Dad will let me move all the plants to our own garden.

I don't stay long. What's the point? I pull up a few weeds, cut back a bit more of the bramble jungle. I've been coming here for nearly a year and you can see progress. It's nowhere near finished—that would take years. But I've turned it from a weed-filled mess to something beautiful, a riot of climbing roses and wildflowers. Maybe the new family will like gardening. Maybe one of the insanely hot boys will carry on my work and one day he'll find out it was me who was the secret gardener and we'll fall in love.

Yeah, right.

I brush compost off my jeans and pack my stuff away. It's another hot day. I close the side gate and walk back out onto the lane, stopping dead when I see Bella walking toward me flanked by Nicole and Caitlin, her two best friends.

"Jesus, Tess—what have you been doing? Crawling in the mud? Rolling round in the bushes?" It's Nicole who says it, and Caitlin laughs. Bella, in the center, doesn't say anything. She doesn't laugh at me like the other two, but she doesn't support me, either.

"Come on, Tess, fess up. Who have you been rolling around in the bushes with?" Nicole says.

"Tess with a boy? As *if*," Caitlin says.

Nicole finds this hilarious. And Bella? She isn't laughing. But she still. Doesn't. Say. Anything.

My hand squeezes the carrier bag. I want to get out the clippers and hack off their stupid flicky hair, silence their mocking words with a trowel in the face. Instead, I keep walking, head down, shoving Nicole with my shoulder as I march past.

My eyes are swimming with hot tears as I round the corner.

"Tess—wait."

I can hear Bella running up behind me, but I don't slow down.

"Hey," she says, stopping me with a hand on my shoulder. "You okay?"

"Am I *okay*?" I turn to face her, letting her see the tears.

"Look—I'm sorry, okay?"

"Why didn't you say anything? Why do you let them be such cows to me?"

She raises her hands and lets them drop. "I...I don't know. But

Tess, come on. You don't help yourself, you know. Look at the state of you—you're not eight anymore, a chubby tomboy in dungarees."

Chubby. She actually said chubby. Yes, I know I'm a state—my T-shirt's too tight and my jeans are filthy. No makeup, hair a halo of frizz. But I've been bloody gardening, not going to a goddamn nightclub.

"You're embarrassed by me," I say, my voice flat.

"No—of course not," she says, but there's a pause before she says it and no conviction in her voice.

"Well, *fuck you*, Arabella Cooper. Just fuck off with your friends. Pretend you don't know me and then maybe I won't embarrass you anymore." I swing the carrier bag and smack her in the arm with it before walking away again, fast enough that I'm out of breath in a minute.

I don't look back to see if she's following. I know she won't be.

Bella comes into my room later that night.

"You awake?"

I close my eyes and stay huddled on my side. She sighs and lies on the bed next to me, on top of the covers. She smells of cigarette smoke and the woods.

"I'm so sorry, baby sis. I was a total bitch. I should have said something. I should have told them to shut up."

"Why didn't you?" I say, turning to face her.

"Because...I don't know. There are no excuses, are there?"

"I wish you didn't care so much about what they think. They're so horrible—nasty, horrible girls."

"They're not all bad," she says. "Nic's really funny and Caitlin can be, like, really kind sometimes."

"Huh. I've never seen that."

"It was just teasing, you know. They do it to everyone, not just you." She pauses and a gurgle of laughter escapes her. "And Tess—seriously—when you came round the corner. You really did look like you'd crawled out of the hedge. You were covered in mud—it was all over your face. And there were leaves in your hair. It was like some wild woman had jumped out at us."

There's no cruelty in her laughter and reluctantly I smile. "Yeah, hardly catwalk-ready."

She laughs again and I shush her, aware of Dad sleeping across the landing.

"I really am sorry, though," she says. "I wish I could be more like you sometimes. You really don't care what you look like or what people think."

I think of the half hour I spent sobbing when I got back to the house, how I wanted to smash every mirror. My eyes still feel swollen and sore.

"What were you doing, anyway?" she asks. "Mud-wrestling?"

I hesitate. Should I tell her? About the garden? I imagine showing her. I imagine it becoming our place, not just mine. But, oh yeah, it's not mine anymore, is it? Bella's pretty boys are moving in.

"Nothing. Just crawling through hedges. As you do."

She laughs again, softly, reaches out to tug on one of my curls. "You're mad, baby sis. Totally nuts. Don't ever change."

"You neither."

She yawns. "Can I sleep in here tonight?"

It's only a single bed and Bella's a quilt-hogger, but I move over anyway, closer to the wall. "Course you can."

I close my eyes and drift off to the sound of my sister's soft breathing.

NOW

CHAPTER 6

ANOTHER SUMMER OF DEATH?

Body found in the woods

Police have confirmed that on August 23, 2008, a body was recovered from woods near West Dean in the Vale of Glamorgan and that another person has been taken to the hospital, where they are reported to be in a stable condition. No identities have been revealed.

IS THIS THE WORK OF A SERIAL KILLER?

Police have revealed the identity of the dead body discovered in the woods near West Dean as that of Arabella Cooper, aged eighteen. It is believed her sixteen-year-old sister was discovered unconscious nearby. Officers have not yet revealed if they are treating the death as suspicious, but after the murders of seventeen-year-old Nicole Wallace and nineteen-year-old Annie Weston, and with Rachel Wells still missing, fears are growing that a serial killer is preying on the teenage girls of this area.

COOPER DEATH "A TRAGIC ACCIDENT"

An inquest has ruled the death of Arabella Cooper a tragic accident, stating that the embankment was unsafe due to an earlier storm and that, under the influence of alcohol, the girls fell. Arabella Cooper's death was caused by a "fatal head injury" from rocks at the base of the embankment. Evidence shows that the severe storm that heralded the end of a three-week heatwave caused part of the embankment to give way, causing the girl's fall.

                              *   *   *

I keep all these newspaper reports in a box under my bed. I've
carried this box everywhere I've lived in the last ten years. Dad
doesn't know. He never knew I pulled the papers out of the bin
after he threw them away without showing them to me. He never
knew I carefully cut out each story and put it in a box. He never
knew I'd lie awake at night crying over the things I overheard in
the village said about my sister, all those gossips whispering in
hushed voices about Bella being a troublemaker, some drunken
hell-raiser.

I took the box to the police station once. Dad doesn't know
that, either. I tracked down the detective who'd questioned me in
my hospital room, and a week after the inquest ruled Bella's death
an accident, I waved in front of him the stories that talked about a
serial killer and screamed at him to do something, to find out the
truth. Because, awful though the idea would be, I wanted to stop
all that gleeful gossip, I wanted there to be some other explanation than a drunken accident in the woods.

I remember the pity on his face. He picked up all those newspaper cuttings from the floor after I'd let them drop and he
smoothed them all out before putting them back in the box carefully and neatly. He was kind, I remember, but kind in the way
you are to a distraught child, or a doddery old woman who's forgotten where she lives.

The inquest said it was an accident so an accident it was. Case
closed. He put the lid on the box and sent me away, and I don't
think I've opened the box since. As my grief grew less sharp edged,
I burned with humiliation and tucked the box farther away under
the bed to gather more dust, telling myself he was right, the inquest findings were right, everyone was right. It was an accident.

But I never threw the box away.

"So what's the plan then? Are you going to become Tanya Nibbington, Norfolk's most famous tree surgeon?"

We've moved on from tea and are halfway down the bottle of wine Sophie brought with her.

"I have no clue. I'm already freaking out about how I'm going to pay the rent on this place."

"But you're still being paid at the moment, aren't you?"

"Yeah—while it's still a suspension. But let's be realistic—they're not going to let me back, are they? After that, I've probably got about three months before I run out of money."

Sophie's silent for a moment. "Plenty of time to find something else—to figure out what you want to do. And if you're stuck, I have a sofa bed, no problem."

"You're an angel. And as much as I'd love to stay with you, I hope it doesn't come to that. Homeless and jobless is not a look I'm going for."

Sophie squeezes my hand. "Hey, maybe there's one tiny positive in all this. You have time now to go back and be with your stepmother. To be there for your dad."

My throat tightens. It's not just the walls closing in at the thought of going back there, it's the whole bloody world. "I can't. I can't go back there."

"But...Tess, your stepmother's *dying*."

"Do you know, I haven't been back there for longer than a day in nearly a decade? Not even to see Julia since she was diagnosed. I've only visited her in the hospital."

"Seriously? That's...shit. Why?"

"Because...I told you my sister died in an accident. But I never told you it was the night of Dad's wedding to Julia. I never told you I was there..."

She looks at me, waiting for more. I swallow hard.

"Look, Soph, it...it was like this. We were out in the woods and we both fell, or something—I was unconscious. When I woke up her body was right there next to me. She was dead. And I still don't remember what happened, how we ended up there."

Everything from the night of the wedding is coated in a layer of fog. I waited, afterward, for my memory to come back. A trickle

of little things did come back—a flash of entering the woods after
Bella, the feel of rain on my head as the storm broke. As I healed
from my injuries, as I watched Bella being buried, as we cleared
her room, I waited, expecting the trickle to become a flood. The
police stopped asking questions after the inquest declared her
death an accident, but still I waited.

The bits I do remember are things I didn't want Dad to know.
I remember drinking champagne and being drunk almost to the
point of passing out. I remember someone half-carrying me upstairs. But who? Max? Dad? God—Jack or Sean? And shouting—
Bella and me, and someone else. So much shouting, barely heard
above the storm. But the fog is like a curtain I can't pull aside.

Sophie leans back. "Shit," she says again.

"Yes. It was. Totally shit. I've never…I was sixteen. Everyone
was saying it was this tragic accident, but I refused to accept it. I
was convinced something terrible had happened, but I couldn't remember. I was plagued by the most awful nightmares afterward—
my sister rising from the grave, stalking me through the woods like
some zombie horror show. I couldn't wait to get away—from the
house, from the woods. From everyone that reminded me of her."

"Christ, Tess, that's understandable, but…"

"I miss her," I say, pressing my hand against my rib cage where
the ache of regret is almost physical. "I miss her so much, but I've
refused to let myself think about her. But she keeps appearing in
my dreams and then last night—it wasn't one of the nightmares—
Bella was here, in this flat, and it was so real."

There are tears in my eyes and I can see Sophie blinking back
tears of her own.

"I'm so bloody angry with myself," I burst out. "I've spent all
these years running from my memories of Bella and everything
that happened, to the point where I've let Dad deal with Julia's
illness all on his own, because I've been too damned scared to go
back. I hate the place. It's become like a phobia I've let run my life.
And now Julia is dying and I'm still running? That whole crap-
fest with Rebecca—it's all tied to this. Ten years and I haven't even

begun to face up to it. I've left the wounds open and raw and festering and where has it got me? I've let down my dad. I've let Julia down. I've lost my job and may end up facing criminal charges. You're the only friend who really knows any of this. I'm a mess, Soph. A stupid, pathetic mess."

Sophie puts down her glass and leans in to hug me. "Oh God, babes, you are, aren't you? A total mess."

I let out a laugh that's half sob and pull away to wipe my eyes.

"And still, knowing all that, admitting all that, I can't face going back there."

Sophie just looks at me.

"Don't give me that teacher look. I know what I *should* do. I don't want to be like this, scared to the point of hyperventilating over some bloody trees and a ten-year-old nightmare. I want to be…"

"You want to be a brave soldier?"

I laugh again. "Yes, I do. Screw Tanya Nibbington—*I* want to be Maeve Larson, intrepid detective, afraid of nothing. I want to go back and say fuck off nightmares, screw you, woods—you're not haunted. I want to dream of my sister without it being a nightmare. I want to be there for Dad and Julia."

She stays silent as my fear and conscience wrestle for dominance.

"Look," she says eventually. "I can't tell you what to do, all I can do is promise that if you *do* go, if you *do* channel your inner Maeve Larson—hell, forget that, if you channel the inner Tess, the one who can take on the horror show that is the eleventh grade and come out alive—I will be here for you, on the end of a phone and waiting with a bucket of wine when you get back."

I waver and the woods crowd into the pause. I can't stand the thought of going back, but how can I let my dad be alone when Julia dies?

My phone rings as I'm clearing up after Sophie leaves. It's a mobile number I don't recognize, so I answer cautiously.

"Hardy-girl?"

My throat closes up at the familiar voice and it takes me a moment to find my own.

"Max?"

His words, his voice, sends me spiraling back in time and disorients me. Me and Bella—Tess and Arabella, named for the Thomas Hardy heroines from the books my mum loved so much. Although, in the books, it's me who had the tragic death. Even though Max always called us both Hardy-girl, it was only me who took it as a caress, for whom the nickname felt like a kiss. Bella always hated her full name, more so after she actually read *Jude the Obscure* and decided Arabella was a complete cow. She took offense at the choice, even though I think Mum just liked the name.

"How are you, Hardy-girl? God, this is a blast from the past. I hope you don't mind me ringing so late. I just got off the phone with your dad."

"He told you about Julia?"

There's a pause. "I can't quite believe it. It's hard to imagine her not being there anymore." His voice breaks. "I feel so guilty for not visiting more."

He doesn't need to feel guilty. After Max's dad got posted abroad, he and Lena were sent to boarding school—they probably saw more of Julia and Greg on school holidays than they did their own parents. Even after she moved in with Dad, he visited more often than Julia's own sons. But then, Jack and Sean had their issues with her. So did me and Bella.

God—her sons and her stepdaughters, all lined up against her in hostility, the only people on her side the children of her best friends.

"Dad said she hasn't got long left—days, weeks, I don't know."

"I'm sorry," he says, his words coming out on a sigh.

I brush my hand across my cheek to wipe away a tear. I do love her some, even if it isn't enough. I loved her for giving us Max. We only got to keep him for a couple of years—Bella's death took him away again, and I haven't seen him since—but, oh, that soaring crush I had when I thought my heart would burst just looking at him. Everyone else had crushes on Jack and Sean, Julia and Greg's gloriously handsome sons, but it was always Max's quieter strength and kindness that tugged at my heart.

"I was calling to see if you wanted a lift back with me and Lena. We're heading down there in the morning."

He makes it sound so easy.

"I was..." I pause. I was what? Am I going to tell him that I wasn't actually planning on visiting my dying stepmother? I can't. I can't say that out loud to Max. Even after all these years, I want him to think well of me.

"Yes. Yes, please," I say. "A lift would be great."

The trees grow taller in my mind, the woods get darker, but it'll be okay. I'll be with Max.

Ten years of no contact and it turns out Max and I live twenty miles apart. I could have got on the train as soon as I phoned Dad to tell him I was coming, but instead I'm waiting for Max, hovering and looking out of the window for his arrival like I used to as a teenager. I chew my lip. Dad sounded so relieved I was coming back. I hate to think how much strain he's been under since Julia was diagnosed. How lonely he must be.

After Bella died, Julia was the strong one, thrown into this family just as we all fell apart. She did all the practical stuff while me and Dad tottered around, shell-shocked and completely messed up.

But there was always that sticking point—if she'd never come into our lives, Bella would probably still be alive. The knowledge has been a festering thorn in my side for ten years and it makes it hard to be in the same room with her without constantly wondering *what if*. The relationship we'd been building, stepmother and stepdaughter, destroyed by Bella's death.

Christ, I'm not sure I can go through with this. I'm wondering if I have time to call Sophie for another pep talk when I hear the toot of a horn and head downstairs on shaking legs.

The sun is out today and I shade my eyes to see him as he gets out of the car. Max. My Max.

"Hey, Hardy-girl," Max says, and I let him fold me up in his arms. He smells different, but his arms feel the same, still give me the same strength as he squeezes tight. Maybe he can help me channel my inner Maeve Larson.

He looks the same but different as well, same lean frame and short brown hair, same brown eyes that I'd wistfully sigh over in the way only a teenage girl can. The years have added a couple of fine lines, turned the teenage lankiness into a more muscled leanness, but he's lost none of the crooked-smile gorgeousness I daydreamed about.

"God, you look amazing," he says. "It's weird, I never thought you and Bella were alike, but look at you now."

I pull away too quickly, almost shoving him away from me.

"I'm sorry—but you walked out and if it weren't for the hair, it could have been her."

Always her, never me. Even if she weren't in my dreams, her ghost would still be with me.

"Where's Lena?" I ask, interrupting him, looking for his sister.

"In the car," he says. I look over and see her through the window. She's slumped on the back seat, asleep, dark glasses covering her eyes.

"Is she okay?"

"Don't ask." He sighs and runs a hand through his hair. "She was drunk when I picked her up."

"At eleven in the morning?"

"Tell me about it."

It used to be indulgence I'd hear in his voice when he talked about Lena, an eye roll, a bit of exasperation, but more tolerance. The disapproval I hear now tells me more about how Max has grown up and maybe Lena hasn't.

"She hasn't changed, then."

I look at him and he shakes his head. "She moves from job to job because she keeps getting fired and every job she takes is worse than the last. Mum and Dad put a brave face on it, calling her work PR, but basically she hands out club flyers in the city center. Then she goes to the club and drinks away her entire earnings."

My smile fades.

"Where is she going to end up?" he says. I don't think he expects me to answer.

"And you?" I say. "I can see you've grown up."

Max touches my hand. He lifts it, traces circles on my palm with his other hand. "I've missed you, Tess."

I pull my hand away and clench my fist. "Really?"

"I called you. Back then. You know I did. You never took my calls."

"Because you *left*." The words burst out. It's stupid to still be angry, but I am.

"Tess..."

"I know you had to go when your parents did, of course I do. But before all those awful days leading up to the funeral, I never saw you, you avoided me. You were like a bloody stranger."

"I'm sorry, but I was freaking out. I was seventeen—one minute we're at a wedding and the next, Bella was dead. And you...I couldn't cope with your pain. It was awful, you and Leo...I couldn't handle it."

"And you think I could? You didn't even visit me in the hospital."

"I'm sorry," he says again. "I know it was wrong. If I could have the time again..."

I shudder. I don't want to live that time again.

"It hasn't felt like ten years," he continues. "I haven't seen Julia and Leo much, but every time they've told me all about you, shown me photos."

They did the same with me—snapshots of Max and Lena, little snippets about their lives, news about Max I'd store up and daydream about, never quite brave enough to pick up the phone and call him, despite Julia's encouragement.

"What about Jack and Sean? Have they shared lovely photos of them, too?"

He hesitates. "They're actually...not too bad now. It's been a long time for all of us, Tess."

I flinch. "You've seen them?"

"Of course."

He sounds surprised. It hurts to hear that surprise. It feels like a betrayal. I'd forgotten he knew them first. That they were all friends years before Bella and I came into the picture. No, not forgotten. I've very deliberately not thought about it because I always wanted Max to be mine, not theirs.

"I see Sean for a drink sometimes. Not often."

"And Jack?"

He shrugs. "Not as much. Jack is...well, Jack is still Jack, I guess. Only not as..."

Not as what? Angry? Scary? Intimidating? Bitter? That's what I remember about Jack. That and his bloody shark smile. At least I always knew where I stood with Sean, with his obvious anger and hate. Jack would smile that wide smile of his, but his eyes...there was never a smile in his eyes.

"You know he got married?"

I nod. Dad told me.

"He got married, had a son. I have to say, I never thought he'd be the one to settle down and be the grown-up."

I can't imagine it. Like Bella when she appears as dream, ghost, or hallucination, whatever it is, I imagine the others being the same age as they were the last time I saw them. Jack, married with a child? Does not compute.

I put my bag in the trunk and climb into the car next to him.

"I never thought this is how we'd meet up again," Max says as he pulls out into the main road.

"Really?" I say. "It seems to me that all our meetings have been surrounded by death."

He winces at my words and I look over at him, this oh-so-familiar stranger, waiting for some memories to come flooding back, but there's nothing. *Did you kiss me back?* I want to ask. *When I made my clumsy love-filled pass at you, did you kiss me back, Max? Was it you who helped me upstairs, was it you, your lips brushing mine?*

But ten years is a river too wide. So we sit in a strange car and my memory remains blank.

Lena wakes up nearly two hours into the journey, as we pull off the highway onto the lanes that lead home.

"Jesus Christ, I need a drink," she says, leaning forward, hooking her arms over the back of both our seats.

Max's face twitches and I squeeze his hand where it rests on the gear stick.

"Bloody hell, fast work, Tess. Ten years apart and already you're holding hands." She laughs as I snatch my hand away.

She's still a damned teenager then, isn't she? Her laughing words reignite the anger that built when I saw Lena in Rebecca Martin's face. All that teenage angst, all the turmoil stirred up by the arrival of Julia, her family, and Max and Lena. I forgot, for a moment, seeing Max again. I forgot he was never really my Max—they formed a gang: Bella, Max and Lena, Jack and Sean. And then there was me, forever on the outside.

She's still drunk; I can see that as I look back at her and she takes her sunglasses off. Her pupils are so huge that her eyes look black, so maybe she's more than drunk. She's wearing that curling half-smile that used to scare me when I was a kid. Back then she seemed so big, bad, and dangerous. She's lightened her hair since last time; streaks of blond run through it. Last time I saw her, she had dyed it black to go with the black clothes she wore, even on the hottest, hottest days. It doesn't surprise me, what Max told me, about the disaster of her life. I never could imagine Lena doing anything more than smoking, hiding out with Bella in the village, swigging stolen vodka, and flirting with anyone who stopped by, for all the outrageous future plans she used to make.

And Max...Max has done just what he planned. Back then

he'd constructed nothing more than sandcastles, but he had his architect's dreams. He'd sketch glorious buildings in the ground with a stick. Fantastic, impractical buildings that belonged in a sci-fi film. I used to pick flowers and make gardens for his houses. We were going to meet up at Chelsea Flower Show the year I won my first award there.

"So what's it like back there?" Lena asks. "Still the same? And how're Julia and your dad doing? It's so shit, what's going on."

"I...don't know. I haven't been back myself for a long time."

"Seriously?"

"Lena—shut up." Max's voice is sharp.

"No way. Goody-goody Tess takes over my role as bad girl by failing to visit her dying stepmum. Halle-bloody-lujah, Lena is not the worst person on stage."

"You don't know anything," I burst out, twisting in my seat to look at her, getting a faceful of her stale, boozy breath. "I'm not 'goody-goody Tess,' I never bloody was. It's been ten years, so shut your drunk mouth and stop acting like a child, okay?"

Lena lapses into silence and, in my mind, Sophie lets off a tiny confetti cannon.

I can do this. I *can*.

CHAPTER 7

My heart speeds up as we reach the outskirts of West Dean. Everything looks the same—the shop, the pub, the dilapidated kids' playground. It's like time has stood still, everyone and everything locked in an enchanted sleep in the years I've lived away in a city that grows and changes by the day. People stop and stare as Max's car passes and I swear I can hear whispered observations filtering in through the closed windows. *There she is, back at last, took her time, didn't she?* It feels like they're swirling all around me, closing in. *Wonder what happened. The sister who lived.* My head is spinning. *Wonder what really happened in the woods?*

"Stop!" I yell to Max, and almost fall out of the car before throwing up on the grass verge. It feels like everything I've eaten in the last month comes up and I stay leaning over, my legs shaking, waiting for the black spots to stop floating in front of my eyes.

"You all right, Tess?"

I can hear the concern in Max's voice. I straighten up and try on a smile.

"Fine. I'm fine. Something I ate, that's all."

He nods, but the frown of concern doesn't go as I get back in. I lean back and close my eyes, taking shallow breaths as my stomach continues to somersault.

The world is getting weird as I feel myself drift—stretching out and warping, a crap song on the radio merging into Bella singing in the garden, wind whistling in through the window becoming footsteps crunching through the woods. Bella and me and Max and Lena, hide-and-seek among the twisted trees. Then there's Sean and my eyes fly open and there's a house in the road, white and crumbling with black staring windows like eyes, and we're heading straight for it. I almost lurch sideways, almost try for the steering wheel to steer us away when it blinks back out and it's just the empty road out of the village again, nothing in front of us but a tractor, slowing us to a crawl.

My eyelids feel weighed down. Something heavy sits on them and they keep drifting closed. The car stops and it pulls me out of a half-sleep. It takes me a minute, because I think sleep has carried me here and this is a dream. We're outside my old house with the ivy and the peeling paint and the broken gate. I expect to see Bella at the upstairs window, Dad in the garden. Maybe even Mum, if this is a way-back dream. Me, seven again, with my mum still around, tall and curly before she got sick, looking just like me.

But I blink and the fog clears and I get that I'm awake. It's still daylight but the house is dark because of the woods directly behind it, huge trees looming up and arching over the house and in its narrowness, the house could be one of them: a tree-house, tall and thin and higgledy-piggledy, with mean windows and a red door. If it were a house on its own in the forest it would be like something out of a fairy tale.

"Here we are then," Max says.

Yes. Here we are then.

Dad comes out and gathers me in a hug and, despite myself, it's so good to see him. I hold on tight, closing my eyes, pretending I'm a kid again, breathing him in, the familiar smell of his aftershave, a lingering hint of coffee on his breath. He smells like home and this hug, this moment, is worth everything that's to come.

He's shaking as I hug him back and I cling on, stroking his back. *Yes, I can do this*, I want to say, to convince us both. *I will be here for you.*

Dad looks grayer and older, thinner, hunched over as he greets Max and Lena, like more than a few months have passed since I saw him last, like years have gone by. I touch my face, expecting to feel lines, sagging skin.

I squeeze Dad's hand. "Come on, Dad, let's go in and see Julia."

*   *   *

"I'm sorry about Lena," Max says quietly, picking up a tea towel and drying the mugs I've washed. Dad nodded off in the living room, so Max and I tiptoed out to the kitchen while Lena went outside to smoke. We're all still waiting for Julia to wake up so we can visit, the last hour spent in halting, awkward small talk punctuated by the ticking clocks Dad has all over the house.

"It's okay," I say, not looking at him. "Like you said—she was drunk."

He pauses and puts the mug he's dried down on the counter. "But I was surprised, too. You haven't been visiting? I know Lena shouldn't have spoken like she did. But Julia's been so ill and..."

I feel like I've been slapped.

"I did visit her in the hospital," I say. "Which is more than Lena bloody did. But I couldn't come back here. When I was sick on the way...it wasn't something I ate, it was coming back here."

He glances toward the window, to the woods outside. "Jesus—still? After all this time?"

"Yes, still. Yes, after all this time. I come back here and I see those woods and I want to pass out or puke or run screaming every time. So yes, I've been a crap daughter, a crap stepdaughter, but I'm here now, aren't I?"

"Sorry," he says, and hesitates. "Do you still not...?"

"Remember? No. A lot of that whole wedding weekend is a blur and I still don't remember anything about what happened to Bella."

"I'm sorry," he says again. "But me and Lena are here with you. We can help."

I want to laugh at the thought of Lena helping, but he chooses that moment to pull me into his arms and I hold my breath instead.

*   *   *

"So—roomies then! It's like being back at boarding school. We can stash cookies and stolen vodka under the bed. Hang out of the window smoking," Lena says.

I stuff a pillow into a pillowcase and raise my eyebrows. With Max in Bella's old room, Lena's having to stay in with me. She's sitting on the edge of the bed swinging her legs, making no attempt to help.

"I don't have those Enid Blyton boarding school moments to reminisce over—me and Bella went to the local school."

"Still got a chip on your shoulder about that?"

I squeeze the pillow between my hands and resist the urge to hit her with it. Why does she always have to be so...so *Lena*?

"And it was never remotely Enid Blyton, anyway," she says. "Just a lot of miserable girls like me whose parents either didn't want them at home or worked abroad. All starving themselves or making themselves sick or slicing up their arms."

"Wow. Sounds...well, it sounds absolutely horrible." I pause. "You know, Bella always wanted to go to boarding school when we were kids."

Lena smiles. "I know. She used to ask me *so* many questions. I'd tell her how shit it was, but she'd still be sighing over it like it sounded amazing."

"Oh. That must have been...never mind."

"What?"

"I was going to say it must have been frustrating. If you were trying to share something you hated and she wouldn't listen."

Lena picks up her pillowcase and lays it on her lap, tracing the floral pattern with her fingers. "It was a bit, I suppose. But she was so damned sweet with it. It ended up making me feel better in a way. All I used to do was moan about it, but she wouldn't let me. She made me find some vague nice things about the whole experience."

"Well, we only have to be roommates for the weekend, so hopefully there won't be any nasty trigger moments."

"Yeah, and no doubt you're already counting down the hours until I'm gone again."

I don't say anything because she's right. A few hours in her company and I've already got a knot of anger and anxiety building inside me.

"It was awful after she died, you know," she says into the silence, her usual mocking tone missing. "For the rest of us as well. I had to go back to that fucking school and our parents pissed off again and it was so shit. Did you ever get, for even a second, how crap it was for us?"

My throat goes tight and any warmth I'd been feeling evaporates. "I'd just lost my sister. I was a bit too caught up in grieving to worry about *your* feelings, funnily enough."

"God, Tess, I'm not having a *dig*. She was the best friend I ever had, you know." She sighs and chucks the pillowcase back onto the bed. "I probably should have come back to visit Julia more, but it was weird, you know?"

I nod. "Yeah. Same for me."

"Poor Julia. And poor Leo. They've had the shittiest time of all, haven't they? While you and me and Max wallow in our own self-indulgent woe-is-me crap."

She's voicing everything I've been berating myself about and it startles me to be so on the same page as Lena. I don't think I like it.

She sighs again and stands up and stretches. "Look, I'm sorry we weren't here for you and Leo and Julia. And sorry I was such a bitch in the car on the way down. It's freaking me out, coming back here. Anxiety makes me bitchy." She pauses and smiles. "Bitchier."

Apology or not, I'm not sure how long I'll last in a room with Lena without it ending up in an argument. I glance toward the window. I can't see the woods from here, but I know they're there. Time to rip the bandage off. If I'm going to stay here and be with Dad and Julia, I can't be throwing up or passing out every time I see a bloody tree.

"I think I'll go for a walk."

*   *   *

The wind has picked up, moaning through the trees behind the house. I zip my coat to the top and tuck my scarf in tight. My phone buzzes as I step away from the house and get a mobile signal again. I have two new voicemails. It could be Sophie, checking to see if I'm okay, full of plans for nights out when I get back. But what if it's Karen, what if Rebecca's parents have decided to press charges? I haven't let myself think of that. I've accepted that in all likelihood I'll be fired, yes. But being charged? Arrested? A police record? I put my phone back in my pocket, letting it be Schrödinger's cat for a while—my future both dead and alive at the same time until I listen to the messages.

I set off down the lane, walking fast, ignoring the woods on my left, but too aware of the trees and shadows. The night Bella died, I was out there in the woods with her, but I don't know why. Then there's a gap and it's like I went to sleep and woke up in the woods, rotting leaves on my face and in my mouth, soaked with rain and streaked with mud. But alive. Bella was lying next to me and I thought...I thought she was asleep but when I got up and looked, her eyes were open and staring and there was blood on her face and...I blanked out again then, woke up in the ambulance.

I stop and hunch over, sliced in two by a spasm of pain so sharp it stops my breath. We were at the bottom of a gully, made slick by rain and a summer storm. They said we fell. They said there was a landslide. They tested Bella's alcohol levels and they were too high for a few glasses of champagne and they said we'd sneaked out drinking and Bella had slipped, pulling me with her, falling and tumbling thirty feet, Bella's life ending on a sharp rock at the bottom.

They found cigarettes in her pocket, a plastic-wrapped lump of dope. Everyone clamored to tell how much she used to drink, how much of a wild child she was. But...but...I never went into the woods at night. Bella sneaked out to drink, yes, and I know she'd take the shortcut home through the woods, but I was never invited along. She'd go into the village, or up to the amusement park with her friends—those cool, hostile girls who ignored me when Bella let me tag along.

I told them. I said all that as I lay in my hospital bed, dehydrated and in shock. Something happened, I said. Something terrible happened. And I think I started babbling about the killer who was on the loose, the rumors and stories that thrilled and terrified us all in equal measure. The "summer of death," the local papers called it—all those stories about a killer who never got caught, who stopped his spree after the previous summer and disappeared into legend.

I was looked at with pity, treated with sympathy and frustration as my memory refused to come back. The inquest ruled it an accidental death in the end, but people still look at me, even now, curiosity on their faces, a question tucked away in their cheeks, not spoken but always there. *Do* you remember? Do you, Tess?

Tess

I look up, whirling round, heart pounding. Who called me? It sounded like they were right next to me, hissing in my ear, but I'm alone. It's mid-afternoon, but with the trees arching up and over, blocking the weak sun, it could be night. The lane is unlit and the woods have faded, become part of the greater dark.

"Who's there?" I say, my whisper sounding too loud. My neck prickles—someone's out here, watching me, following me.

I close my eyes and there she is, clear in my mind: Bella stepping out from behind a tree in her tank top and jeans, a dark smudge I know is blood on her forehead.

Once upon a time, she says. *Once upon a time, two girls went into the woods . . .*

I can't breathe. My heart pounds and I can't take a breath. In the back of my mind, I hear shouting. Me, shouting at Bella, then another voice, tantalizingly familiar, a male hand pushing my tangled hair out of my eyes, wiping away a tear. What is it? When was this? It won't come into focus.

Come on, she says, beckoning me into the trees. *Come into the woods. Let's finish the story.*

I shake my head and back away, turning and running back toward the house. No, I can't do it. Not the woods, not the woods, never the woods.

CHAPTER 8

Max and Lena have gone out shopping and Dad's pottering around downstairs when I step into Julia's room. I tiptoe in quietly in case she's still sleeping, but she's awake. More than awake: she's up, buttoning a jade-green cardigan over her purple striped pajamas.

"Julia—you should be resting."

She looks up and gives me a tired smile. "All I've done in the last two days is sleep. Right now I need to be up to greet my guests." She holds out her arms. "Hello, Tess."

I go over and hug her, careful not to squeeze because she feels so thin and fragile. Last time I saw her, in the hospital, she was bloated from the medication, given a fake bloom of health by the chemotherapy drugs. The fake bloom is all gone now and I have to work hard to hide my shock at how ill she looks. She hasn't lost that bright shock of red hair, but even in the half-light, I see how much more gray is threaded through the red.

"Don't," she says, seeing me looking and touching her head. "I wanted to dye the roots before you came, but I can't do the chemicals anymore."

"I'm so sorry..." I begin, guilt heavy in my gut.

"Don't," she says again. "I don't want you weeping and wailing around me, all guilt and regret. Too late for that. Was I pissed off you didn't come home for your dad? Yes, of course I was, but I also get it. I know how you feel about this place. I remember how bad you were after Bella died, how badly you needed to get away. And you're here now, aren't you? Let's not waste any more time."

I take a deep breath and force a smile. "Okay. Of course. And I'm here for as long as I need to be here. I promise."

"Good. Then you can start by helping me downstairs."

I frown. Downstairs? She's out of breath already, just from getting out of bed and putting on a cardigan. Looking around the room, I see right away where all the furniture from downstairs has gone: the red armchair with the sagging seat, the oak side table, a china vase filled with flowers. All Julia's favorite things have been brought up here—Dad has surrounded her with them. There are framed photos on the table—of me and Bella, Dad, her sons, and little Ellie, forever young.

I see what Dad has tried to do, but it can't take away what this room now is. If anything, it highlights it, and I wonder if Julia feels that too, if all her favorite things remind her that soon it's all going to be gone. The room smells wrong, despite the flowers. It smells like hospitals. It smells like death. I can understand why she wants to leave it.

"I don't want to see everyone gathered around my bed like I'm going to drop dead in the next five minutes," Julia says. "The sun's out—I want to be in the garden, in the fresh air."

I draw in a shaky breath. What do I say? I can't pretend she's going to get better, I can't tell her some miracle is going to occur. She and Dad have already gone through this, sitting in front of the consultant as she told them there was nothing else they could do. Did she scream and rage and smash things up? I would, I think, but I can't imagine it of Julia, who's always smiled in the face of everything. Instead, I can picture her smiling and shaking the consultant's hand and walking out and comforting Dad and smiling through it all. Smiling as he brought up the chair and the ornaments and the photographs, smiling to make him feel better.

But there are tears in her eyes now, so I summon my inner strength when all I want to do is fall sobbing at her feet.

"Well, come on then, let's do this. Pimm's in the garden in February it is."

Julia smiles faintly. "Maybe not Pimm's. Maybe a cup of PG Tips might be better."

I hook my arm through hers. "Ah, you say that, but when you

experience the tropical forty-five-degree temperature in pajamas and slippers, I'm sure you'll change your mind."

It's a slow journey downstairs. We pause every couple of steps, Julia holding on to the banister with one hand and on to me with the other. But it's worth it for the genuine smile on her face as we step out into the winter sunshine and she stops to take a deep breath.

"God, it's like I've been in prison for twenty years and this is my first time outside."

"Well, we're not going to stay out long," I warn her. "It's bloody freezing and you're wearing pajamas. Dad'll kill me if you die of cold on my watch."

"Oh, crass death joke, Tess. Really crass."

"But better than the weeping and wailing and guilt-ridden apologies?" I ask, eyebrows raised.

"Definitely," she says, nodding. She lets go of my arm to grip my hand. She's so thin I can see all the tendons raised in her hand. I can feel her bones, too close to the surface. It feels like if I squeeze, even gently, I'll crush them to dust. "Look after him for me, will you? After?"

"Dad?"

She nods. "He's being so strong, but he's gone through this too many times. I'm worried."

I put my other hand on top of hers. "I will, I promise."

"He sits in there with me, surrounded by all that...*stuff*, and he looks so lost."

"I'll be here for him. I won't let him be alone."

"I wish...I wish the boys would come. Now, while I'm still well enough to sit in the garden."

I look away, pulling my hands free of hers. Those bloody boys.

Julia reaches for one of my curls, tugging it and letting it go. It's what Bella used to do, and my eyes fill with tears. I don't know if they're for Bella or for the shadow of Julia that's left.

*   *   *

Max and Lena come through the gate as I'm settling Julia on the bench, a fleecy throw snatched from the living room wrapped around her.

"Julia," Max says, coming straight over and giving her a hug and a kiss on the forehead.

"Hello, gorgeous," she says, smiling up at him, raising a hand to stroke his cheek.

"Enough of that," he says, smiling back. "You're married, remember?"

Lena comes over and plonks herself next to Julia. "Whoa, Julia, babe—I hate to break it to you, but you look worse than I do, and I have the *mother* of all hangovers."

"I have to say, Lena, cancer is definitely worse than a hangover."

"Yeah," Lena says, grabbing the hand that Julia lets fall from Max's face. "It's fucking shit. But we can help, can't we, Tess? Paint your nails, do your hair, get some color on your face."

I perch on the arm of the bench. "If that's what Julia wants, of course we can."

"Who *doesn't* want a free pamper session?"

I look to Julia for an answer but instead she just says, "Oh, it's so *good* to see you all here." She leans her head against my shoulder. Lena's still holding her hand and Max is crouched down in front of her.

Dad comes out of the house then and Lena waves at him. "Hey, Leo, come and join the party. I was about to break open the Prosecco."

Dad's face lights up at the sound of Julia's laughing response and I'm glad—even with the woods looming up around me—so very glad I came.

I go in to help Dad make tea, leaving Julia laughing with Max and Lena. He smiles at them out of the window as he waits for the kettle to boil. "This is what I hoped for," he says. "Look how happy she is to see you all again."

I wrap my arms around myself, watching him put teabags in the old brown pot we've had forever, steam rising as he pours in boiling water.

"She really loves Max and Lena, doesn't she?" I say.

"She practically brought them up after their dad accepted his job abroad."

"At least they're here for her. Not like her own sons."

Dad shrugs. "They don't carry the same resentment as Jack and Sean. It was always Julia rather than Greg they were close to."

I haven't seen Jack or Sean since the wedding, when they were witness to Bella's death. They're tainted with it, covered in the leaves and mud and death that covered my sister. I hoped, when I left home, never to have to see them again.

"She told me she wishes they were here," I say.

Dad turns away from the window and pours the tea. "Sean's here."

"What?"

"He's at Dean House."

I think of that sense of being followed earlier. Was it Sean? Watching me?

"How do you know?"

"I saw him going in. I went to speak to him, but he's refusing to visit. I haven't told Julia he's in the village. It's bad enough they won't return my calls, but if she found out Sean was here and still not visiting..."

My hands shake as I put my mug down, and tea spills on the table. "Those fucking boys," I say. "Jesus—the last thing I want is them back in the house, but can't they even give her this? After all this time, they can't even visit her once before she dies?"

"Tess..."

"What? I'm not going to pretend to be nice, just because they're Julia's sons and she's ill."

"No, that's not what I meant. Will you try?"

"Try what?"

"Go and see Sean—try and get him to visit his mother."

* * *

I wait until Dad and Julia have gone to bed before I talk to Max and Lena. We sit in the kitchen so our voices don't carry upstairs.

"What's up, Tess?" Lena asks, fiddling with a bottle of wine and a corkscrew. "You've been trailing round with a face like a smacked arse all evening."

"Julia wants to see Sean and Jack again."

Lena looks blank. "Well, duh—they are her sons. Why wouldn't she want to see them?"

"But wanting something and it actually happening is...I asked Leo and he said they wouldn't even talk to him. I don't think they'll be popping in with grapes and flowers anytime soon," Max says, peeling the label off the bottle of beer he's drinking.

I rub my hands through my hair. "God, I'm so torn. The last thing I want to do is see them again, but Julia...Dad says Sean is here. Over at Dean House. He's actually here and hasn't come to see her. He's such a shit. Is it really going to be good for her to see them again? When they haven't bothered in all these years? Won't it make things worse—or is that just me wanting to believe that because I don't want to see them?"

"I don't know. If it's what Julia wants."

I sigh and look at Max. "I know, I know. Maybe you should speak to him? You're still friends—he's more likely to listen to you than me or Dad, isn't he? Perhaps Dad didn't manage to explain how little time Julia has."

Max and Lena exchange a glance and then look back at me. "He knows, Tess," Max says. "I called him before I called you. He basically told me to stay out of it, that it was none of my business."

"So I'm our last shot at getting him here?" I shake my head. "I haven't set eyes on either of them since the wedding. I think...did I have a fight with Sean? It's another thing I can't bloody remember. There was something...something Bella said. I..."

My voice dies as lightning flashes in my mind. A thunderous

roar and Bella...Bella's voice shouting, screaming at me. Oh God, the storm, the woods, it's that night. I'm remembering...what am I remembering?

"Tess? Are you okay?"

"Shh," I say, pushing Max's hand away and standing up. There. Clearer. Bella's crying, she's in her jeans and tank top, soaked by the rain. We're in the woods.

"What's going on?" Lena says.

"Wait," I say. "I'm...I was thinking about Sean and I'm...Oh God, I think I'm remembering something. Something Bella said in the woods."

"Tess?" Max sounds alarmed. "You look pale. Sit down. Take a breath." He takes my arm and guides me to a chair.

Lena's there, in my face. "What did you remember? What did Bella say to you?"

"Leave it, Lena," Max says, and they start arguing and their voices drown out Bella's and it's gone. The moment, the memory, whatever it was, is gone.

"For God's sake," I shout, interrupting them. "I almost remembered something. It could have been important."

There's a long silence.

"Are you sure?" Max asks. "Sure it was a real memory? After all this time?"

"Maybe it's being back here." I realize my hands are shaking. Lena shoves a glass of wine at me and I wrap my hands around it. "Seeing you two again, spending time with Julia. Maybe...maybe if I did get Sean and Jack back here, I'd remember it all."

There's another long pause that seems to last forever.

"But do you *want* to?" Lena says into the silence.

"Of course I do. I was there when she died. I was the last person to see her alive, the last person she spoke to, and I don't remember it." I take a breath. "And...I had this dream. After Dad called to tell me about Julia. And it was so vivid. Bella was so real. What if it wasn't a dream—what if it was some kind of memory coming back?"

They look at each other and back at me and I can see the wariness on their faces.

"Forget it," I say, pushing my chair back. "I'm going to bed. I'm exhausted."

I go upstairs and shower. When I go back to my room, rubbing my hair dry, I hear a noise from outside and go over to the window. Lena and Max are in the driveway, huddled under the light, Lena with a cigarette in her hand. I keep the light off and stay hidden by the curtain. Lena's voice is raised and Max appears to be trying to calm her down, his hand on her arm. She shakes it off and points at the house. I step farther into the shadows, wishing the window was open so I could hear their argument. Max looks rattled, Lena angry. What are they arguing about? Me? Julia? Being back here? Or is it an older argument?

Max looks up then and I swear he looks right at me even though I'm hidden by the darkness and the curtain. He's frowning and looks like a stranger. I step away so I can't see them anymore. I guess he is. He doesn't look like the boy I once thought I loved, but then, wasn't that boy part invention anyway? I guess he always was a stranger.

What will Jack and Sean be if even Max has become a stranger?

I feel warm breath on the back of my neck and freeze in place, scared at who I'll see if I turn around. I take a deep breath and dive into bed, closing my eyes. But despite my exhaustion, I can't switch my mind off and my eyes snap back open in the darkness. Even long after Lena has come up and fallen asleep, I lie awake.

THEN

CHAPTER 9

OCTOBER 2006

"Guess what?" Bella bounces into my room and throws herself onto the bed next to me.

"Watch out," I mutter, scooping up the pages of my essay she's lying on. "I've been working all bloody week on this coursework."

She nudges me and grins. "Guess what, guess what, guess what?"

"What?" I say, tucking the crumpled pages inside my textbook.

She sits up. "They've moved in."

"Who's moved into where?"

She rolls her eyes. "The new family—into Dean House."

I turn away to put the book back in my bag, letting my hair fall over my face. I can see dirt under my nails, still there from gardening at Dean House over the weekend, no matter how much I've scrubbed them. That's it then. No more secret garden.

"Oh, right—the Insanely-Hots."

"There's actually three kids—the two boys and a sweet little girl. The boys go to private school."

"How do you know?"

"I saw them in the village, practically stopping traffic, so I asked Mrs. Wilson about them."

Of course Mrs. Wilson would know everything. I doubt she let them buy anything in her shop until they'd answered twenty questions.

"Apparently they go to boarding school somewhere near Oxford. How cool is that?"

"I can't imagine all boarding schools are like Malory Towers." I laugh at her. She sounds like she's eight again, pleading with Mum and Dad to send us away to school for midnight feasts and lacrosse matches.

"God, I know that, but I bet it's better than our crappy school and they are certainly better than the juvenile idiots we have to put up with."

I don't care. The boys at our school are all obnoxious and poisonous, but I'm not boy-obsessed like Bella, like she has been pretty much since she started at secondary school. But then, she's gorgeous, whereas I get called Colossal Cooper and Tessie the Elephant every time the boys see me lumbering round the netball court. Not that Bella knows that.

I stand up and stretch. I've been hunched over that history essay for hours. "Want to go to the woods?" I ask, pulling the curtains wider. The sun shines in, lighting up Bella's blond hair, making her face glow. It's the perfect Indian summer day and, outside, the woods look lovely and cool and dark.

She shields her eyes and shakes her head. "We can't," she says. "The new family is throwing an impromptu barbecue—they've put out an open invite for the whole village."

An hour later, Bella's thrown on jeans and a T-shirt and looks stunning, her hair tousled, scuffed Converse on her feet. Whereas I've been primping for ages and still hate what the mirror tells me. I've spent too much time outside and my cheeks are red, my nose burnt. My hair's a nightmare and my jeans are too tight. I've put on a baggy T-shirt to cover the bulges but it just makes me look fatter.

Dad's waiting downstairs with a bottle of wine and a cake he bought from the shop to take as housewarming presents. He looks like he wants to go as much as I do, uncomfortable in a jacket and jeans, a silly grown-up weekend look that's just plain weird on him. He doesn't go out anymore, not since Mum died. It's been me and him, home every night and weekend, reading our books, watching rubbish on TV, driving Bella mad as she paces about, swept along by a restless breeze we don't even feel.

*   *   *

Dean House looks different from the front. I never went in that way when I was gardening there—I've always gone through the side gate, approaching from the woods, stealth spy style. From the front, it's a dump, always has been, but now there's scaffolding up, new tiles shining on the roof, new windows replacing the rotting wooden framed ones that used to be there.

A man and a woman greet us as we walk up the path. The Insanely-Hots indeed—they don't look like the parents of my friends. For one thing, they're too young. The man, who introduces himself to us as Greg Lewis, with his shiny hair and wide smile, looks so much younger than Dad that he could pass as his son. And his wife, Julia, has red hair and a big laugh. She's not supermodel pretty, but her smile lights up the world. Neither of them looks old enough to have teenage sons. Julia's carrying a wriggling toddler, a little girl with blond wavy hair who totters over to us when her mother puts her down and shows us the doll she's holding, a battered naked Barbie with wild frizzy brown hair.

"She looks like you," the little girl says, holding the doll up to me.

Everyone laughs and I blush as everyone looks from the doll to my own wild curls. Great. Bloody great.

"Tess likes the outdoors and getting her hands dirty too much to worry about her hair," Dad says, and Greg Lewis turns to smile at me.

"So you're a gardener? You'll have to come over and help me with mine."

I can feel my cheeks get even hotter and I stuff my hands in my pockets like he might see the dirt under my nails and know what I've been doing. "Um, yeah, I guess I could..."

But he's already turned away, laughing now with Dad, and I feel stupid. God, Tess, he was just being polite, it wasn't a real invitation.

I look around and spot the boys right away, two strangers standing apart from a sea of familiar faces. I see Nicole and Bella's other friends have already found them, though, all hovering with adoring smiles. Bella was right—they are both so good-looking; shiny and different. The boys have darker hair than their kid sister, but all together they could be a family straight out of a fairy tale, too pretty to be real. The older one is smiling, but the younger one looks like he might bite.

"Let's say hello," Bella says, hooking her arm through mine.

I pull away from her and step backward. "No thanks," I say, moving into the shadows. "I don't like the look of them. But you go ahead."

She shrugs and saunters off to join her friends. Nicole waves to her. She looks over at me for a second, then smiles and leans in to whisper something to the boys. They glance over at me. The younger one doesn't smile, just stares, but the older one laughs. My face goes hot imagining all the horrible things Nicole could have said.

"Why don't you go and join them?" Julia says with her dazzling smile.

"Or you could play Barbies with me," the little girl says, brandishing the naked Tess-doll.

I look to my dad for rescue, but he's been led off by Greg to a crowd of men holding bottles of beer.

"She doesn't want to play with your dolls, sweetie. I'll just get the boys to... Jack? Sean? Come over and say hello to Tess," she calls.

Oh no. Oh please.

They walk over, the older one still grinning.

"Boys—this is Tess, one of our neighbors. Why don't you take her to hang out with you?"

The younger one is still staring at me, unsmiling, and my face is getting hotter.

"No," I say, too loudly. "I *want* to play Barbies."

The older one—Jack—laughs again. "Of course you do."

Three weeks later, one chilly, bright Saturday morning at the start of half-term, Julia Lewis pays us a visit. It is the day after Ben

Matthews kissed me at school. He walked back to his gang of friends afterward and I heard one of them ask him how it was and he said, "She tasted fat." It was my first kiss and it was coated in humiliation.

Julia brings more than her three kids. She brings Max and Lena, the children of her best friends. "They work abroad," I hear her say to Dad in a hushed voice. "Poor things—they hardly see their parents."

My plan to stay with the adults and keep little Ellie company is stalled by the sight of the boy, Max. Forget the Insanely-Hots, he's the handsome prince, the white knight, the happy-ever-after; he's all of them. He smiles at me and it melts away the humiliation, it melts away the elephantine layer of imaginary fat that has settled on me like a real weight. His smile makes me feel I can stand next to Bella and not in her shadow.

Then the spell is broken as Bella bounds up. "Come on," she says. "We'll show you the woods."

Bella leads us through the woods to the fallen tree at the top of the embankment by the stream. "Look," she says, laughing, pointing to our names carved into the wood. "We did this last year, made it our tree." She pulls a penknife out of her jeans pocket and holds it out to Max. "Want to sign?"

I frown. It's supposed to be our tree. Our woods. Our place. I want to snatch the penknife out of Max's hand, but...But. I also want Max to carve his initials next to mine. I'd have added a love heart around them in my imagination. Tess and Max, sitting in a tree, k-i-s-s-i-n-g.

But it's Bella's name he carves his own next to and Lena adds hers on the other side, so the three of them are huddled together, not enough space between them so it's like one name—MaxBellaLena—a solitary, wobbly-lettered Tess alone three inches away.

"You too," Bella says to Jack and Sean, holding the knife out. "You've got to add your names too."

The magic of the woods is receding; instead I smell the dankness of the stream and wet leaves, feel sharp twigs and damp mud under my feet. I hear the trees rustling—whispering, feel the breeze get colder on my cheeks.

They're all looking at Bella as Jack takes the knife. It's like I'm not even there and I pinch myself to make sure I exist.

Worst of all, Max is looking at Bella and all of a sudden I realize his smile is just for her. It was always for her.

DECEMBER 2006

"Tess? Will you babysit Ellie tonight? Greg and Julia want me to go to the pub with them."

I look up from my homework. Again? It's the third time this month. I guess I don't mind that much—I'm not doing anything else and they pay me to do it. But it stings a bit that they always ask me and not Bella. Because they know I'm always available and they know Bella is always out. It's the Christmas holidays—why can't Jack or Sean babysit their own bloody sister?

Oh right. Because they also have a social life. Even though they've been away at boarding school, they still came home to a ton of Christmas and New Year's party invitations. I know this because Bella told me. Because she's been invited to all the same parties and I haven't been invited to any.

"Or..." Dad's still hovering. "If they can find someone else, you could come to the pub with us, if you like? You've barely left the house this holiday."

Yes, that's it, Dad. Rub it in that you have a better social life than me. Pity me enough to take me to the pub with a bunch of forty-year-olds where I'll sit in the corner with a Coke and a bag of chips while you all get drunk.

"No thanks," I say, slamming my book shut. "I'd rather babysit."

"Tess—don't be like that."

"Like *what*? I've said I'll do it, haven't I? Go and get wasted with your new friends."

I stomp up the stairs, the guilt kicking in before I'm halfway up. Jeez—I should be pleased Dad's getting out there, not crying at home about Mum more than two years after she died.

It's just...I throw myself onto my bed and stare up at the ceiling. It's just it's not only Dad who's been sucked into the glamorous lives of our new neighbors. It's Bella as well—all excited by the new boys in town, who only appear with their private school accents on school holidays or for the odd weekend, exotic and rare enough to never get boring. Between them going back after half-term and breaking up for Christmas, all I've bloody heard is Bella and her mates going on and on about them, obsessively stalking them on Facebook. Bella was round there the day they came home for the holidays. Her and Nicole and Caitlin swooping down on the boys, dragging them out. Jack's nearly eighteen now, he gets served in the pubs, sneaks drinks to the others while the barman turns a blind eye. Max and Lena were there as well—their mum and dad aren't coming home for Christmas. Bella told me all this and I spent a couple of days hoping Max might come over to see me.

Bella and I never go to the woods anymore. Or even to the beach. I like the beach better in the winter. All wrapped up in layers and hats and scarves, we sometimes have the whole place to ourselves. But now, she's out most nights with her friends and Jack and Sean, sneaking in at eleven, smelling of booze and cigarettes, falling into my room to tell tales of who's hooked up with whom and more. Me holding my breath, hoping she won't tell me Max has got off with one of her friends.

Like Dad, she took pity on me the first time. Begged me to come along. But then we got there and Nicole loudly said, *Christ, we'll never get served with her tagging along*. And it was true—the barman's blind eye wasn't quite blind enough with me there and he refused to serve alcohol to anyone.

None of them spoke to me except Bella. Did Max even notice I was there? None of them noticed when I slunk off home after half an hour. Not even Bella.

She hasn't asked me since.

So yes, Dad, I'll babysit. Why the bloody hell not? What the bloody hell else am I going to do? I roll over and punch the pillow. Maybe Bella will end up spending so much time with them, she'll realize what idiots they are and I'll get my sister back.

I'm making hot chocolate for Ellie, testing to make sure it's not too hot before adding mini marshmallows. Bella is helping her change into her pajamas so when Julia and Greg pick her up, they can carry her from our house to the car and then straight to bed at their house.

"Read," Ellie says, tottering into the room in her Peppa Pig jammies, weighed down by a heavy hardbacked book, Bella walking behind her.

I frown as Ellie drops the book on my lap. "Why did you give her this?" I say to Bella, who shrugs and doesn't look up from her phone.

"It's a kid's book, isn't it?"

It's more than a kid's book. It's the book our mother used to read to us, full of creepy fairy tales that started giving me nightmares after she died. I kept it hidden after that because I didn't want to look at it, but I also kept it treasured because it was something precious to Mum. It isn't something a four-year-old with sticky fingers and a penchant for scribbling on any paper she finds should have.

"I tell you what," I say to Ellie with a big smile. "We can read later but let's play Barbies now, okay?"

It's easy to distract her with dolls.

Bella sinks down on the sofa next to me. "Do you think he likes me?" she says, picking up a Barbie in a wedding dress.

"Who?"

Not Max. Please don't say Max. My heart still flutters when I see him. Max is the reason I said yes to that disastrous night at the pub, even though I knew Bella's friends and Jack and Sean would be there.

Bella drops the doll when her phone beeps and she picks it up with a smile. "Never mind," she says. "I'm just popping out for a bit. Cover for me if Dad comes back, okay?"

"Bella?" I call after her as she shrugs into her jacket. "Do you want to do something tomorrow? Just us two?"

She hesitates and opens her mouth to answer but then her phone pings again and she's distracted, staring down at the screen. "Sure," she says, hand on the door. "If I have time."

"It's okay," Ellie says after Bella slams the front door behind her. She pats my hand. "I'll still play with you."

I laugh and pick up another doll. "Thanks, Ellie—we'll have way more fun, won't we?"

"I wish I had sisters," she says, struggling to push a doll's foot into a pink boot. "I wish you were my sister."

I hug her and kiss her blond curls. She smells of chocolate and strawberry shampoo. "You can be my secret baby sister," I say.

There's a tap on the front door as I'm covering Ellie with a blanket. She crashed out on the sofa just before nine after an epic Barbie session consisting of four weddings and two parties.

I hurry to the door, not wanting Ellie to wake up cranky and tired. I step back in shock when I see Sean on the doorstep.

"Hey," he says with a half-smile as I just stare at him. "Thought I'd come and pick Ellie up—relieve you of your babysitting duties."

"I thought you were out with the others." Who's Bella with if not Jack and Sean?

He shrugs. "I wasn't in the mood for the pub tonight."

"Um . . . okay. Ellie's just fallen asleep."

"Right," he says, staring at me. "Can I come in anyway? It's freezing out here."

I notice he's only wearing a thin, long-sleeved T-shirt and no coat. How's he supposed to get Ellie home? Carry her two miles in her Peppa Pig pajamas? "Oh. Yeah. Yes, of course. Sorry."

"Looks like she's had fun," he says, looking at the scattered dolls all over the floor.

I lean to start picking them up, stacking them in the toy box she brought with her. I never babysit at their house—they always bring her here. I don't know why.

"I think she likes having another girl to play with," I say.

Sean smiles. We're talking in low voices, little more than a whisper so as not to wake Ellie. "Yeah—she's never impressed when me and Jack play."

"You and Jack play with *dolls*?" I can't imagine it. Not in a million years. Cutting the heads off the dolls—yes. That I can imagine. And the two of them telling Ellie to leave them alone, that I can also imagine.

Sean's staring at me. "You don't like us very much, do you?"

I gape, not knowing what to say. "I don't...it's just..."

"You never say a word to me or Jack. You hang around like a timid little mouse. You don't know us at all, so how come you have this permanent sneer on your face when you look at us? You did it just then. She's our kid sister—do you think we never get roped into playing with her or looking after her?"

I back away from his fierce rant. No—he's the one with the sneer, the attitude, him and his brother with that mocking smile, always looking like he's laughing at me.

"If I'm a mouse, it's because of you. No one's ever bothered trying to talk to me—I'm just Bella's frumpy bloody sister. And maybe I don't want to be patronized and treated like I'm Ellie's age, so that's why I don't want to hang out with a bunch of...a bunch of *knobs* who think they're God's gift."

"So you have no reason to dislike us. You're not interested in getting to know us at all. You're just jealous *you're* not getting any attention. Oh, poor Tess. How hard done by you are."

"Fuck off," I hiss.

"I will," he says, getting up. "I don't know why I bothered coming round."

He slams the door on his way out and Ellie wakes up with a grumpy wail.

I grit my teeth. I hate him. I hate both of them, Jack and bloody Sean.

New Year's Eve and we're over at Dean House with the rest of the village. Bella's wearing a black slinky dress and is laughing with Max and Lena, putting her hand on Max's arm as she leans in to talk to him. I've refused to wear anything but jeans and I'm sitting in a corner playing with Ellie.

"Come on, buttercup, it's time you were in bed," Julia says, coming over and scooping Ellie up. "Let's leave Tess to play with people her own age, shall we?"

Ellie wails as Julia carries her away and part of me wants to wail right along with her, left alone in a corner with a half-finished Disney princess jigsaw puzzle. Sometimes it's so much easier to play with Ellie, the pair of us invisible in a corner.

This house is weird. They've lit candles and strung fairy lights around the room, filled every surface with bottles and glasses, but under all the party stuff, it looks like they haven't bothered doing anything. The paper's peeling on the walls and the floorboards are bare. It's cold and creepy and damp and I don't know how they can stand living here. It's like they did all the essential stuff—sorting the roof and windows—and then got bored and gave up, so the inside still has the creepy haunted-house vibe it always had.

No one else seems to see it. Probably because everyone is drunk except me. Even Dad's necking back the wine, standing over by the fire with Greg Lewis.

Now Bella is dragging Max off to dance and I get up to leave. I'm halfway to the door when I see Sean coming in, so I about-turn and duck out the back door instead, taking refuge in the garden.

I take a deep breath as I walk around. There are so many weeds. Half the roses I spent months nurturing are being choked by them.

My hands itch to get stuck in, pull away the tangled brambles, give the flowers a chance to breathe and grow. But a flare of light at the far end of the walled garden tells me I'm not alone. Someone's out here smoking a cigarette. As my eyes adjust to the dark, I see it's Greg Lewis. He raises a hand and beckons me over.

"Hello, Tess. Are you having a good time?"

I shrug and fiddle with an ivy leaf clinging to the wall.

"I know what you mean. It's a bit much, isn't it?"

I'm surprised. He's been circling the room with Julia, life and soul of the party, his loud laugh cutting through the noise all night, dancing with everyone.

"Julia's the party animal," he says in explanation. "I'd prefer a quiet night down the pub." He grinds his cigarette out under his foot.

"I need to do something about this garden in the spring," he says, kicking at a weed sprouting from the ground. "Sean used to help me in the old house, but he's away at school most of the time now."

"Sean likes gardening?" I can't hide the note of surprise in my voice.

He smiles. "Sure. You do too, don't you? Leo said something. You should talk to Sean about it—it's always difficult to find things in common when you're the youngest, isn't it?"

I bow my head at the pity in his voice. Oh God—have they been discussing me on their nights down the pub? Poor, friendless Tess.

I turn away.

"Hey," Greg says, touching my shoulder. "Sorry. That was a bit patronizing, wasn't it?"

"I don't *want* to get drunk and smoke and take drugs in the woods, that's all. I don't want to be one of those idiots. How does that make me the sad case?"

I wince as I realize I've just told Greg in so many words that drinking and smoking and taking drugs is what his sons get up to when they're out with Bella and her friends. I don't even know if it's true or if it's just what I'm afraid of.

"It doesn't," he says. "Not at all. It makes you the sensible one. You just keep being you, Tess Cooper."

"What's going on?"

I spin round at the new voice and see Sean watching us from the back door, silhouetted by the kitchen light.

"Tess is out here getting some fresh air," Greg says, stepping away from me.

"Is that right?" Sean says, and he's staring at me, a frown on his face.

"Yeah—is that a problem?" I realize I don't want pity and sympathy from Greg—that's just making me feel worse. I want a *fight*. I want Sean Lewis to snap back at me, give me a chance to vent all this . . . frustration and jealousy and God knows what.

But he doesn't. He laughs and shakes his head, then turns away and heads back inside. As he pulls the door open, I hear everyone cheering and the chimes of Big Ben from the TV.

Great. Happy bloody New Year.

NOW

CHAPTER 10

"Hey, Soph."

"Hey, stranger. How's it going? How are you coping being back there?"

"Well, I had to get Max to stop the car so I could throw up as soon as we got to the village, so that gives you a bit of an indication."

"Shit."

"Yep. But...I'm still glad I came back."

"How are Julia and your dad?"

I lean back against the pillows and close my eyes, soothed by the sympathy in her voice. It's only eight in the morning—I'm amazed she answered; Sophie likes a lie-in on a Saturday. My eyes are gritty with tiredness—I can't have slept more than two hours. "They're...God, I was going to say they're fine, that automatic ridiculous answer. But they're not. Of course they're not. Julia is dying—she's so ill, it's torture to see. And Dad. My poor, poor dad. He's...struggling."

"At least you're there."

"Yeah. I guess. What's happening there?" My heart thumps as I wait for her answer. The pause before she speaks is too long.

"I...I don't know really. I told Karen what's happening with Julia. They're holding off on things as long as they can."

"So I don't need to worry about being arrested at the funeral then?"

I'd meant it as a joke but there's another pause. "I'm sure it won't come to that."

Those pauses. Her tone. Rebecca Martin's parents must be making trouble. It doesn't take a detective to interpret her silences.

"I feel so awful about what I did, Soph. I'm here and it's like I'm sixteen again and remembering what I was like then. I can't quite believe I did that to Rebecca. She's a *kid*. I wish I could see her, try to explain..."

"Jesus, Tess—don't even think it."

"No, no, I'm not. I just wish I could go back in time and undo it."

"Yeah. Me too."

I sigh. "So, Max and Lena came back with me. I wasn't sure it was a good idea, but Julia seemed so happy to see them. But they're... they're reminders of Bella. Every time I look at them, I see her."

"How was it seeing your old boyfriend again?"

I snort. "He was never my boyfriend. But last night... It was weird. I was talking to him and Lena about Sean and... I think I was remembering things. From the night of Bella's death."

"Oh God, really? What did you remember?"

"I'm not sure. It was vague and muddled. I didn't sleep last night, so my brain is a mess, which isn't helping. It was a flash of us out in the woods, her yelling something at me. And I keep seeing this other moment. From the wedding, I think. Someone's talking to me—a man. But I can't make out the words or see their face. And now..." I grip my phone harder. "And now Julia wants to see her sons and although I don't want them here, I'm thinking I should try..."

"For Julia?"

"Sean's here. Back at his old house. Dad wants me to try to get him to visit." I pause. "And maybe seeing him—seeing Dean House again, walking past the woods, maybe it'll trigger another memory. I don't want to. I want to run as far away in the other direction as possible. But I think I need to, Soph, if I ever want to move on and not pass out every time I come near the place."

Sophie's turn to sigh. "I guess. But..."

"What? Say it. Whatever you're thinking."

"I'm worried. You have so much going on—with Julia, with school. God, Tess, I know you're determined to tough it out, but maybe one step at a time, yeah?"

"But Julia wants to see Sean and Dad's asked me if I'll talk to him." I sit upright. "I'll sort it out, though. And it'll serve Sean right if I puke all over him. Don't worry about me."

"Can't help it. That's my job as chief best friend."

I laugh. "I have to go."

"Okay, babes. Call me tomorrow, okay? Let me know how it's going."

I hear a noise as I end the call and get up with a frown. Lena's standing outside the door. She's wearing the same clothes as last night and looks like she slept about as much as I did.

"Sorry," she says. "I could hear you on the phone and I didn't want to interrupt."

"Were you *listening*?"

Lena raises her eyebrows and ducks round me. "Um—no. Why would I? I just need to get something."

How long was she standing there? She might not have meant to, but she would have heard every word.

I rub my eyes, heavy-headed and groggy. "Where's Max?" I ask. I wanted to take Max with me to talk to Sean. They're still friends; surely he'll be more persuasive than me face-to-face, even if Sean told him to eff off on the phone?

Lena rolls her eyes, pulling creased clothes out of her bag. "Oh, he dashed off at seven for some emergency meeting."

"On a Saturday?"

She shrugs. "Don't ask me. It's bad enough I couldn't sleep and was up before the bloody sun rose. I was not conscious enough to ask questions."

"When will he be back?"

She shrugs, pulling her T-shirt over her head. "Hopefully in time for me not to have to get the train back tomorrow. He's not gone far—it's some project of theirs near Cardiff." She finishes changing and smiles at me. "What, you thought Mr. Ambitious had dropped everything to rush to Julia's side? It was good timing, was how he put it. He gets to put the whole weekend on expenses."

"Good timing? Julia dying is *good timing*?"

She winces. "I don't think that was what he meant exactly."

I waver in the doorway. Could I take Lena with me? No. She's too combative. She's hardly likely to persuade Sean into visiting. Get him in a headlock and try dragging him here, yes, but not persuade him nicely.

I put a hand on my stomach. Shit. I'm going to have to do this alone.

Dad is in with Julia, holding her hand. I pause in the doorway. They're talking in low voices, Dad leaning in toward her. It looks too intimate, his hand in hers, the smile on his face, so I pass by without going in, blowing them both a kiss.

I argue with myself the whole time I walk to Dean House. Do I really want Sean in my life again? Even for Julia's sake? I could lie, couldn't I? Tell Dad I went there and he refused to see me. Julia doesn't even know he's here. I waver but my feet keep walking the familiar route.

It's not even nine o'clock when I get to Dean House and I wonder if I've been foolish to march over so early before my courage failed. Will Sean still be here? And if he is, what if I wake him up and he's pissed off? As I hesitate, thinking about leaving, I hear running footsteps behind me, Lena's voice calling my name.

"What is it?" I say. "What are you doing here? Is it Julia?"

She shakes her head. "Hang on a sec," she says. "Let me get my breath." She looks over at the house. "I heard a bit of what you were saying on the phone. Sorry—I wasn't eavesdropping but I couldn't help it. I thought I'd come and see Sean with you but you'd already gone by the time I'd got ready. I needn't have run though— you haven't even made it past the wall yet."

"I was actually contemplating running back home and hiding under the bed."

She lights a cigarette and grins at me. "Might be a good idea. Save it for later when it's an acceptable time to down some Dutch courage before knocking on the door." It's not like Lena to be so cautious. She's always been more of a dive-in-and-worry-about-it-later person. Hence my not inviting her along.

"Hey, do you remember how sexy Greg Lewis was? Bella used to insist he was far hotter than Jack and Sean. Older man and all that. I never really saw it myself. I've known him since I was three."

I flinch at her mention of Greg. I've not thought—not allowed myself to think—about him for a very long time.

I remember overhearing Bella and her friends talking about him, how I would squirm at their speculation about the tragic figure living alone in the monster house after everything happened. He was handsome and brooding and alone and I'm sure, in that creeping hot summer when there was a killer on the loose, Bella and her friends weren't the only kids who thought of him, hiding away in his creepy house. It added an edge, a frisson of danger, to the average boring teenage crush.

"He was old enough to be her dad." I try to keep my tone neutral, but the smile Lena gives me tells me I failed.

"Bella told me she used to talk to him."

My cheeks burn. *Our secret*, Bella said. Not a secret at all, then. She told Lena and God knows who else. I feel the old jealousy stir. He was *mine*, it shrieks. How dare she claim him as hers?

"She said she used to visit without us and she spoke to him." Lena glances over at me. "What do you think happened to him? Do you really think he ran off because of the wedding?"

I forgot to wonder. I'd stopped going over there a few weeks before the wedding. And then Bella dying overshadowed him disappearing. Julia became ours, the boys never bothered visiting the house or clearing it out. Greg Lewis disappeared and the weeds grew and the dust settled and we all...forgot. I feel the familiar piercing guilt. I doubt Jack and Sean forgot, did they?

I shiver, remembering the dust that had already settled over the house when I went there with Bella the night before the wedding. "Maybe he's still there, locked in a forgotten room."

"Nah—I reckon he's probably living it up in Marbella," Lena says.

"But why wouldn't he contact his sons?" Something's nagging, tugging at the string of my lost memories, but I can't get hold of it.

"How do you know he doesn't keep in contact? How do you know he hasn't arranged to have all his stuff shipped somewhere?" Lena pauses. "I came here once, on my own. I was pissed off with Max and Bella—they were hanging out together, leaving me out, whispering and sneaking off," she says with a funny smile on her face.

My shoulder jerks, can't help it.

"I sneaked over the wall and I saw him..." Lena's voice dies.

"Saw him what?"

"Saw him watching you." She looks at me. "You didn't know I knew? You didn't think Bella and I would be curious about where you kept sneaking off to?"

No, I didn't know. That last year, I didn't think Bella even saw me anymore. Not until...

"Don't worry," she says. "I didn't tell anyone then and I won't now. You were in the garden, sweaty and...well, you weren't looking your best, Tess, to be honest."

I grit my teeth. She can't say anything without the cut, the jab.

Lena laughs. "Sorry," she says. But she doesn't mean it. She might as well add, "No offense."

I shrug. "So he was watching—so what? He used to teach me about gardening."

She grins. "It was what he was doing while he was watching." She leans forward and whispers in my ear.

I recoil, pull away from her and her disgusting words that spread through me like a virus.

"No—he wouldn't. Jesus, Lena!"

She laughs again. "I swear, Tess. He was watching you, all

sweaty and grubby in your shorts and his hand was down his pants. Swear it."

She's lying, taking all my own worried thoughts and turning them into a nightmare she wants to grow inside me for some sick reason. It makes me wonder what else Bella told her. She wouldn't have, would she?

"Why the hell would you even say that?" I mutter, shoulders rigid with tension.

"You know why Julia really left him, right?" Lena says, lighting another cigarette.

"The relationship broke down after Ellie died. Everyone knows that."

Lena laughs. "Right. That's what he *wanted* everyone to think."

"So what was the real reason?"

Smoke from Lena's cigarette blows in my face and I wave it away.

"He used to fuck teenage girls," she says, and I step away from her, her words a slap in the face.

She's staring at me. "Yeah—you know that, don't you?"

Oh God—the way she's looking at me. Bella must have told her.

"Of *course* I don't know that—how do you know?"

She raises an eyebrow. "How do you think?"

Greg and *Lena*?

She laughs. "Only joking. As if I'd touch an old man."

He wasn't that old.

"It is true, though, about him and teenage girls. Jack told me once. He caught his dad touching up one of his girlfriends. I think that's why he ran off. I think he got caught."

I remember the way Greg touched Bella's hair that day I saw them together.

"Come on, Tess," Lena says, nudging me. "Are you trying to tell me he never touched you all those times you were . . . *gardening* together? No sweaty little rolls in the mud? You can tell me, I'll keep it a secret."

I turn away from her, jumping as a bird swoops past. "What are you even doing here? It's not to see Sean, is it?"

"I had to get out of that house," she says. "God—the *smell*." She shudders. "I can't stand it. Seeing Julia like that—wasn't she always larger than life? Didn't she light up any room she was in? I didn't want to come. I wanted to remember her like she was. All those parties, do you remember?"

Not big, formal parties. Impulsive get-togethers. Max, Lena, and their parents on their infrequent trips back to the UK, Dad, Julia, me, and Bella. A few neighbors sometimes, regulars from the pub. Bring a bottle and tuck in.

"So why are you here?" I ask again.

"Max. He made me come. He'd have killed me if I'd refused." She shakes her head and kicks the wall. "I'm out of here as soon as possible on Sunday, though. I've said all the goodbyes I need to. I don't need to stay and watch her die."

"What about Max—will he stay?"

She shrugs. "He has to work, so I don't know." She glances at me. "Still got that crush, Tess?"

"Don't be daft. I was just asking."

"I never got why you used to follow Max around with those big, puppy-dog eyes when Jack and Sean were around. God, those boys—were any boys ever so brooding and beautiful?"

They terrified me as a teenager. Not like Max, so steady and kind. Jack and Sean weren't storybook brooding; they were bitter, too much rage too close to the surface, so much worse after Julia left them for us. And all of it aimed at Bella and me: the usurpers, the thieves of their mother's love. It wasn't thrilling, being with them, it was frightening.

Lena grabs my arm. "There he is," she says, pointing at a shadow in one of the windows.

"Right," I say, walking toward the gate. "I'm going in—I'm going to *make* him come and see Julia." I glance back at her. "Are you coming?"

She shakes her head and pulls a face. "Second thoughts, too many ghosts for me in there. Not all of them dead. Sorry, Tess."

I'm at the gate when her voice stops me.

"Do you ever wonder where we'd all be if Bella hadn't died?"
I look back.

"Would we all still be friends?"

"I don't know."

"I never had a friend like her—not before, not since. It felt like we were the sisters sometimes."

The old jealousy stirs. "It's been ten years, Lena."

"And my life has been pretty much shit ever since she died." She looks lost and it dampens the embers of jealousy.

She wipes a hand across her face. Was she crying? Lena? Impossible to tell under the sunglasses. But then she smiles. "Ignore me," she says. "My hangover's making me sentimental. Go on then— go catch yourself a Lewis boy."

I look back once more as I get to the front door. She's still there, but she's looking away from the house, toward the woods. I wonder if she sees it too, every time she comes here, Bella and me, half-buried under leaves and mud. I bet she's thinking what they all must have been thinking back then. Why did Bella have to be the one who died?

He comes to the door after my third knock: Sean Lewis, still stupidly handsome. More so, I think. Age suits him. Ten years has added muscle and character. The intensity that was so odd at seventeen is sexy at twenty-seven. You would always give this man a second look if you saw him out. But then you'd see it, the simmering anger and something else lurking, and maybe then you'd go back to your boyfriend and feel safer and a bit happier. But he also looks tired and so much like his father, it makes the words I came to say stick in my throat. My dad, the man Julia left them for, is inches shorter, thinner, plainer. A quiet man, so bloody ordinary. But no one would feel uneasy looking at my dad. He was a man to feel safe with and I know Julia did. Greg—he never looked like someone's father, he never looked safe.

I have another flash of memory—sharp and bright and loud. Me and Sean, dancing at the wedding, but not out on the lawn

with everyone else, swaying instead in the trees at the edge of the
wood that bordered our garden. Is that real?

Sean looks at me and shock is replaced by a half-smile. He
reaches out like he's going to hug me and I recoil. My instinct is to
run, just like it was back then, and my reaction stalls him. His face
floods with color and the smile disappears, replaced by the more
familiar blankness I was never able to read.

"Tess? God—you were not who I expected to find on my
doorstep."

After the wedding, after Bella died, Jack and Sean disappeared
again. Jack had already moved out of Dean House by then and
Sean never came back to visit. Neither of them ever came back to
stay. Has Julia even seen them since?

"I'm here for Julia," I say. I came over here planning to unleash
all my anger, to drag him back kicking and screaming to see his
dying mother. But he has shadows under his eyes and I wonder if
he sleeps, if he's been lying awake remembering the last time he
was here, if he lies awake thinking of all the years he never got to
spend with his mother and it twists me up inside because I know
that pain. God, it almost killed me when my own mother died, all
the grief for everything we weren't going to be able to do together.
She would never meet my boyfriends and give me advice, never
watch me get married, never get to hold any children I might have
in the future. The pain of it is still there, muted but sharp enough
to hurt.

Sean is looking at me and I think he must be able to see it all
on my face. My heart races and a long-ago voice whispers in my
head. *He's dangerous*. Who said that? Was it Bella? Or Lena or
Max? I don't remember. It was the night we all got drunk and
things got hazy, a few days before Bella died.

Run, Jack's voice whispers in my memory.

Run.

"You'd better come in," Sean says, stepping aside to let me in
the house. The hallway behind him is dark and I can see a coating
of dust and cobwebs over everything. As Sean steps aside, I'm hit

with a tang of mildew and rot and dust that coats my throat and makes me cough. The house smells rotten and I take an involuntary step back.

"No thanks," I say. "I don't want to come in."

As I take another step away, Sean stands there, looking lost. I notice a rolled-up sleeping bag propped against the wall.

"Are you *staying* here?" I ask.

He nods. "I figured it was easier than going back and forth from a B and B in the village."

"But..." I look beyond him at the dust and the decay. "You can't stay here—there's no light, no heating. For God's sake"—it's out of my mouth before I've thought it through—"come and stay with us."

"It's not like you to be so concerned for my welfare. From what I remember, you used to be all about getting me out of your house, not into it."

"And from what I remember, you used to be Mr. Hostile, all snotty arrogance and scowls."

He smiles, a big warm smile. "Ugh—yeah. The scowly teenage years. What little shits we were."

A returning smile tugs at the corners of my own mouth and the disorienting feeling I got with Lena, that I'm sixteen again, fades. But there's still something nagging at me. *Why* is Sean being so nice? Christ knows, he has no reason to. Why is he even here, if not for Julia? I grit my teeth.

"So what's going on—why are you skulking around here instead of spending time with your mother? Your *dying* mother?"

"I am going to see her."

It wrong-foots me. I came in expecting to have to fight to get him over to see Julia.

"I wasn't going to. I told Leo and Max I wouldn't. I was going to come back to the house, do what I had to do, and leave without visiting. I thought..." He pauses and shakes his head. "I thought I'd have more time, you know? When Leo rang to tell me about the cancer—God, it was only six months ago. I thought she'd fight it, get through it. I put off calling and visiting, but I always thought I'd have time. Then Leo told me she was dying and my instinct was still to stay away, but it's my last chance, isn't it? Last chance to..."

His voice trails off and I hope the missed words are *last chance to say goodbye* and not *last chance to scream accusations.*

"So why are you *here*?" I say again, spreading my arms to indicate the abandoned house, the darkness, the dust. "Are you hiding?"

He kicks a cardboard box next to him. "We've sold the house."

"Sold it? That's a bit sudden..." I stop and laugh. "Sorry. What a stupid thing to say."

"Yeah—not sure you could call ten years of the house being empty a sudden sale."

There's a silence that should be awkward, but somehow it isn't. One thing about Sean, he's good at being quiet. "Maybe the new owners will finish what your dad started—make this place fabulous." I think of the gardens with a pang.

He smiles and shrugs. "Doubt it. We've sold it to a construction company. They're going to build a whole load of new houses on the site. Initial work starts Monday—they'll be clearing the grounds, emptying the house before pulling it down." He looks at the box. "I told Jack I'd come here and pack up anything we wanted to keep, but...I don't know what to take." He picks up a pottery ornament from the box, blows the dust off. "I don't know...was any of it really Dad's? It's just stuff, isn't it? None of it important. If it was important, he'd have taken it with him."

"Has he..." I stop to clear my throat. "Has he ever been back?"

"Look at this place—it's not been touched in all the time he's been gone." He laughs, a bitter edge to the sound. "At least Mum didn't run far."

Greg went missing a few days before the wedding. Already having to deal with the fact that their mother had broken up the family and was marrying another man, the boys—because they were still boys then, Jack not yet twenty, Sean almost eighteen—had to then deal with their father running off. What must that have done to them? I lost my mother and my sister, but they didn't leave me voluntarily—they were taken. But Julia and Greg... how could they?

"Look, I get that you and Julia have all sorts of unresolved stuff going on, but she doesn't have much time. She wants to see you now," I say. "Seriously, if I had the same opportunity—to see my mum or sister again..."

"I've already said I'm going to see her." He shakes his head and kicks the box away from him. "Fuck it—I don't want any of this stuff."

"Will you come now?" I ask. "Please. You can't stay here—you'll get ill, the state of the place."

He stares at me for a long time and I wonder what he's looking for in my face. Is he seeing what Max saw—the ghost of Bella?

He nods once. "Okay. I'll come."

I turn away, planning to wait out on the lane, wanting to be farther away from the house, when Sean calls me back. "I found something I wanted to give you." His voice trails off as he holds out another box. "I thought it was Dad's."

I open the box and hold my breath at what's inside. It's Bella's camera, the one Greg gave her, and a book.

"It's Dad's book," Sean says as I take it out. "He's written on the inside."

I open the book. *To Arabella, who sees the world in a special way. Love Greg.*

"She was friends with him," I say, stroking the cover of the book, not looking at him. "He gave her the camera."

"So why was it back in Dean House?"

"I don't know. Maybe she gave it back to him. She stopped using it." I stop and blink. Wasn't Bella carrying the camera the night before the wedding? That strange night she brought me here?

"There's still film in it," Sean says, and we stare at each other.

It stops my breath, the realization that on this film are the last photos Bella took. Could I still develop it after all this time? I clutch the box to my chest. I can try. I can get the film developed, see if...see if there's some memory of my sister trapped on there, some precious moment I can get back.

Do I hear a whisper or is it just the rustling of trees? For a moment, it sounds like my sister whispering, *yes yes yes*.

CHAPTER 11

I go out onto the lane and text Dad while I wait for Sean, so he can warn Julia. The grass at the back of Dean House stretches out and down to the border of the woods. A mist has settled and the trees are half-hidden, truncated. Instead of trees, they're a regiment of brown-suited soldiers, silent and still, watching me.

There's a pheasant on the grass, picking for worms with the smaller birds. It's a scene that should be idyllic, but it's not my house, not my view, and at the end of it all, always at the end of it all, the woods, the woods.

My head is full—of Julia, of Sean and Jack, the summer of death when everyone in the village lived in the grip of fear. I don't want to be here. I want to be back in my flat, listening to city noises, smelling wet pavement and car fumes, the greasy breakfasts frying in the café on the corner. Two-for-one cocktails with Sophie, picking up city boys. Familiar comforts of a life I've adopted, the Tess I've become since leaving here. God, I even want to be back in the school corridors among all that noise and commotion, being mocked by Rebecca Martin.

"You ready?" Sean appears next to me.

I nod. "I'd forgotten how beautiful it was here."

The pheasant takes flight and he smiles. "It is, isn't it? I haven't been back in so long. I might take some time while I'm here, explore the coast, take some walks."

I stare at him, frowning as we walk out into the lane. "You've changed so much."

"Have I?"

"You were always so..." I spread my hands out.

"So what?" He's smiling again.

"Grumpy. Hostile. Always lurking and scowling and, well, scaring the shit out of me."

His smile turns to laughter. "Was I really? That's not how I remember it. You think *I* was hostile? It used to come off you in waves."

A smile tugs unwillingly at the corners of my mouth. God, I wouldn't be a teenager again if someone offered me a million dollars. Sean's portrayal of us as truculent little jerks makes me think of Rebecca Martin again.

"There's this girl I teach, she's like that. So abrasive. Challenging me with every look and word. I guess…it's all an act, isn't it? It was with me."

Sean nods. "Do you like it? Teaching?"

If I squint into the morning mist, I can almost see Bella, the day she told me she didn't want to be a photographer anymore, that she was going to do a teaching course instead. Did I ever question her about it? It was such an odd and abrupt change—she'd wanted to be a photographer since she was twelve.

"It's something I've been asking myself recently." I cringe inside as I remember the time Rebecca Martin had annoyed me so much that I scrawled a D across her Shakespeare essay when it was worth at least a B, if not an A. "I don't think I'm a very good teacher. I think I'd make a better landscape gardener. That's what I wanted to do when I was a kid."

He smiles again. "You know that's what I do, right? Gardening? I work in the gardens of a National Trust house across the river in Gloucestershire."

"Really?"

"And Jack went into construction. With Max as an architect, we could build ourselves a whole town."

The front door opens as we approach the house and Dad and Julia step out together. It makes my chest hurt to see the effort Julia has made—she's dressed, hair brushed and soft around her face, radiant smile at the ready for her son. I step away from Sean.

"You go on," I say. "I'll give you some time with your mum. But, Sean?"

He glances back at me.

"Don't...don't upset her, okay?"

He gives me a look I can't interpret and I have an urge to grab him and pull him away, but it's too late, Julia is there, touching his arm, touching his cheek, tears in her eyes as he bends to murmur something in her ear.

I turn away.

It's much later in the afternoon when I open the front door and hear raised voices coming from the kitchen. "You have got to be fucking kidding me," I mutter, clenching my fists. I'll bloody kill Sean if he's come in and upset Dad or Julia.

The kitchen door opens and Sean comes storming out, slamming it behind him. He's scowling but stops short when he sees me in the doorway.

"What have you done?" I say. "What have you said to Julia? She's dying—you can't bring all your baggage into my house and upset her in her last days. You—"

"Oh right, of course you'd assume that, wouldn't you? Mum's gone up for a rest, actually, before you get on your high horse. And it wasn't me shouting, it was Max and Lena."

"What?" I glance toward the stairs and Julia's closed door. "Come outside a minute.

"Why were Max and Lena shouting at you?" I continue when we're far enough away from the house not to disturb Julia's rest.

He sighs and runs a hand through his hair. "I told them about the house being sold and they went off on one."

"Why?"

He shakes his head. "I don't even think it's the house...Mum wanted it sold. When she got ill, she wrote me and Jack a letter. The house belonged jointly to Mum and Dad—they never got around to changing that before Dad ran off. It meant...Mum had to have Dad declared legally dead so she could sell it. I think that's what rattled Max and Lena."

"You think Greg is *dead*?"

Sean hesitates, then shakes his head. "No, of course not. But I don't think he's ever coming back. The house is falling apart—it's been falling apart for years and it's not like any of us are going to live there again, is it? Mum wants...she wants it done before she dies and me and Jack end up tangled in probate."

"I'm sorry," I say. "I heard shouting and I just thought..."

"I'm glad I came over," Sean says. "Glad I came to see her."

"Did you manage to clear the air?"

He smiles faintly. "Clear the air? That's a diplomatic way of putting it." He shrugs. "It was fine, Tess. Awkward on both sides, but we managed to have a conversation."

I wonder if they did, or if they were both so careful to step around the bigger issues that the conversation was nothing but small talk. Not my business, though, unless it hurt Dad in any way. I had to leave them to sort it out.

"And is she okay about the house being sold already?"

"Do you really think Julia cares what happens to the *house*? She and Dad split up nearly twelve years ago. She's glad we're finally able to get rid of it. All she cares about right now is seeing Jack again before she dies."

"Do you think he'll come back?" I want him to say no.

Sean frowns. "I'll drag him back if I have to."

I flinch and pull a face. Fucking Jack.

"What's your problem?" There's a sharpness in Sean's voice I know I deserve. "I know he was a bit of a dick back then but, come on, it's been ten years. You teach hundreds of obnoxious teenagers—surely you can handle Jack now? He's nearly thirty. Christ, we're all nearly thirty."

He's right. Why do I have this fear, almost panic, at the thought of Jack? Lena was as obnoxious back then as Jack, but I didn't have that same fear when I saw her. Irritation, yes. Exasperation, even, but not fear.

"Because he made my life a misery back then, he really did. How much can he have changed? He's going to come back and...and...upset Julia, I know he is. Because he's..." I pause, take a breath. "I'm sorry, I know he's your brother, but...it's not even just him—it's both of you. Ever since we met you, it's like you were surrounded by death. Ellie, Bella—even Nicole. First your little sister, then Nicole—and I know Jack was with Nicole. And Bella, was he with her too? Or was that you?"

"What exactly are you saying, Tess? What exactly are you accusing us of?"

"I'm not. I'm sorry." I swallow. "But please don't—" That weird panic is back, building in my gut. "Please don't bring him back. He'll upset her. It's what he does. He'll upset everyone."

He frowns. "So despite the apology, we're still the bad guys? Still unwelcome in the Cooper household. Well, it's not about you, is it? It's not about what you want." He pauses, sighs. "Never mind. You should be getting inside. It's dark. Getting late."

"What about you? Are you staying with us or...?"

"You don't want me staying with you, not really." He glances back at the house. "I'll go back to Dean House. I have my sleeping bag, a flashlight. One last night."

I shiver. I'd never spend the night there. I should ask him back into the house again. I should insist. I open my mouth and close it again. I can't.

He's right. Deep down, where that fluttering panic lives, they're still the bad guys.

CHAPTER 12

I have to tell you, Tess. I have to tell you have to tell you...

I wake with a gasp, Bella's voice, barely heard above the roar of a storm, still echoing in my head. I'm shaking, not in my bed. Christ. I'm in the hallway, my hand on the latch of the front door. I'm sleepwalking? I pull my hand away, fingers stiff and sore. Oh God, the door is unlatched. If I hadn't woken up, would I have gone outside in my pajamas, gone wandering off still asleep? I rub my face. It's cold, but my forehead is damp with sweat and my heart is pounding.

"Tess?" It's Dad's voice, pitched low. He's at the top of the stairs, bathrobe on.

"It's okay, Dad," I whisper. "I...I couldn't sleep. I came down for some tea. Go back to sleep."

I have to wait a moment after he goes before I can force my trembling legs to move. What was that? Was it a dream that sent me down here, trying to escape the house? To go where? Or was it a memory? Not as vivid a vision as when I dreamed Bella back alive in my flat, but Bella's yelling voice—*I have to tell you...*It hurts my stomach and makes my head throb. Was that real? From the night she died?

I look at the clock on the wall. It's four a.m. I'm not even going to try to go back to sleep now. I rub my hand across my mouth. I can taste vomit, sour in my throat. God, this place, being back here, what is it doing to me?

Ten o'clock and I'm sitting in the kitchen, nursing a fourth cup of tea, showered and dressed.

"Dad?" I say as he comes in, reaching for the teapot. "I need to go back for a couple of days—I have a meeting at work." My voice wobbles on the last words. I finally called Karen back, arranged to call in at school today at five. Well after all the kids will have left for the day. Karen's suggestion.

Dad smiles and squeezes my hand. "Of course. It's okay—Julia's stable at the moment. You know, if they need you at work, that's okay too. If you came back again this weekend..."

I shake my head. "It's fine. I've arranged things. I'll be back to-morrow."

I'm going back with Max. Lena left yesterday on the train and I haven't seen Sean since our argument outside the house.

"I have my meeting today, then I'm seeing Sophie, and I'll be back on the train tomorrow morning."

"It's so good of you to do this—taking all this time off."

I feel guilty about not telling him the truth, letting him think I'm making some huge sacrifice, taking unpaid leave. But the truth will make him worry, and Christ knows he doesn't need more worry at the moment. Which is why I'm also not telling him I was on the phone with the doctor as soon as it opened, making an emergency appointment. I frightened myself with the sleepwalking. I can't be here for Dad and Julia if I'm scared to close my eyes at night.

"I'll do a big shop when I get back—cook that chicken casserole you love."

His face lights up for a moment. "Julia loves that, too. It might encourage her to eat."

"Tess? You ready?" Max pops his head through the door.

I nod. "I'll be right there." I lean forward and kiss Dad on the cheek. "I'll see you tomorrow, okay? Ring me if anything...if you need anything."

Lost in thought as we set off, it takes me a while to notice Max seems as preoccupied as I am. A sideways glance takes in the frown on his face, his hands white-knuckled on the steering wheel.

"Are you okay? You seem a bit down," I say as we pull onto the highway.

"I'm okay. A bit weirded out by the Dean House sale, I guess."

I raise my eyebrows and he looks across at me. "I know, I know. It's not my house, I haven't been back there in forever but..."

"But?"

"You know we've known Jack and Sean forever, right? We used to live three streets apart when we were little kids. But childhood friends grow apart, it's natural—we had nothing in common apart from our parents being friends." He pauses to change lanes.

"Then Mum and Dad moved abroad for Dad's job and they shoved me in the same boarding school as Jack and Sean. We never hung out in the same group and I didn't even have Lena to balance things out. And then on school holidays, we'd go visit Mum and Dad for a couple of weeks in the summer and then get shunted off to Julia and Greg. We never used to see Jack and Sean—they had their own lives, their own friends."

Did I even notice this back then? They came as a package, Jack and Sean and Max and Lena. I saw them as a unit. But—is that why Max stood out to me, beyond the obvious? Because I sensed he was the odd one out as much as I was?

"But when they bought Dean House and moved to your village, things were different," Max says. "Jack and Sean didn't have their old gangs or places to go. Jack and Lena used to moan about how boring it was, but I loved it—the beach, the woods, God, even those discos up at the amusement park, remember? Coming here...we all hung out together and it felt like a proper holiday. I used to look forward to school holidays again, meeting you and Bella. I guess what I'm feeling now is like someone's sold my favorite holiday house out from under me. I know it's silly."

"No, I get that." I glance over at him. "Sean thought you might be upset over them having Greg declared legally dead."

"Right," he says after a pause. "I am, of course. It was a bit of a shock, that's all."

He lapses back into silence for a few more minutes. It's good Max is driving—the road slips and slides in front of me, stretching and contracting. I'm hoping I might get some proper sleep tonight, away from the village, that this new insomnia has to do with being back home. I haven't slept for more than a couple of hours for nearly a week now. My eyelids get heavy and I feel myself drifting off.

"Hey, listen," he says, pulling me awake again. "Enough brooding. When we get there, why don't we have dinner and catch up? With everything that's been going on, it seems like we've hardly spoken."

Ten years ago, I would have done anything to hear him ask me out for dinner, caught up in the agonies of first love. But ten years ago, I had a sister and something approaching a normal life. Max is all tied up in the horror of what had happened and I don't know how to unpack it all. I don't know whether he sees any of that in my face but he smiles and shakes his head.

"Sorry—forget I said anything. Bad timing, I know. Our moment got missed, I think."

Moment? Did we ever have a moment?

"It's not that. I've arranged to have a drink with my friend, that's all."

I haven't thought much about Max. I haven't allowed myself to think about him. But, equally, now that he's back, I don't want him to disappear. I don't want to stop thinking about him again.

"But I'd love to have dinner," I say. "Why don't you come with me to meet Sophie? We can eat afterward and if it gets too late, you can stay at my place—I have a sofa bed."

"So Sophie, your friend, she's another teacher?"

"That's right. I met her on my first day in the job and we hit it off right away. She's fab—you'll love her."

He shakes his head. "You know, I never pictured you as a teacher. When Julia told me...actually, that's not entirely true. I could imagine you as a primary school teacher. I remember how great you were with Ellie."

"Yeah, well, she was a great little girl. Easy to love."

"Yeah. But secondary-school kids? Classes full of Seans and Jacks and Nicoles? Why put yourself through it?"

"It was...oh, I don't know. After Bella died and everything that happened, I stopped gardening, I didn't want to do it anymore and I was...lost, I guess. I fixated on teaching because that's what Bella said she was going to do."

"Bella? Teaching? Come on! I thought she was going to art college to do photography?"

I sigh. "I think she got disillusioned. Decided she didn't have the talent to make that a career. And actually, I think Bella would have made a great teacher. Better than me, anyway."

"That's kind of sad. How both of you gave up on your dreams."

I shrug. "We were only kids, really. Kids change their minds day to day on what they want to do with their lives." I smile. "And it's never too late, is it? I'm only twenty-six, nothing's set in stone."

"Thinking of ditching the teaching and running off to dig borders for a living?"

Does he have to sound so patronizing?

"Why not?" I say it lightly. "I'm sure there are courses I could do. Or maybe I'll follow Bella's other path and take some photography classes."

He laughs and shakes his head. "God, she used to be a pain with that camera of hers, didn't she? Always sneaking up and taking candid shots of us all." He glances at me. "I'd love to see those photos again, wouldn't you? I wonder what happened to her camera."

I open my mouth to tell him Sean found it, that it's currently shoved in a cupboard in my childhood home waiting for me to develop the film, but he hasn't finished.

"She was taking photos a couple of days before the wedding, I remember," he says. "She took a couple of...embarrassing ones I didn't want shown around." The frown is back on his face.

I'd forgotten about the camera in the last couple of days. I must get that film developed. I bite my lip. What could possibly be so embarrassing that Max still remembers it now?

"I never found it after she died," I say. Not strictly a lie. I'm not sure why I'm keeping it quiet that Sean has found the camera—I think I just want to see these embarrassing photos for myself before sharing. With anyone.

We stop for coffee and I have to lean against the car for a moment as we get out. The sun's glare hurts my eyes, needles of pain digging in, getting inside my head. It's like the world's worst hangover.

"Tess? You okay?"

"Sorry. I'm . . . not sleeping at the moment. Being back in the village and all the worry about Julia, you know?"

He touches my arm. "Come on, let's get you some coffee."

"You go on and get them; I'm going to splash some cold water on my face."

Hidden away in the bathroom, I take two Tylenol, washing them down with water scooped up in my hand. But even the coldest water on my face can't wake me up, and in the fluorescent light of the restroom I look terrible, skin so pale it looks gray, eyes red-rimmed and black-shadowed. I look thinner than I did last week, when my dead sister stepped out of my dreams and into my flat. I blink and see a reflection of the door swinging shut. I didn't notice anyone come in or out, didn't see anyone standing next to me at the mirrors. How long did I zone out for?

Max drops me at the school and arranges to meet me later at the pub with Sophie. I take a deep breath as I walk toward Karen's office, trying to quell the rising flutter of nerves. Last week—what I did to Rebecca Martin—it doesn't seem real. It doesn't seem real that it's been less than a week since I was teaching here. One weekend at home and the rest of my life seems an eternity away.

"I'm sorry, Tess, but we've had to let you go. What you did, it was gross misconduct, so we have no choice other than instant dismissal." Karen doesn't bother with small talk and I'm glad.

"It's okay. I knew this would happen."

"I know you're going through a lot with your stepmother, but there was nothing else the school could do."

"I'm so sorry, Karen. I'm so, so sorry for what I did. I honestly . . . I don't understand why I lost it like I did. I have no excuses and I totally understand you have to fire me."

Karen sighs and leans back in her seat. "I think we've convinced the Martins not to go to the police with this. It's all we can do for you, I'm afraid."

A sliver of relief slips through me. "Thank you."

She shakes her head. "I wish I understood what you did as well, Tess. We've collected your things." She nods at a small box on the desk in front of her. "You realize you can't come back onto school grounds after this, don't you?"

There's a touch of anger in her voice and I bow my head. How much trouble have I caused the school?

"I'm sorry," I say again, picking up the box.

She follows me to the door. "I hope . . . I hope you sort things out."

I feel tears burning at the back of my eyes as I walk through the empty corridors, a half-empty box in my arms.

Someone gets out of a black car in the parking lot as I walk toward the main gates.

"There you are—we've been waiting for you to come slinking back."

Oh, I really can't deal with this now. I glance up toward Karen's office window, but the blinds are down.

"What do you want, Mr. Martin?"

"What do I want? You attack my daughter, go into hiding, and you're asking what do I want?"

"I'm not going to discuss this with you now." I juggle the box in my arms as it threatens to fall.

"Fired you, have they?" Mr. Martin says, staring at the box. He's not a big man, but he's blocking my path, all self-righteous anger shining bright on his red face. Has he been sitting outside the school all day, waiting for me to come back? How close to the edge is he? I can't reach my phone to call the police without dropping the box and alerting him and we're too far from the school building for anyone to hear if I call for help.

"I said, I'm not going to discuss this now. You need to be home taking care of your daughter."

He freezes. "Don't you tell me what to do with my own kid— it's you she needs protecting from, you stupid bitch."

"No," I say through gritted teeth. "It's not me she needs protecting from. Don't you care that some man is sending her bloody photos of himself naked? Don't you care that he asked her out when she was fourteen fucking years old? You were told all this, but all you seem to care about is getting one over on me and the school. It's not me she needs protecting from, it's the forty-year-old man sending her pornographic photos."

I realize he's shaking, all the red-faced swagger gone.

"Get out of my way. And don't you dare come near me again or it'll be me going to the police. You'll be on the school CCTV."

He stands back and stares at me, shaking his head. "You're insane. Fucking insane."

God, how did this get so complicated? That time I saw those pictures on Rebecca's phone, it was instinct that made me take it. She was laughing and bragging about having sex with some forty-year-old, but I saw something else in her face; I saw the shadow of Nicole Wallace and Annie Weston and Bella and *me*. I saw me in her face. And I wanted... I wanted to protect her, that was all.

My foot's bouncing and I can't seem to keep it still. I can see the others in the doctor's waiting room watching me. They probably think I've found a lump. Or I'm bleeding from somewhere I shouldn't. But it's not me that won't stop bleeding. God, I don't know what I'm going to say. I made tea in my sleep and had a conversation with my dead sister. My stepmother is dying and I threatened to throw a student out of the window. I've barely slept for a week and, when I do, I nearly sleepwalk my way out of the house. Every way I look at it I sound crazy. I probably *look* crazy right now.

It wasn't an accident, Bella whispers as I wait to get called in, and I shake my head to get rid of her voice. No, not her voice. *My* voice. My subconscious.

Everyone's looking at me as I hunch over, arms wrapped around myself. My nerves are taking their minds off whatever brings them here and I can't get angry with them because I do the same when I'm in the doctor's waiting room. Who doesn't? The ten-year-old magazines, gray carpet, gray chairs, the smell of antiseptic and the sounds of sniffing and coughing—what else are you going to do to kill the time? The yellow man with the shakes, the sneezing, coughing, wailing kids—easy-peasy. But the ghost-pale woman in the corner staring straight ahead? Less easy to diagnose. Oh no, wait. That's me, reflected in the window. Foot still bouncing, ready to take off for space, then a buzz and my name is called. I take a deep breath and get up.

The doctor has a bald spot, shiny and red. It reminds me of someone, a fleeting memory that's there and gone before I can catch it. I can't help but notice it because he stays bent over the keyboard he's tapping away on even when I come in and sit down. Maybe he'll notice I'm here if I reach over and rub it, Aladdin style.

"I'm having trouble sleeping," I say weakly when he finally looks up. I see his gaze slip away from me, to his computer. He'll look me up now to check that I'm not an addict looking for a prescriptive fix. He'll give me some pills to help me sleep and send me away. I have to try again.

"It's more than that. More than insomnia. I'm sleepwalking and... and I'm seeing things."

That gets his attention. "You're seeing things? Spots? Floating black spots in front of your eyes? Flashes? Prisms?" He's getting out that light thing, ready to shine in my eyes, ready to look into my brain for some physical thing to hack off, burn out, drown in pills.

I shake my head. "No—real things. Well, not *real*. I think I'm hallucinating and talking to... a person. My sister."

"You're seeing your sister?"

A gurgle of laughter escapes, almost a snort. What am I doing here? "Yes. I saw my sister last week. In the middle of the night. And I haven't slept properly since."

"And you think it was a hallucination?"

"My sister's dead. She died ten years ago. So yes, I think it was a hallucination."

He frowns, taps something into his computer. "What was she doing?"

I laugh again, clamp my hand over my mouth to try to stop it coming out. What was she *doing*? That's what he's asking? The doctor looks flustered now, out of his depth. What can he prescribe for this?

"I haven't been sleeping," I say again. "I've been under a lot of stress at work. And there's a serious illness in the family. But these dreams or hallucinations or whatever they are—they're so real. So vivid. More than a dream."

"Hallucinations, though—that's fairly extreme. I think I need to refer you on. I'll organize some tests for you; blood tests, a CT scan. And I'll arrange for you to see a consultant."

I shake my head again, reach over, and put my hand over his to stop him from typing in whatever he's typing. He snatches his hand away like I've got something contagious. I think I've crossed a doctor–patient line.

"I'm sorry. Sorry. But...do you think it could it be real? No. That's not what I mean. I know it's not real. But there are so many things from when she died that I don't remember. Do you think the strain I'm under could be unleashing some repressed memories?"

He's frowning and there's a sheen of sweat on his forehead. "Miss Cooper. Tess—this is something we have to treat. If you're hallucinating...it could be a symptom of something else, beyond the insomnia. Repressed memories? I don't know, but nothing said to you by a hallucination can be real. And if you're at the stage where you believe that it is..." He pauses but he doesn't really need to finish. I've just heard myself and I sound crazy. Full-on, bat-shit crazy. He pushes a prescription and a letter across the desk to me. "The prescription should help with the sleep issues and you may find the problem...disappears if you sleep. But I've also put in a request for a consultation for you. To rule out any physical issues first and foremost. If nothing comes from that, we can look at a psychiatric evaluation."

"Forget it," I say, jumping up, swaying as I go momentarily dizzy. "Forget it—all of it. I don't need drugs or psychiatric help. It's probably just really vivid dreams, right? I'm sure it happens all the time."

The doctor calls after me as I leave, clutching the prescription and referral letter. My cheeks are burning and heart thudding as I hurry away. Damn it—I do not need a psychiatric evaluation, or a bloody CT scan. I'll take the pills if that's what I need to sleep while I'm back home. It's just being back there, isn't it? The fragments of memory, the dreams, the sleepwalking, it'll all go away when I leave, won't it?

I pause on the corner, waiting for the pedestrian light to turn green. But if they really are memories, if being back there with everyone is finally causing me to remember—do I really want it to go away?

Sophie is already in the pub, two ridiculous cocktails in front of her, complete with paper umbrellas. It soothes me seeing her and I go over with a smile.

"Maeve? Maeve Larson, super detective?"

She turns and grins at me, getting up to give me a hug. "Isn't that you on your undercover case to solve the crime?" She winces. "Sorry. That came out wrong. I didn't mean..."

"Oh don't. Don't be daft—just pass me a bucket of alcohol. I have had one hell of a day."

"Ah. The meeting."

"Yep. That's it. Teaching career well and truly over."

"Shit."

I don't want to tell her about my run-in with Rebecca's father. Or my visit to the doctor, or the box of sleeping pills now sitting in my bag. It'll make her worry. Even more than she's obviously worrying now.

"Soph, it's okay. Not how I would have chosen to go, but at least... well, at least I can have a shot at finding something I really want to do now, right?" I pull a face and take a huge swig of the too-sweet cocktail. "So long as it isn't anything that requires references."

"Well, cheers to the future career of the indomitable Miss Tess Cooper," she says, clinking her glass against mine.

"Listen, I hope you don't mind, but Max gave me a lift back, so I asked him to join us."

"Ooh, the heartthrob? The lost love of your life?"

"I wish I'd never told you about him."

She laughs. "I promise not to reveal all the details of the crush you told me about."

"Good," I say, looking at the door. "Because he's just walked in, so *behave*."

He's wearing a suit and as he walks across the pub I realize he looks like all the other city boys crowding the bar downing pints. And such a contrast to me and Sophie, both in jeans. It strikes me as a bit odd—I mean, I know he said he was calling into work, but why not change into something more casual to meet us? Unless he plans to take me somewhere suit-worthy for dinner. I hope not—I want to be somewhere I can kick my shoes off, lean back, and eat comfort food. I look at Sophie. She's forever mocking the city boys—I don't want her to see Max as one of them.

"Hey, Tess," Max says with a big smile. "And you must be Sophie? Can I get you both a drink?"

It'll be fine, I tell myself as he comes back over with a tray of drinks. He's Max.

*   *   *

"Well?" I say, leaning in toward Sophie as soon as Max leaves to find the men's room.

"He's certainly good-looking," she says.

I wince. "You don't like him."

"It's not that. What's not to like? He's charming, attentive, tells good jokes..."

"But?"

"It's not really a but. It's just...I don't know. He's almost too charming. Like it's an act. I'm sorry—I'm being a cow, aren't I? He's probably being his most charming self to impress me and I'm being a right surly bitch." She sighs. "He just seems so different from the person I thought you'd end up with. He's so ambitious and...and...*well groomed*."

I snort with laughter and spit some of my drink out, spraying her with strawberry daiquiri.

"Oh, nice, Cooper. Very nice," she says, wiping her face with a napkin.

"Sorry, but—he's too *well groomed*?"

She grins. "You know what I mean. He's so smooth and slick. You like gardening and running, your wardrobe runs to jeans and Lycra. But I guess opposites attract and you can't listen to me when I've only known him for the time it takes to down three strawberry daiquiris."

Opposites? I never used to think of us as opposites.

"But seriously," Sophie says, touching my hand. "If he's the one good thing that comes out of such an awful time, then I'm all for it."

She smiles up at Max when he returns and reaches for her coat. "Well, guys, I'm off. Don't do anything I wouldn't." She winks at me as she says it and dissolves into laughter as I shove her hard on the shoulder.

"So where do you want to eat?" Max asks after we've waved Sophie off in a taxi. "I saw a nice Italian place on my way here."

I'm hit with a wave of exhaustion. Three cocktails on no sleep was probably not a good idea. "Would you mind if we just went back to my place? I can cook something, or order takeout."

He hesitates, then smiles. "Sure. No problem. Lead the way, Hardy-girl."

"This is it—not much to see. Kitchen and living room—bathroom through there. And my room."

It's hardly a tour—I can stand in one spot and see every room in my flat, but it's mine and it's safe. Quiet. I always used to be able to sleep here. Max wanders round, looking at the kitchenette with its shiny cream units, the big brown sofa that doubles as a bed for guests. I want him to see past the bland rented flat furniture and see the things that are *me*: the shelf I've put up in the kitchen with all my vintage teacups, the books, the ornaments. Nothing valuable, but each one treasured. But his eyes skip past the shelf and the battered leather chair that sits next to the plain sofa. Does he notice the turquoise cushion with the pink and orange pompoms that sits proudly against the brown leather? I hadn't noticed how much in the corners and shadows I've placed these pieces of me. Shy, hidden expressions of personality. They look hesitant; they look staged.

The bathroom's probably most obviously me, with every surface crowded with bottles of bubble bath and lotions and potions. I can't remember if I've picked all the clothes up off the floor, so I don't open my bedroom door.

"Wow," he says, staring down at my flashing answering machine. "You have a *lot* of messages."

I feel a sick thud. They'll all be from the school.

"I'll listen to them later," I say, turning my back on the blinking light. After all, the deed is done—doesn't matter if I listen to them or not, now, does it?

"You don't have any plants," Max says, looking around.

"No, I don't like houseplants. I like plants to live outdoors."

"I never imagined you living somewhere without some kind of garden."

"Can't afford a house or even a garden flat on a teacher's salary."

"Not here, no. But then, I never imagined you living in the city, either. You were always a country girl."

"*Were* being the operative word there. You haven't seen me in ten years. I was sixteen then, a kid. So were you."

"Didn't expect you to have changed that much, though."

"Oh eff off, Max. Stop being so sanctimonious. God, so I'm a teacher in a flat, so what? I'm not a goddamn crack dealer, am I?"

He laughs and he's Max again. "Sorry—sorry, Tess. I'm being an ass, I know I am. It's weird, that's all. It's been so long, and I guess I was expecting you to still have dirt under your fingernails and leaves in your hair."

He means it to be light-hearted, but I see dead Bella in his words, dirt under her nails, leaves and blood in her hair. Didn't he tell me how much I looked like her now?

"I haven't changed that much—look." I lean past him and un-lock the glass door to my small balcony; it's the reason I took this flat—my outdoor space, my garden. It's full of color—big pots of green and purple, a tall shrub in burgundy red. I have window boxes of herbs and just about enough room for one wrought-iron chair among it all.

Max laughs again, a bigger, happier laugh. "Your secret garden in miniature," he says, and I nod. Yes, that's it. All mine, hidden away four floors up.

"Why don't you sit out here while I go and see what I can cob-ble together to eat?"

I bring him a beer and leave him sitting in my secret garden, half-hidden among the plants, looking out over the city. I go into the bedroom and am hit with a wave of tiredness so pow-erful I sway like it's a real wave. I sit on the bed, then sink back onto the pillows. Just five minutes, that's all. I just need five minutes...

"Tess?"

I can hear someone calling me but I ignore the voice because I'm looking for Bella. It's dark here and I can't see but I know she's here and she has something to tell me, something important. I just have to keep looking...

"Tess."

My eyes fly open. Max is bending over me, shaking my shoulder. I blink away sleep—I was asleep. Actually asleep. I look over at the clock—eight thirty. I only slept for an hour, but I still slept.

He smiles down at me. "I was wondering what happened to you."

"I'm sorry," I say, my voice sounding slurred and drugged. "I haven't been sleeping..."

"It's not surprising," he says, sitting on the bed, trailing his hand down my arm. "With everything that's going on with Julia."

I shake my head. "It's not just that. I've been having dreams. About Bella." I can tell Max, can't I? He was there, he'll understand the turmoil in my head.

His fingers stop their slow stroking.

"I think I'm starting to remember things. I thought I was just having really vivid dreams, but I think they might be memories. And I saw Bella, like, so vividly. I know it's not real, but...she said her death wasn't an accident."

"What? The inquest..."

I sit up. "I know what the inquest said. But I didn't want to believe it then and maybe I was right not to. I'm remembering other things too, fragments from the night of the wedding."

He's frowning down at me, no sign of his beautiful crooked smile, and I wish I hadn't said anything. I don't want him looking at me with the same wariness the doctor did, like I'm off my rocker. I reach up and impulsively kiss him. I think he's going to move away, then he kisses me back and, instead of pulling away, he sinks down on me, onto the bed, and I'm no longer tired, not one little bit. My heart is pounding as he pauses and looks at me.

"Tess—are you sure?"

I remember the first time I saw Max, when Julia brought him for a visit. He came in last and I think I loved him right away in the way only fourteen-year-olds can fall in love—full, instantly, from head to toe, of shivery, pulse-racing love for a lanky teenage boy with brown hair and a crooked smile. I loved him without pause for two more years until the day of the wedding when, for the first time, I thought he might love me back and I think we almost kissed. Almost. I probably would have exploded if we had. Just plain exploded from all that bottled-up love. But we didn't kiss. Bella died instead and I didn't see him anymore. And not once, in all the years since, have I ever felt that soaring love for anyone else. So am I sure?

I pull him back toward me and reach for the buttons on his shirt.

When I wake up, Max's arm lies heavy across my belly. I lift it off and look over at the clock again. My stomach rumbles. We never did have dinner. The pizza we ended up ordering is congealing in the kitchen. It's nearly five in the morning. I slept again, this time for nearly six hours. With that and the hour earlier, it's more than I've slept in days. But I'm wide awake now and I know my sleep's over for the night.

I could lie here for the rest of the night next to Max and watch him sleep, the culmination of all those dreams when I was fourteen, fifteen, sixteen... But my leg twitches and I'm already getting restless. The sex was awkward, self-conscious. We weren't comfortable together, it was clumsy and... I wanted to stop and I think he did too. He turned his back as soon as it was over, pretending to sleep. I know he was pretending by the tension in his shoulders, the unevenness of his breathing. It was sex by numbers and when I close my eyes, I mourn for the daydreams all shattered in thirty sweaty minutes. I need to get out. There's an all-night grocery a couple of streets away. I'll go and get bread and milk, attempt to make the morning after less awkward.

I hesitate when I step outside the building, looking into the patches of darkness between the street lights, half-expecting Sean or Jack to be hiding there. Silly—they don't know where I live. They haven't sought me out in ten years; there's no reason they would now. It's being back there. It's spooked me. I should feel reassured being back here, in my safe place, my safe new life. I've made drunken late-night forays to the grocery before, seeking snacks after a night out with Sophie and the others. But at five o'clock in the morning, the streets are empty, the roads quiet. It's as quiet as back home, where the woods haunt me. I hesitate before striding out, head down, taking a route that's lit all the way.

"Where the hell have you been?"

"What?" I look at the clock—it's five thirty. What's he doing awake? He's standing in the kitchen, shirtless, bare chest shining pale under the fluorescent light. I look away. All those years of me dreaming about having Max in my home, half-naked, but in this brightly lit reality I just want to throw a T-shirt at him and make him cover up.

"I woke up and you weren't there. When you didn't come back, I got up and you were nowhere. Where the hell have you been?"

"I went to get breakfast." I put the milk and bread on the table.

"In the middle of the night—on your own? Are you insane?"

"It's hardly the middle of the night—it's nearly six. And it's quite safe around here, I do it all the time."

"Jesus, Tess. I thought it was Lena who had the death wish, not you. It only takes one night, one crazy to be out on the prowl. You of all people should know that." He's scowling, face twisted in unfamiliar hostility. It's a stranger's face, someone angry at more than me just going out for bread. His fists are clenched and he looks like he's spoiling for a fight.

I stiffen and push past him. I'm cold and I want to get in the shower. "It's not a big deal—I couldn't sleep, so I thought I'd get us breakfast. I thought it would be a nice thing to do. I'm fine—I didn't see anyone." I'm trying to placate him.

"You couldn't sleep? Not even with these?" He holds up the box of sleeping pills I got from the doctor. I freeze, looking at the crumpled-up pharmacy bag on the sideboard. He's been looking through my things? I curl my hands into fists. No, not now. I don't want an argument at five thirty in the morning, not with Max. Never with Max.

I push past him without answering and close the bathroom door behind me, my hand hovering over the lock. No, no need for that. It's Max.

I pause as I get undressed. The bathroom cabinet door is open. I'm sure it was closed before.

I come out of the shower, tying the belt on my bathrobe, with my hair wrapped in a towel. Everything looks wrong, a little bit out of place, like someone's been shifting furniture around while I was out. The drawer is open in my dressing table, a door ajar in the living-room cupboard. I find Max making coffee in the kitchen. He has a cabinet door open and he's rummaging for something.

"What are you looking for?"

He glances back. "Painkillers. I have a headache."

It explains the bathroom cabinet, the open cupboards and drawers. He's looking for Tylenol, that's all. I open a drawer and pass him a box of pills. In the time I've been in the shower, he's got dressed, shoes on, bag by his feet.

"Where are you going?"

"I'm going to head home."

"At six in the morning?"

I don't really want to hear the real reasons he's going, but in the morning half-light I can't bear to hear his excuses, the awkward lies, either.

"I listened to your messages," he says, and I stiffen.

"I'm sorry, but you were gone and I was worried. God, Tess, you're in trouble, aren't you? What did you *do*?"

"You shouldn't have listened, you had no right."

Max stares at me. "I can't do this. I don't need another messed-up woman in my life. Lena is enough to deal with. Coming here was a mistake. I thought I wanted..." He hesitates and I think he's going to say something else, something big, but then he ducks his head. "Sorry, Tess."

I could push it, but I don't want to face the fact that this was just a one-night stand that Max already regrets. An awkward after-sex moment made more awkward by the fact that I literally ran out the door as soon as it was over. Did he really wake up because he sensed I was gone? Or did he wake up to sneak out only to find I'd beaten him to it? I tried to have sex with the Max I used to hero-worship but that's not who fell asleep next to me. In my sleep-deprived paranoia, I see more than regret on his face. I see distaste.

I nod, take the coffee he holds out, turn away to drink it so he can't see my face. "It's okay—it's fine. I get it."

It's no big deal. He's not my first one-night stand, not the first man to walk out on me. Hell, it's not like it's the first time *he's* walked out on me, is it? Where was he after Bella died? He left, disappeared. They all did. It was just me and Dad, Julia hovering on the edges, for such a long time.

"Jesus, Tess—don't. Don't do that. It was my fault. I could tell you weren't into it, but I wanted...Lena warned me."

"Warned you of what? Warned you against sleeping with me?"

"She said I shouldn't try and make something happen, when..."

More secrets, more whispering behind my back. "*I* kissed *you*."

"But what were we doing? Trying to rekindle something that never happened? I wanted some time with you away from the house, but I didn't intend..."

Don't, I want to say. *Don't tell me you felt sorry for me, don't tell me you always knew I had a crush on you, that our half-assed sex was out of pity.*

"I'm sorry," he says again, hovering awkwardly. "But I'll still give you a lift to the station."

"You don't have to. I can get the bus."

"No, don't be silly. I practically drive past it. I'll wait for you to get ready."

Now? We have to go now? I walk away from him, closing the bedroom door behind me and sinking onto the bed.

Well. Could I have screwed up in a more spectacular way? But it's not just me, is it? After we had sex and I came back from the shop, he seemed...what? Angry. Resentful. Was that just because he was worried about me—me going out, the sleeping pills, the messages? This whole thing seems like more than a spontaneous mistake, almost like it was planned, staged. Which is ridiculous, isn't it? It was me who asked for a lift, me who invited him here, me who kissed him. But...

I know it's my paranoia, but the Max who was in my flat last night—the Max standing in my kitchen right now—it's not the Max I remember. It's not the Max I thought I knew.

CHAPTER 13

He's tense on the drive to the station, not talking. I look across at him and see what Sophie saw last night—a well-groomed stranger. I close my eyes. Despite the amount of sleep I got last night, I'm still exhausted. I feel myself drifting and force my eyes back open.

I look back at the road and that's when Dean House stutters into view—it's there, right in the road, right in front of us, and someone's running out of it—toward the car, arms waving. It's Bella, fear on her face. And behind her, there's someone else—someone—

"*Look out!*" I shout as Bella runs into the road, and I reach to grab the steering wheel.

The car swerves, Max pulls hard on the steering wheel and the car lurches back to the left. There's an awful screeching, grinding noise and the car spins and turns.

Oh God, oh God, I don't want to die.

I wake up on a stretcher in a hospital corridor. Max is standing next to me, a bruise on his forehead but otherwise okay.

"What happened?" I say, my voice croaky.

"There was an accident—you grabbed the steering wheel and the car crashed, don't you remember?"

I wince and close my eyes. Oh God. "I'm like the grim reaper version of King Midas—everyone I touch dies."

"I'm not dead."

I look at his bruised face. "I did my bloody best, though, didn't I? You could have died."

"It was an accident."

I look away. I could have killed him. I could have killed him and me. If I close my eyes I can see it again—the house looming up in front of me, Bella in front of the car, shadowed by the trees. Was I asleep when I saw it? Had I drifted into a dream? Or was it a memory—someone chased Bella out of the house. That's what made me reach for the steering wheel. Someone was chasing her right into the path of the car.

I reach out and grab his arm. "I'm sorry. I'm so sorry, but I thought I saw..."

He pulls his arm away from me. "What? What did you see? I didn't see anything. It was an empty road and you just screamed. You grabbed the wheel and drove straight toward the wall." He shakes his head. "You'd drifted off—one minute you were asleep, the next all hell broke loose." He looks away from me to where my dad, a nurse, and a uniformed police officer walk toward us. He leans down to whisper in my ear. "But don't worry. I told the police you must have grabbed the wheel to avoid an animal or something. I didn't see anything but...tell them that. Tell them you did it to avoid hitting a dog or a cat or something. You don't need to be in more trouble than you already are."

"I'm sorry," I say as my dad and the policeman reach me. I don't know whether I'm apologizing to Dad, to Max, or to the police.

"There was a cat," I say. "I saw a cat in the road and I acted instinctively. I don't know what happened."

I turn my head away and it explodes with pain. I close my eyes and feel myself drifting. I don't want to because the woods are there, waiting for me in my dreams. They're always waiting.

The hospital is quiet. I don't know what time it is, but when I close my eyes, I see a house made of bones, ghosts haunting every room. As I drift, I find myself walking through the woods toward Dean House and I sense Bella next to me. I can smell dirt and blood and dead leaves. I can hear something dripping on the ground and I won't turn my head to look at her because I'm scared of what I might see.

"Let me tell you a story," Bella says.

"Stop it, Bella," I say. "I don't like your stories."

"That's because they're not really stories."

"Maybe there'd be more happy endings if they were."

She brings her death-smell closer and I close my eyes. "Listen. Let me tell you about the time two girls went into the woods and only one came out..."

I wake with a gasp and sit up, hunched over in the bed. No, no, no, I don't like that dream.

Dad picks me up from the hospital.

"I'm so sorry," I say as I climb into the passenger seat, doing up my seat belt with shaking hands. "How's Max? How's his car?"

"Don't worry about it," Dad says, leaning over to kiss my forehead and stroke my hair. "It's not your fault. Max doesn't care about his car—we're just so relieved it wasn't worse. You and Max are both fine, that's all that matters."

"But...how did he get home? How's he going to get to work?"

"He's been signed off work for a few days. He really is fine, just a nasty bump to the head."

"So is he...?"

"He's back at home with Julia, yes. Lena too. She came back when she heard about the accident."

So all we need is for Jack to resurface and the whole gang will be back together. My throat closes. No, not the whole gang.

"*You* should be with Julia, not dealing with more crap."

"Don't, Tess—it was an accident. You couldn't help it. Julia's okay. She's sleeping, she doesn't know anything about it." He glances at me as he starts the engine. "Max said...he mentioned something about the strain you're under. Some trouble at work."

I close my eyes and turn away, suppressing a surge of irritation. Max chose to tell Dad now? When his wife is dying and his daughter was just in a car accident? Who else has he told?

"It's fine, Dad," I say stiffly. "Seriously—it's all sorted." No need to tell him it's sorted by me being fired.

We drive past a huddle of smokers ignoring the no smoking

signs outside the front of the hospital. My hands are curled into
fists on my lap. I could have killed Max, killed myself. The
thought won't go away, it keeps getting bigger, ballooning in my
brain and my chest so I can barely breathe and I can't think about
anything else.

I still don't understand what happened. I closed my eyes for
a second—was I really asleep like Max said? The vision—the
memory—of the house, someone chasing Bella, was so real and
vivid. It has to be real, doesn't it? But when did that happen? Was
it the night of the wedding? Is that what sent Bella into the woods,
me running after her? Were we running away from someone else?
I try but I can't see the person chasing her out of Dean House. All
I can see is Bella, fear on her face as she ran in front of the car.

I shake my head. Memories coming back or not, I'm becoming
a danger to more than just myself. I need to start taking those
sleeping pills. Hallucinating, sleepwalking...and now I'd almost
killed Max.

It won't go away even now, though. We're driving through the
town, but in the front of my mind, tucked between the terraced
streets, there's the sound of the wind rushing through trees, the
feel of a storm gathering.

The sky is gray, thick with cloud. Reluctant to fully commit to
day, it could be twilight, slipping back into night without the sun
ever making an appearance. Dad slows the car as we approach
Dean House. He's pale, his hands tight on the steering wheel.
A uniformed policewoman stands by the gate. People in forensic
suits are moving around inside the tangled garden.

"Wait! Stop. What's going on? What's happened? Is it Sean? Is
it..."

"No, Tess, Sean is fine." He pauses. "The property developers
that bought the house came in yesterday to start work on demolition."

"And? So? Why are the police there?"

Another pause. "They found bones."

My scalp prickles. "What?"

"In the woods. Just outside the garden at Dean House, but within the boundaries. The new owners brought in the diggers and they dug up human bones."

I'm instantly thrown back ten years. A body in the woods. Like Bella. Like Nicole and the other murdered girl. My vision goes dark and I think I'm going to pass out. There's a roaring in my ears, a roaring that sounds like screaming, that sounds like rain and wind rushing through trees and mud sliding down a bank and... it sounds like death.

"Who?" I whisper. "Is it another girl? Is it another murder?"

Dad shakes his head. "I don't know. The police have been there most of the night, that's all I know."

I turn to face forward again, afraid that Bella's ghost will creep into my waking world if I keep looking. Bones—they've found bones. Who is it?

"Let's get out of here," I say to Dad. "Please."

Dad reaches out to stop me from opening the door when he pulls up outside the house.

"Wait, Tess."

I can see Max watching us from the window.

"What is it?"

"Jack's here."

I sink back into the car seat.

"I'm sorry—I know you two don't get along, but Julia wanted to see him so badly. Sean spoke to him. Persuaded him to come back."

Part of me wants to beg Dad to turn around and drive away again, but I'm not sixteen anymore.

Dad shakes his head. "He turned up last night. It was him that told us about the police being at Dean House. We're all in shock, Jack and Sean most of all. It's their house—or it was. We're expecting the police to turn up any minute and I'm frightened about how the stress will affect Julia."

"Does she know?"

"No. I've asked everyone to keep it quiet."

"But won't the police want to speak to her as well?"

His hands tighten on the steering wheel again. "I won't let them. She finally has all her family here, a chance to say...I won't let them ruin it."

And I can't ruin it either with a stupid, decade-old fear of being in the same house as Jack.

"It's okay," I force myself to say. "We'll sort it between us. We won't let anyone spoil this for Julia."

Dad sighs. "Jack hasn't actually seen her yet. But she knows he's here. If you'd seen how happy she was..."

Jack joins Max at the window, watching us like he can hear our conversation, and I want to duck down in my seat and hide. He looks so much like his brother, but his hair is longer, darker, swept to the side. He has stubble that's almost enough to be a beard, but the eyes are the same, that light, light blue. The difference is the smile. Sean rarely smiles, but Jack's smiling out at us, like we're not here waiting for his mother to die, like bones haven't just been found in his garden, looking happy to be here.

Jack steps out of the house as we leave the car and Dad frowns.

"Go on in, Dad," I say.

"Are you sure?" But he's already looking up at Julia's window.

"Go on. I'll get my bag and I'll be right behind you."

I wait for Dad to go in before I turn to face Jack.

"Hey, Tess," he says. He reaches for my bag but I snatch it away from him.

"Hello, Jack."

He smiles. "It's been a long time."

I grit my teeth. "So is it just you, or do we have the pleasure of meeting your family?"

His smile gets wider. "You don't sound like you'd consider it a pleasure." His smile drops. "And no, I came alone. This isn't how I'd want my wife and son to meet my mother."

"I'm sorry. About Julia."

He sighs. "Yeah, it is a bit of a shit show, isn't it? Julia, what-ever the hell is going on at Dean House, and you, Tess—I hear you tried and failed to kill off our darling Max. What the hell did he do to make you try the whole murder/suicide thing?"

"Ha ha, very funny, Jack. As always, it's so lovely to see you. And so unchanged."

He grins. "Funny how that doesn't sound much like a compli-ment."

"It wasn't meant to be."

"Well, is that any way to be with a poor man whose mother is dying and whose family home appears to have become a grave-yard?"

"I can't say you look like you're either grieving or in shock."

"Funnily enough, neither do you." He bursts out laughing. "Your face, Tess, so furious. You are so easy to wind up. You know, Max is unnerved by you. Told me you walked out of your flat and he thought you were a ghost. He said you were just like Bella." He pauses. "I don't see it, though. You're the good girl, aren't you, Tess? Always were. Nothing like your sister."

I turn away from him.

"So *virtuous*," he continues. "I remember you tattling to your dad and Julia about catching Bella drinking with me and Lena. Little *saint*."

"Stop it."

He laughs. "Don't like the reminder, do you? Don't like remem-bering how miserable you made Bella, how much trouble you got her into." He steps closer. "Especially when it was all a lie—your Goody Two-shoes act. You were never who you pretended to be."

I take a step toward the house and he sidesteps with me. "Oh, stop being so bloody juvenile."

"You thought no one saw, didn't you? Thought everyone bought the mouse act. But I don't need to see the scar on my brother's face to remind me who you really are."

He's talking crap. He hasn't changed a bit, despite the wife and child. This is another wild chase through the woods. But he's right about one thing—I'm not a scared little mouse, not now. I could do to Jack what I did to Rebecca Martin—grab him by the throat. My hand curls into a fist and I want to do it, grab him and punch him.

"I wish we'd never moved to that damned house," he says.

"Me too."

He laughs softly. "Poor Tess—does it keep you awake at night, thinking of the lives you could all have had if we'd never come to town?" He sighs and looks around. "I swore I'd never come back to this shithole." He falls into silence and I hover, wanting to walk away but unable to move. I'm undone by the momentary vulnerability I see in Jack's hunched shoulders and defeated expression.

"Who do you think it is? The body they found?"

His face goes blank. "I have no idea. I haven't been here in a decade."

"But it's bones they've found, that's what Dad said, not a body. So it could have been there that long." I shiver. "What if it's another girl? There was another one, wasn't there? Who went missing and no one ever found."

He pulls a face, back to the Jack I remember. "Jeez, I came out here to wind you up for some light relief. I think I'll go back inside, watch Max freaking out some more. It's more entertaining."

"Max is freaking out?"

"Bodies in gardens don't exactly fit in with his plans for the week."

We both turn as the front door opens and Lena steps out, a cigarette in her hand, flanked by Max and Sean. It goes unspoken that we're out here so that anything we say about the discovery in Dean House doesn't drift up to Julia, but now that we're gathered here, no one has anything to say. Max won't look at me. Is it because of the car accident or the disaster of our night in my flat?

The others look like strangers and the gap where Bella should be is like a gaping wound only I can see and feel. I think about the murdered girls, the summer of death, the killings that stopped and never got solved. Max is white-faced, a shaking mess, the bruise on his forehead an accusation I look away from. Lena's pacing up and down and Jack and Sean...their faces are inscrutable. What's going on in their heads? It was their house, their dad's house. Very soon, the police are going to be here to ask questions.

"They might not be human," Max says. "It could just be animal bones."

But none of us believes that. Jack actually laughs. "Seriously, Max? I hope that forensic team can tell the difference—I don't think the police want to talk to us about the bones of some dead dog."

"Sorry," Max says. "I'm not...it's just...*Jesus*. A body? In your garden? What the hell is going on?"

"Not quite in the garden," Jack says. "But close enough. Technically, the land they found it on belongs—belonged—to us."

I find I'm shaking, trembling from head to foot. It's too close to where Bella died. It's too close to where Julia lies dying. It's too much damned death.

"It's our house," Sean says, looking at his brother. "Or it was. The police are going to want to speak to us. Can you stay? Will it be okay with Dani?"

Dani. Jack's wife. It's disorienting, looking at him and seeing this grown man, married with a child. He keeps doubling in my mind, replaced with the Jack I remember from ten years ago.

Jack shrugs. "It's fine. She'll understand."

"But the bones could have been there for decades," I burst out. "They could have been there before any of us ever came to this village."

Sean shrugs. "But until they work that out, they're going to want to talk to anyone who has a connection to the house."

"Well, shit—that's all of us," Lena says. "How the hell am I meant to explain that to my boss if I have to take more time off?"

"Well," Jack says. "I, for one, hope they hurry up and get it over with." He glances back at the house, up at Julia's window. "Julia too. I hope she hurries up and dies, puts us all out of our misery so we can get on with our lives."

I drop my bag on the ground and turn to walk away. I don't think I can do this, not without punching him in the face. It's like I'm sixteen again, Jack's mocking laugh chasing me into the woods. But I don't even have that sanctuary anymore, do I?

I walk fast, but don't get very far before I have to stop. I'm still wobbly from the accident. My ribs ache when I take a deep breath and my legs are shaking. I wrap my arms around my tender ribs and lean against the wall.

"Are you okay?" It's Sean who's followed me. Am I hurt it's not Max? No. I don't want the awkwardness of that conversation right now. It's laughable—hilarious in fact—that of all the people now gathered in my house, Sean is actually the easiest one to speak to.

"You told me your brother had changed."

"He has. He's just winding you up, Tess. You were always so sulky and tongue-tied around him, he liked it when he managed to pull your strings and you went off. He liked *you* when you got mad."

I shake my head. "I think it's you who's kidding yourself that he's changed. He was a shit then and he's a shit now. Five minutes in his company is enough to tell me that."

"I think he's having problems with Dani." Sean sighs and leans against the wall next to me. "If I'm honest, they've been having problems since Charlie was born. Then Julia dying and now this. It's all an act, Tess. What he says and how he acts—it's not real. It's a defense mechanism, that's all."

"Who do you think is buried there?" I ask, half dreading his answer. "Do you think it's that other missing girl?"

"I don't know. I'm trying not to think about it."

I shiver as I think of him staying at the house, on his own with a sleeping bag and a flashlight and a body buried in the woods.

"Did you see anything? Or sense anything when you were there?"

"What are you talking about?"

My face floods with color. "Nothing. It's just—it's odd, that's all. That this happened now, right as you come back, that it's on your property. I—"

He laughs. "Oh please! You don't think I was there burying bodies, do you? Did you not listen before? They found bones, not a freshly buried corpse. God, you are *priceless*."

"Oh shut up, Sean, I didn't for one second suggest that. I am not *stupid*. But do you think the police won't be asking those questions? About what you were doing there alone? And what if the bones are really old? Didn't they speak to you all when those girls died before?"

"They spoke to bloody everyone. They spoke to your dad, didn't they? And Bella?"

"Bella was Nicole's best friend. Of course they talked to her." I swallow. "And Jack went out with Nicole."

"Jack went out with *everyone*."

We're facing each other now, almost shouting, my sore ribs forgotten. I hear my words repeated in my head and it sounds awful. Am I really suggesting that Jack or Sean...?

I step away from Sean, confused, anger fading. "Look, I'm sorry, okay? I shouldn't have said that. I didn't mean to imply anything, honestly."

He frowns at me and shakes his head. "I don't understand you. I don't get you at all."

That. There. His words. Like an echo. Like a conversation we've had before.

I smile as I complete the echo. "Well, I don't get me, either."

He looks confused for a moment, then his frown fades and he almost smiles back. "You shouted that at me once, didn't you? It made no bloody sense."

I shrug. "Yeah, well, I rarely do make sense."

A police car drives slowly past us.

"They're going to drag it all back up, aren't they? Even if the bones they've found have nothing to do with those murdered girls. It's going to be the summer of death all over again."

THEN

CHAPTER 14

JANUARY 2007

Dad's late. It's dark outside and the Bolognese that Bella and I have cobbled together is going gloopy in the pan. He's always home by six. And he's meant to be going out tonight for his regular pub quiz with Julia and Greg. I've already got the box of toys out for Ellie, ready to welcome the new dolls she got for Christmas. I grin. Bella's staying in tonight—it'll be her first experience of an epic Barbie marathon. I think she's kind of looking forward to it. Yes, she rolled her eyes and played sulky, but she also went rummaging in the attic for the last remaining Barbie from our own doll days—a sad, shorn-haired thing, its head colored purple with felt-tip pen.

"Where is he?" Bella's frowning and looking out of the window. The clock is creeping toward seven. "Do you think he went straight to the pub?"

I shake my head. "No, Ellie's coming here. He always waits for Julia and Greg to drop her off and they go out together."

She turns to look at me. "Why do they bring her here? Isn't that a bit weird? Most babysitters go to the kid's house, don't they?"

I shrug. I don't tell Bella I think it's because Julia knows how uncomfortable I am around her sons. I think Julia knows I might say no to babysitting if she asked me to go to their house.

Bella rings Dad's office and they tell her he left at five thirty like he always does, but it's past seven now and as usual he doesn't have his mobile phone on. Bella's worried, too. She doesn't say anything but I can see her glancing at the clock and it tightens the knot in my stomach even more. It's freezing outside, the roads lethal with black ice. When I hear his car door slam, my whole body floods with relief and I flop down onto a chair and laugh.

"Where were you?" we shout in unison as he comes through the door.

He's white-faced and shaky and the look on his face terrifies me because it's the same look he had when he came home from the hospital with Mum and they sat us down and told us about the cancer.

"Something awful has happened," he says, and there's a break in his voice. Bella rushes over and hugs him but I'm frozen in place, wanting nothing more than to put my hands over my ears and not hear whatever he's going to say.

"Julia was driving...she had Jack and Ellie with her. And the roads were so icy..."

Stop.

"She hit a patch of ice and the car crashed."

Stop.

"And Ellie...Ellie's side took the impact. She died. Oh God—Ellie's dead."

Bella starts crying, hysterical sobs that hurt my ears. And I...I can't breathe.

Ellie. Little Ellie with the blond hair and the Barbie she named Tessie after me, that she declared was her favorite ever ever doll. Ellie, who I've babysat for so many times she has a box of toys here in the house.

Ellie, my secret baby sister.

Shh, I want to say to Dad. *Stop*. Don't say any more. Don't say any more and it won't be real.

APRIL 2007

I hear crying and freeze halfway through taking my coat off. I walk as quietly as I can to the kitchen and peek through the half-open door. Julia is in there with Dad and the pitiful sound of her sobbing makes my own chest ache. I press my hand to it and swallow past the lump in my throat. Julia has been round a few times since Ellie died, but the gap next to her is so huge, neither Bella nor I have been able to bear being around her. It's probably awful of us to avoid her like that, but it's like she's been ripped in half—I can practically see the raw, bleeding seam where Ellie used to be attached.

We haven't seen so much of Greg and nothing of the boys. Jack dropped out of school and he's got a job working for a builder friend of Greg's and he's living away. Sean went back to boarding school after the funeral and hasn't been seen since. And Greg...Bella says he's taken it really hard, but has kept himself and his grief locked away.

Even though it was me who knew Ellie best from all the babysitting, it was Bella who went over there with Dad afterward. Bella who kept going round, helping out. I haven't been able to.

I'm sorry, I want to burst in there and say. *I'm sorry I've been so crap at showing sympathy and I miss her too*. I do, I really do. I cried so much over that box of stupid toys the day after we heard. Hugging Ellie's beloved Tessie Barbie, eyes swollen, chest aching, and nose streaming. She was four. Only four bloody years old. I can't...I can't even...I can't bear it, even now, three months on. I reach out to push the door open but then I see Dad put his hand over hers and the moment seems too intimate to interrupt. The ache of sympathy turns into something else and I creep farther away instead of closer.

"I don't understand how he could do that," I hear Julia say, and it stops me in my tracks.

He? Who is she talking about? I thought she was crying over Ellie.

"What's going on?" Bella's walking downstairs.

I put a finger to my lips and nod toward the kitchen. I go up the stairs and meet her halfway. "Dad's in there with Julia. She's upset."

Bella frowns. "Is Greg with her?"

I shake my head and she sighs, making as if to go into the kitchen. I grab her arm. "Don't—Julia's crying."

"She should be crying with her husband, not our dad. He's over there alone."

"Since when do you care so much about Greg Lewis? I thought it was Jack or Sean you cared about."

"Oh, stop it, Tess, stop being such a juvenile. He's falling apart over there. Dad's supposed to be *his* friend, not hers."

"Come on, Bella, she lost her little girl. She lost *Ellie*." My voice breaks but Bella's still scowling.

"Well, she should have been more careful, shouldn't she? She should never have been driving when it was so icy."

I gasp and recoil.

Bella is white-faced, her lips pressed together. "It's what Greg thinks, too. And the boys. Even Max and Lena. Why do you think none of them are here? That's why she should be at home, trying to sort things out with *him*, with Greg."

I can't believe she's saying such awful, awful things. God—if Julia heard what she was saying...

"You...you *bitch*."

Bella's shoulders stiffen. "Grow up, Tess. Stop fucking hiding."

Bella comes into my room that night. I'm half-asleep but sit up as she climbs onto the bed next to me.

"I didn't mean it," she says, and I know she's talking about what she said about Julia earlier.

"I know you didn't, big sis."

She leans her head against mine. "It's so fucking awful. I hate going over there and seeing them in such a state in that empty dump of a house, but I feel bad if I don't because they—especially Greg—seem so alone. No one else even bothers."

I bite my lip. She sounds so sad. I should be going with her. I'm being so selfish letting her go on her own.

"And I don't like the way she's latched on to Dad."

I think of Dad putting his hand on Julia's. "Don't be daft. They're friends, that's all."

"Wasn't Dad supposed to be *Greg*'s friend? Greg doesn't know about her little visits to Dad. He doesn't have a clue. That's not right, is it?"

No, it's not right. But nothing about this is right.

I walk through the woods, humming a song I heard on the radio that got stuck in my head. We're into the second week of the Easter holidays and the sun is out. It's not warm enough for the beach yet, so I've pulled on a sweater and come adventuring in the woods, a bag full of snacks and a book on my back. Dad had Julia over again, but after Bella's comments before, I feel a bit awkward round her now, guilty that they seem to be getting closer while Greg's over at Dean House on his own.

I slow when I hear voices coming from the clearing and as I step into sight, I immediately wish I'd turned tail as soon as I heard them. It's Bella, but she's with Jack and Sean and Lena. I almost do turn around, but then Max steps into view from behind a tree and hunches down next to them. He's the one who looks up and sees me, calling my name with that delicious smile on his face.

I didn't know they were here. Bella never mentioned a word.

"Well, great," Lena says, "the gang's all here. Come join us, Tess. We're going all Scooby-Doo, trying to solve a mystery."

I go over and try not to look all disapproving when I see that Lena's holding a cigarette and that Jack has a bottle of something that's definitely not Coke balanced between his knees.

"Mystery?" I say, hovering self-consciously, not wanting to commit to staying by sitting down.

"You know that girl who went missing?" Lena offers me the cigarette packet as she speaks and I shake my head. Bella takes one though.

I do, vaguely. Some girl, Annie something, a couple of years older than us, from a town not far from here, had been reported missing a few days ago. "She ran away, didn't she?"

"Well," said Lena, "that's what everyone *thought*."

"So I take it you have another theory?"

"It's not a theory," Jack drawls, a funny smile on his face. "They found a body."

"*Her* body?"

He shrugs. "It hasn't been confirmed yet, but it wasn't far from where she lived, so..."

I shiver and plonk myself down on a log next to Bella. "God. That's...horrible. What happened? Was it an accident?"

Jack leans in toward me. "She was strangled—it was murder."

I jerk away from him and Bella sighs. "Stop it, Jack, you're scaring her."

"No, he's not," I snap. "God, Bella, I'm fifteen, not five."

"Ooh, *meow*. Cat-fight alert," Jack says, laughing.

"We thought we could do our own investigation," Lena says, flicking her cigarette into the stream. "Go to the town where she lived, see if we can find out who might have done it."

I notice Sean hasn't said a word since I got here. He stands up, kicking at the dead leaves on the ground.

"That's the stupidest idea ever," I say. "It's dangerous and... *stupid*."

"Ah, poor Tessie *is* scared," Jack says. "You were right to leave her out of this, Bella. Why don't you go home to Daddy?"

I grit my teeth and stand and walk away. I hear someone following but don't stop until I hear Bella call my name.

"Wait up, Tess," she says.

"I hate him." I shout it without meaning to. "Him and his brother. Did you hear him?"

"He was just trying to wind you up."

"Well, he bloody succeeded. Why the hell is he here in the woods talking about some poor murdered girl when his own sister just died? I don't think he cares about Ellie at all. He's probably glad she's gone."

"*Tess Cooper*," Bella gasps, grabbing my arm and giving me a shake. "What a horrible thing to say!"

Tears are burning in my eyes as I stare at my sister. "It's true," I say, my voice breaking. "And I can't believe you're here with them joining in with all this morbid...*shit*."

I turn and march away from her. Poor Julia. No wonder she's spending so much time with Dad when her own sons are so *awful*.

MAY 2007

I wait for Bella outside the house, heart thudding, desperate to share the gossip.

"Guess what?" I say as soon as she opens the gate. "Julia's gone."

"What?" She's frowning, looking down at her phone, not at me.

"Julia packed her bags and left! She's left Greg, run off somewhere." I can hear the tremble in my voice and I look at Bella, wanting her to reassure me or share my fear or...I don't know what I want her to do.

"She *left* him? Jesus...are you sure?"

She sounds shocked but already she's back on her phone, tapping out a text.

I clench my fists, feeling a surge of irritation. Doesn't she believe me? Is she texting one of her mates to ask *them* about it? Who does she think is going to know more than us? Julia's been coming round to our house more and more recently, but when I asked, Dad said he knew nothing about her leaving. No one in the village seems to know where she's gone or why she left, but it's all anyone is talking about.

Her phone dings and her face goes blank as she reads her text. "Wow," Bella says, finally looking at me, her voice flat. "That is...strange. How are the boys taking it? And Greg?"

"The boys are both away, I think, and no one's seen Greg."

"Right." She walks past me and I grab her shoulder.

"What's going on? Don't you even care that your precious Greg's wife has walked out?"

She pushes me, two hands shoving me so hard I stagger. "Stop it, Tess. Bloody grow up. He's not my Greg and of course I care. But she'll be back—her and Greg...you've seen them together. Of course she'll come back."

"Wait," I say, as she moves past me. I glance toward the house to check that Dad's not around. I ignore Bella's impatient sigh as she turns back to me, her arms folded.

"I think Dad knows," I say.

She frowns. "Knows what?"

"I think Dad knows where she is. I think he's been going to see her. I heard him on the phone."

Bella's face goes white.

"I'm worried, Bella." I get the words out at last. "I'm worried Dad's the reason Julia left Greg."

Bella shakes her head. "No. No fucking *way* is that going to happen."

JUNE 2007

We sit in shock. Me and Bella, the distance between us closed by this...this *thing* that's happened. Dad is downstairs with Julia. *With* her. He came home from the pub with her and they were holding hands and laughing. Bella saw them from her bedroom window and came and woke me up. Together we watched as Dad leaned in and kissed her, her fake red hair shining under the outside light.

I was right. Awfully, horribly right.

But neither of us can quite believe it. This is why Julia left Greg? For my dad? Ten years older, four inches shorter, my permanently broke dad?

Bella suddenly starts laughing. "Can you fucking believe this?" she says.

I start laughing too—what the hell else are we supposed to do?

"Girls? Are you still awake?"

Dad's voice calling up the stairs cuts through our laughter. He's waiting in the kitchen when we go downstairs, still holding Julia's hand.

"What's going on?" Bella asks.

Dad glances at Julia. "We...that is, I...Julia's going to be staying with us for a while. With me."

"What?" I half laugh as I say it. This has to be a joke, right? Or a dream. It's a bloody bad dream.

"We've become closer. In the last few months. Since..."

"No fucking way." Bella's voice cuts Dad off. "You are not serious?"

"Bella..."

"No. Just no. She is not moving in here—into my mother's house. Into my mother's bed."

"Bella—come on," I say, stepping up to touch her arm.

She shakes me off. "Stay out of it, Tess." She turns to Julia. "And you—what is this? You kill your own daughter in a crash, so you think you can move in and get two new ones?"

"Arabella," Dad says again, his voice raised in anger. "How dare you—"

"How dare I? What the damned hell is this? You two have been sneaking around having some seedy affair and now you're moving her in? What—are you going to move Jack and Sean in as well, expect us to play happy fucking families?"

She whirls around, looks at me. "Are you happy with that, Tess? Having Jack and Sean in your house?"

I shake my head, struck dumb by her rage. Julia's face crumples and I feel awful. I like Julia, I really do, but this...

"And Greg? Your *husband*, Julia?" Bella is still shouting. "What's he going to have to say about this?"

We're interrupted by a hammering on the front door. Bella and I stare at each other. Oh God—it must be Greg.

But when Dad comes back into the room, he's trailed not by a furious Greg Lewis, but by Mr. and Mrs. Wallace, Nic's parents.

Mrs. Wallace is crying and Mr. Wallace rushes straight up to Bella. "Is she here? Is she with you?"

Bella looks startled. "Nic? No—I haven't seen her today."

"But last night—she was with you last night?"

Bella shakes her head. "What? No, I haven't seen her all week. What's going on?"

Mr. Wallace sinks into a chair. "She left a message yesterday to say she was sleeping over here. So we didn't think...but then she didn't come home. And she's not answering her phone. No one knows where she is."

Dad crouches next to him. "Steve? I think you need to call the police."

Dad's thinking about that other girl, the one who was murdered, I know he is. It was only a couple of months ago and they never did find who did it. But...that was miles away. It would never happen *here*, not to someone we *know*.

I bite my lip to stop words I'd regret from pouring out. Nicole is the worst of Bella's friends. I don't believe she's really missing, not properly. She's forever pretending to be with Bella when really she's off with some boy or at a party she doesn't want her parents to know about. She's probably gone off to see Jack—she was all over him at their New Year's party. She'll turn up, basking in the attention. She isn't worthy of Bella's concern. She isn't worthy of Bella's friendship. Wouldn't it be better if she really had disappeared forever?

I wake with a start. What was it—what did I hear? The night silence is thick. I can hear my breath, quick and harsh. I strain my ears and hear it eventually—voices from downstairs, rising and falling. I get up, stuff my feet in slippers, and pull on my bathrobe. Bella's door is open. I can see her sleeping in her bed, a tangle of blond hair, a bundle under the quilt. It eases my thumping heart—it wasn't her sneaking in or out that woke me. I creep down the stairs and the voices get louder. I recognize Dad's voice, but not the other male voice. They're in the kitchen, the door ajar. I hesitate outside, wavering between advance and retreat. In the end, I do neither; I tuck myself away in the shadows behind the door instead to listen.

"Jesus, Steve, I'm so sorry."

Dad's voice. And Steve? It must be Steve Wallace, Nicole's dad. Nicole—Bella's missing friend. God, it's been awful the last couple of days. The police even spoke to Bella. I don't like Nicole, I never have. She's been stepping up the bitchy, snide comments, even in front of Bella, always covering herself by laughing after and saying *only kidding*. Like saying only kidding does anything to lessen the cruel comments. It's like stabbing someone and then trying to cover it up with a bandage. I know it was her that started the Tessie the Elephant nickname, now picked up by half the school.

When the Wallaces turned up saying she was missing, though, I never thought something might have actually happened to her. I thought she'd run off to see Jack, or some other boyfriend, run off to piss off her parents.

But she hasn't come back.

I risk a peek around the door. Mr. Wallace has his head in his hands. There's a bottle of whisky between him and Dad on the table, two half-full glasses.

"I shouldn't have shouted at her," Mr. Wallace says. "But those texts on her phone... She got so mad at me, screaming about how she was seeing a real man, who was going to take her away. Jesus Christ, Nicole is only seventeen and the things in those texts—they were sick, Leo, perverted."

I hear the scrape of a chair, the chink of glass against glass and tuck myself back into the shadows, holding my breath.

"Who do you think it is?" my dad says.

"She was seeing Jack Lewis—I told the police that. But Greg bloody covered for him, said he was away working and it couldn't be him. Oh yeah, he had alibis for the whole lot of them when Nic went missing."

I let my breath out in a whoosh. I did honestly think Nicole had sneaked off to visit Jack.

"That bastard. I know he's lying, covering for his boys. There's something about that family. Nicole was always over there. You need to watch your girls, Leo. You need to protect them."

I feel sick. God, all the time Bella's been spending over there—with Jack and Sean, with Greg, even. Dad doesn't know any of that. No, I'm being stupid—Jack and Sean, they're not much older than me, they wouldn't have done anything awful to Nicole. And Greg. Well, he's *nice*. He's *kind*.

"Did you tell the police about the texts?"

My stomach flips as I hear Mr. Wallace start to cry. Grown-ups shouldn't cry. Dad did after Mum died, but I only ever saw it at the funeral. I wanted to close my eyes and cover my ears then. It frightened me seeing my dad cry.

"Of course. And I told them it had to be one of the Lewis boys, but they checked their phones and there are no messages to Nicole. They must have deleted them, or got another phone," Mr. Wallace says. "So the police think she's just run off and she hasn't. She's seventeen, they keep saying. She'll come home when she's ready. There's no evidence anything's happened to her."

"They could be right."

"*No*. She would have texted one of her friends—Bella or Caitlin—even if she didn't want to talk to me or Liz. But no one's heard from her. Something's wrong. Something bad has happened, I know it." His voice rises. "What if she hasn't run off with Jack Lewis, Leo? What if whoever killed that other girl has got her?"

Bella won't come out of her room. She's been out with Caitlin all the time since Nicole went missing, searching their local haunts, asking everyone they know if they've seen her. But today...the news has been on nonstop since we got home from school, the same story repeated by all the local channels. A body has been found in the woods. Not our woods—a few miles away, but close enough. No identity yet, but enough of the reporters have said it's a woman to convince Bella it's Nicole. Nicole Wallace, queen bitch, dead in the woods. I know I couldn't have wished this into happening with my wicked thoughts, but it feels like I did. I never said the words out loud, but I think Bella heard them anyway. I went up to her room to say...I don't know what I was going to say, but I didn't get chance anyway. Bella just stared at me and her face was cold and blank. A million unsaid words passed between us and then she slammed the door in my face.

The village is alight with rumor and the rumors all say the same thing. Nicole Wallace was murdered like that other girl.

I didn't wish this into happening. I didn't. I wouldn't.

NOW

CHAPTER 15

The house is different at night. During the day, it's cozy and warm, cradled in the encroaching trees. At night, there's nothing to see out of the windows but blackness. Creaks that go unnoticed during daylight become sinister and my breath comes out in white plumes. I sit up in bed. It's barely ten o'clock, but I haven't slept for three nights, not since I got back from the hospital. I've tried, but my eyes keep snapping open, staring into the dark. The creak of a floorboard sounds like a groan. I can hear voices downstairs but I don't want to be around Jack and the others.

I get up and pull on leggings and sneakers, zip up a fleece hoodie. I can't stay indoors listening to the house get quiet as everybody else falls asleep. My mind gets too busy, sends creeping thoughts down unwanted corridors, asking what if and why and when... thoughts of death and blood and ghosts. And bones. God, bones...

Neither Jack nor Sean said anything when they came back from the police station and all our questions are hovering unspoken, thick and heavy in the cold air. I hear them as whispers in the night. *Who is it? Who is it? Whose bones are they?*

I tiptoe across the landing and almost scream, hands over my mouth as the bathroom door opens and Sean steps out, rubbing his hair with a towel. I take a step back toward my room but it's too late, he's seen me.

"Is Julia...?"

I shake my head.

He looks at me. "Where are you going?"

"Out for a run. I couldn't sleep. I was restless."

He sighs. "Same here. I can't stop thinking about the police swarming all over Dean House. Want some company?"

Not you, I want to say, but the presence of his dying mother in the house stops the words from coming out. And also...he looks so sad. He looks lost, shoulders slumped, eyes tired and shadowed.

"I prefer to run alone," I say instead.

He cocks his head. "At ten at night?"

I shrug. I've run later than this. Not here, though.

We both pause by Julia's room. "How was she when you saw her?" I ask. It's not really what I'm asking. I'm asking if he and Jack have made things worse. If they took their hostility and anger and stories of buried bones into their dying mother's room.

"We didn't scream recriminations and throw things," he says with a ghost of a smile. He knows what I'm asking.

The landing feels too small with both of us here. The house feels too small. It always did, when they were in the house. I wasn't running back then, but I used to spend more time out of the house than in it while they were here. Even now, I feel as awkward and self-conscious as I did at sixteen in his presence. I turn away, eager to leave before the walls close in even more, and his voice stops me.

"Do you think she ever knew what her leaving did to us?" he asks.

I hesitate. Do I tell him I tried not to think about it? Tried never to think about them? "Yes. I do. Sometimes...she used to cry."

"But was it for me and Jack, do you think? Or for Ellie?"

"I don't know. I never asked."

"I was going to. It was one of the things I came back to ask, before it's too late. But when I went in to see her...I can't be angry anymore. She's dying, there's nothing left of the woman who made me so angry." His face twists and I think maybe there is still some anger left there.

"Jack got expelled from school after Ellie died. Did she ever tell you?"

I shake my head. "I thought he dropped out."

We're talking in whispers. Julia's door is ajar and I take another step away. Sean follows, standing too close, so I can smell the toothpaste on his breath, the fading scent of shower gel. His hair is still damp.

"He refused to go back after her funeral, so Dad got him a job, packed him off so he wouldn't embarrass the family. And then Mum left. We were there, floundering after Ellie's death, and she just walked away and left us. She didn't tell us, didn't come and see me at school or go and see Jack. We just got a call from Dad to say she'd walked out. No one hears anything from her and then a few weeks later she moves in with Leo. Jack was so pissed off when she moved in here—he walked out of his job to go and see Dad."

"I'm sorry." As I say it, my heart is hammering. When Julia moved in it was the same time as Nicole went missing. Didn't Greg claim both the boys were away—Jack working and Sean at school? "Did you come back as well?"

"No. I stayed at school. I know Dad tried to persuade Jack to give school another go but he flat-out refused, so Dad packed him off to work with yet another of his construction mates."

"Did he . . . was he here long?" How long was it between Nicole going missing and her body being found?

Sean looks at me oddly. "I don't know. A couple of days or so." He pauses. "He said he was going to see Dad, but I think he was looking for Mum."

The shock of Julia moving in got lost when Nicole went missing. Nicole's murder stopped any of us from wondering about Dad and Julia's relationship and how long it had been going on. They must have been seeing each other in the months before she left Greg, but Dad never said a word. And if Jack was looking for her, why not just knock on the door? He knew where she was. Was he spying on us? I think of all the time I used to spend alone in the woods back then and repaint it in my imagination, Jack watching from behind every tree. I go hot at the thought of what else he might have seen.

I wonder if the police know that Jack Lewis was in town when Nicole was murdered. I wonder if they know his dad lied about him being away the whole time.

"We didn't invite her, you know. It was as big a shock to me and Bella as it must have been to you and Jack. We had no idea." That's not strictly true, though, is it? I was worrying about it for weeks before Julia actually moved in.

Sean laughs softly. "It wasn't your fault, though we blamed you—you, your sister, your dad. We made you the villains so we didn't have to blame our mother for choosing you over us."

"I'm so sorry about Ellie. She was such a lovely little girl."

He smiles. "She was such an adorable little pain. We were teenagers. The last thing we wanted was a toddler to babysit, filling the house with pink and dolls."

I go downstairs and he follows me. Jack and Lena are laughing in the living room, the door closed. I resist the urge to open the front door and start running in case Sean chooses to follow me. The thought makes my heart beat faster in a peculiar mix of fear and...something else. Perhaps I'm not as immune to the Lewis boys as I thought. Instead, I go to the kitchen, fill the kettle, put teabags in the pot.

"We never..." I hesitate. "We never thought we wanted a stepmother, never thought we needed one. The shock of her moving in with us...of her getting together with Dad...I'm sorry. We were teenagers, obsessed with our own problems. We should have spent more time thinking about the family she left behind when she came to us." I make a face. "Julia became ours whether we wanted her or not, and you and Jack were being so awful to her, I cast you both in the roles of the enemy."

He sighs and takes the mug of tea I hand him. "She did try and sort things out with us. She was always trying to get us here. But we were too angry. We took Dad's side and refused to have anything to do with her."

I assumed, when he arrived, that he would still be full of all the burning anger that scared me when I met him first. But I don't think it's there anymore. I stand a couple of feet away and I don't feel the same edginess, the needle-like prickle of uneasiness that used to make me think just his presence could give me a static shock.

It's muted now, dampened by sadness. I don't know if it makes me any easier in his company. I watch him, leaning back against the counter, shoulders curved, head bowed, hands gripping tea made in a flowery mug.

The split-second urge to lean over and push his hair out of his face, though, that's new.

He looks up and my cheeks burn as I wonder if I blanked out for a second and actually did it.

I think of the bones at Dean House and wonder how long they've been there. Bella's voice from my dreams is still whispering, always whispering the same words: *It wasn't an accident.* It makes me clench my hand into a fist. Feeling a bond with Sean—feeling sympathy—isn't why I'm here.

"So what have the police said to you—about the body they found in your garden?" It comes out too loud, my tone harsh. I want to be angry with him. "Have they linked it to the old murders?"

He frowns. "They haven't told us anything. They just wanted to know how long it is since we lived there, if anyone else has lived there since." He stops. "And they wanted to know if Dad had been in contact."

"What's this—filling Tess in on the fiasco that is the police investigation?" Jack says, walking into the kitchen. He goes to the fridge and pulls out a beer. I want to snap at him for making himself so much at home. He laughs and shakes his head. "Oh, of course now they're interested in finding Dad, but when he went missing? They did not give a shit."

"But...did he really go missing?" I ask. "I thought he packed a bag and contacted you and..."

"A couple of texts to say he had to get away. And then we never heard from him again. Fuck knows what happened to him—he said he was off to Germany to work with a mate, but there was never any sign of him leaving the country, no activity on his bank account. We told the police all that back then and they did a half-assed search, but they were basically—*he's a grown man, no risk to himself or others, who left of his own volition.* In other words, fuck off and stop bothering us."

"I never...I'm sorry. I assumed he'd kept in touch."

"Oh, don't pretend you ever gave a shit," Jack says, striding out of the room, beer in hand.

I recoil. "So he's changed, has he?" I say to Sean.

"Tess..."

"Maybe you should mention to the police that he was lurking around spying right around the time Nicole Wallace got murdered."

Sean steps back, face pale.

"Oops," I say. "Did you forget what you just told me screws up his alibi?"

Pushing past him, I step out into the night.

CHAPTER 16

A few days later and I still haven't slept properly through the night. My legs are heavy as I climb the stairs and the thought of a full night's sleep makes me cry with longing. I haven't taken any of the sleeping pills the doctor prescribed yet, but maybe I should. I hate the thought of medication, but it would only be while I'm here.

Lena's already in the bedroom, standing at the window in the dark, looking out at the night. She doesn't turn when I go in.

"Are you okay?"

She glances back at me, her face solemn. "Not really. It's really getting to me—the body in the woods."

I shiver. "Yeah, I know what you mean."

"Do you think they'll ever be able to figure out who it is? If it's just bones that are left?"

"I don't know. They can work miracles these days with DNA, can't they?" I join her at the window. "Do you think it's that girl? The one that went missing?"

She's quiet for a long time. "It's got to be, hasn't it?" She shakes her head. "The whole world thought it had stopped—poor Nic. No one ever found out who killed her and no more bodies were found and everyone forgot about her, didn't they?"

I frown. "I doubt her family did."

"No. And Bella never would have, if she was still alive."

We both stand in silence.

"Do you think there are more?"

"More what?"

"Bodies. Remains, whatever. In the woods. They're going to look, aren't they? They're going to tear this village apart." She sighs. "Do you ever wonder about Greg?"

"What?"

"His behavior toward teenage girls. It was...creepy. And the timing. They move to the area and suddenly teenage girls start going missing and getting murdered."

All the hairs rise on my arms and I tense up. She turns from the window to look at me. "You should tell them, Tess."

"Tell who what?"

"You should tell the police. Tell them what Greg was like. What he was like with you."

I back away from her, shaking my head. "What are you talking about?"

She sighs. "Bella told me. I'm sorry—I've never said a word to anyone else, ever." She pauses. "But you should tell the police."

I back away farther and the room retreats. My head is full of a roaring storm, me screaming at Bella, her shouting back. "What exactly did Bella tell you?" I ask, too loudly.

She looks at me with her eyebrows raised. "Like I said—how creepy he was with you both. What did you think I meant?" She pauses. "But you should tell them. And if you won't, I definitely will."

I'm not going to even try to sleep with Lena's words whizzing around my head. No one ever understood the friendship I had with Greg. Isn't that why I kept it secret? Because people would see the girl I was then, fifteen going on sixteen, and Greg nearly forty, and they'd see it as wrong. What I always saw, though, before I messed things up so spectacularly, was a lonely man who'd lost his daughter, whose wife had left him. At first, wasn't that what I was to him—a surrogate daughter? My fault, everything that went wrong, not his. I don't believe, never did believe all that crap Lena was spouting about him. It wasn't my experience, so how can I go to the police and implicate him? Without knowing who is buried in the woods?

I trudge downstairs, frowning when I see the front door is ajar.

I hear a cough and take a step outside. Jack steps out of a patch of darkness, cigarette glowing in his hand.

"What are you doing out here?"

"Obeying the no-smoking-inside rule," he says, flicking the cigarette away.

"In the middle of the night?"

"One for the road before I tuck myself up in beddy-byes."

I stand on the step, wishing I hadn't come out. I have nothing to say to Jack and I can't hover here awkwardly forever. I'm about to turn away and go back inside when he speaks again. "I was out here, all maudlin in the dark, thinking about families."

I fold my arms and take a step closer to him. "Understandable, with Julia..."

"None of us have the conventional family setup, do we? You and Leo, Max and Lena with their parents jetting off without a look back. And me and Sean." He stops and laughs.

I raise my eyebrows. "I guess out of all of us, you're the only one with anything approaching a conventional family—wife and child, house in the suburbs."

His laughter stops. "Yeah, that's not going so great."

"I'm sorry."

"Are you?" He sounds amused. "You probably think it serves me right, don't you, Tess?"

"No. No, of course not." I'm glad it's too dark for him to see my face properly.

"Did you know our respective dads had a fight once?"

"What are you talking about?"

Jack shrugs. "Not long before the wedding."

I shake my head. "No, he never..."

"I followed Dad over here and pulled the two of them apart. It was such a shit time—Mum living with you, Dad was a mess, Nic had been murdered."

My heart skips a beat, catches up in a sick gallop. I remember Bella telling me how uncaring Jack had been over Nicole's murder. And Sean has revealed that Jack was around when the murder happened. But in the moonlight, he doesn't look uncaring, he looks haunted.

"I used to dream about her, after she died. I'd dream we were out together and then I'd look over and she'd be dead, a corpse walking and laughing next to me."

My throat feels tight—the description of his dreams is so close to my recent ones of Bella.

"You were here, though, weren't you? When she was killed," I say. "Sean told me. Well, he let it slip."

He's looking blankly at me. "No—Sean's got that wrong. I was abroad. Working with one of Dad's crews. I didn't find out about it until I got back in the country."

"But Sean said..."

"He got it wrong. Or he was lying."

"Why would he lie?"

Jack shrugs. "Ask him, not me."

I shake my head. "No, I think it's you who's lying."

He leans toward me and grabs my arm. "What the fuck are you accusing me of? I can prove I wasn't here, but I won't have you going around saying shit like that, jeopardizing my marriage. My son is barely more than a baby and I have a good job, a reputation. I will not let you fuck with that."

There's no hint of sadness or softness left in his face. He's all fierce rage and all my old fears are back, screaming at me to run.

I don't expect to sleep after my confrontation with Jack, but I drift off and slip right into a dream. What's different is this time I know I'm dreaming. I know I'm dreaming because I'm in the woods and Bella is sitting on the fallen tree by the stream where we carved our names. I know it's a dream but it feels so real—Bella looks like she did back then but I'm not sixteen, reliving a memory. I'm me as I am now, in my pajamas, feet bare, the taste of toothpaste still in my mouth. I can smell the dankness of the stream and wet leaves, feel sharp twigs and damp mud under my feet. I can hear the trees rustling, whispering, feel the breeze on my cheeks. It doesn't feel like a dream; I feel like I'm really here, in the woods. In the dark. I can hear Bella breathing. But I don't know how I got here. It's like I blinked and when my eyes opened, I was here, standing next to a fallen tree with my dead sister.

"I don't want to be here," I whisper, and she sighs.

"You need to remember."

I shake my head. I'm not sure I want to, not anymore. Not now that they've found that body. It's brought everything home: the summer of death, the summer Bella died. If I remember now, I'll never be able to unsee it and I'll never be able to sleep again.

"We came here that night. Once upon a time, two girls went into the woods and only one came out..."

I shake my head again. No. No, we didn't. That's not how I want the story to end.

"We came here that night and you have to remember."

"No, I don't." It comes out as a shout. "Why? What's the point now? It won't bring you back, will it? You're dead. You're fucking dead, rotting in the ground. You're not here. We're not here. If I remember, it'll..."

"It'll what, Tess?"

"It'll change how I see you," I whisper.

The blood is back on her forehead. Mud on her top, leaves in her hair. If I remember, what will I see?

I hear a noise, something coming toward us through the woods, something big, crashing through the trees. Bella looks behind her then back at me, her eyes wide.

"You have to remember, Tess, but for now you have to *run*."

I wake up with a gasp and I know it was a dream—I'm back in my bed at Dad's house. But my legs are burning like I've been running and I'm sweating and in the dark there are shadows on the bedcovers that look like mud.

I get out of bed, my legs trembling. Lena's asleep in the bed next to me. My door is open, but I remember closing it before I went to sleep. When I look, my feet are muddy and there's blood on the bottom of one of them, a stinging cut that could have come from a sharp stone. Oh God, I've done it again, but this time I got out of the house, went sleepwalking through the woods, talking to my dead sister. Bella keeps telling me to wake up, but I can't because I don't know the difference between asleep and awake anymore. Am I awake now or still in the dream?

There are no other lights on. No sounds coming from any of the other rooms. There was something off in the dream I had, something off that nags in my memory. Lights. There were lights. Not in the woods—coming from behind us, from up at Dean House. A flickering light in the windows, like someone was in there with a flashlight. Did I dream all this? Did I?

CHAPTER 17

There's a strange car outside when I go downstairs next morning and Lena's hovering outside the closed kitchen door.

"What's going on?"

Lena turns, looking pale and shaken. "The police are here," she whispers. "They wanted to speak to Jack and Sean."

I go over—I can hear muffled voices but can't make out what they're saying.

"Have you heard anything?"

Lena takes my arm and leads me away from the kitchen door. "Not really. Jack raised his voice, but I couldn't hear what they were saying properly. It's got to be about the body they found, though, right?"

She paces the hall, all nervous energy, but I just feel cold. Have they found out who it is?

Jack comes storming out of the kitchen, shoving past me and Lena, almost sending me sprawling, but Lena still has hold of my arm and she steadies me. Jack goes outside, slamming the front door behind him. I hear his car start, hear gravel flying as he drives away.

Two men follow Jack out of the kitchen. The one in front wears a suit. I get a sickening lurch of recognition as I look at his tired face and balding head.

"Tess." He nods at me, doesn't smile.

It's the detective who came to see me in the hospital after Bella's death.

He doesn't say anything else, just walks out with his colleague.

Lena and I both turn back to look into the kitchen. The door is open now and Sean is sitting at the kitchen table, his head in his hands.

"It's Dad," he says, when he looks up and sees us there.

"Greg?" I say, looking around stupidly, like I'm expecting him to pop out from behind the door. "He's back?"

He shakes his head. "No...the body. The *bones*. It's Dad. He's dead."

Max breezes in as Lena and I stare at Sean in shock. He looks happy—he's whistling as he walks through the front door. His hair is damp and he smells of shower gel. Where has he been?

"What's up?" he says. "Jack just almost ran me over out there."

Sean gets up and walks past us without a word, going upstairs.

"The body they found," I say through numb lips. "It's Greg."

"What? How can they know?" Max says, dragging his hands through his hair. "It's only been a couple of weeks—they found *bones*, not a body. How can they possibly know?"

"A DNA match," Dad says, coming downstairs. He looks ill. "They wanted to speak to Julia, but she can't...she's in no state to deal with this."

I sink down onto a chair on shaking legs.

I don't understand what this means. I was so sure it was going to turn out to be another teenage girl. Another lost victim of the summer of death.

I don't know how long we sit there, me, Max, and Lena. Dad excuses himself and goes back up to Julia. Lena's drumming her fingers on the table, Max just looks in shock. And I'm...I'm remembering every conversation I had with Greg Lewis. I flinch at the thought of sharing that with the police. But they won't want to speak to me, will they? Jack and Sean, of course, even Max and Lena as friends of the family. My heart rate speeds up. But we, Dad and I, were pretty much his closest neighbors. And he and Dad were friends before Julia...

"I think they're wrong," Max says into the heavy silence. "How can they know this quickly?"

"They took DNA samples. Back then, when he went missing." It's Jack. I gasp—I didn't hear him come back.

There's a creak on the stairs and Sean comes in to join us, closing the kitchen door behind him.

"They asked so many questions about Dad—when he went missing, had anyone heard from him in the time he'd been gone." He pauses and looks at Jack. "I thought they were asking about him as a *suspect*, because it was his property the body was found on."

Jack is pacing around the room, red spots high on his cheeks, no sign of his fake smile.

"Jack...Sean...I'm so sorry," I say, reaching out a hand toward Jack. I move back as Jack whirls around, looking like he wants to punch somebody.

"No," he says, shaking his head. "Max is right—they've got it wrong. It can't be Dad."

Sean gets up and puts a hand on his brother's shoulder but Jack shakes him off.

"Jesus," Jack says, looking ill. "Did it happen right away? Did he ever go to Europe or were we all here for that fucking wedding, dressed up and getting drunk while our dad was rotting in the garden?"

"Maybe he came back," Lena says. She's white-faced, her arms wrapped around herself. "They can't know yet when he...he could have come back anytime."

"Did he?" Jack's looking at me. "You were the only one still here after the wedding. Did he come back?"

I shake my head. "I never saw him, I swear."

"Christ, I don't even have those fucking texts he sent anymore. I lost that phone years ago." Jack runs his hands through his hair and sinks into a chair.

"The police will be able to tell us when it happened, won't they?" Sean says, sitting next to his brother. "Not exactly, but roughly? When and how..."

"Could it have been an accident?" Max says, and Jack and Sean both stare at him.

"An *accident*?" Jack says. "He buried himself in the fucking woods by *accident*?"

Max shakes his head. "Right. Yeah. Sorry, I'm not thinking straight."

"I'm going up to ask Julia what she knows," Jack says, getting up.

"No," Sean says, grabbing his arm. "She's dying up there—you can't go barging in screaming accusations."

"You think the police won't have questions for her?" Jack looks like he's going to hit his brother. "Why are you so defensive about her all of a sudden? Have you forgotten she left us? Dumped us for a new family?"

"She's dying."

"Yeah—and now we know our dad has been dead for *years*, buried on his own damned land."

"It has nothing to do with her."

"Doesn't it? How do we know this whole new family of hers didn't put him there?"

I take a breath and hold it. The very air feels violent and I daren't move for fear of setting it off.

"We don't know anything—that's for the police to find out," Sean says, his voice shaking, and it reminds me again that the police will have questions for all of us about our relationships with Greg Lewis.

I get up and walk out of the room. Lena follows me.

"Well," Lena says, staring at me, "this is a turnup, isn't it, Tess? Bet you weren't really expecting it to be Greg...Or were you?" She leans in closer. "You have to tell them now, Tess. You have to."

I glance past her and see Jack watching us. I have to resist the urge to run.

THEN

CHAPTER 18

From the *Western Vale News*, June 25, 2007:

SECOND BODY FOUND

The body of a second teenager has been found in a wooded area near Porthcawl, police confirmed last night. At this stage, there are no more details, but following so soon after the murder of Annie Weston in April, less than twenty miles away, this latest discovery has raised speculation that the deaths are related.

June 27, 2007:

NICOLE WALLACE MURDERED

Police have confirmed that they are treating the death of Nicole Wallace as a murder inquiry and the same team investigating Annie Weston's murder are working on the case.

Two murders of two teenage girls in the same area have led to local concern that this could be the work of a serial killer. While the police will not confirm they are looking for the same person in connection with the cases, they are warning local teenagers to avoid going out alone after dark.

*　　*　　*

JULY 2007

I haven't been back to the garden since the Lewises' New Year's party. I didn't mind when the house was empty. Even if I'd been caught, all I was doing was making it nicer—weeding and pruning the overgrown plants. It wasn't like I was one of the kids trashing the place and spray-painting the walls. But the boys are away, Sean off with some of his posh private school friends and Jack wherever he's working and Ellie is…gone. Julia is living at our house and I guess Greg is at work. He's away a lot, building his houses, growing his empire. I don't know why they bothered moving here in the first place.

It's not too bad, is my first thought when I step into the garden. The side gate is locked now, but the wall is low and easy to climb, even for me. I haven't touched the place in nearly a year, but someone has. No new weeds and the roses look better than when I was looking after them, glossy leaves and massive blooms. There are even some new plants, gathered in pots by the back door, waiting to be planted. Did Sean do this? Greg said he was the gardener in the family. Or was it Julia who did it? Was she going to take over our garden now, erase any lingering trace of my mother from the overgrown mess our garden had become since Mum died?

I stroke one of the leaves on the climbing roses, careful not to touch the thorns.

"So you're my phantom gardener."

I spin round, ready to run when I hear the voice behind me. "I'm sorry—I thought you were away." I stop. "Not that I come here when the house is empty. I'm not…"

"It's okay. I'm not planning to call the police. Sean's given up and God knows I could use the help."

There's laughter in his voice and I can feel my cheeks glowing as I look at him.

"Here," Greg says, holding out some clippers and a pair of gardening gloves. "I've had them ready for when you returned."

"I'm sorry about Julia," I say as I pat compost around the newly planted rosebush. He'd left me alone for an hour but then came out with two mugs of tea, standing watching me so I felt an itch on the back of my neck from his presence.

"It's fine, Tess," he says, passing me a watering can. "I'm not going to pretend I'm happy about it, but her leaving was in the cards as soon as Ellie died."

His eyes are bright with tears when I glance up. I don't know what to say to him. His daughter died and now his wife has left him and come to live with us. It's all so *wrong*. He should hate us; he should be chasing me away from his house with a pitchfork. Instead, he's letting me help him garden and he's made me a cup of tea. The sun shines down on him and the light makes him look younger and a million times better-looking than his sons.

"And honestly, I don't know. We'd been having problems for a while."

The moment grows more awkward. I don't want to hear about his marital problems. I feel hot and uncomfortable as he sighs. He's right behind me and I can feel the sigh on the back of my neck.

"You know we're not actually married?"

I almost drop the clippers I'm holding.

"We got together so young—not much older than you. Julia fell pregnant with Jack and we moved in together. Never quite got around to the whole marriage thing. I suppose that made it easier for her to walk away. No messy divorce. The house is half hers but she hasn't asked for anything." He pauses. "Not yet, anyway."

"Not necessarily a good thing," I mutter. "That it was so easy for her to walk away. Not good for you or the boys, anyway."

"I'm glad you came," he says. "It's good to have someone on my side." Am I on his side? How can I be when the other side is my dad? "Most people have avoided me—no one seems to know what to say." He touches my hand as he says it, the slightest brush of skin against skin, but it makes me shiver. He's like his sons and nothing like Max—there's that spark of danger that Bella and all her friends drool over, in his hand on mine, but it makes me want to run and hide.

"Come back anytime," he says, and when I look down I see he's not trying to hold my hand, or whatever ridiculous notion passed through my mind, he's pressing a key into my palm.

*   *   *

I stop dead, key to the side gate in my hand, at the sound of female laughter. I frown at the thought of going into the garden and finding Greg with a new girlfriend. I've been coming around every afternoon for a month and sometimes he's been there, sometimes not, but it's always been just him. He's so easy to talk to. I tell him about Bella, about school, and about Max. Not mentioning any names, but just talking about my feelings. And he listens and advises and...it feels like I'm talking to a friend. In fact, he's easier to talk to than any of the girls in school. I never used to be bothered that I didn't have a best friend because I had Bella, but recently...bloody hell, how sad is it that forty-year-old Greg is the nearest thing I have to a real friend?

I waver, thinking of running. But no, why should I? He gave me a key, told me to come anytime. I push the gate open and walk around the side of the house, faltering when I get to the garden and see Bella standing there with Greg. She's wearing tight faded jeans and a T-shirt that barely skims her belly button. My face gets hotter as I tug my own baggy T-shirt down over my jeans.

"Hey, Tess," Greg calls, and my sister turns and sees me, her eyebrows rising in surprise.

"What are you doing here?" she asks, like this is her place.

I lift the trowel and fork I'm carrying in response. "Helping in the garden," I mutter.

"Look what Greg's lending me," she says, holding up an ancient-looking camera. "The boys told him I was into photography."

"But you already have a camera." Dad gave her one for Christmas, one that cost a fortune.

"I know," she says, turning the camera in her hands. "But this is a classic. I can't wait to use it." She reaches up and kisses Greg on the cheek and I feel the kiss like a sting. "Thank you so much."

Greg smiles and touches her hair. He did the same to me the other day—he rubbed my curls like I used to see him doing to Ellie, four-year-old Ellie. He rubbed my head like I was a toddler. He does the same to Bella, tousling her blond hair, but my stupid brain sees it more as a caress. My hand clenches on the trowel and fork in my hand, hard enough to make my palm ache.

SEPTEMBER 2007

"So this will be your room while you're here," I hear Julia say. I press so hard on the paper, my pen goes through and ruins my essay. I clench my teeth. Bella's standing at the door listening as Julia gives Jack and Sean a tour of the house. She's so desperately eager. I've heard her on the phone loads of times, pleading with them to come visit, phone calls that have always ended abruptly with no goodbyes. Do they hang up on her? She's been living here for nearly three months and today's the first time she's seen her sons in person since she left Greg. Bella has been moved in with me and they've given the boys her room.

Julia's been rushing around, tidying and sorting, one minute singing, the next nervously pacing. I'm feeling much the same. Nothing to do with *them*—but Julia said she'd invited Max and Lena down for the weekend too. To make things easier for Jack and Sean, she said. I'll put up with them for a week if it means seeing Max again. They weren't even supposed to be staying originally. They were meant to be home at Dean House, but Greg announced he was going to be away working, so here they bloody are. I don't even know why—Jack's eighteen, so why can't they bloody stay on their own over at Dean House?

"They'd better not touch any of my stuff," Bella mutters, pulling the door a fraction wider.

"You haven't left anything private in there, have you?"

She laughs. "Course not. I wouldn't trust them."

"You don't fancy them anymore, then?"

She throws herself onto the bed. "Oh, I don't know...when they moved here, they were like these shiny new things. I did fancy them—who wouldn't? Jack at least, Sean's a bit..." She pauses and pulls a face. "He's a bit solemn and scowly, isn't he? But Jack, God, he's so funny and bloody gorgeous. I really thought he liked me back."

"But?"

"But he got together with Nic," she bursts out. "I was pissed off with both of them. But then Nic died and Jack didn't even seem *bothered*. And that seems so wrong. God, I know it was just a sex thing with them, Nic told me that. He always talked to me more than her, about Ellie and other stuff. But he should have cared more. Or at least pretended he did—he knew she was my friend."

Her voice breaks. It's been horrible since Nic died. Bella's been pestered by journalists and surrounded at school by people pretending to be all sympathetic but really just desperate for the gory details. She spent days shut away in her room after they found Nic's body, refusing to go out with Caitlin, even avoiding Jack and Sean and Max and Lena.

"I'm sorry," I say, going over and squeezing her hand. "You've had such a crap time. And Jack is a total...*shit*."

She gives me a wobbly smile. "At least I've still got you, though, baby sis."

"Always."

She sighs. "I know you didn't like her. I don't blame you—she was a total cow to you. But she was my friend and I can't get past how she died. I can't...I knew she was seeing someone and I knew she was using me as an alibi when she met him. I thought it was Jack and it pissed me off because I liked him as well. So I can't get past the knowledge that while she was being murdered, while she was lying dead in the woods, I was sulking. I was jealous because she was seeing the boy I liked."

"Come on, big sis, you and Nic were arguing all the time. And you always liked the same boys. She didn't tell you she was pretending she was with you when she went missing, did she? You couldn't have done anything to prevent what happened."

"Doesn't stop me from thinking it, though. And I miss her. I keep catching myself going to text her to rant about the whole Julia and Dad thing, and then I remember."

I chew on my lip. I should have tried harder to get Bella to talk to me about all of this, but she shut herself away and refused to open her door when I knocked. She never comes down to eat the dinners Julia cooks, she's cold with Dad, downright rude to Julia, and snappy with me. But I should have tried harder. Maybe it would have been easier if Julia weren't here, if it was just me and Bella and Dad.

"I wish..." My voice trails off.

"You wish what?"

"I wish Julia hadn't come here," I say, giving up on my essay. I shove my books back in my bag and lie back on the bed. "We were fine before, weren't we? The three of us? I wish they'd never moved into the bloody village." I feel a twinge of guilt as I say it. Julia's impossible to hate, she's so bloody sunny all the time. And her being here has made Dad really happy. But...

"I know," Bella says, sitting next to me. "Every time I walk into a room and she's there, I get a jolt of surprise. It's not like our house anymore." She sighs. "And now we've got Jack and Sean as well and that's going to be just *weird*. Is this going to be a regular thing? Is she going to insist they spend Christmas here?"

I shudder at the thought.

"We have to do something about it," she says.

"Like what?"

"I don't know. Make their lives so miserable they all want to leave?"

"What about Dad? He likes her." He loves her, I think, but I can't say those words out loud.

There's a knock on the door and Julia pokes her head round. "Hey, girls," she says. "Are you going to come out and say hello to Jack and Sean?"

Bella ignores her, but I can't, so I reluctantly get up and follow her out. They're sitting on the twin beds Dad set up in Bella's room, bags at their feet, still wearing their coats.

"Oh look, it's our new sister," Jack says in his drawling voice, and I feel myself blushing. Sean doesn't say anything. He glances at me and away, a frown on his face.

Julia sighs. "Be nice, Jack." She says this but she walks away, leaving me alone in the room with the boys.

Jack laughs and pats the space on the bed next to him. "Come and sit down, sister Tess," he says. "Let's get cozy. I'll be nice, I promise."

"Hey," he calls as I back out of the room. "On second thought, send the hot sister in—I'll be extra nice to her."

Sean follows me as I escape downstairs, stopping me in the hall with a hand on my arm.

"What do you want?" I almost shout it. "Why are you even here? It's not like you're kids who need babysitting while your dad's out of town."

"I was going to explain about Jack," he says stiffly in his posh private school accent. "He didn't want to be here—I persuaded him because I thought it might be a good idea to mend some bridges, to actually be here full-time for a few days. Clearly, you're not of the same opinion."

"No, I'm not. And neither is Bella," I say, shaking him off, my eyes hot with tears I'm determined not to shed. "We don't want you here. None of you. I wish you and your bloody mother would fuck off and leave us alone. How do you think your poor dad's going to feel when he gets back to find us all here playing happy families while he's on his own? It's sick. It's wrong."

He shakes his head and steps away from me. "My poor dad? Jesus, you as well?"

Me as well what?

"Where have you been?" It's eleven o'clock and Bella is tiptoeing into my room. I went to bed half an hour ago, but couldn't sleep knowing Bella was still out.

"Shh," she says, glancing toward Dad and Julia's room. She squeezes past me and collapses on my bed. "Isn't it supposed to be Dad standing with folded arms telling me off for being out late?"

"He went out for a meal with Julia—I told him you were home asleep."

She laughs. "And he believed you? Did you put a pillow under my quilt to be a fake me as well?"

I perch on the edge of the bed, pushing her feet out of the way. Her shoes are muddy and they've left a smear of dirt on my quilt. "Dad's only got eyes for his new girlfriend at the moment."

"Which is why I'm able to go out every night."

"You stink of booze and you're filthy. Where the bloody hell have you been?"

"Up at the amusement park. I came back through the woods."

"At this time? God, Bella, that's so bloody dangerous. They haven't found whoever killed Nicole. He could be still out there."

"Oh, don't worry, I had company." She's smiling up at the ceiling, lost in whatever memories she has of her night.

I ate alone as Dad and Julia were out, and spent the rest of my evening doing homework.

"Were you with them?"

"Who? Jack and Sean?"

I've barely seen them this week. Julia's barely seen them. I think that's why Dad took her out, to cheer her up.

"Were you really up at the amusement park? Or did you go to Dean House?"

There's a pause and then Bella sits up and looks at me. "Why would I go there? Jack and Sean are here."

"Greg's back, though. I saw his car in the village earlier."

"Do you have some kind of problem with him giving me the camera?"

"Of course not. He can do what he likes."

"He's not yours, Tess. Seriously, if you're going to get your first crush, he would be the wrong choice. Like, really wrong."

"Will you get your dirty feet off my bed?" I say, shoving her again. "And I haven't got any stupid crush. I'm nearly sixteen, not twelve."

"You wouldn't know it sometimes, *baby* sis."

"I don't care who you were with, or where, but I do care that you're not doing any of your coursework. How are you going to get into that photography course if you fail all your exams?"

"I don't want to do photography anymore," she says. "Not at college level, anyway. I'm thinking of applying for teaching courses."

"Teaching? You?" It's my turn to laugh. "You hate little kids. God, you'd be the worst teacher in the world."

She gets off the bed. "I'm talking secondary school, not primary. I actually think I'd be good with older kids, but thanks for the support, sis."

"Sorry, but . . . you've wanted to be a photographer forever."

"Yeah, well, the teacher pretty much said the last lot of work I did was shit."

"Come on—you're so talented, I'm sure she didn't . . ."

"You don't know. You weren't there, were you? She wouldn't even let me put them in my portfolio. A whole month's work. So what's the point?"

She's been going out a lot taking photos with the camera Greg gave her, staying late at school to develop them. I glance over to the corner where she's stashed her portfolio and sketchbooks.

"Oh, forget it," she says, sounding exhausted. "I'm going to sleep."

I lie awake for ages, waiting for Bella's breathing to slip into that deep, even rhythm that tells me she's sleeping. Then I get quietly out of bed and go and get her portfolio, unzipping it slowly so I don't wake her. There's just enough light shining through our half-open door so I can see the photographs, but I instantly wish there wasn't.

Bella normally photographs the woods and the beach, gorgeous moody black-and-white shots of the mist among the trees, of the violent splash of water as the sea hits the rocks. These new ones are life studies—Bella glimpsed behind the lens through a mirror, half in shadow but clearly naked. A man, face not shown, but again, clearly naked, half-covered by a rumpled sheet. God, is it Jack? All that stuff she said about not fancying him anymore . . . I've seen them talking. I've seen the way she smiles at him.

I push the portfolio away from me. They're not pornographic in any way, but they're so intimate and so . . . *wrong*. They're not shit, like Bella said, but I can see why her teacher wouldn't let her put them in her coursework folder. I don't understand. I don't get why she would even take these into school to show. Bloody hell, maybe it's good she's not going to do photography at college—I can't imagine Dad going to her exhibitions if these are the type of photos she wants to take now.

NOW

CHAPTER 19

Julia is with me in the kitchen, both of us scraping potatoes for tonight's supper. She's noticeably thinner but she was determined to come downstairs to have dinner with everyone. Personally, I'm tempted to hop into the bed she was so insistent on leaving and hide under the covers until this awkward "family dinner" is well and truly over. Would anyone even notice? In the simmering tension between Julia and her sons, there's little room for anything else.

"You know what I'd love?" Julia says, putting down the knife and potato she's holding. "To have one more party. Not a big one, just family. And Max and Lena, of course. Maybe a couple of people from the village. One last hurrah—some champagne, a big curry or chili for everyone to help themselves. Some really loud music. Loud enough that we get complaints."

I make myself smile. God, if she knew what was going on. "That sounds amazing. Why don't we organize something—for the weekend, maybe?"

She shakes her head. "No, we can't. Much as I'd love to." She pauses. "Leo told me about Greg."

"Oh."

"I know you all wanted to keep it from me, he told me. But it was impossible really. The police want to speak to me as well."

"I'm sorry. It's...it's so awful. Awful that he's dead and that we've all thought he was alive and living his best life somewhere abroad and awful that you have to deal with this now as well as..."

"As well as dying myself?" She pushes the knife and bag of potatoes away from her. "I've been trying to work out how I feel.

Shocked, yes. But should I be sad? I am, in a way. For Jack and Sean, mostly. And for Greg. I don't want to think about what happened or how he must have suffered. I loved him. For such a long time I loved him. But that's so far in the past. I think even the boys had come to terms with the fact that he was never coming back. But none of us thought..."

I put my hand over hers. There are tears in her eyes. "It's okay to be sad about it, you know. Doesn't matter how long the relationship had been over."

She nods. "I know. I just don't want Leo to see it."

"You know, your party idea...it could be what everyone needs. Not a big thing with loud music, but maybe something smaller, a few drinks, everyone sharing stories about Greg and..." My voice trails off. What am I saying? That's the last thing I want.

Dad pops his head round the door. "Tess? Time to go to the police station. I'll give you a lift." He comes in and leans to kiss Julia. "Do you want to come for a ride, Ju? Get some fresh air?"

"No, thanks, baby. I'm tired. I think I'll go and rest."

"I'll see you for supper," I say, squeezing her hand.

She looks exhausted. "I think I'll skip supper, actually. I'm not hungry at all."

I watch as Dad helps her up. She's been resting more and more, the determined energy she found when I arrived with Max and Lena fading.

God, I wish we could throw her a party. Fuck Jack and Sean and Greg. I'd love to hear Julia's laugh again, listen to her singing along badly to some party mix CD.

Dad drops me at the police station. He wanted to wait but I insisted he go back to Julia, telling him I'd get the bus back. I know they've already spoken to Max and Lena and that's not helping my nerves. I can't settle. I shift in my seat, look around the room. It doesn't look like I'd imagined it to from all the books I've read where suspects are questioned. It's less bleak and official looking.

It looks like a meeting room in an office. But then I guess I'm not here as a suspect, am I?

The door opens and a man walks in, smiling. "Tess? Detective Levinson—do you remember me?"

I do. He's the same detective who came to see Jack and Sean, the same man who spoke to me after Bella died, bald spot bigger, more lines on his face. I realize he is the familiarity I felt when I sat in front of that doctor. He reminded me of the detective with his wary, pitying expression.

I remember my disorientation when I woke up in the hospital; the detective's face when he had to tell me Bella was dead. I also remember my meltdown afterward, my frantic insistence that someone had killed Bella, stupid, wildly shouted accusations without anything to back up what I said.

"Do you mind if I tape our chat?" he says now, fiddling with a tape machine. "You can say no, that's fine—you're here entirely voluntarily, but it'll help if we have the whole conversation to refer back to."

I hesitate. I want to say no, but how will that look? I shrug. "That's fine," I say. "I don't think I'll be able to help you, though. I haven't lived here for a long time."

"We're aware of that. I'm sorry to hear about your stepmother. And your recent accident, as well."

I touch the fading bruise on my head. The accident? What does that have to do with anything?

"We spoke to Mr. Rees."

I look blankly at him for a moment before I get it. Mr. Rees is Max's dad in my head, but they mean Max, don't they?

"He's very concerned about you. He told us you haven't been sleeping. That you wrenched the steering wheel out of his hand and caused the crash."

What?

"No," I say, shaking my head, cheeks burning. "There was a cat. It was...instinct to grab the wheel. I grabbed the wheel to avoid a cat."

"Mr. Rees claims he didn't see anything in the road."

That's not what Max said in the hospital. He was the one who told me to mention the bloody cat.

"What does this have to do with anything?"

"Just trying to establish your state of mind, that's all. But you're right—it has nothing to do with the discovery of Greg Lewis's body, does it?"

I feel winded. "It's definitely him, then?"

He doesn't answer. He opens a folder and flicks through some pages.

"After your sister died, you kept insisting it couldn't have been an accident. Why was that, Tess?"

"I don't know. I was confused, grieving...I had a head injury, for God's sake. What has this got to do with Greg?"

"He was reported missing around the same time. I'm sure you understand we're exploring any and all connections at the moment."

"He could have come back. He doesn't have to have died then, does he?"

"Did you see him? The day of the wedding? Did you see something that night?"

I shake my head. My vision doubles, then clears. "No. I don't remember. I told you that."

"You still don't remember? After ten years?"

"It's a condition. It's in your bloody reports."

Detective Levinson flicks through a few more pages. "Ah yes— dissociative memory disorder. At the time, the doctor wasn't sure whether it was temporary, or even whether you really had this at all. The amount of alcohol in your system..."

"I don't fucking remember." I'm nearly shouting, half out of my chair.

Detective Levinson leans back in his chair. There's a faint smile on his face. "Okay, forget that for now. Let's talk about Greg Lewis."

I rub my eyes. They're gritty, my eyelids heavy. My head is pounding and I just want to lay my head on the table and sleep.

"I barely knew him." I look down at the table as I speak, echoes of past conversations with Greg running through my mind.

"Really? Living so close—and with his ex-partner becoming your stepmother?"

"Well, the circumstances hardly invited neighborly confidences, did they? I was a kid."

"Sixteen when he went missing."

"And he was forty."

"It's been suggested to us that Greg Lewis very much liked befriending teenage girls."

My cheeks burn with a thousand memories. "I don't think I was his type."

"And your sister? Was she his type?"

I curl my hands into fists under the table. "Who's telling you all this? Is it Lena? God, she makes things up all the time. Or Jack? You know he's lying. He's always hated us, hated my dad—hated his own damned mother for leaving."

Detective Levinson leans forward. "Listen, Tess. With this new discovery, you have to appreciate that we're looking at any connections with Greg Lewis, however old. And in light of the suggestion that he instigated relationships with young girls. If he hurt you, or tried to hurt you—if he went after your sister...those are mitigating circumstances."

Mitigating circumstances for *what*? They think *I* did it? What has Lena told them? I fold my arms. "I don't remember what happened to Bella. I didn't see Greg Lewis. I hadn't seen him for a long time even before he disappeared. Can I go home now?"

"Okay. No problem. One more question before we let you go. How was your father's relationship with Greg Lewis?"

"My *dad*?"

"Your stepmother left Mr. Lewis and moved in with your father. I'm assuming there was tension? With you all living so close?"

I shake my head. "No. It was fine."

"He was fine with his partner leaving him and moving in with another man two miles down the road? So soon after losing their daughter?"

"Look, I'm not sure what you're implying here..."

"I'm not implying anything. I'm asking—did Greg Lewis ever come to your house?"

"Not that I recall."

He raises his eyebrows. "More memory loss?"

"No, not memory loss. It didn't happen. There was no tension, no confrontation."

Detective Levinson looks at the other detective sitting next to him, who hasn't said a word.

"Okay, Tess, that's it for now. We might have some more questions for you later, but for now...get some rest. You look like you need it."

CHAPTER 20

I'm rigid with tension as I walk away from the police station, my breathing uneven—too-fast breaths punctuated with gasps as the enormity of this whole thing hits: I've just been questioned by the police. The *police*. About a murder. Doesn't matter that I know nothing about what happened to Greg; the fear still sets my heart galloping. By the time I get to the bus station, I have to stop and lean against the wall, force myself to take slow, even breaths to dispel the black floating spots in my vision. Is this a panic attack? No, stop. Calm down. I just need to calm down. My hands are shaking and I'm not sure my legs will hold me if I move from my hunched position against the wall. A man slows and asks me if I'm okay. I nod and force a smile. What am I supposed to say?

I can see the local bus for my village a few stops away, but I can't make myself go over there. I get my phone out. I could call Dad—he'd come and pick me up, I know he would. But he's with Julia and I don't want him to see me like this. I call Sophie but, of course, she's in school, so her phone goes straight to voicemail. I don't want to leave a message, I want to speak to her. I want to see her. The bus home is starting up, ready to leave, but instead of running toward it, I walk in the opposite direction, toward the train station across the road.

I'm sitting on the floor outside Sophie's flat, waiting for her to get home from school. The urge to run away has passed, that stupid urge that made me jump on the train instead of the bus. I can't ring Dad—what can I tell him? That I panicked and ran away because I couldn't cope? He's there, watching his wife die, fielding questions from the police about Greg's death, and I've bloody run away.

I hear someone coming up the stairs and I get to my feet just as Sophie appears. She's got her head down, fumbling in her bag for her keys, so she doesn't see me until she's a couple of feet away, then she looks up and jumps a mile.

"Jesus *Christ*, Tess, you almost gave me a heart attack. What the hell are you doing here?"

"I'm sorry, I'm sorry. I knew you were teaching and I really needed to see you." Hearing Sophie's voice releases something and I start crying, my words coming out in hitching breaths.

"Okay, calm down. Is it Julia? Is it...hell, hang on a minute, let me open the door."

As soon as we're inside the flat, she turns to wrap me in a hug. "I'm sorry, I'm so sorry," she mutters as she steers me to the sofa. "Is it Julia? Did she die?"

I shake my head. "No, it's not Julia."

She lets out a long breath. "Oh, thank God. I thought...you were so upset." She looks over at me and frowns. "What happened to your face?"

I touch the fading bruise. "Oh yeah, long story. Minor car accident, but don't worry, I'm fine."

"You're *fine*? Tess, you are clearly not *fine*."

"I'm sorry. I freaked out. I was panicking and I just needed to see you. There's been...a lot going on." An echo of Bella snorts laughter in my head at the understatement. I keep looking straight ahead, irrationally afraid that if I turn my head, it won't be Sophie sitting next to me, it'll be Bella, mud and leaves in her hair, dripping blood onto the sofa.

"I came from the police station," I say, and there's a wobble in my voice. I swallow and try to keep it together. "They found... they found a body. At Dean House. Julia's old house."

"What? Fuck!"

"It's Greg."

"Who's Greg?"

"He's Julia's ex. Jack and Sean's dad."

"Shit."

"And he was..." I pause. "I knew him."

Sophie's chewing her lip, waiting for me to say more.

I take a deep breath. "I knew him as more than Julia's ex, or the boys' dad. And I..." I can feel sweat building under my hairline. "I lied to the police about it. I told them I barely knew him."

"Is it...is it suspicious, then? But you haven't been there. Why would they speak to you?"

"He was buried in the woods. Nothing left but bones. He's been there a long time. He went missing, you see, right before Dad and Julia's wedding."

"When you were still there. Oh crap. And you lied? Why?"

"Because I did something terrible," I burst out. "No," I say at the look on her face. "Not that—it wasn't me. But if I tell the police I knew him, and I tell them what I did, it's going to look bad, Soph."

My hands are trembling as I wait for her to ask.

"I don't want to know," Sophie says.

"What?"

"Don't tell me, Tess. If I don't know, I can't...I won't lie for you. Not to the police. And if what you did was so terrible, I couldn't not tell them. So don't tell me at all."

I want to cry at the distance that's suddenly stretching between us. I rushed here to see her, because she's Sophie, my best friend. I want her to reassure me, tell me it isn't so terrible after all, I didn't do anything. The things I said couldn't have done that much damage.

But the fear on her face, my own growing panic—I can't shake it. Since I found out the body in the garden is that of Greg Lewis, I can't shake the conviction that what I did back then, what I said, whoever put Greg there, it was because of me.

"So what do you want to do now?" She says it stiffly. "Are you staying? You're welcome, of course, but what about Julia and your dad?"

The awkwardness between us is like a solid presence I can't breach. I shake my head. "I have to go back to Dad's. It was stupid to run off like that. I don't know what I was thinking."

"You don't need to rush straight off. Why don't you stay tonight?"

I bite my lip. I could. I could call Dad, he'd understand. "You could come back with me if you want?" I say. "See Julia and my dad and..." I let the words trail off as I see the look on her face. "I'm sorry. The last thing you need is to be there with all the crap that's going on, isn't it? Julia, the police...I'm sorry. It has nothing to do with you."

"I wish it didn't."

"What do you mean?"

"How am I supposed to ignore what you just said? Shit, Tess, it sounded like the start of a confession."

I stare at her. "A confession to what?"

"Shit," she says again, shaking her head. "I'm sorry. I don't know what I'm saying. But..." She pauses. "I think you need to come back. Back properly, I mean, to your own flat. As soon as possible. You're not...God, ever since you got that phone call from your dad about Julia you've been like a different person. Everything that happened at school, this, now, you turning up in hysterics, being questioned by the *police*?"

I find myself moving away from her, shifting farther down the sofa. Yes, I am like a different person. Hysterics aside, even I can see that. What I don't know is which Tess is real—the Tess Sophie knows, or the person I am back home.

CHAPTER 21

I get back to Dad's house just after eight. I couldn't stay with Sophie in the end—the unfamiliar awkwardness got too much. But she hugged me as I left, clinging to me and whispering apologies. I hope—I really hope—that when all of this is over, we'll be able to get back to where we were with our friendship. That the Tess I am with her is stronger than the Tess I've reverted to being since I came back here.

"Where have you been, then?" Jack calls after me as I head into the house. He's standing outside, smoking a cigarette. "At the police station the whole time?"

"I went to meet a friend," I say, moving past him.

"So what did the police want to talk to you about?"

I blink. "Nothing much. Just general questions—did I know Greg, that sort of thing."

"And what did you say?"

"That I barely knew him."

He's looking down at the ground, scuffing the dirt. "I still can't believe it's him. I thought... I never thought he was dead. Not really. I always assumed he'd come swanning back into our lives one day."

I want to keep walking. I don't want to feel sorry for Jack. All the thoughts and fears I've been having... feeling sorry for him doesn't fit. I *need* him to be the villain. I need to be angry with him. But...

"I'm sorry," I say in a low voice, and he glances up, a frown on his face.

"You're sorry for me? Don't be. It's not like I'm mourning someone who's been present in my life, is it? Neither of my parents have and I'm all grown up now." He pauses. "She's not likely to die today, then? My darling mother? Not if you're okay going out and leaving her."

"Do you even care? I don't get why you're still here—you clearly have no intention of spending any real time with her. Every time she gets up, you leave the house."

"Well, today's the day, I think. Liquid courage," he says, brandishing the pack of cigarettes. "Time to find out what dear old Mama knows about my dead father."

"Don't you dare upset her." I say it fiercely, my hands clenched into fists at my sides. "The last thing she needs is you barging in shouting at her."

"Why do you assume I'm going to march in there shouting?"

I realize his mocking grin is missing. He sounds flat, almost subdued.

"When have you ever given me reason to assume you're not going to storm in and stir things up, upsetting everyone?"

He opens his mouth, closes it, then surprises me by laughing. "You're right. It's this place, isn't it? Being back here with everyone. We all fall into the roles given us a long time ago. Me, the bad guy, you, the grumpy mouse."

My fingernails dig into my palms. That's not who I am. That's never who I was.

"I'm not trying to be mean," he continues. "But it's true, isn't it? You think Lena is really still such a wild child away from here, at the age of twenty-eight? And you're a teacher, bet you're totally different in your real life." He shakes his head. "It's why I'd never dream of going back to a school reunion or shit like that. The kid everyone bullied could be CEO of the biggest fucking company in the world, but the moment he stepped into that reunion, he'd be the scared victim again."

"So it's not real, is it—Jack the *bad guy*?"

He smiles. "About as real as Tess the scared mouse is now." He pauses. "But I was given my role a long time before I ever met you.

Harder to break." He glances up at the house. "Especially when it's your own mother who made you the bad guy."

I wait for him to go inside first, taking a steadying breath. He's unsettled me, thrown me off balance. He's right. We've all come back and slotted into the same roles and I'm as guilty as anyone of putting Jack straight back into the bad-guy slot. But I won't let myself feel sorry for him because I don't think it's just a role he's playing.

I open the front door and drop my bag on the floor. I'm already wishing I hadn't said anything to Sophie. And I didn't, really. I didn't tell her anything, same as I didn't tell the police anything. But that's the problem, isn't it? The more I don't tell, the more I have to hide. Oh God—why didn't I just say I knew him? That I used to do his bloody gardening—that's all I had to say. Maybe I should...I could call the station and...and...but they'll want to know why I lied. And that leads to the fight I had with Bella and that would look so bad.

No. I can't call them now. It's not like I did anything, is it? Not like I put Greg Lewis in the ground. I hear Dad's voice and poke my head into the kitchen to say hello, but he's on the phone, a frown on his face, and he doesn't even look at me.

Dad puts the phone down and I stare at him.

"What's wrong?"

"They want me to go down to the station tomorrow morning to answer some more questions," he says, sinking into a chair.

"Questions? Why would they need to ask *you* questions?"

"Tess..." I'm pacing the room and Dad's voice stops me in my tracks. "Jack told the police about my fight with Greg."

"I heard about that. But it's nothing, right? A stupid scuffle over Julia marrying you?" My shoulders are hunched, my hands hovering like they want to cover my ears. A flash of memory, one I don't want: *You told me he was the monster*, Bella's voice echoes in my head, full of so much pain. Did you tell Dad, Bella? I shriek silently. Did you tell?

Dad rubs a hand across his eyes. He's sleeping about as much as I am, constantly on the alert with Julia.

"Before the wedding, you and Bella were out and Greg came round looking for trouble. He was shouting at Julia. I lost my temper. I hit him, Tess."

I look at my dad, so small and even tempered. I can't imagine it. Surely Greg would have wiped the floor with him.

Dad looks at me. "I know, I know. It's the only fight I've ever been in and I... regret it."

"What... what was he shouting at Julia about?"

"He was saying awful things about Ellie and the boys." Dad frowns. "Does it matter?"

I shake my head. Bella didn't tell. I'm safe.

"He didn't fight back. I kept hitting him and he just took it," Dad says, staring down at his hands. "I never realized how angry I was with him. All the things Julia told me when she moved in. I just... I *wanted* to hurt him. I hit him and he fell and his nose was bleeding and I hit him again, pulled him up and hit him again." He shakes his head. "He didn't try to hit me back or defend himself. It was like he wanted me to keep hitting him."

"But..."

"It was right before he disappeared. I expected the police to come knocking after the fight. I thought that was his plan—to let me attack him, to not fight back—and then he'd go to the police and have me arrested. But they never came. He disappeared and they never came."

I close my eyes. Behind my eyelids, Bella is sitting next to Dad, looking so sad. I open my eyes again to make her go away. "Tell them Jack lied."

"What?"

"Tell them you argued but never fought. It was ten years ago—Jack has no proof."

"I can't lie to the *police*."

"Why not? You didn't do it, did you? You didn't kill Greg."

"Of course not, but I can't lie."

Not like you did, the ghost of Bella says to me, still with that sad look on her face.

"Stop it," I say to her, shaking my head.

"Stop what?" Dad says, frowning.

"Nothing. I was..." I can't tell him I was talking to my dead sister.

I didn't lie, I say to her silently. I just didn't tell them everything.

You didn't tell them how often we went to the house, she says. *You didn't tell them we were friends with him. Why didn't you tell them?*

It wasn't relevant, that's why. It would have looked bad—like it looked bad to Sophie and I didn't even tell her everything. It would have sent them looking in the wrong direction, focusing on the wrong things. Just like this supposed fight Dad had with Greg.

"It's not relevant," I say to Dad. "Your fight with him doesn't matter. It'll make them suspicious of you when you didn't do anything. You should be home here with Julia, not wasting time at the police station."

I start pacing again and the Bella in my head paces with me. I'm telling myself as much as Dad. It's not relevant. We worked in the garden together, that's all. Why give them reason to look at us more closely? We didn't *do* anything.

"Tess, are you okay?" Dad says, getting up.

"I'm fine. Fine. Worried about you, that's all. Why does Jack have to stir everything up?"

"His father is dead."

"And we had nothing to do with it. Nothing."

"But what if I did?" Dad says, his voice shaking. "I hit him, knocked him down. What if he had a head injury?"

"What—and then he went home and buried himself in the woods?" My voice rises as I echo Jack's words.

Dad's pale. He looks smaller and older. He doesn't meet my gaze and it sends a jitter of fear through me.

"It's not lying, not really, if you just deny it," I say. "Or...or just make it sound less like a fight and more like a...a minor disagreement. It's your word against Jack's. They won't be able to prove anything."

It's like Bella steps out of my head. I swear I can feel her breath on my cheek. *How many more lies?* she whispers.

"What did you tell the police?" I confront Jack the moment he comes downstairs.

There are shadows under his eyes.

"Leave it, Tess," he says, getting the coffee out of the cupboard.

"Leave it? You've sent them after my dad."

He slams the jar down on the counter and turns to face me. "I told them the truth. My dad is dead. He has a fight with your father and two days later, he's gone."

"Do you really think his death has anything to do with my dad?"

"I don't know, do I? I didn't know he was fucking dead." He shakes his head and runs a hand through his hair. "You're so damned selfish. My father was murdered, my mother is upstairs dying, and you're having a tantrum because I told the police the truth."

"Dad didn't do *anything*."

"Then he has nothing to worry about, does he?"

Of course he doesn't. So why is that knot of fear in my stomach growing?

CHAPTER 22

I close the front door quietly. I don't want anyone knowing I'm going for a run. I jog slowly down the lane, footsteps heavy on the ground, sounding reluctant at this slow pace. My ears are straining for the sound of following steps but there's nothing but my own steady rhythm, my own breathing, getting faster as I up the pace.

I can think more clearly out here alone. About all of them, about Bella . . . and about Greg.

Bella and I both thought Greg was our friend and maybe he was. But *was* there something wrong with him, or was Lena just making stuff up? Were the police just fishing with their questions, or do they genuinely believe he might have had something to do with Nicole's and Annie Weston's murders? And there was that other poor girl who went missing and was never found. I think of the great expanse of the woods and the back of my neck prickles. I can see it more objectively now, ten years on, how others would have seen that friendship. He was odd, strange—why did he keep inviting Bella and me round? Why was he happy to keep both . . . *friendships* a secret? We were teenagers, he was forty, living alone in that creepy house. It wasn't right. With me, there was never any hint of anything weird, but I was . . . I was nothing. Clumsy and plain and nothing.

Bella was different. Beautiful, bright, shining Arabella. If Bella went round there after the fight we had . . . It may have been an accident, but he could have killed my sister. I never thought of Greg back then. Not really. He'd already gone, moved away, he'd texted Jack from abroad, or so Jack says. I was relieved he'd gone, a problem gone away without me having to deal with it. But he could have come back, couldn't he? Could have been at Dean House the night of the wedding. But if it was Greg, who then killed him?

I'd begun to think it could have been Jack. I thought Jack might have been the one who killed Nicole and the other girl. Jack with his fake alibi.

Maybe they were in it together.

I can't tell the police this, I have no evidence. Would Sean even admit telling me about the fake alibi? I think of how I told Dad to lie to the police about the fight. Why would Sean tell the police if it implicated his brother? He's not going to believe his brother or his father were murderers any more than I'd ever believe Dad had something to do with Greg's death.

But Bella's death wasn't an accident. I believed it then, but I let myself be persuaded by what everyone else was saying. I let them convince me it was and it's possible I would have gone the rest of my life thinking that if I hadn't come back here. Or was I thinking it earlier? Was I thinking it when I took Rebecca's phone to the police, convinced she was being abused?

My phone dings and I slow as I pull it out of my hoodie pocket. There's a text from an unknown number—*party at dean house*! I frown and look up. I'm almost right outside Dean House and as I step closer to the gate, I see a light flash in one of the upstairs windows.

My heart races as I look at the house. The front door and windows are boarded up, warning signs still in place, police tape across the door. Did I imagine that light? The text must be a joke. Jack, probably. Or Lena. The police seem to have finished their searches at last. They've been digging for weeks, looking for more bones, sweeping through the house, looking for clues. Useless, though, surely—half the neighborhood kids have broken into Dean House on dares in the decade it's been empty. The number of real parties that must have been held there—what evidence could they possibly hope to find?

My phone dings again and I gasp and almost drop it when

Bella's face pops up on the screen. *partying allll night—i'll sleep when i'm dead!* flashes underneath the photo. My hand is shaking as I fumble with the phone. Of course, as I look more closely, I can see it's not really Bella—someone's snapped an old picture of her, laughing, spinning with a bottle in her hand. She's in Dean House—I recognize the wood paneling from the living room, the striped wallpaper above. When was this taken and who took it? Greg? Jack, Sean?

My heart is galloping. I can imagine her over there now, dancing and laughing and drinking and even though I know it's not real—there's not going to be some time bubble of a decade-old party going on behind the boarded-up windows—I push the gate open and walk up the path.

I walk past the police tape, round to the back where they haven't bothered boarding anything up. The window at the back of the living room is unlocked. It's swollen with damp and I struggle to push it up. I have a moment where sense comes back and I think it's a sign—I should go home. But then the window loosens, opens with a creak, and the dust and dead air wafts out.

I climb through into the living room, stepping down onto the dusty floorboards. It looks the same—as though nothing has been touched in ten years. I haven't thought about this place in ten years, I haven't let myself think about it. But if I had, wouldn't I have assumed something would have changed? That Greg would have returned, or the boys would have come and emptied the house, or the house would have been sold earlier, done up as a renovation project?

I can see evidence that the police have been in here; things moved, out of place, flurries of footprints on the floor, already fading as another layer of dust coats them. But it's like the very air is the same, stale, starved of oxygen, every breath dust-laden. The whole house is a time capsule, undisturbed, waiting to be opened, secrets revealed. But there's no spinning, laughing Bella, no sign of a party or anyone else here. I frown, and my gaze catches a small suitcase sitting next to the armchair, old and battered, dark blue, worn white at the edges. I take a breath and hold it. I remember this suitcase. I came to garden once and it started raining. Greg wasn't around and I looked in the window, hoping he'd offer shelter from the stinging rain. He was in here, sitting in that same armchair, the blue suitcase open on his lap. He was crying, lifting things out of the case, putting them back in, crying over them, weeping. I backed away, feeling like a voyeur, spying on his private moment of pain, and walked home in the biting downpour.

He disappeared soon after that and I remembered the case. I remember now thinking I'd seen him packing up his life, getting ready to leave. I imagined him taking this case on his adventures around the world. I chew on my lip. Did the police have the case out, looking for evidence? But why leave it here?

Unless it wasn't the police. Unless it was whoever sent those texts, messing with me. I should go now, call Detective Levinson. But...if it is someone messing with me, what might they have put in the case?

Curiosity and fear build inside me, tug me forward until I'm bending down, hand on the zipper of the case. It's a Pandora's box—but will it be worse for me to open it or for the police to do it? Other people have ventured here, evidenced in the graffiti on the walls, the empty bottles that litter the garden. Kids, teenagers, here on dares to hang out at the monster house. Other people have done worse than open a suitcase, but it feels like I'm committing a crime as I lift the lid. Greg is still here, unseen, reproaching me.

It is his life inside, but not clothes and passport packed for a trip away. It's bundles of letters and photographs, the hidden history of a man I never really knew. His own time capsule within the time capsule his house has become since he left.

I don't read the letters, it's an intrusion too far. But I flick through the photographs. Some of them are old, 1980s judging by the clothes and hairstyles. I recognize Greg from his smile, rub away the pang in my stomach as I look at him smiling at a girl with her arm slung around him whom I recognize as a young Julia, looking like a red-haired Princess Di with a big frosted pink smile.

The decades pass as I flick through the pile. The boys appear, grinning toddlers, mischievous boys, then Ellie. Julia disappears, the photos empty of people, are just of the house, the village, the gardens, the sea.

I stop as I get to the last one and my eye twitches. I stuff the photograph in my pocket and close the case, rubbing the dust off my hands and backing away. The photo I've taken shouldn't be here: it's a school photo, a smiling class of teenagers. I recognize the uniforms because it's my school. I recognize it because we have the same photo in an album at home. It's Bella's class, my sister smiling in the second row. Three girls along there's another face I recognize. Nicole Wallace, murdered in that summer of death. Bella's classmate. Bella's friend.

The police can't have left this suitcase here. They would have taken this photograph, wouldn't they?

I walk back across the room, chased by whispering ghosts, and get halfway when I freeze, all the hairs rising on the back of my neck, my chest tightening until I can barely breathe. Blood whooshes in my ears, pulsing to the beat of my heart. There's something laid under the desk by the boarded-up front window.

It's a pair of shoes. My legs are shaking and I can't take another step. I recognize those shoes. They're Bella's. They're the shoes she was wearing the night she died. She wasn't wearing them when we were found. She was barefoot then, her feet scratched and muddy, suggesting she'd run through the woods barefoot. They didn't ever find the shoes; no one believed my insistence that she was wearing them when she set out. Because I didn't see her leave, because I don't remember anything. But her shoes weren't at home, weren't in the hall where they always were, a pair of scruffy old white Converse, frayed edges and grass stains around the toes.

I searched the house for them afterward, searched everywhere, even in the most unlikely of places, but I never found them. I even went back in the woods, in case she'd taken them off there. But they were never there. I hold my breath and make myself walk over to them. They are her shoes—same frayed edges, patches of light green, one lace with its ragged end taped up. There's even the faint hint of her initials in faded marker on the inside from when she'd wear them for school PE lessons.

Someone else has been here and put the shoes here for me to find. It makes me aware that I'm here alone at night and no one knows where I am. Except the person who sent me those texts. The person who left the shoes here for me to find.

I grab the shoes, turn, and run. I fumble with the window, convinced for a panicked moment that it won't open, that someone has crept up and sealed me inside the house, but it opens and I almost fall out, setting out at a run, not bothering to close the window behind me.

I run home, almost falling several times, a stumbling, lurching run along the unlit lane. No one follows, but in my mind, he does, the monster, breathing fire, my death in his eyes. I won't sleep tonight, I won't even try. He'll keep chasing if I close my eyes, Freddy Krueger with his razor fingers, waiting to kill me in my dreams.

Back at the house, I put the shoes on my bed, expecting them to disappear if I close my eyes. My trip to the house has already taken on a surreal edge—it feels like a dream but I know it's real. I hug Bella's shoes to my chest. This is real, my visit to the house was real. Someone's had these shoes for ten years and they've left them and the blue suitcase for me to find. I was right. Someone else was in the woods with us that night. Someone else knows what happened to Bella.

CHAPTER 23

Dad's already gone to the police station when I get downstairs the next morning. Sean is in the kitchen, a cold cup of coffee next to him. I don't have time for breakfast and I'm not hungry anyway. I hug my bag close to me. Sean and Jack were both around last night—it could have been either of them over at Dean House, leaving the shoes for me to find.

"It's already in the papers," Sean says as I turn to leave.

"What?"

"Just the local paper, a snippet, talking about the 'find' at Dean House, speculating about the police presence. It mentions the other deaths, the unsolved killings of those two girls and the rumors from back then."

My hand convulses on the door handle, knuckles white.

"It's all going to come back, isn't it? Everything that happened that summer? This is just the start." There's a heaviness in his voice, a dread echoed in me.

The local paper is still in the hall, open on the table where Sean must have read it. I pick it up with shaking hands. Sean is right. As soon as the news is released that it's his father's body, there's going to be more than bones dug up in the coming weeks.

I wanted that ten years ago. God—I wanted that when Bella appeared in my flat. I wanted the police to see Bella as a victim, not a silly girl who got drunk and fell to her death. But now? The thought of the police back here, squirreling their way back into our lives while Julia dies upstairs, the thought of all the questions they'll be asking Dad right now. The thought terrifies me.

Bella is at the back of my mind, whispering the start of the story again: *Once upon a time, two girls went into the woods...*

I drift off on the bus. I'm on my way to the police station, Bella's shoes in my bag, and as the rocking of the bus sends me into that weird netherworld of half asleep, half awake, I see Bella is sitting next to me on the bus. I've tuned in halfway through a conversation. All Bella, me silent next to her.

Is this a dream or a memory?

"I never thought it would be him," she says. "Never, ever." She turns to look at me, all glowing eyes and pink cheeks. She's wearing a dress. Bella never wore dresses. She looks radiant. "We talked, after you stormed off. I understand now. I understand why he took us there."

"You *understand*?" My voice is stiff, my hands clenched around my bag. My eyes flutter open—did I say that out loud? The woman in front shifts in her seat. She probably thinks I'm mad, talking to myself. I close my eyes again, letting myself drift. If this is a lost memory, I need to find my way back to it.

Bella rolls her eyes. "Don't be like that. You were the one who stomped off. You were the one who said those awful things to him."

"You said you hated him."

"That was before I knew him. He's like us, Tess, he really is. He's angry because of what she did. He's..." Her voice trails off as she gets lost in her memories of whatever he did or said to steal her away.

I could finish her sentence but I don't think she'd like what I had to say. He's dangerous. He's manipulative. He's using you. He's wrong and everything she's doing is wrong.

I'd forgotten all this. I'd forgotten this bus journey. I'd forgotten her words.

Wait. Where are we going? I try to pull out of the dream.

"This didn't happen," I say, and she laughs. "I didn't get the bus back with you. We didn't have this conversation."

The bus is fading, the landscape outside blurring.

"But didn't you always wonder?" she says. "We never talked about it, did we? Dad told us about marrying Julia and we never got around to talking about it."

I pull awake with a gasp and the woman in front turns to look at me. "Are you okay, love?" she says, a wary frown on her face. I stumble up out of my seat and go to the front of the bus, pressing the bell for the next stop.

I get to the police station just before eleven, walking the last mile. My head feels spacey, weird.

"Is Detective Levinson here?" My voice sounds strange again as I speak—faraway, not mine. I'm aware of curious glances as I'm shown into an office. There are three messy desks, but I'm the only person sitting in here. People walk by, slowing as they look at me. Am I shaking? God—am I even dressed? I check myself— yes, clothes, shoes. No coat and I haven't brushed my hair or put any makeup on, but I'm dressed at least. God, I can't remember the last time I slept properly. My eyes hurt. My head hurts. I have to start taking those sleeping pills. I will. Tonight.

"Tess? Have you remembered something?" Detective Levinson comes in, taking a seat opposite me, moving a pile of paper into a tray.

"Is my dad still here?"

He frowns and shakes his head.

I push forward the bag I put the shoes in. It's just a messenger bag, hardly a sterile evidence bag, but they might still be able to get fingerprints off the shoes.

"They're her shoes—Bella's shoes. The ones she was wearing the night she died."

He looks at me but doesn't open the bag.

"I found them in the house—Dean House."

"You've been in the house?" He frowns. "The house—the grounds—that's a crime scene."

"I'm sorry, but I thought...I thought if I went there I might remember something. But when I went in, Bella's shoes were there, lined up side by side, left there for me to find."

"By who?"

"By whoever killed Bella." My voice rises and Detective Levinson sits back in his chair, his face going blank.

"Did you see anyone else there?"

"No. But there's something else. There was a suitcase. It belonged...it must have belonged to Greg Lewis. And I looked inside and there was a photograph, a school photo of Bella's class when she was sixteen or seventeen. And Nicole Wallace is in the photo as well. Why would he have had that photo?"

Detective Levinson leans back, rubs a hand across his bald head.

"And I got these texts..." I get my phone out but my voice dies as I open my messages. The texts aren't there. I scroll up and down but they're not bloody there. Someone must have taken my phone and deleted them. It has to have been Jack or Lena. My heart thumps. Or Sean or Max. Any one of them could have spied on me tapping in my passcode.

"Did you tell anyone else you were going to the house?"

"No, but there were other, new, footprints in the dust. They were..." My voice trails off and I go cold. They were small, I was going to say. A small foot, clean in the dust next to my prints. I've had so many of these blank moments now, these fugues where time passes, where I'm not asleep but I'm not awake either. Black holes in my memory. Those footprints, that other path of prints, so new—were they mine?

The other day, when I thought I'd been sleepwalking, talking to Bella in the woods, seeing lights at the window of Dean House...did I actually go inside? Did I find the shoes somewhere else and put them in the house? I was in the woods, with Bella, and I thought it was a dream. Oh God, what else have I been doing in my sleep? Were those text messages even real?

I shake my head. I didn't...I couldn't. "Will you check? Will you look?"

There's that look again—half pity, half wariness. They might send someone out, but what are they going to find? Footprints in the dust that could all belong to me.

My head is pounding, my eyes are gritty. I shouldn't have come. I'm not helping. All I'm doing is convincing the police I'm unhinged.

Maybe I am. I see my dead sister, don't I? It's more vivid than dreams. How long before the questions are about me, how long before my doctor is asked and he tells them I'm hallucinating? Max has already told them I caused the car accident by grabbing the wheel. It's possible none of this has anything to do with Bella, it's possible it's my own guilt over walking away from Greg and our secret garden. I want him to be guilty to justify it.

I remember...I do remember Bella putting on the shoes. She changed in the afternoon, swapping satin bridesmaid shoes for the comfort of sneakers. But can I really say one hundred percent that she was still wearing them when she went into the woods?

I close my eyes, remembering my obsession with finding them after she died. My dad was so worried, following me around the house as I tore through cupboards and drawers, insisting we find them, insisting they were evidence. But evidence of what? What the bloody hell did I think those shoes were going to tell me?

Detective Levinson's hand is on the bag, but he doesn't open it. He isn't interested in a pair of shoes no one ever believed she was wearing. He thinks I'm doing what they all thought I was doing back then—making stuff up, trying to throw doubt on the accident verdict. The difference between now and then is that, for the first time, I'm starting to wonder the same thing.

When I get back to the house, Jack is sitting in the garden, a lit cigarette balanced on a saucer next to him on the old wooden table. He's wearing sunglasses and I can't tell if he's looking at me as I walk up the driveway.

"Been for a nice trip out?" he says, and there's amusement

in his voice. He's laughing at me. If I still had the shoes, I'd throw them at him. *Was it you?* I want to yell to his smug, grinning face.

"What are you doing here?" I mutter, and he shrugs. "Don't you spend any time at home? Shouldn't you be trying to sort out your marriage?"

He smiles a twisted smile. "Dani understands I need to sort things out. She, at least, is sympathetic to the fact that my mother is dying and my father's body has just been found."

"Sorry," I say, my cheeks burning. I can't have a conversation with Jack without ending up in awkward moments like this, feeling fifteen again.

He laughs. "Are you? You should be—you're part of the reason we're having trouble, after all."

"Me? What...?"

"Apparently, I'm too distant. Apparently, I don't commit. I blame it on my mother fucking off to another ready-made family." He leans forward and the chair creaks. "Though I don't think my mother has done any more good for you than she did for us, has she, Tess? You with your half-life, scared to sleep, and Leo watching her die, wasting away himself. And Bella...well, Bella certainly hasn't come out of it well."

I clench my fists, wanting to smack his stupid, laughing face. "Do you have to be so poisonous, all the time?"

His smile drops. "It's all I've got left."

"It's not true. You have your brother. You have your mother upstairs—she's not gone yet."

"Which is why I'm here and not at work or home with my wife and son. To spend *quality* time with my dying mother."

"So why are you out here? Why aren't you upstairs?"

He puts the cigarette out, reaches for the packet, and lights another one. He offers the packet to me and I shake my head.

"She doesn't want the curtains or the window open. The sun's out but her room is like a crypt."

"The daylight hurts her eyes." She told me this last night. She sleeps most of the day. Like me, she's awake most of the night. For the first time, my growing insomnia is a good thing because I'm awake to spend time with her when the demons come, whispering their death messages to her.

"All the clocks are wrong, have you noticed?" he says out of the blue.

I blink, wondering if I've missed half a conversation. He's smiling at me again and I think I did zone out.

"What are you talking about?"

"Your dad has so many clocks—one in every room—but they all tell different times."

I shake my head. "So?"

"I don't mean a few minutes out. I mean hours out. It's a different time in each room of your house. Don't you think that's strange? Midnight in the kitchen, four o'clock on the landing."

I frown. Dad used to be religious about winding and synchronizing all the clocks he's collected over the years. I got used to the ticking; it was like a heartbeat underlying everything. After a while, you stop hearing it. Have I noticed a slip in the rhythm since I've been back? Clocks ticking and chiming out of sync, adding to the loss of equilibrium I've felt.

"Dad's got more important things to do than wind clocks."

"Maybe the clocks and times are for each of us. Julia's is the one closest to midnight, seconds ticking by too slowly."

"Was it you who sent those texts?" I blurt out.

Jack leans forward and I can see myself reflected in his sunglasses. "What are you talking about?"

I wish he'd take the damned sunglasses off. His confusion sounds genuine, but if I could see his eyes would I see amusement instead? I can't even show him the texts I'm accusing him of sending.

Jack tilts his head. "You look tired, Tess. Max was filling us in on the strain you're under—losing your job and everything. You really should get some sleep."

I stiffen. Max told him? He told the others as well?

"I remember last time you were this stressed. It wasn't long before the wedding, was it? Poor Sean. I suppose he was lucky not to lose an eye."

"Oh, fuck off," I shout, and march off into the house. He's right—every clock is telling a different time. I get my phone out to check the correct time, but the battery has died. Without it, I'm lost. It's midnight and four a.m. and noon and eleven thirty all at once. Jack follows me in and laughs when he sees me holding the clock in the living room. I put it down and flip him the bird.

"You're back," I say, rushing over to Dad as he walks in the door. He looks exhausted, gray and haggard.

"Is Julia okay?" he asks.

"She's fine. I've been sitting with her. I didn't tell her where you were."

"Thank you," he says. "I was going to come straight back but I needed some time alone before I came home to Julia. God, I need a drink."

I follow him to the kitchen. He gets a beer from the fridge. He sits down and pours it with a shaking hand.

"How was it? Did you tell them...?"

"I didn't lie, if that's what you're asking. I told them the truth—that he came around looking for trouble. That I hit him and he left and I didn't see him again. They kept asking the same things over and over."

"But they let you go. That's good, right?"

"They don't have any reason to arrest me yet, but I don't think I'm off their list." He looks up at me. "They asked me about you also—how well you knew him. I told them I don't think you knew him at all. That's the truth, isn't it, Tess?"

I take his empty bottle and turn away to put it in the recycling bin. "That's right. I barely knew him."

"They were insinuating that you and Bella both knew him,

that both of you spent time with him that I didn't know about."

I wonder what Lena has told them. "They were probably just trying to needle you," I say.

"There were other questions too..." He pauses, takes a long swallow of his beer.

I get a bottle of wine and a glass, sit at the table with him and pour it.

"They asked about Nicole Wallace and the other girl who was murdered."

"They asked *you* about them?"

He shakes his head. "They were asking about the murdered girls and Greg."

I stare into my glass. I don't even want to think about it. That would make my insane teenage infatuation even more twisted than it was. I feel the same childish surge of frustration I felt back then: if only Max had liked me back, if only Bella hadn't flirted with him, making him blind to anyone but her, if only...then I never would have felt so stupidly lonely that hanging out with a man my father's age turned into something that never should have been.

"But what's the connection? He's dead. He was murdered himself, wasn't he?"

"It's the timing, I think. Of course there was never anything to suggest it was him back then, but he disappeared and the murders stopped. And now he's turned up dead."

"So what do they think happened?"

He looks at me and there's a question in his eyes. "I think they're wondering if another girl fought back and won."

I breathe in and hold on to the breath until I'm dizzy. I close my eyes and Bella is there, leaves in her hair, blood on her face.

Tell him, she whispers, and I shake my head, black spots appearing before my eyes.

Tell him? Tell him what? That I did go there, alone, at night? That he might have been a serial killer and I tried to kiss him and how, even now, with this new knowledge, I feel not relief that I got away unscathed, but the same sting of humiliation at his rejection? That's what made me say all those things to Bella. She was so mad, so angry. Oh God, he could have been a serial killer and I gave her a reason to go after him.

THEN

CHAPTER 24

OCTOBER 2007

It's raining and I pull my hood up, hunch my shoulders, and walk faster. It's that drizzling, clinging rain and it creeps under my hood and soaks my face. I slow down when I get to the village. There's a man with a microphone, another man with a camera behind him, and they're talking to Bella and her friend Caitlin. I stop a few feet away and try to listen in but the man with the microphone spots me and turns around.

"Would you like to be interviewed about the missing girl?"

"What?"

"Another teenage girl has gone missing. Does it worry you that there may be a serial killer in the county?"

What? I look at Bella. Her face is set and still, fists clenched at her side. She hasn't mentioned Nicole's murder in weeks, but right now she looks like she's going to be sick.

"Do you feel safe walking home alone knowing a killer is on the loose?" the reporter asks, stepping closer with his stupid microphone.

"Leave her alone," Bella calls in a low, fierce voice.

"I don't want to be interviewed," I mutter, marching past Bella and Caitlin.

There's another news van parked by the post office and I can see a camera crew inside, interviewing Mrs. Wilson. Christ knows what she'll tell them—probably all about Bella and her gang marauding around the village. We'll have more journalists banging on our door next.

I'm trying to think if there's been anyone else missing from school recently. But we would have heard if anyone local had gone missing, wouldn't we? After Nicole's death, there were assemblies and memorials and endless counseling sessions offered to all the girls. And when no one was arrested, the same message was drummed in over and over again. Stay safe. Make sure someone is with you if you're out at night. Make sure someone always knows where you are. It made the village, this tiny, sleepy village where no one locks their doors, dangerous. It made every stranger a figure of suspicion. And it made me so mad at Bella that she carried on like nothing had happened, still going out and walking back through the bloody woods in the middle of the night. God, Nicole was her friend. Why wasn't she worried that the person who murdered her was still out there?

I hear footsteps behind me as I leave the village and walk up the lane that skirts the woods. I feel a squeeze of panic and my heart pounds. I huddle deeper into my coat and speed up, my walk now a half run.

"Tess—wait up."

I stop to catch my breath, shaky with relief to hear Bella's voice. She jogs to catch up to me.

"Finished your interview? Did you enjoy your fifteen minutes of fame?"

She shakes her head. She isn't wearing a coat and her hair clings to her face in wet tendrils. Despite the drowned-rat look, she's still stupidly beautiful. "I didn't do an interview. I couldn't, not after Nic. It was Caitlin who was talking to them."

"Who is it? Is it someone else from our school?"

"No. It's some girl from the next county. No one we know."

I shudder. "You don't think it's the same person, do you? A serial killer like that journalist said?"

She shrugs. "No idea—she could have just run away or something. Fuck—I don't think we've ever had any murders around here before." She frowns and wraps her arms around herself. "You shouldn't keep walking home from school by yourself."

"And you shouldn't still go out at night."

"I don't go out alone."

"That doesn't matter—you should stay home until whoever's doing this is caught."

She shakes her head and walks on ahead. "Leave it, Tess."

"I'll tell Dad if you don't stop," I call after her.

"Tell him," she says. "It won't make a difference."

"Have you got a death wish or something? What is *wrong* with you lately?"

She spins round, stands in front of me. "You don't have a bloody clue, do you?"

"A clue about what?"

"Oh, forget it, little sister. And if you tell Dad about me going out, I'll tell him about your little secret."

"What secret?"

"Your lovely friendship with Julia's ex. Your little gardening jaunts."

I flinch. "I don't think he'll be worried about me doing some weeding for a neighbor."

"Oh, don't you? Really? It's all entirely innocent, is it? Is that why you wash your hair and put makeup on every time you go weeding?" She laughs. "I don't think it's me with the death wish."

"What do you mean?"

She sighs and shakes her head. "Just . . . be careful, okay? Maybe we should both stay home a bit more."

A thorn pierces my palm through the gardening glove and I suck in my breath.

"Are you okay? Let me look," Greg says, pulling off my glove. There's a drop of blood on my palm. He wipes it away. "I don't think you'll die from blood loss," he says, smiling, still with my hand in his.

No, there is no more blood because it's all gone to my face. Bella's stupid words have spoiled this. All I can think about is what if Dad walked into the garden now and saw Greg holding my hand. Saw me with my freshly washed curls and lip gloss, alone with Julia's ex? It makes this feel sordid and wrong, but it doesn't make me want to snatch my hand away.

"Have you heard about the other girl who's gone missing?"

Greg lets my hand go and I watch another drop of blood well up. "Impossible not to hear about it around here."

"She wasn't from our school, but she was close enough that everyone thinks the killer might have taken her."

"The local gossips are loving it, aren't they? No thoughts for the poor girl's family. Although I hear she's a troublemaker—wild," Greg says.

That's what the tabloids are saying: a "wild" girl, just like Nicole. Doesn't mean they deserved to be killed, though.

"It's got everyone talking about Nicole again. You met her, didn't you? At the first party you had?"

He turns away, starts scooping up weeds and putting them in a green garden bag. "I don't remember her. The kids were there for the boys, none of them spoke to me."

That's not entirely true, though. I'm sure I remember a very drunk Nicole dragging a laughing Greg onto the dance floor at their New Year's party. Nicole, with her arms draped around his shoulders, watched from various points round the room by me, Julia, Jack, Sean, and Bella.

NOVEMBER 2007

"Where are you going?"

Bella's stuffing things into a small rucksack. She looks up and grins. "On an adventure. Want to come?"

It's been so long since we did anything together. Ellie dying, Julia moving in, Jack, Sean, Max . . . so many things driving a wedge between us. I only ever go to the woods alone now.

"Where?" I ask again.

I want to go, I do, I do. But I want it to be just me and her—

Tess and Bella on a big adventure, not trailing round some shopping center after her and her sniggering mates.

"It wouldn't be an adventure if I told you. Go on, come with me. Please."

I never could resist when she gives me puppy-dog eyes.

We walk to the bus stop and it is, for those ten minutes, just like old times. Bella walks next to me, swinging her rucksack, rattling on and on about nothing at all and I'm happy to walk next to her listening. It's such a gorgeous day, I can't believe it's November, cold but bright, the ground crunchy with fallen leaves, red and orange and yellow, speckled with frost.

"So, come on—are you ever going to tell me where we're going?" I say as I see the bus approaching in the distance.

"Okay," she says, laughing. "We're going to meet Jack and Sean."

"What?"

"Sean's going to sneak out of school and Jack's off work—we're going on a picnic."

"A *picnic*? In November? With Jack and Sean? After everything you said about Jack after Nic died?"

She shrugs and holds up a hand to flag the bus down. "Yeah, I was upset about how Jack was over Nic. But I saw...it was a defense mechanism, the way he was. We talked and...I was wrong. They're actually..." She turns to me and a smile grows huge on her face. "Oh, Tess, he—they are actually pretty amazing."

Which one, I wonder as I take a step back. Which one of the brothers has put the smile back on my sister's face?

"Come on then," she says, stepping onto the bus.

I shake my head and take another step back. "No way. I'm not going anywhere with them. You shouldn't either—they're... they're *dangerous*."

She laughs. "Dangerous? Oh Tess, don't be daft!"

I watch her climb onto the bus, that massive smile still on her face, and I waver, rising onto the balls of my feet. If I run, I could make it, jump onto the bus with my sister, off on an adventure with the "amazing" brothers, the Insanely-Hots. Or I could wait while the bus pulls away, taking my sister on an adventure while I stay at home. Safe. Alone. No massive smile anywhere near my face.

I'm still wavering when she turns back to me, two tickets in her hand. "Max and Lena might be there," she says, and it breaks my trance. I jump onto the bus after her, snatching my ticket out of her hand as she laughs.

I know it's a mistake the moment we get off the bus and I see Jack and Sean already waiting. Jack's eyes are hidden behind sunglasses but he's grinning that hateful grin of his. Sean is leaning against the bus stop, hands in pockets, shoulders hunched, looking down at the ground rather than at us. Bella said they were taking us for a picnic, but neither of them is carrying anything.

"Where are Max and Lena?" I say as I follow Bella off the bus.

Jack cocks his head. "Is that the only reason you came? To see the lovely Maxie-boy?"

"Shut up, Jack," Bella says, rolling her eyes. "Stop winding her up. Where are they? And where's this picnic you promised?"

"They couldn't sneak out of school. Not as practiced as us. And the picnic was a bit of a red herring to get you here."

"To get us where?" Bella says, looking round at the dead-end street. We're in a town half an hour's bus ride from our village, nothing about it standing out as worth a visit—a few tired-looking cheap shops, some ugly houses.

"Come on," Jack says. "You'll see."

He leads us away from the town center, Bella and Sean flanking him, me trailing behind, wishing I'd never come. It's a two-hour wait until the next bus home, so I'm stuck with them until then. And I swear it's colder here—my toes are going numb in my sneakers. Some bloody adventure.

We've been walking for fifteen minutes when Jack stops. We're well out of the town center, surrounded by trees and fields. Jack stands by a fence bordering a scrubby field surrounded by woods.

"This is it," he says, looking back at the rest of us.

"This is what?" Bella says, a note of irritation in her voice.

"This is where the other girl—Annie Weston's body was found."

I take an involuntary step back from the fence. Next to me, I hear Sean take a sharp breath in. He didn't know where Jack was bringing us either, then.

"What the *fuck*, Jack?" Bella almost shouts. "Why the hell would you bring us here?"

"Relax, we're not about to be jumped by a serial killer. They've arrested someone, didn't you hear? They tracked down Annie Weston's ex, some twenty-year-old druggie. Bet they'll find a connection to Nic." He sounds fierce as he says it. "They still haven't found that other girl, either. I tell you, if I could get hold of that bastard..."

I haven't heard. Wouldn't it be all over the local news if they've caught the killer? How come Jack found out first? Maybe the police told him. He was Nicole's boyfriend, after all. Bella says his indifference was pretend, a defense mechanism. For the first time, I can see it. The fierce anger in his voice...and something else. There's relief in his voice as well. If they've arrested someone, he's off the hook.

I look at Bella. She's white-faced and shaking, biting her lip. "You are such a shit, Jack Lewis," she says.

"Oh, come on," he says, frowning. "We should be celebrating. They caught the bastard. They caught the shit who killed your best friend and my girlfriend."

"Yeah, her fucking *best friend* is dead, you stupid shit," I yell. "Your girlfriend is *dead*. Celebrating? Are you bloody mad or just a total dick?"

"Whoa," he says, throwing his hands up. "The mouse has teeth. Who knew?"

"Shut up. Just shut up for once," I shout, shoving him with both hands. "Why do you always have to ruin things? Why do you always have to upset everyone? Is your own life so miserable you have to make everyone else miserable too? Julia leaving probably had nothing to do with Ellie—she probably left because of something you did, because you are such a *shit*."

My voice rings out, loud enough to be heard in the next county, I swear. I want to swallow the words instantly. It's Jack's turn to go white, no sign of his cocky grin.

I'm sorry, I want to say. *I shouldn't have said it. I lost my temper, I shouldn't*...But, oh no, those words won't come out, will they? Not in light of their shocked faces.

"I'm going," I mutter. "Are you coming, Bella?"

Bella glances at Jack, who's standing now with his head bowed. She shakes her head at me and touches his arm. "No—you go."

I spin and march away, hurt weighing me down. Yes, I was wrong to say what I did, but I did it for Bella. And she's staying with *him*? To check that *he's* okay?

"Wait," Sean says, catching my arm. "You can't walk back on your own."

"*Relax*," I say, a mocking copy of Jack's words. "We're not going to be jumped by a serial killer, remember?"

"Why are you being like this?"

"Like what? Sticking up for my sister? Calling your brother out for such a stupid stunt bringing us here?"

"No. Cruel."

I stop walking and take a shaky breath.

"Saying that to him about Ellie and Mum...that was cruel."

"What—more cruel than bringing us to a murder site?"

He takes a step toward me and I stumble away from the anger on his face. "Does it not occur to you that Jack could be hurting too?" he says. "Oh no, why would it? If it doesn't affect you, it doesn't register, right? It's fine to be a bitch if it's just to Jack and Sean."

There's a lump in my throat. I want to say sorry again. Explain that the words burst out in anger and I didn't mean to be cruel. I don't want to be cruel. But I'm not apologizing to Sean Lewis.

"Well, maybe it's hanging round you lot that's turning me into a bitch."

"That's easily solved," he says stiffly. "I'll make sure we keep well away in future." He turns away and walks back toward Jack and Bella.

"Good," I shout after him. "You do that."

Bella gets home just before seven. I jump up off the bed to greet her. "I'm sorry. I shouldn't have had a go at Jack like that. Not about Ellie."

Someone's stolen the smile from her face and, instead, she looks pale and sad. "It's okay, Tess. It's not me you have to say sorry to."

"Yeah, well, I tried saying sorry to Sean and he was an idiot about it."

"You should say sorry to Jack."

I quail at the thought. "How was it?" I ask, avoiding her suggestion. "Did the boys know any more about the man they've arrested?"

She shrugs, facing away from me as she bends to pull her shoes off. She wore her white Converse and I notice mud all over them. Did they actually go into the field? Tread on the ground where a girl was raped and murdered?

"Not really," she says quietly.

"It has to have been the same person, though, right? The same person who took that other girl and...hurt Nicole?"

"God, Tess, I don't know, okay?"

I wait for a moment, chewing my lip. "So what did you do?"

"Tess...I'm tired. Can we talk about it later?"

I open my mouth to argue, but Dad's calling us to come downstairs. He and Julia are in the living room, big smiles on their faces. I look at Bella and she shrugs and raises her eyebrows. I frown. Is that a bruise on her cheek? Revealed as she tucks her hair behind her ears?

"Girls...we have some news. I've asked Julia to marry me."

There's a roaring in my ears as I stare at the diamond ring on Julia's finger and all concerns about Bella's "adventure" are instantly lost. I want to be sick, hurl up the whole of the casserole we had for tea right in their faces. Married? They're getting married?

"Wow," Bella says in an odd, flat voice. "That's...big."

Dad's smile fades. He looks sad again, sad like he hasn't for a long time, not since the dark old days after Mum died.

"Congratulations," I say in a false-bright voice, too loud. "That's...that's brilliant news, isn't it, Bella?" I look at her and will her to play along.

Her gaze bounces from me to Dad and back again. She turns back to them and smiles. "It is," she says. "Great news. I'm really pleased for you both."

"Has anyone told Gr— Mr. Lewis?" I blurt it out in the middle of the awkward celebrations and they all turn to look at me. Dad glances at Julia and back at me.

"We wanted to tell you girls first. Julia's going to ring the boys and I'm sure they'll tell their father."

It's only six months since Julia walked out on Greg. How is he going to feel when he finds out?

The next day, Bella slams out of the house early. I follow and find her sitting on the fallen tree at the top of the embankment looking down into the stream. I sit down next to her, my jeans biting at my waist. Bella jumps up, starts pacing around, smacking trees with a long branch she's picked up.

"We'll stop it from happening," she says, sending leaves whirling as she spins around.

I drop a stone in the dank water of the slow-moving stream. "We can't. How can we? What could we do?"

"He's married to Mum," she shouts, smashing the branch onto a rock, breaking the wood in two.

My hand grubs in the damp earth for another stone. "Mum's dead."

Bella comes over and sits on the dead tree next to me. "God, poor Jack and Sean. It's bad enough she's *living* here."

My hand curls in the mud. Something squeezes tight in my stomach. She sounds all worried, not about Greg, stuck on his own, or Dad rushing into things when they've only been together a few months, but about those bloody boys.

"Oh yeah, poor Jack and Sean. I don't get you, Bella. After Nicole died, you were so anti-Jack, and yesterday, you went off giddy as hell at the idea of spending the day with them."

Bella kicks free the stone I've been reaching for. "Oh stop it, Tess," she mutters. "You're such a bore sometimes."

Her words sting.

"Do you think they've told Greg yet?" I blurt out. "Someone needs to—before he hears it from some village gossip."

She looks up at me and frowns. "Are you still going over there? Tess...you have to stop. It looks bad, a fifteen-year-old visiting an almost forty-year-old man living on his own."

My cheeks burst into flames. "We're only gardening. God, stop treating me like a child."

She shakes her head, still frowning.

"And you weren't so bothered about seeing him yourself when he gave you that camera, were you?"

"But I'm seventeen and..."

I roll my eyes. "Oh wow—two whole years older. Yes, old woman, I guess that makes the world of difference."

She smiles at my sarcasm. It's reluctant, but it's a smile.

"So what are you going to do?" I say before she can lecture me any more. "About the wedding, if you're so dead set against it?"

She looks at me and then away, smiling over my shoulder. I hear the crack of a twig breaking and whirl around to see who my sister has invited to the party, heart simultaneously lifting and falling at the sight of Max and Lena.

Lena looks at me and laughs. "Jeez, Tess, the look on your face!"

"What are you doing here?"

Lena glances at Max. "Bella sent an SOS. So we fled."

"Won't you get in trouble?"

She smiles. "Probably. But I'm eighteen, Max is seventeen—they don't keep us penned in anymore. Our friends will cover for us until we get back."

It strikes me in that moment as horribly sad that, if anyone notices they're missing, the only people who'll care will be teachers. Their parents, off on the other side of the world, haven't got a clue what they're doing. It also makes me wonder how they can sneak out so easily today but not yesterday. Did Jack even invite them? I don't think he was expecting me to tag along, either. I think he just wanted it to be him, Bella, and Sean. The thought makes me nervous and uneasy.

"We can help you stop the wedding. It's simple," Lena says, lighting a cigarette and passing the packet around to the rest of us. "We've done this before, right, Max?"

Max shakes his head. "Our parents are still together."

"I don't mean we've done this, exactly. I mean we've manipulated the situation to suit our ends. *Oh, Mummy and Daddy*," she says in a fake little-girl voice. "*We're so sad and lonely without you. The only thing that'll make us feel better is a new computer and a new phone and a holiday*."

Max looks uncomfortable. But it isn't me he glances at with his cheeks stained red—it's Bella. It's Bella he wants to see him at his best.

But Bella is laughing with Lena and I'm jealous, wishing I could be as cool and carefree as Lena. All I seem to do these days is nag and moan, and it's obvious that Bella's fed up with me.

"You have to provoke Julia into looking bad," Lena says. "Show her in a bad light in front of your dad. Get him to the point where he has to choose between you and her."

I frown. Yes, the thought of them getting married is freaking me out, but I don't want to split them up. It's actually been nice having Julia in the house. Dad laughs a lot more and she cooks a brilliant chili and everything seems that much brighter. "That's a bit mean, isn't it? Julia's always been really nice to you, having you to stay in the holidays."

Lena rolls her eyes. "Well, that's all stopped now, hasn't it? We haven't had any invites to stay at *your place*, have we?" She sounds bitter.

Ah, now I get her eagerness to mess things up between Dad and Julia. She wants things back how they were.

She turns to Bella. "Come on, Bella. What was it you were saying as we arrived? You'd do anything to stop it from happening?"

Max has wandered off and I follow him deeper into the woods.

"I'm sorry about my sister," he says when he turns and sees me following him.

I shrug. "She's just playing up to Bella. My sister will soon figure out there's nothing we can do about this bloody wedding—not without hurting Dad. We don't want a new stepmother, but we do want our dad to be happy. And I like Julia, so things could be a lot worse."

"It wouldn't be that bad, would it?" he says. "Forget what Lena said. If they get married, we might be here more as well."

A warmth fills my belly at the thought. There'll be an engagement party, a rehearsal dinner, the wedding itself. All with Max in the house with me. I step closer to him and my arm brushes against his. All the hairs on my arm rise.

He turns to look down at me and my heart starts galloping. Is this it? Am I imagining it or is he bending to kiss...? I reach up but he steps away and my kiss lands on the air instead of his lips.

He smiles, staring into the middle distance. "Ha," he says. "Can you imagine Bella in some frilly bridesmaid's dress?"

Yes. Yes, I can. She'll look beautiful.

I can see he already knows. I've come to tell him myself so he doesn't have to wait for his sons to tell him, but I can see by the way he's slumped at the table that he knows. I back away. Should I leave him alone? I don't know. I don't know what to do. Then he moves and I see Bella's jacket chucked over the back of one of the kitchen chairs and I realize how he knows so quickly. She gave me that look when I asked if anyone had told him about the wedding, like I was stupid for even asking. Then the moment my back was turned, she comes rushing over to tell him herself.

I back farther away and manage to walk into the table, sending it scraping along the paving slabs. Greg looks up at the noise and catches my eye. He smiles and gets up.

"Hey, Tess," he says, appearing at the back door. "Were you knocking? Sorry—I didn't hear."

"It's okay," I mutter. "I just wanted to..." My voice trails off.

"I heard," he says, and I nod. "You just missed your sister. She came to tell me."

There's an awkward silence.

"Are you...are you okay?"

"You don't need to worry about me," he says with a smile. "But what about you? How do you feel about it?"

"It's a bit of a shock. They've only been together a few months. But I guess if they're happy..."

"You don't sound exactly thrilled for them." He pauses and steps outside. "Come on—the roses need pruning."

We garden in silence for a few minutes while all my stupid feelings stew inside me.

"Why do boys always go for the obvious?" The words burst out and Greg smiles, handing me a pair of clippers.

"Ah. Max?"

My answer is in the way I duck my head at the mention of his name.

"Because they're boys," he says. "It takes age and experience to look past the obvious. Aren't girls the same? Would you have fallen for Max if he were short and ugly?"

His words make me feel young and stupid because he's right. I fell for Max before I'd even had a conversation with him because he was gorgeous. And the reason he's only my friend, the reason he hasn't fallen right back, is because I am definitely not gorgeous. I am ordinary. But does it make me feel any better to know I'm as bad as him? Of course it doesn't, it just makes it obvious my feelings for him will be forever unrequited and it bloody hurts.

"Tess," Greg says, taking the clippers from me before I cut through the rose I'm supposed to be pruning. "You're funny and creative and you're going to grow up so lovely. You're only fifteen—what's the hurry?"

What's the hurry? Bella has always been the person I've talked about everything to and that is another stab wound, knowing I can't tell this to her because she wouldn't understand, because she's never been ordinary, because I've seen Max look at her the way I look at him. How long before she looks back and sees what I see? *That*'s the hurry. I don't have bloody time to wait to *grow up lovely*.

God, sometimes I wish I were an only child.

"Come on," he says. "I'll walk you back. It's getting late—you shouldn't be walking alone."

I shrug. "They've caught someone for the murders, haven't they? We're back to being a nice, safe village."

He pauses, halfway through putting his jacket on. "Actually, they've released the guy they arrested."

"What?"

"Rock-solid alibi, I heard."

"But..."

But that means the murderer is still on the loose. I think of Bella roaming the woods on her own at night. I think of Jack and Sean taking her to murder sites and I shiver.

A few days later, I'm back at Dean House and for once I go to the front door rather than round the back of the garden, but there's no answer when I knock. I realize I haven't been inside the house since that long-ago New Year's party. Greg sometimes brings out drinks and biscuits when we garden, but he always goes in by himself. I go around the side to knock on the back door instead and freeze with my hand poised to knock. I can see him in the kitchen and he has someone with him. Her back is to me, but I'd recognize her blond hair anywhere. She's clutching the jacket she left behind the last time she was there. He reaches over and touches her bowed head and jealousy races through my body, hot and painful. It's like the Max situation all over again. He's never once invited me into the house, but Bella is in there *again*.

All her false warnings to stay away—is it because she has something going on with him herself? Did she leave the jacket there deliberately to have an excuse to come back? Exactly how grateful is she for that camera he gave her? The hot jealousy has solidified into sharp needles that stab and stab. I clutch the clippers I brought back with me tight in my hand, wanting to stab something myself. She already has Max mooning around after her, plus all the boys at school. Is this where she's been every night when she told me she was up at the amusement park with her friends? Here, alone in Dean House with Greg?

I hate her sometimes. I do, I do.

MARCH 2008

"He likes you, you know," Bella says, leaning down to pick up a stone, smiling back at me over her shoulder. We're cutting through the woods on the way to Dean House. Well, I am, gardening tools in a messenger bag, scruffiest jeans on. Bella's dressed up to go out. But she insisted on walking me over there first. Because apparently it's not safe for me to be out in the woods alone, but it's fine for her.

"Who?" I say, my heart beating faster. Max, I'm thinking. Tell me it's Max.

"Sean."

"*Sean?* Really? Urgh—no. Are you winding me up?"

Bella laughs. "I see him watching you. And why are you looking so horrified? He is gorgeous—you should be thrilled."

"But he's so scowly and brooding. He scares me a bit, to be honest. I can't imagine ever . . . you know." I blush, glad it's dark in the woods so she can't see.

She smiles. "Brooding and scowly is sexy—like Heathcliff."

"Heathcliff was a total psycho. And anyway, it doesn't matter because I don't like Sean."

She turns and faces me. "Who do you like, then?"

I frown. "You know who I like."

The smile drops from her face. She looks...what? What's that look on her face? Goose bumps rise on my arms.

"Still? It's still Max?"

"It'll always be Max."

"He's all wrong for you, Tess. I know you like him because he's so kind to you, but I don't think he sees you that way. He sees you like a sister."

"You don't know that."

I recognize the look on her face this time. It's pity. "I do know," she says. "He told me. He's embarrassed by the way you moon around after him. It makes him uncomfortable. It's why he hasn't been hanging out at our house so much."

A twig breaks behind me and I hear laughing. We both spin round to see Jack and Sean stepping out of the trees. Oh God—how much did they hear? And what the bloody hell are they doing here? I expected Sean, it's the Easter holidays, after all, but Jack should be away working, not here to torture us.

"Well, looky what we've got here," Jack says, his eyes alight with glee. "Two little piggies ripe for hunting."

Bella rolls her eyes. She folds her arms and glares at both of them but I can see she's trying not to smile. "Why don't you fuck off, Jack Lewis?"

He steps closer to her, an eyebrow raised. "That's not what you said last night."

I look at Bella, startled. She was with Jack last night?

He leans toward her like he's going to kiss her, but she pushes him away. He staggers back a step and laughs again. Bella turns to me. "Go on home, Tess," she says, like I'm a toddler.

Jack looks at me. "Yeah—run, little piggy."

I turn away and start walking, determined not to give in to the urge to run. I hear Bella say something, then her laugh turning into a scream. I hear a crashing sound—someone running through the trees toward me.

"Run, little piggy. Run before we eat you all up."

I want to go back to Bella, I really do, but in the woods, in the dark, I'm finding it hard not to panic as the rustle of leaves and crunching of feet on broken twigs tell me someone is getting closer.

I speed up, breaking into a run.

"You go that way," I hear Jack's voice call. "Cut her off."

I don't know if they're talking about me or Bella, but I run faster, fumbling in the messenger bag until I find the clippers, and run on, clutching them in my hand. I'm getting scratched in the face by low-hanging branches, my chest burns and my legs ache, and the footsteps behind me are getting closer.

I scream when a hand grabs my arm, pulling me back. I whirl round, get slammed against a tree.

"Shh," he says, putting a hand over my mouth. "Calm down, it's only me."

Sean. Standing right in front of me, breathing as fast as I am, his hand over my mouth, smelling of cigarettes and chocolate.

I struggle away from him, shaking and nearly crying. "Get off me," I say, wanting to punch him. He likes you, Bella said. Well, that's bollocks. Total bullshit. I hate him. I didn't want Sean liking me. I wanted Max.

"Wait, Tess," he says, reaching out to grab my arm again. "Don't run. I wanted to talk to you. I wanted to—"

"Fuck off," I yell. "You and your bloody brother can fuck off. I wish your whole damned family would fuck off and die." I swing my arm up to slap him and only remember the clippers in my hand as they connect, slicing at the side of his face.

He staggers back, his hand over the cut, and I clap my own hand over my mouth as if I could swallow the words back down.

"I'm sorry," I say. "I never meant..." I drop the clippers and they land in a pile of leaves and broken twigs.

"What the hell is going on?"

I turn to see Greg marching toward us.

"I could hear shouting and screaming from back up at the house. And I come out here and see my own son chasing down a girl?" He stops. "What happened to your face?" he asks Sean.

Sean half turns away from me, his shoulders hunched. His foot kicks the clippers farther into the undergrowth. "It's fine. I cut my face on a branch. It was a game."

"A game?" Greg says, looking from Sean to me. "Tess doesn't look like she's enjoying your game very much." He reaches out a hand to me. "Come on, Tess, come on back to the house. I'll get you a drink and give you a lift home. Leave Sean to his games."

I hesitate, looking back at Sean, but whatever was going on, the moment has passed. I want to apologize again, explain I forgot I had the clippers in my hand. I did, I really did. But he's scowling at me again, all sneering hostility. I tighten my lips and take Greg's hand.

NOW

CHAPTER 25

Max and Lena are back. Lena doesn't seem to care how much work she's missing, but I'm surprised by Max—Max, who's so ambitious that he combined his first visit to see Julia with a work thing. But perhaps they sense, like me, that time's running out. They've already been up to see Julia and now we're sitting in the garden in the early spring sunshine. We've made it to March. We've made it through the dark of winter. Soon the clocks will change. I went through the house yesterday, putting all the clocks right. I noticed this morning, though, that some of them have already lost time. And things aren't right, there's none of the anticipation spring should bring. It's not warm enough to go out without coats, but I think they feel it too, the heaviness of impending death. I tried to persuade Dad to sit out with us—he seems to be shrinking under the weight of it and it frightens me that he might fade when Julia dies, sucked dry by the presence of death.

"You're quiet, Hardy-girl," Max says. He's wearing sunglasses and I can't see his eyes as he looks at me, but I can see myself reflected in the lenses and, like Dad, I look smaller, shrunken. I did sleep last night, but it was a sleep full of broken dreams, all nightmares. I didn't wake up refreshed. If anything, I feel worse today, the world more disjointed. I still haven't started on the sleeping pills—I'm worried I'll fall into a dream I can't climb out of.

Max, since he got here, has become another Max again. The awkwardness that's hovered around us since our disastrous night in my flat seems to have gone, on his part at least, and he keeps touching me—my arm, stroking my hair. I think I'm alone, feel a touch, turn, and he's there, a smile on his face, like nothing happened, like he didn't practically run away screaming after sleeping with me, that I didn't almost kill him by grabbing the steering wheel and crashing his car. But it's the painted-on smile I first saw that night in my flat, the one Sophie saw and didn't like. I don't know where I am with him—he's like the spring weather, going from sunshine to rain in seconds, and it keeps me off balance. Instead of leaning closer as he gets more affectionate, I find myself stepping away, hiding when I see him coming.

Detective Levinson called this morning. They checked the house but found no sign of anyone being in there other than the window I'd left open. The wind and rain had blown in, erasing those paths of footprints. He said there was no sign of a suitcase anywhere in the house. If I didn't have the photograph I took, I'd wonder if it was ever there. He didn't give any indication he doubted anything I said, but I heard it anyway as he told me the only fingerprints they could pick up off the shoes were mine. I didn't mention that I'd taken the photograph, because when I went to the album at home to find its twin, it wasn't there. The page was empty.

"I'm okay," I say to Max with a smile, putting my own sunglasses on.

There were more stories in the newspapers today. I walked to the village shop and there was Dean House, on the front pages of several of the national papers. It's only a matter of time before Bella's death reappears in connection with it. The local paper has already run a story asking, WHATEVER HAPPENED TO ARABELLA COOPER? I haven't told Max and Lena. I don't know if they've seen the stories as well, if they're just avoiding discussing it with me. It sits between us—between me and Max, anyway. Lena appears to be asleep, face white under her dark glasses and newly dyed black hair. She looks the same as she did back then, regressing, like I am.

"Tess?" Dad appears at the back door and I'm glad to get up, away from Max's mirrored gaze. "Will you sit with Julia awhile? She's awake and she asked for you."

I nod and go upstairs, putting the sunglasses away as I enter the gloom of her room. The curtains are closed, only a narrow shaft of light coming through the gap in the middle. She's awake and watching me as I walk across the room to sit by the bed.

"Hey, lovely," I say. "It's a beautiful day out there. Maybe later we could go out in the garden for some fresh air?"

She shakes her head and winces. "I don't think so, Tess. I'm so tired."

I swallow down a lump in my throat. How stupid of me—that optimism when I spoke to Sophie, my ridiculous hopes of remission. The strength that got her out of bed those first few days when we came back...looking at her now, I don't know where she found it.

"I wanted to tell you..." she says, and I wait for her to catch her breath and continue.

"I wanted to talk to you about Ellie. About the accident and after..."

"You don't have to," I say, touching her hand. Leaning closer, I realize her breath smells sour, as though the rot inside her is creeping out. I resist the childish urge to hold my breath—*don't let it in, don't let it get you too.* "Dad told me. You don't need to talk about it."

"I want to," she says. "I need to. My boys won't listen and I want...if I tell you, you can try to explain to them why I had to leave."

In the darkness of her room, leaning in close to hear the whisper of her voice, holding her cold, thin hand, her story becomes a fairy tale—not a Disney version, but a Brothers Grimm tale, a Hans Christian Andersen tale.

"I always wanted a daughter. We tried for years after Sean was born but nothing happened and I thought it never would. When I got pregnant, I was convinced it would be another boy. For a few weeks, Greg even tried to talk me into an abortion—money was tight, there was no room for another baby, the house was too small. But I couldn't and then she was born. She didn't look like any of us. She was like a changeling child with blond fairy hair and dark eyes.

"I've never known a baby so quiet. Jack and Sean used to cry for hours, red-faced temper tantrums even as the tiniest of babies, but she slept through from only a few weeks old and barely cried at all." She stops to take a breath and I pass her a glass of water, holding it steady when her hands shake.

"Everyone loved her—Greg, the boys, anyone who met her, and she was...she was mine in a way the boys never were. They had their football and rugby with Greg and I was just Mum who did their washing and cooked their tea. And when Greg insisted they go away to boarding school, they seemed even further out of my reach. But then I had my little girl who loved tea parties with her dolls and loved wearing pretty dresses and it seemed complete." She stops talking and closes her eyes.

"And then you lost her," I say, remembering Ellie, my pretend baby sister. There's a lump in my throat and my voice is more of a whisper than hers.

"We should never have gone out that day—the roads were too icy."

"It was an accident," I say, words so many people have said to me over Bella's death. Does it make Julia feel better to hear them? Did it ever make me feel better? No. Of course not.

"We should never have gone out," she repeats. "Sometimes I dream that she's still alive. I dream that we stayed home that day and played with her dolls. And then I wake up."

My eyes fill with tears. It's awful. So awful. But what plays in my mind are Lena's words—about why Julia really left. "Was there another reason you left?" I whisper. "To do with Greg?"

She looks at me and there's something in her face. Is it fear? But then the door opens and Sean comes in, walking to the other side of the bed to sit in the red armchair.

"I was paralyzed by my grief," Julia says—to me, but her other hand reaches toward Sean. He looks at it but doesn't take it, remains hunched in the chair.

"I couldn't function, couldn't do anything. I wasn't there for such a long time. I know I let Jack and Sean down, but I couldn't..." She coughs and her face spasms in pain.

"Julia," I say, squeezing her hand, wishing I'd never asked. "Don't—rest..."

"I have to," she says again. "I'm sorry, Sean. I'm so sorry."

"You left," he said, his own voice raw. "You came out of that...fog and you left. You were only a couple of miles down the road, but it might as well have been a thousand. You stopped calling, put us off when we wanted to visit."

"Your father—"

"Don't blame Dad."

"He blamed me."

Sean reacts to that, getting up and turning away from us to face the curtained window.

"Greg got angry—at first he raged at the world for taking his little girl away, but then he turned that rage on me."

"I never saw anything," Sean says.

"He never did anything in front of you, but when we were alone, he said things—awful things. He made my guilt grow. He hated me; he told me I killed her. He said I murdered her."

Sean turns. "Stop it."

"He started drinking more. One night he pushed me against the wall and put his hands around my throat. There was so much rage on his face." She looks back at me. "I was already close to your dad by then but nothing had happened—it was too soon after he lost your mother, way too soon after I'd lost Ellie, but we...we helped each other. We became friends." She turns her head toward Sean. "I couldn't stay. We weren't a couple anymore. I couldn't stay and wait for him to start using his fists."

"But you left us behind," Sean says. "Packed us back off to school and left without telling us. You could have told us; you could have had us to visit every other damned weekend. Christ, you weren't the first parents to split up, but it was like you wanted to leave us as well as Dad."

"I never planned to leave you. Greg made you go back to school so soon after Ellie died, made Jack go off to work when he left school. I couldn't stay, I couldn't. But I tried—I called you. I called you both and you wouldn't take my calls."

"We were angry," Sean bursts out. "You ran off without a word, moved in with another man, for God's sake. But we would have listened, eventually. If you'd kept trying."

Julia rubs her eyes. "I know. I left it too long. And when I made you visit . . . it was too late. You hated me then."

"I never . . ." He stops.

I remember what he was like at seventeen, the bitterness and the anger, the way he looked at Julia at the wedding. Death takes more than just the victim. It destroys everyone else within touching distance.

Julia's eyes are drifting shut, her voice getting slurry. "I always thought I'd have time. That enough years would pass and we could become a family again. My boys and my stepdaughters. That I could forgive Jack and he would forgive me . . . I'm sorry, Sean. Tell your brother, won't you? He won't listen to me. I've tried . . ."

Her breathing slows, becomes even. What does she mean—forgive Jack? Forgive him for what? I stay in the chair, wait for Sean to storm out or sit back down. He comes over to the bed and takes Julia's limp hand, still held outstretched toward him.

"No one ever talked about Ellie," he says, staring down at his mother. "We all just suffered alone." He sinks back into the chair. "You became a target for all the pain and anger. We could blame you."

We sit in silence then, the son and the stepdaughter, holding Julia's hands, willing her to keep breathing.

"I wish . . ." he begins, and his voice trails off. I wait another three of Julia's breaths before he continues.

"I wish I'd come to visit her sooner. Before she got ill. I've wanted to for a long time, but my anger, my resentment—it was like a voice in my head. It kept saying *no, she should come grovel-*

ing to you on bended knee." He sighs. "And Jack ... Jack fed into that, always telling me she should come to me, not the other way round. I let his and Dad's bitterness feed mine." He looks at his mother. "I used to take such childish pleasure in refusing her calls. I was angry at her for calling; then, when she gave up, I was angry at her for not calling. It became easier for us to pretend we had no parents. We never bothered coming back after the wedding."

"We always think there's going to be more time," I say, thinking of Bella, our strained relationship that last summer. How many nights have I spent aching with regret, curled up around it like a physical pain, thinking the same as Sean—I wish, I wish, I wish?

"At least you're here now." At least Julia is still alive.

"It's too late, though, isn't it? Fucking deathbed reconciliation— that's not what I wanted."

"No, of course not, but that's all you've got."

He flinches. Does he hear it in my voice? Bitterness. No, it's not enough, yes, it's too late for him to restart his relationship with his mother, but at least he has this time, however long it is, to talk to her, to mend what's broken.

I want that with Bella. Is that why I'm seeing her so vividly in dreams and hallucinations?

Julia gasps and her eyes fly open. "Tell her," she says.

"What?" I lean closer. "Tell who what?"

Her eyes are glazed and unfocused. "Tell Bella to be careful. Tell her to watch out for him. She doesn't know ..." Her voice drifts off and her eyes close again. I glance up at Sean and he's watching his mother, white-faced.

"She doesn't know what she's saying," he says in a low voice, but it sounds to me like Sean knows exactly what Julia meant.

Jack comes slamming into my room, the door banging behind him. "Is it true?"

I step away from his anger and bump into the wall. "What? What are you on about?"

"Lena told me about your little gardening dates with my dad."

It stings. I don't think I really expected her to keep quiet about it, but still...

"I used to help out with weeding and stuff—so what?"

"So what? So my father has been murdered and you've been claiming you barely knew him. You've been lying—and not just to me and Sean."

"I never mentioned it because it's not important. It was a...an after-school job for a couple of months, that's all."

He steps closer, close enough that I can feel his breath on my face. "Do you know what? I'm beginning to think the whole fucking lot of you were in on it. You, your dad, your dead sister."

"Really? Where's your proof? What are you going to tell the police? That I helped your dad in the bloody garden?"

His hands clench into fists and for a moment I think he's going to lunge at me. Then he seems to get himself under control, shaking his head and letting out a long breath. "Damn you and your family," he says. "I swear, if I ever find out any of you had something to do with my father's death..."

My heart's pounding, but I don't let myself look away from him. "Are you threatening me? Because I'll tell you something, Jack, it's not my gardening activities the police seem to be interested in, it's the relationships your beloved father had with Bella and Nicole and God knows how many other teenage girls. Maybe you should ask yourself if the reason he ended up dead is anything to do with that."

He goes pale and, in the absence of his usual big fake grin, I realize with a shock that he knows. He knows the stories about his dad and teenage girls. And if he knows, maybe Lena wasn't making up stories and Julia did leave Greg because of it. And if Julia knew...

My heart thumps harder. If Greg killed Bella and those other girls and Julia and Jack knew about him...

"What the hell are you doing, Jack?" It's Sean, standing in the doorway.

Jack steps away from me and looks at his brother. "Why don't you ask little miss schoolteacher here? Turns out she knew Dad a *lot* better than we thought."

"Is it true?" Sean asks quietly after Jack has left the room.

My heart is still thudding and my legs are shaky, so I sit on the bed. Sean—does Sean know as well? "Not like he's insinuating. I helped him out in the garden for a while, that's all."

His eyelids flicker. He glances out onto the landing, then pushes my door closed. "I knew," he said. "Dad let it slip once."

"So you know all I was doing was gardening! You can tell Jack and—"

"Dad said you had a crush on him. That things were awkward and he didn't know how to deal with it."

My face floods with color. "That's not true. I never...God, your dad was old. It was Max I..."

"Yeah, that's what I said to him at the time. We all saw the way you were with Max, it was pretty obvious. I guess...my dad always liked to think women liked him. That's probably what it was, right?" He pauses. "I mean, he never..."

He stops and shakes his head. "Never mind. Forget I said anything." Then, as he turns to leave, he says, "Watch out for Jack. When he gets something in his head, he's pretty relentless."

CHAPTER 26

I'm back at the police station in front of Detective Levinson—a polite request to make a formal statement. Again, it's been stated I'm here entirely voluntarily, but that casual call set off a thrum of fear that hasn't gone. I was expecting it—of course I was, after Jack's threat. There's no way he wasn't going to go straight to them about my...relationship with Greg. I was so stupid to lie to them about knowing him. How's it going to look if I tell the truth now? But if I don't...if I don't, then I have to sit here and lie to the detective's face, tell him Jack's the liar, not me.

Sophie's face is in my head, the worry and wariness when I tried to explain. Shit. I've made something so small, a lonely teenage girl helping out in a garden, into something huge and suspicious. And if it's true—about Greg and teenage girls...

My throat is dry by the time I finish going through my statement and I'm ready to get up and go when Detective Levinson stops me.

"So, Tess...I wanted to ask again. How well did you know Greg Lewis?"

I sigh and lean back in the chair, clutching the bottom of it to stop myself from folding my arms and hunching over defensively. "Look—I know what this is about. Jack got the wrong end of the stick. I used to...way before he disappeared, I used to do some gardening at Dean House."

"I see. You didn't mention this before."

"Because, like I said, it was way before he left. I'd stopped going over there a long time before the wedding." I look down, remembering how I...omitted telling him about visiting Dean

House the night before the wedding with Bella. It wasn't relevant, was what I told myself then. But now... what was Bella trying to tell me that night?

There's a long pause I can't resist filling. "You're wasting time, you know, talking to me and Dad—it's Jack you should be talking to. Did you know he was in town when Nicole Wallace went missing?"

He still doesn't say anything.

"And Greg... I think Jack did it."

"You think he murdered his own father?"

"You're the one who keeps asking about Greg and the murdered girls, Nicole and the other one." I lean forward. "What if Greg killed the girls and Jack found out, so he..."

"You seem certain it was Jack."

"He took us to where one of the girls was killed once, took us right to the murder site. You don't know him—he can turn on the charm, but it's all pretend, it's all lies."

"Mr. Lewis has a different story to tell, Tess. He told us you were violent as a teenager."

"What?" I laugh. "Is he kidding?"

"He told us you gave his brother the scar on his face."

I lean back in the chair. I can feel my face getting hotter and hotter. "No. That was an accident. A misunderstanding. Something *he* started."

Detective Levinson glances down at the file in front of him. "Mr. Lewis says you attacked Sean Lewis with a pair of garden clippers, causing him to require eight stitches. His statement says, 'If my father hadn't turned up, she would have stabbed him.'" Detective Levinson looks up. "Is this true?"

I shake my head. "Of course not. Not the way he tells it. He wasn't even *there*. He's twisting things—it's what he does."

"But it's not the only occasion you've lost your temper and got violent, is it?"

I fold my arms, hunched into a defensive position. I know what's coming.

"You've recently been fired from your job for attacking a student. And the father of the student has put in another complaint—that you verbally attacked and threatened him in the school parking lot and that you were insisting his daughter was being abused by a pedophile."

"That's a lie," I almost shout, standing up. "*He* attacked *me*. *He* was waiting for *me*. I never said anything about a pedophile. I was trying to warn him."

"You were very...upset at the thought that a teenage girl might be having a relationship with an older man?"

"Of course—I'm...I mean, I *was* her teacher."

"It's not because it has bad memories for you of Greg Lewis? Or your sister?"

I shake my head and sit back down, fold my arms again. "I told you, I helped him out in the garden; he was a family friend, that's all."

There's a long silence as Detective Levinson stares at me.

"Okay, Tess. Thanks for coming in—that's all for now."

CHAPTER 27

I'm on my way to Dean House when my phone rings. It's Sophie.

"Tess—are you okay? I'm sorry, but I've only just seen your message."

"Message?"

There's a pause. "The text you sent. I was in class when it came through."

"I didn't send you a message."

A longer pause. "Yes, you did. Scared me shitless, actually."

I didn't send her a message—I didn't. Where was my phone this morning? I had it on charge, but I'm sure it was in my room with me. But what about when I showered? When I went downstairs to get coffee? Jack and Sean are still in the house. So are Max and Lena.

I squeeze my phone so hard I'm surprised it doesn't break. "What did the message say?"

"It . . . it barely made sense. You were rambling about the police and murder and the bones they found . . . Tess, I'm worried about you. The police came to the school and Rebecca's parents came in."

"It's fine. I'm fine. There's . . . the police are asking all of us questions. But there's nothing to worry about, is there? I didn't *do* anything."

"Are you sure?"

I gasp.

"Sorry, I'm sorry," Sophie says. "But what you said to me about lying to the police. And your behavior—ever since your dad phoned about Julia and you knew you'd have to go back. The Rebecca thing, that message—everything's wrong, Tess, everything."

"Jesus, Soph. I can't believe you're even suggesting..."

"I'm not. Not really. But I don't think you should stay there anymore. Remember when you asked me to come home with you? Meet your dad and Julia? You acted so strange. It was like you were *scared*. Not just reluctant to go back to a place full of bad memories, but actually scared of the woods and the village." She stops. I can hear her breathing. "I think...the memories you're suppressing. I think it's more than what happened to your sister."

I can smell mud and wet leaves and the copper tang of blood. I don't dare turn my head in case I see Bella next to me, forced out of my dreams, a hallucination as horribly real as when she appeared in my flat, dripping blood. Or worse—what if it's Greg? I don't want to see that.

"I have to go," I whisper to Sophie, and end the call before she can say anything else. I walk away fast, head down, focused on the screen of my phone as I scroll through my texts. There. There it is—the text to Sophie:

I'm scared, Sophie—the police are after me. The bones, the body, it's murder and they know, they know. Should I tell them? Should I tell them the truth?

I didn't write that. But it came from my phone. My heart beats faster. *Did* I send this? Half-asleep, am I doing more than sleep-walking? No. No. Someone else sent this. Any of them could have got hold of my phone—Jack or Sean or Lena—even Max. But why? Why would they do it? I can delete it—delete all my bloody messages. But it will still exist on Sophie's phone. I heard the worry in her voice. She thinks I had something to do with Greg's death. If my best friend thinks it's me...Oh God. She's so honest. If the police ever spoke to her, would she lie for me? I don't think she could. I wouldn't want her to have to do that. I put my phone in my pocket and shake my head. No. I didn't do anything. I have nothing to worry about. I'll keep my phone hidden and, once I get some proper sleep, I'll be able to think more clearly. I need to hold on to the promise I made to Dad and to myself. I'm getting my life back on track.

*   *   *

The walled garden at the back of Dean House, my secret garden, has been left untouched so far by the demolition team, halted by the police investigation. The police have been here though, digging, looking for more bones. I saw it from the window when I broke in. It was as overgrown as the rest of the garden, untouched for years since I stopped coming here, but the stubbly apple trees and overgrown rosebushes pushing up through the weeds used to have their own kind of wild beauty. Even without my attention, even left alone, the apples still grew, the roses still bloomed.

But the police swarmed through, trampling plants as well as weeds, killing the beauty. After another night of no sleep, I left the house early, getting a spade and a trowel and gardening gloves from my dad's shed, making my way down the lane in the half-light, a flask of tea and a roll of green plastic bags in the rucksack on my back.

I should leave it, abandon it, like everyone else has. I have Dad's garden to concentrate on now, that's going to be a project to heal both of us. But...I need to do this. Dean House and its inhabitants are so tied up in my lost memories—doesn't it make sense that I'll remember more if I go back to the gardens? Although...I think of Sophie's words. Do I really want to remember? But there's the class photo I found, Bella's shoes. Those damned texts. Someone's messing with me, planting things to make me paranoid and suspicious. To make *me* look suspicious. If I don't remember, I have nothing to fight back with.

The gloves protect my hands from some of the brambles, but they're soon smeared with blood from the sharpest thorns as they cut through the canvas, prick my palms with dozens of holes. I don't stop, chopping at the thickest, most stubborn roots with Mum's old clippers, clearing away the choking weeds from the roses that still climb the walls. Too early for them to flower, but there are a couple of buds.

I've been working for two hours and am taking a break and

drinking tea when Sean climbs over the wall and joins me. He's carrying a bag, which he puts down on the ground. He doesn't say anything but takes the second plastic cup I offer him, drinking the tea I pour into it. As he stands next to me, I can see the faint scar on the side of his face. We never talked about it. I went off with Greg and didn't see the boys again until just before the wedding. And even then we didn't talk about it.

"What are you doing here?" I ask, as the silence gets too much.

He shrugs. "I saw you marching off, guessed you'd be coming here."

I think of the texts. The light I saw flashing in Dean House before I found Bella's shoes. Everything the police seem to suddenly know. How different Sean is to how I remember him. "Why would you assume that?"

He glances at me. "Because I can't stop thinking about it either—Dad. Everything that happened back then. It all started and ended here, didn't it?"

No. For me it ended in the woods with my sister dead next to me. But he's right about it all starting here. I should want to run now—it could well be Sean sending texts, planting the shoes. But...I no longer feel that edge of fear round him, like I do with Jack. And the longer I think about those long-ago days, I wonder if I ever really did feel that about Sean, or if he was just tainted by the danger I felt emanating from Jack.

He likes you, Bella whispers in my head.

Sean was always quieter than Jack, a bit awkward. Stilted. A bit hostile and grumpy, yes, but no more than I used to be. Most of his hostility resulted in me attacking first. In the midst of the glamorous confidence of the others—Bella and Lena, Max and Jack—we stood out. Was I blinded by his status as one of the "insanely hot" boys? Did I always mistake shyness for arrogance, misery for hostility?

When I stand up to carry on gardening, he stands next to me, pulling up weeds, clearing brambles from the hidden roses. He doesn't have gloves to protect him from the thorns and his hands are soon scratched and bloodier than mine, leaving smudges of dark red on the gray stone wall we're slowly uncovering.

He doesn't stop, doesn't speak, not even when the blood starts trickling down his hands and dripping onto the ground. I look at him and realize he's crying, silent tears streaking his cheeks. I don't know if his tears are for Greg or for Julia, but he works relentlessly, attacking the weeds like this is a battle, and maybe to him it is, pulling away the killing weeds to let the plants breathe and grow again.

It starts to rain, but we continue working side by side, working our way along the wall until it's clear; no more weeds, no more brambles, just crumbling gray stone and climbing roses. Sean stops then, at the corner of the wall, breathing hard, his hands a bloody mess. He seems calmer and I am too, the coiled anxiety I hadn't even realized I was carrying gone, the ache in my shoulders now from the exercise rather than tension.

I still have the sense that something is coming, something is going to happen. I know this is pointless, that there are only days until the bulldozers crush all this to dust, but it feels important. It feels right to be doing this.

"The doctor came again," Sean says. "I knew, of course I knew, that there wasn't going to be any happy-ever-after for her. God, I can see her deteriorating every time I step into the room. But still, I hoped..."

"Of course you did. We're here tending a garden that's about to be demolished. Aren't we always hoping for a miracle?"

He laughs. "Miracles? I never had you down for someone who believed in miracles."

"Not believed in—hoped for. Every night after Bella died, I went to bed wishing with all I had that I'd open my eyes and she'd be back, sleeping in her bed."

"Yeah. I get that. I used to do the same after Ellie died."

"Does Jack know about the doctor's visit?"

"He was there when the doctor came down." He sighs. "He's only seen her twice since coming back."

"Fucking Jack."

Sean kicks at a stubborn weed pushing up through the ground. "That's my brother. A one-man wrecking crew."

"What is he so angry at? Still? Is it because she left?"

"Jack stores things up. He broods. And he doesn't forgive."

"But you do?"

His eyes are still red. "It made me bitter for too long, her leaving. I don't want that bitterness to fester after she's gone."

"When you turned up, I thought nothing had changed. But *you* have, at least."

"Jack did, as well, after your sister died."

"Did he?"

"He and Bella...they had something. A connection. He met his wife soon after and it was odd, a bit creepy how like Bella she was."

Sean must see something in my face, because his own shuts down, becomes expressionless. "I'm sorry," he says. "I don't mean to bring back any bad memories."

I shake my head. "No, it's okay. I guessed there was something between them, even though Bella never said. I tried to talk her out of it. I never saw anything in...Jack worthy of my big sister's affections."

He smiles. "You were going to say my name then as well, weren't you? I think you saw what you wanted to see. Until I surprised you at the wedding. Then you saw."

Saw what? My memories of the wedding are hazy, disjointed because of the amount of champagne I drank. I have flashes of trying to be happy for Dad and Julia because they were so obviously in love. I don't remember if I succeeded in pretending to be happy for them—everything got overshadowed by what happened in the woods that night and no one was happy—real or pretend—after that.

Jack and Sean didn't come to Bella's funeral, I do remember that. So much for the connection Sean just told me about.

"I was wondering," he says suddenly. "About the camera. And what might be on the film. Have you had it developed yet?"

I shake my head. "I've sent it off, but haven't had the photos back yet." I pause. "Shit—I should have told the police about it, shouldn't I? As soon as they found the body. I didn't think."

"I think you should wait to see what's on the film before you mention it."

"Why would I wait...?" I stop. "You're worried, aren't you? The police have been asking questions about Greg and the murdered girls. You're worried that what's on that film could implicate your dad in some way... or Jack."

"A photo came through on Dad's phone once. Of Nic Wallace. Smiling in her underwear. Jack deleted it before Dad saw it—said it was a mistake. That she meant to send it to him." He pauses. "But I always wondered. Especially after Mum left and then Nic went missing."

"Have you told the police?"

His silence gives me my answer.

"You have to. You have to tell them—"

He interrupts me. "Tess—what if...?"

"What?"

"What if Bella was involved in Dad's death?"

"What do you mean, 'involved'?"

"Perhaps Dad was what I'm scared he was. Bella and Nic Wallace were friends, weren't they? She could have found out and..."

"And what? Murdered him and buried his body? She was eighteen, she was... she was *good*." I put the memory of the night before the wedding out of my head. Her tears, her weird behavior as she made me go with her to Dean House.

"Come on, we all know she was more of a rebel than the good girl you're suggesting. We were strangers to the village but even when we first moved here, we heard stuff about her and her friends—that they were the ones to go to if we needed booze or to find the parties."

"What—so because she drank and went to parties, that makes her a murderer? Who the hell are you to say anything about my sister? What—you were Mother Teresa, Mr. bloody perfect?"

"Of course not, but..."

"But nothing."

"You've put her on a pedestal, acting like she was perfect. Oh no, there can't have been anything going on with her and Jack, oh no, she can't possibly have been involved in anything *bad*."

"Shut up."

I don't want to hear it. I don't want to remember the times when I didn't put her on a pedestal, when all my feelings for her were jealousy and resentment and anger.

"You were always misguided—especially when it came to her. You wouldn't listen. There could be something on that film, something important."

The camera that holds the last photos Bella took looms in my mind and I'm remembering Max asking oh so casually about it, all this interest surrounding decade-old things that should have been forgotten by everyone but me. The woods surrounding us seem to creep closer and I think of Sean following me here, where there's no one else for miles around.

"Stop it, go away. Get the fuck away from me," I hiss. "I was right. You and your brother are bad news, here to stir things up. Leave me alone, Sean. Leave my memories of my sister alone."

CHAPTER 28

"Tess—wait up!"

I glance back. Max is jogging toward me.

"Where are you going?"

"Only into the village. The tension in the house is getting a bit much."

He slows to a walk next to me. "Tell me about it. Understandable, I guess. First Julia, now Greg..."

"I just wanted to get away for a bit. Not talk about Julia or Greg or the police investigation."

"Suits me. Mind if I tag along? It seems like forever since we've talked."

I do mind, really. Max is as much a part of the tension as any of the others. More so, really, with the elephant in the room that is our night in my flat. We walk in silence for a while.

"Look—I'm just going to say it, okay?" Max says, breaking the silence. "I'm sorry I was such a dick after the night we—"

"Oh, please don't. Let's agree to not talk about that as well, shall we? I think we both know it was a big mistake."

"Wait," he says, touching my arm. "Was it? I guess the timing was a disaster, but it's something I've thought about for a long time. Haven't you? And it was good, right? Maybe, after all this...we could go out, try again."

I'm floored by his words. He's been thinking about it, about me? That's not how I remember it. I remember him treating me like a kid sister. I remember him mooning after Bella, definitely not me. And good? That night was awkward, weird—and by no stretch of the imagination good sex.

It throws me, this reversal. My crush on him was so

all-encompassing and now, ten years later, he's looking for—what, a *relationship*? And I'm scrabbling for excuses. A way to let him down gently, because it's Max, who I used to think I loved when I was sixteen and he was eighteen.

But when I look over at him, his self-conscious half-smile, the awkward arm on mine, I think again that it's like he's playing a part. I don't believe what he's saying—I don't think *he* believes what he's saying. So why is he doing this?

"Shit," he says, stopping dead as we turn the corner near Dean House.

There's a camera crew and a TV news van outside the walls.

"I think we should go back," he mutters.

My chest feels tight. It's like I'm being forced to stay trapped in my old house with everyone. A week, two weeks ago, I thought I wanted that. Because I wanted to remember all the things that are lost. But I'm no longer sure that's what I want. What I do remember is already so awful; how bad are the memories my mind is suppressing?

Only two hours' sleep last night. I've started making a note, part fear, part fascination. What happens when it's no sleep at all? How long can a person live without any sleep at all? I've forgotten what I look like without the dark shadows, without the red-rimmed eyes and the pale skin. I take the unopened box of sleeping pills out of my bag. Why am I so afraid of taking them? A medicated sleep could take away the dreams, stop the sleepwalking—but what if it doesn't? What if I end up trapped in sleep and the nightmares get stronger, pulling me out of my bed, wandering the woods...

I think Sophie was right. Being back here is not good for me. But what can I do? Not only would it look bad to the police if I suddenly leave, but how could I explain it to Dad? I see him looking at me as I make tea, worry on his face. I don't want to add to it; he has enough to worry about watching his wife die, while the police hover with their questions and insinuations. I don't talk about it, but it's obvious—my insomnia makes itself known in my outward appearance during daylight hours as well as in the dead of night.

"Are you okay?" Dad asks for the hundredth time.

"It's the quiet," I say. "I'm not used to it anymore. I'm used to falling asleep to the sound of cars, and music and voices. Don't worry about me, Dad. I'm fine."

There's a knock at the door and we look at each other. Dad gets up and goes to answer it. I hear voices, male, but not voices I immediately recognize. Dad's frowning as he comes back in, the look of worry still on his face. He's followed by two men in suits. Detective Levinson is one; the other is younger, shorter, with the same light brown hair as Max.

"Tess? The detectives—they want to talk to you."

I put my teacup down and stand up. "To me? What about?"

Detective Levinson steps forward to talk. "Nothing to worry about—just a couple of things we want to clear up." He looks at me and Dad, standing in front of him.

"Please," he says. "Sit back down, have your tea. I know this is a difficult time and I'm sorry for disturbing you." They both glance up as he speaks, Julia's dying presence making itself known.

"Would you like tea or coffee?" Dad asks, and makes himself busy when they accept. I stare down into my own cup. I know why they're here. So does Bella, existing only in my head, my dreams, but hovering unseen over there next to Dad anyway, face solemn, in her death clothes.

"Have you found something out?" I ask. "About Mr. Lewis?"

"That's not why we're here," Detective Levinson says. "We wanted to talk to you—to you both—about Arabella." There's a pause. "We know your memory of your sister's accident is still incomplete..."

It wasn't an accident, Bella whispers, and I wince. How can no one else hear it? It's in my head but it's so loud. How can they not read her words on my face? The walls are closing in, the air is getting heavier.

"Excuse me a moment," I say, scraping my chair back. I barely make it to the bathroom before bringing up everything I've eaten in the last twenty-four hours, retching up stinging strings of bile. Bella has followed me. I can hear her breath in my ear, smell the perfume she used to wear. *Tell them, Tess,* she whispers, fast, urgent. *Remember what happened, remember that night...*

I wash my face with shaking hands. What are they saying downstairs? Is Dad telling them more about my insomnia, is he telling them I'm fragile, is he telling them the strain I'm under? I think of my hands on Rebecca Martin, dragging her toward me by her tie, my threat to throw her through the window.

I make myself go back downstairs, force myself to sit back down at the table. "I'm sorry," I say. "But what does Bella's death have to do with Greg Lewis?"

"The initial time frame, as far as we can establish—it looks as though Greg Lewis died around the same time as your sister."

I lean forward. "But he left. Jack got a text from him. He left the country, didn't he? Took his passport, his phone..."

"There's actually no evidence he went anywhere. No travel records, no further contact. It's possible the text did not come from him."

"What? But it was his phone, it..." Oh. My voice trails off. They think the murderer might have sent Jack that text, to stop anyone from looking for Greg.

"Wait," I say. "Jack's always insisted his dad sent him a text, but did anyone else ever see it? He could have been making it up, couldn't he? If it was him who..."

"We're speaking to everyone who knew Greg Lewis. But today we wanted to talk to you about your sister."

I suck in a breath and hold it. I hadn't realized, for a moment, what they were getting at. Greg had gone abroad by the time Bella died, so I never thought...But if he never sent the text, then he might never have been abroad. He could have been lurking in the woods the night of the wedding.

"Can you take us through what you remember after the wedding? The night your sister died?" Detective Levinson asks. There's sympathy on his face, caution too. He's gained an impression of me from whatever Dad and Max and Rebecca Martin have told him, from his memory of me at the hospital, coming to him raving about Bella's shoes. One I'm not going to be able to undo.

"It was the night of the wedding. I'd gone upstairs—I had a bit too much champagne and...I don't know if I fell asleep or not, but it was late and everything was quiet downstairs but Bella's bed was empty. She was...she had insomnia sometimes. There were weeks where she couldn't sleep." My face is hot. I clutch my cold cup of tea so they won't see my hands shaking. "On warm nights, when she couldn't sleep, she would sometimes go into the woods."

"Alone?" This is from the younger officer. I don't like what I hear in his voice. I remember the questions after Bella died, about her drinking, about drugs and boyfriends. They tried to paint such an ugly picture of her and it wasn't true.

"Yes, alone," I say. "She didn't go calling for her friends in the middle of the night."

"But you went into the woods with her that night."

"I saw her empty bed. I went down and saw her leave the house. I knew where she'd be heading."

That's not entirely true. I was worried she was going back to Dean House. That was why I followed her.

"And then?"

"I remember going into the woods. It was hot, we were in the middle of a heatwave, and I remember the relief of going into the trees. It was so much cooler; that's why Bella went there. I told you all this back then."

"Please—tell us again."

"I got spooked. I heard a noise, a twig breaking or something behind me. I called for Bella but she didn't answer. I got scared, I started running and...I don't know. I must have hit something, or fallen. I don't remember anything else."

Detective Levinson leans forward. "Can you remember where you entered the woods?"

"From the lane."

"You were both found a long way from your house. Not far behind Dean House. It's at least two miles from here."

"I know, but I don't remember going there. I don't remember anything after those first few minutes of entering the woods."

He leans back. "How well did you know Mr. Lewis?"

I freeze. "You've asked me all this. I told you before—I barely knew him." I glance at Dad. "I used to...help him out in the garden a bit when I was younger, that's all."

I can see Dad's startled look.

"And your sister? Did she know him?"

I hesitate. *Our secret*, Bella said to me once. *Don't tell.* Bella's death and Greg's death, so close together. I don't want it to have been Greg who killed Bella, but I also don't want them thinking Bella could have had something to do with Greg's death, not when she's not here to defend herself. "No," I say. "She didn't know him. Other than as Jack and Sean's father."

"What about the other deaths?" I say as they get up to leave. "The murdered girls."

"There was never any evidence linking him or anyone in this area to those murders." But he pauses before he says it.

When Bella died, when the two of us were found in the woods, the stories appeared all over again, speculation that Bella was the third victim, that I was the survivor. We became front-page news, until the inquest ruled Bella's death an accident. A drunken mishap, the press then said. Teenagers out of control. It was like they were angry that we weren't victims of a serial killer, like we'd tried to fool them. So they printed their horrible stories about Bella, and people came forward and whispered lies to them, making Bella and Lena and their friends sound like hell-raisers, making Bella sound like she deserved what happened to her.

All my denials and questions back then, when I refused to accept the Bella painted in the press, when I begged the police to keep investigating, were greeted with sympathy, pity in their eyes as they patiently restated the inquest findings, the amount of alcohol in Bella's system.

Today, though, it's not pity I see in their eyes as I ask the same questions. It's speculation.

I sit in the rotting wooden chair in the middle of the walled garden at Dean House. I've been working for two hours and I've managed to clear all the weeds.

I'm not free of ghosts. Bella appears and disappears. Greg stands behind me giving instructions. I close my eyes and lift my face to the sun and the world tilts so I have to clutch the splintered arms of the chair to stop myself from falling sideways. But it's still more peaceful than Dad's house, too full of Sean and Jack and Dad's grief, while Julia fades upstairs. I can't breathe there. Sean was right about the air. It's been sucked out of the house and what's left is dry and dead. I have a permanent bad taste in my mouth that only dissipates when I'm here, with my hands deep in damp earth, feeling life begin to grow again.

"Tess?"

I jump and the chair tips. For a moment, I tilt, ready to fall with the chair on top of me, then a hand steadies the chair, steadies me. My intruder steps out of the sun and I see it's Lena. I get up and brush the dirt off my jeans.

"I guessed you'd be here when I couldn't find you at your place." She looks around. "Um—why are you gardening in a place that's about to be demolished?"

My face warms. I'm surrounded by garden bags and tools and I don't know how to explain what I'm doing here.

"I used to look over the wall sometimes when me and Bella went to the woods," I say. "Before the Lewises moved in. It reminded me of the secret garden from the book. I wanted to make it beautiful again."

There's a pause. We're surrounded by diggers and police tape and and DANGER—KEEP OUT signs—and nothing I say will explain why I'm here weeding.

Lena raises her eyebrows. "So you really only used to come to help Greg...um...pull up his weeds?"

"Oh, fuck off, Lena. The man is dead. Stop with the dirty insinuations."

"But they're not insinuations, are they? Greg Lewis was weird. The stories about him...they weren't just stories. Bella knew. Jesus—even Jack and Sean knew, though they might deny it. And you? You know, don't you?" She's looking at me so intently.

I shake my head. "Whatever Bella told you, it wasn't true. I swear it."

She tilts her head. "Yeah? You might want to work on sounding more convincing when you spin it to the police."

"What are you doing here, Lena?" I pick up a trowel and start hacking at the roots of a stubborn weed in one of the pots.

"I was going through some of my old photos. I brought them with me—thought there might be some nice old ones of Julia I could show your dad."

I straighten up. "Oh. That's...thank you, Lena. That was really thoughtful."

She rolls her eyes. "Do you have to sound so surprised? Anyway—I found a couple of others. Of Bella. And you. I thought you might be interested." She pulls half a dozen photos out of her bag and holds them out.

The first one is a photo of Sean and Jack together, unsmiling skinny boys, already so bloody handsome. There's a photo of Jack with Greg and Bella. Bella's next to Jack and Greg stands behind them, an arm draped over both their shoulders. Bella's face is tilted up and it's Greg she's looking at, not the camera, not Jack. It makes me twitch.

And then there's another photo I don't understand. It's Bella, looking just as I remember her, smiling and happy, her camera strap hanging off her shoulder. But standing next to her, standing too close to her, is Sean, and they look...they look together. Both seventeen, arms around each other, they stand together looking like boyfriend and girlfriend. I don't remember this. Sean's words about Bella and Jack, about their *connection*—was it just a smoke screen?

I stroke Bella's smiling face in the photo. Was it after this weekend that she stopped sleeping, started sneaking out at night? I don't remember it being a sudden thing. Wasn't it gradual, the change in my sister? Gradual enough for me not to notice anything strange. She just changed. But doesn't everyone at seventeen?

"Surprising, huh?" Lena says. "I always thought it was Jack she had the hots for. But looking at these—well, it could be Greg and Sean, right?" She reaches for the photos but I pull them out of reach.

"It's okay. You can keep them," she says. "But you might want to show them to the police."

CHAPTER 29

I close the door to my room and sit on the bed, spreading out the photos Lena gave me on the quilt. I bite my lip. Am I imagining it? The closeness I see between Bella and Sean? Does it even matter? I hesitate and take photos of them on my phone and send them to Sophie. She's got the distance from this that I lack—she'll be able to tell me if I'm being paranoid. I wait a few moments, then FaceTime her, closing my eyes as I wait for her to answer. It's only been a few days since I've seen Sophie, but with all that's been going on, it feels more like months, like Jack's stopped clocks have done their trick and locked me in a never-ending time loop where I bounce from Julia's deathbed to questions from the police and back again, over and over. I'm wrung out, exhausted, and, right now, all I want in the world is to be sprawled on the sofa of my city flat with Sophie, sharing a bottle of wine and watching crap on Netflix.

"Tess?" I feel a wave of relief as Sophie's face fills the screen.

"Hey, Soph. Did you see the photos I sent?" I ask.

"Why? What's going on?"

"I'm sorry, Soph. I know I've been a bit . . . It's Jack. Jack's messing with me, he's been messing with me for weeks. That text—I never sent it, I swear. It was Jack. He thinks I had something to do with Greg and he . . . he's trying to . . . I don't know what he's trying to do, but he's manipulative. He's dangerous."

"Dangerous? Really? Tess, whatever the hell is going on here, it's not good. You should come back home."

"How can I? Look, I went over there. To Dean House. And I found Bella's shoes—they've been missing since she died. Someone left them there for me and...and...Please. Look at the photos I sent you."

She hesitates and sighs. "Hang on, I'll have a look."

I wait, my teeth clenched, for her to come back on the line.

"What is it you want me to see?" she says. "They're just snapshots, aren't they? Of your sister and..."

"Look at the way Greg's looking at her. And the other one—it's Bella and Sean. They look like they're together, right?"

There's a long pause. "I don't know. It just looks like the camera caught her and Greg mid-conversation. And the one with Sean? I don't...I don't get why it's a big deal even if they were together. It was ten years ago, wasn't it?"

"I always thought it was Jack she was with. But when I saw that photo...if they were together, it gives him a motive. It gives both of them a motive, doesn't it? A love triangle."

"Tess...they're not investigating your sister's death, are they? You told me it was an accident. I know you had that weird dream, but that's not proof of anything. Shouldn't you be concentrating on Greg's death, on sorting things out with the police so you're not lying to them?"

I look round, check the door is still closed and no one is listening in.

"It's all related, I know it is. Whoever's messing with me knows something about how Bella died. Otherwise, why leave the shoes? Why take my phone and send texts?"

She doesn't believe me. I can tell by the frown on her face and I can't blame her. I'm rambling, sounding paranoid, sounding bloody *insane*. If I left now, went back to my old life, how long before the distance made me not believe it myself? It would take on the patina of an old fairy tale. And I'd be letting Dad and Julia down.

I shake my head but there are tears in my eyes. "I can't leave. I'm sorry, Sophie, I'm not coming back. I'm going to take a landscape gardening course at a local college near here and stay with Dad."

"You're not coming back at all? But...you have to apply for the course and get in. I thought you'd come back for a while at least. You can't just abandon your whole life. What about your flat? Your friends? What about me?"

"I'm sorry, but I have to be here. For Julia. For Dad."

Sophie sighs. "Listen, Tess," she says in a lower voice. "Okay, that's fine. The course sounds great—perfect for you. I'll support you all the way. But start it in September and come back home now. I'm worried about you. What the hell is going on, Tess? Are you in trouble?"

My door opens and I jump, dropping the phone, scrabbling to hide the photos. "Is everything okay?" It's Max's voice, Max's hand on my shoulder. Fake Max, a stranger. I pick up my phone and there's Sophie, my best friend, who only knows the lie of me, the fake Tess I've been since I started teaching.

I have to stay. I have to know what happened to Greg, what happened to Bella. I have to see this through.

I force a smile at her. "I'm fine, Sophie. Seriously—I'm fine. There's stuff going on but I have to be here—for Julia, for Dad. You understand that, don't you?"

She's still frowning. "No, not really."

I don't want her to say anything else, not with Max in the room. Can she see him, hovering at the edge of the screen, his hand still there on my shoulder? "I have to go. I'll call you, okay?"

I look up at Max after ending the call, force a smile.

"Are you okay? That conversation sounded intense."

"She's worried about me."

"Well, she doesn't need to be. I'm here." He looks down at the photo still scrunched in my hand, the others only half-covered by the quilt. "What's that?"

"Nothing," I say, stuffing the photos in my pocket. "I'm going back downstairs."

Sean is in the kitchen making toast. "Want some?" he asks, eyebrows raised.

"I thought you were sitting with Julia?"

He nods and cuts his toast in half. "I was. But your dad's up there now, so I left them to it."

I drop the photo of him and Bella in front of him. "Lena gave me this."

He looks at it and puts his toast down. "So?"

"It looks..."

"It looks what?"

"It looks like you're together." Even as I say it, I feel stupid. Sophie was right—so what if they *were* together?

He laughs. "Seriously? Me and *Bella*? You couldn't be more wrong."

He likes you, Bella whispers, and I shake my head.

"Forget it," I say, shoulders stiffening. He sighs and turns away and the tilt of his chin elicits a whisper of memory—his chin brushing against my cheek as he whispered something in my ear, my face turning toward his...He's almost at the door when I call him back.

"Sean? Did I...did I kiss you once?"

He looks back at me and smiles. "I wasn't sure if you'd forgotten or if you were deliberately not mentioning it."

"It was at the wedding, wasn't it?"

He nods. I remember now. I remember his cheek brushing mine, the satin of my bridesmaid's dress against the wool of his suit. I remember pressing myself against him, his arm around me. I remember my head swimming with unfamiliar alcohol, reaching up and brushing my lips against him, how his arm tightened around my waist and we kissed.

"Why?" I whisper. This is what I don't remember. I hated him then, didn't I? Him and Jack with their hostility and bristling anger, didn't I hate them both like they hated us? But Bella had told me Sean liked me. Was that what made me do it? After the sting of what she said about Max, was it that I wanted to kiss someone who liked me back?

"You were angry," he says.

"At you? I kissed you because I was *angry*?"

His smile fades. "Not at me. You were angry with Max. You'd drunk nearly a bottle of wedding champagne and you were looking for a fight. Instead we talked and we kissed. Then you basically passed out, so I helped you upstairs and that was it. I didn't see you after that."

I shake my head. I don't understand how that day ended up so fragmented. I'm sure, after they found us in the woods, I'm sure the day was complete in my head. It was what happened in the night that's gone from my memory. It's like the insomnia is stealing old memories as well as sleep from me.

"Why would I be angry at Max?" Max was my friend, my crush. I should have been kissing him. I thought I was. Didn't I keep that memory, precious and soft until it got tainted by Bella's death and the aftermath? I thought...Bella told me Max didn't want me, but my anger never got directed at him. I resented Bella, not Max.

"Because of what he was up to with Bella," Sean says, and there's a roaring in my ears and it's like an alarm. No, I don't want to hear this. I'm actually shaking my head and Sean steps back into the room, puts his mug on the table.

"It was never me. She never looked at me. But I don't think she would have done it if she'd known how much you liked him."

Not Bella and Max. No, it wasn't true. I push past Sean, out through the front door, not caring that it's raining. Bella walks alongside me as I march into the rain, arms folded, stamping through puddles, head down.

"You knew I liked him. Don't tell me you didn't know," I shout into the wind. "I told you. All those nights you couldn't sleep, all the secrets we whispered to each other. I told you that night in the woods."

She's there in the gap next to me with her perfect hair and perfect cheekbones and her bare feet and her bleeding head, but she won't answer.

"Talk to me, damn it, *talk to me*. You're quick to talk when *you* want to, aren't you? Talk to me."

A car slows, the driver staring as he passes. What does he see? A madwoman yelling at nothing in the middle of a downpour. That's what I am. Bella hasn't come back to me. What a stupid bloody idea. I don't even know who Bella is.

"Enough," I say, calmer, pushing my sodden hair away from my face. "Enough of this. Go, Bella. Leave me alone. Your death was an accident, that's all. I have to let you go. I have to get some help and some sleep and let you go."

Max is waiting for me when I get back to the house. I guess from the look on his face he's already spoken to Sean. The rain has stopped and he's sitting on the wooden bench outside the house. I sit beside him, feeling the damp from the wood seep into my jacket.

"I had such a crush on you back then," I say.

He glances at me. "I know. I knew."

I wince. "Was it that obvious to everyone?"

"Pretty obvious." He's laughing at me.

"Oh God..."

"Listen, Tess—about Bella..."

I put a hand up to stop him from talking. "Don't. Please don't. It's ancient history and it really doesn't matter. I'm...it's being back here. Sometimes I feel like I'm sixteen again and then I realize how ridiculous it is to get hurt by something from ten years ago. It's not like you were my boyfriend, is it?"

The woods loom up behind us but for once I don't care. There's no monster in the woods, no monster in Dean House. Bella's death was an accident, a senseless, pointless accident.

"But I think you should know. I did like you, you know how much I liked you—we were friends. And Bella..." He pauses. "It was just sex."

"I always thought it was Jack, or even Sean, she was seeing. I honestly never thought it was you."

"It wasn't really. It was only a couple of times before the wedding. After...she took me into the woods."

"The *woods*?"

"Come on, Tess, I was seventeen. I'd have had sex anywhere."

I close my eyes and see them, a teenage Max and Bella, walking through the woods together. In my mind, they sink to the floor in the same place she died and, in my mind, he pulls off her shoes first, those battered old white Converse.

I open my eyes. When did Max come back for the weekend? I assumed when he came to the house that he'd just arrived, that he was in his flat in the city, nursing his own wounds from our disaster of a night together, but maybe . . . maybe he was in town a day or two earlier, visiting Dean House with a dead girl's shoes.

I hear a noise in the trees behind us and jump up off the bench. "Like I said, it doesn't matter," I say to Max.

THEN

CHAPTER 30

AUGUST 2008

Wake up, Tess.

I open my eyes and Bella's sitting on the edge of my bed, fully dressed and smiling. She's smiling but there's tension there; she's practically vibrating with it. I can smell alcohol and cigarette smoke.

"Where have you been?" I whisper.

"Out."

"Well—duh. I know that," I say, sitting up. I look at my clock. It's two in the morning. "What were you doing?"

Her smile widens. "Not sure you're old enough to know all the details of what I've been doing."

As my eyes adjust to the dark, I can see her makeup's smudged, her top is half-buttoned. Her lips look swollen and bruised, there's a red mark on her neck.

I look away, feeling the distance, almost like a physical thing. I know Bella's had sex before, but I've never asked her about it. Sex still scares me. I haven't even had a proper boyfriend, haven't come anywhere close to wanting anything more than a kiss off anyone.

What was it like? I want to ask, but I don't. I'm curious, but my fear of it is greater than my curiosity.

"Who were you with?" I ask instead.

"You don't know him," she says, but her smile fades and her gaze flickers away from me.

She's lying.

"Do you want to see a photo of him?"

I don't want to—what if it's Max? But she's already opening her faded suede bag and she pulls out a battered photograph. She laughs as she hands it to me. I recoil and drop it. I was expecting a snapshot, the two of them arm in arm, maybe. Instead it's a close-up of a boy's torso and he's clearly naked. His face isn't in the shot and it's blurred, obviously a sneaky shot taken as he lunged for the camera, but it's intimate and it hits my hidden fears full-on— a nipple, a smattering of chest hair, a snaking line of darker hair leading downward. Nothing pornographic, only the chest, but I swear I can see what they've just been doing, I can smell the sweat and...other things and it totally freaks me out.

Bella laughs again. She leans over and kisses me on the forehead. "You're still such a child," she whispers, as if she were a hundred years older.

And for a second, as her smile dies again, she looks like she is, ancient and sad, and as she pauses, I wonder if she wants me to say something, to *do* something. But the moment passes and her shoulders droop as she puts the photo away.

"Tess, what are you doing here?" Greg asks.

I don't really have an answer. I never come here at night.

"I wanted...it's the wedding soon and Bella said Jack and Sean were away for the weekend and I thought...I thought you might be lonely." I wince at my own words. It sounds ridiculous— a sixteen-year-old girl asking a forty-year-old if he's lonely. He doesn't laugh though. He smiles and opens the door wider.

"I'm fine, but come on in. Do you want a drink?"

I follow him into the kitchen and watch as he pours two glasses of whisky, adding water and ice to mine. I take a sip and try not to pull a face.

"You haven't had any more nonsense from the boys, have you?"

My face warms as I shake my head. Sean can't have told him it was me who cut his face. I haven't been back to look for the lost clippers. "I haven't seen them since..."

He sighs. "I had a word with them. I'm sorry. They're so bitter, but it's not fair for them to take it out on you."

I don't tell him I've pretty much been hiding from them. I'm mortified by what I did to Sean's face, but it's his own bloody fault—him and Jack. I hate them both, I do, I do. I've barely spoken to Bella in the last two days, since her two-in-the-morning visit to my room with *that* photo. The bitter sting of her words about Max is still raw, and my fear that the faceless boy in her photo could be him...the house has never been so full and so silent.

"How are the wedding preparations going?"

"Awful," I say. "Even Bella's got all caught up in it, going shopping with Julia and everything. Max and Lena's parents came back this weekend and it was all anyone talked about and..." My voice trails off before I can confess that it's me who feels lonely. Left out and alone. I was hoping to spend time with Max but he trails round after Bella and Lena the whole time. And Jack and Sean...even Bella is spending more time with them than me. I can't even hang out with Dad anymore, like I used to when Bella was off with her mates, because he has Julia now.

That's why I came over here. Because it struck me that Greg is the only other person involved in this who's as left out as me.

He drains his glass and stares out of the window at the dark garden. "I think it's a mistake," he says.

I think he means me coming here and hover awkwardly, drink in my hand, wondering if I should go.

He turns to smile at me. "The wedding, I mean. She never wanted to be married, to be a wife. She's too much of a free spirit. Julia's never going to be happy with Leo—he's too quiet and ordinary."

Quiet and ordinary like me. I take the insult to both of us and swallow it down. I don't actually think he's right—I've seen Dad and Julia together. Maybe she just didn't want to be Greg's wife.

I have an urge to show him I'm anything but quiet and ordinary and when he reaches for my glass to refill it, I lean in and kiss him.

He jerks his head away and I burn up with humiliation, feel it filling me like hot, molten lava.

"Christ, Tess...I think maybe you should go home. I'm sorry I gave you a drink. I didn't...we'll blame that. Come on, go home, we'll forget this ever happened."

"It's my sister, isn't it?" The words burst out of me. "I saw you with her—you invited her into the house. You never invited me inside until tonight."

"Because you're usually covered in mud from the garden. Bella came once to tell me about the wedding, that's all." He shakes his head. "Don't try to be one of *those* girls, Tess. It's not you."

"Those girls? What girls?"

"Your sister and her friends—acting and looking so much older than they are, flirting, outrageous. You're a *good* girl, Tess, I've seen that. Don't try to be like them."

There's disgust and anger in his voice as he talks about Bella and her friends and I think of Nicole, the biggest flirt of them all and I think of the secret boyfriend I overheard Mr. Wallace talking to Dad about. I never...I knew Nicole was seeing Jack, so I thought...And he sees Bella that way too?

"So—what? You'd have kissed me back if I was one of those *bad* girls? Even though I'm only sixteen? Have you kissed many of those bad girls? What about Bella?" I pause, swallow. "What about Nicole?"

He has a wary look on his face. "You can't go around saying these things. You can't tell anyone about this, or spread stories about me and your sister. I have sons your age."

A surge of satisfaction dilutes the hurt. He's right. I have the power here.

"No, it doesn't look good, does it? You spending all this time with a sixteen-year-old girl, just the two of us. Especially considering two teenage girls were murdered last year and they're still looking for the killer."

He takes a step toward me and I feel a lurch of fear. Why did I even come here tonight? What was I thinking? Does he see it on my face? He stops anyway, runs both his hands through his hair.

"You need to go," he says. "I don't think it's a good idea for you to come back."

*   *   *

The following night I wake up, disturbed by the door opening. It's dark, middle-of-the-night dark. I'm sweating, my nightshirt clinging to me, my hair damp on my head. Bella comes in and, silhouetted in the light from the landing, I can see she's disheveled, hair tangled, her feet bare. She climbs into bed next to me and I can smell damp earth, dead leaves. She must have been in the woods; I know the smell. Her arm is cold against mine and she's shaking.

"What's wrong?" I whisper.

She doesn't answer, curled away from me, cold and shaking.

"Where have you been?"

"I went to see..." Her voice drifts off and her shoulder stiffens when I touch it. Her T-shirt is torn.

"Doesn't matter, Tess," she whispers, barely audible. "I just want to sleep in here with you tonight."

"Okay," I say. I close my eyes as my sister trembles next to me, but I'm no longer sleepy.

I can feel there's something wrong, something awful. There's a wrongness in the room with us. "Bella?" I whisper. "Please...tell me what's wrong."

She's so tense next to me. "Do you ever wish they'd never moved here? Julia, Greg, all of them? Do you ever wish...?"

I bite my lip. "All the time."

She sighs, a deep, shuddery sigh. "Go to sleep now, Tess. It's fine. It'll all be fine. Just go to sleep."

NOW

CHAPTER 31

Jack is in my room when I get back to the house, looking at the books on the shelf. I stand in the doorway, shoulders tense.

"What are you doing in here?"

He glances back at me and smiles. "I was bored—looking for something to read, but the choice is a bit limited." He pulls the book of fairy tales off the shelf and holds it up. "Seriously? You kept this? How old were you when you moved out again?"

I march over and snatch it off him. Of all the books on the shelf, why did he pick up that one? He's watching me, waiting for a reaction, and I work hard to keep my face blank. "My mother gave it to me," I say, putting it back on the shelf.

"Your mother. How sweet. And weren't you lucky to end up with a second mother in the end?"

I need a shower. I need to sleep. I do not need Jack and his games.

"You need to stop punishing Julia," I say, and he laughs.

"You're telling me what to do?"

"She doesn't have much time left. You'll regret it if you keep this anger up until the end."

He puts his hand on my arm and I step away, bumping into the bed.

"Feeling jumpy, Tess? How come? Where were you, anyway?" He looks out of the window at the darkening sky. "Looking for the rest of the bodies you buried?"

"Fuck off, Jack."

He laughs again. "You haven't grown up much in the last ten years, have you?"

It's this place, being back here with Jack and his brother, Max, Dad, and Julia. I swear I feel myself regressing by the day.

"I've grown up more than you," I say. "I'm not some silly girl in the woods anymore, scared of the big bad wolf. At least I'm not still bearing a grudge from more than a decade ago."

"Aren't you? Aren't you still carrying around all the baggage from ten years ago? Isn't that why your drawer is full of sleeping pills and you still have fairy tales on your bookshelf and morbid reminders of your sister everywhere you look?"

"Go and talk to her," I say, pushing him toward the door. "Go and talk to your mother while you still have the chance."

I slam the door behind him and collapse onto the bed. Damn him. How long was he in my room? I look around and see my bedside drawer half-open. I still have the unopened box of sleeping pills the doctor prescribed. I get them out of the drawer and read the label. Will she come back? Will I dream of Bella again if I take these pills? Or will a medicated sleep push her away? Tears burn my eyes. It feels like I'm killing her, like she's going to die all over again if I take a pill and sleep properly. I know it's not real, I know I need to get well, but I don't want to say goodbye to her again.

I lie down, curled on my side, the pill box clutched in my hand, and I feel her curl up behind me, like she used to do sometimes when she couldn't sleep. Her hand touches my hair and I close my eyes.

"Tess? *Tess*."

Someone's shaking me, grabbing my arm, pulling me out of the house, but I'll have to go back through the woods then, oh please don't make me go through the woods...

"Wake up, come on. It's time to wake up."

I sit up with a gasp and bump heads with someone who falls back, swearing. Sean's sitting on my bed, bare-chested, rubbing his forehead. It's dark, night outside.

"What? Why..."

"You were having a bad dream," he says. "I heard you shouting."

My heart is racing, my back is wet with sweat. "What time is it?" I whisper.

"Just after three."

I've slept. Properly slept, for hours, longer than I've slept in weeks. I look down but I'm no longer holding the box of sleeping pills. My fists are clenched tight but empty. I lean over the side of the bed—nothing.

"What are you looking for?"

"I had some sleeping pills, from the doctor. I don't know what I've done with them." I was holding them when I fell asleep, wasn't I?

He picks up my hand, still curled tight into a fist. "What were you dreaming about?"

"The house. The woods. Bella. Same things I always dream about."

He's stroking my wrist with his thumb and I shiver. I swallow, my throat dry. He's staring straight ahead. I don't think he even realizes he's doing it, but I'm hyperaware he's on my bed, half-dressed, in the middle of the night and all I keep thinking is *I kissed you. It was you I kissed* and it feels like I'm sixteen again and I'm tired and awake and hurting and sad and I want...I just *want*.

He turns to look at me and I almost do it, almost lean in again, kiss him again, but I don't have to because he leans in this time. It's the briefest brush of his lips and then he's gone, up and out of the room and I'm left again wondering if he and the kiss were a dream.

I get up to turn the light on and look for the sleeping pills. I won't take one tonight, it's too late, but maybe tomorrow. Maybe tomorrow it'll be time to start getting better. I pull the quilt aside but they're not there. Frowning, I crouch to check under the bed again. Then I open the drawer of the bedside cabinet in case I put them away without remembering. But they're not anywhere—

not on the windowsill or in my bag or any of the drawers or wardrobe. There are still red lines on my palm, the imprint of the edges of the box like a fossil on my skin, so I know I was still clutching the box when I went to sleep.

Did Sean take it? Is that what he was there for, not to wake me from a nightmare but to take the pills away? But why would he? Why would anyone not want me to sleep? I go to my half-open door and peer out. There are no lights on in any of the other rooms and the house is silent. But the hairs have risen up on my arms and they won't go down.

When I wake again after an hour or two of broken sleep, the first thing I see is the wardrobe door open when it was definitely shut before. It creeps me out, the thought of someone in here going through my things when I was asleep. I get up and open the door wider. The camera—Bella's camera—is gone. It has to be Sean who took it. I close my eyes and picture him leaning toward me, his skin against mine. I thought I wanted...I don't know what I wanted. I thought I wanted Max, but when I close my eyes and think of him, all I see is him and Bella in the woods. Sean must have taken the camera to give it to the police, but I've already dropped the film off at the post office. No one-day service here, it's been posted off and I have to wait five long days to find out what's on Bella's last photographs.

I massage my temples, trying to ease the throbbing headache that's settled in like an unwelcome visitor. It's been weeks now since I slept through the night. The world has taken on an edge both sharp and blurry, I have to be careful when I stand or turn because dizziness strikes. Voices seem too loud and I keep drifting, finding time has passed and I have no recollection of it. It's not the weird missing hours I've experienced—these moments are smaller, more frequent; I step out of my room and then I'm in the kitchen, I'm in the shower, then back in my room dressed. It's like someone is cutting moments out of my life, cutting out the in-between bits so everything is on fast-forward. But fast-forward to what? The nights, though, the nights without sleep pass more slowly than ever.

Jack is coming out of Julia's room as I step onto the landing. It doesn't make me happy to see that he's finally talking to his mother. It makes the anxious knot in my stomach bigger, a knot that gnaws and nags and aches. I push past him and go into Julia's room. She's awake and I can see she's been crying. He's told her, I think. Told her about Greg and his twisted conviction that me or Dad or Bella had something to do with his death.

"What did he do?" I say, sitting next to the bed. I touch her hand and she smiles at me.

"Nothing. It's okay, Tess. I'm upset because...he won't listen. He won't talk to me. I can't get through to him like I have to Sean and it makes me sad. I hoped, when they came here, I hoped I'd have time to make things right with them. But I won't, not with Jack, I won't have time, I'll never have enough time."

"Did he say something? To upset you?"

She shakes her head. "It's the not saying anything that upsets me. He doesn't talk about me leaving and he doesn't talk about anything that happened afterward. He refuses to even hear Ellie's name when I try to explain."

"I'm sorry," I say, reaching down to kiss her forehead.

"I wish he would just tell..." Her voice trails off.

"Tell what?"

Her face twists. "Nothing. I shouldn't have said that."

There's something there, in her eyes. Something she wants me to see without her telling. The back of my neck prickles and I turn to look at the open door. Nobody there. But when I look back down at Julia, there's fear on her face and I know someone was there. I go over and close the door.

"What are you hiding?" I whisper to Julia. "Is it about Greg? Greg and...and Bella?" I turn my face away, afraid of her answer.

"What? No...*no*. But don't, Tess. Don't ask me." She pauses, takes in a deep breath that makes her wince. "And don't ask Jack. I don't want him to think I'm telling tales."

Telling tales about what?

I go straight to Jack's room after Julia falls asleep and find him staring out of the window, a bottle of whisky in his hand.

"Why can't you let it go?" I say. "She's *dying*. Can't you even pretend?"

"Did she tell you a sob story about our poor baby dead sister and that's why she left? Or did she tell you some other story?"

There's an edge to his voice. He keeps his tone light but that edge tells me he's wary of what Julia might have told me.

"She didn't say anything other than wishing you would for-give her."

"Really? No other deathbed confessions? No morphine-fueled lies?"

"What are you afraid of?"

His face shuts down. "I'm not afraid of anything Julia has to say."

"Doesn't seem like it." I shouldn't provoke him. I don't want to push him into anger. "She left because she was grieving. She knows it was wrong to leave you. Can't you forgive her? Now, af-ter all this time? Can't you understand and forgive?"

"It's not me who won't forgive."

"What?"

He walks out of the room, over to the bathroom, the bottle still in his hand. There are only a couple of inches left in the bottom and I think he's going to drink it, but he upends it in-stead, letting the liquid pour down the sink. "Doesn't matter. Forget I said anything. But stop thinking it's me who's stayed away, who can't bloody *forgive*. Ask yourself why she used to refuse to see me when I was fucked up and a grieving mess. Ask yourself why I've ended up carrying around so much ugliness that my wife tells me to stay away so my own kid doesn't grow up like me."

"What are you talking about?" His questions have settled

like rotten seeds in my belly, spreading roots of nastiness, whispering questions I don't want to hear. Why did she leave her sons behind? After her daughter had died, why wouldn't she then cling harder to her remaining children, like Dad did to me after Bella died?

Jack leans in close to whisper in my ear, booze-scented breath filling my nose. "Made you think, didn't I? Made you wonder?"

Dad is in the kitchen when I go down at seven, staring out at the woods. He looks dazed.

"Are you . . . is Julia okay?"

"She had a bad night. The doctor . . . the doctor doesn't think it will be long now. He's adjusted her morphine doses, put a syringe driver up so she's not in any pain, but it makes her . . . it's like I've already lost her."

I go over and wrap my arms around him.

"She didn't want this," he says. "This long, drawn-out end. She wanted to be at home and she wanted to say her goodbyes and she wanted it to be *peaceful*. And easy. I see her in pain and struggling, or doped up on morphine with no idea where she is and I want to . . . I want to . . ."

His voice breaks and I hold him tighter as he cries.

He pulls away and wipes his eyes. "I sat with Julia and realized how many of your mum's and Bella's things are still here, how we've lived surrounded by death and memories for so long."

He shakes his head. "I wonder sometimes if I should have gotten rid of their things. I could never bear to. But it means they're always here. I've never stopped to think how hard that must have been for Julia."

I shiver. Bella's here now, her breath warm on my neck.

"Julia never pushed me. She never asked me to clear away their things. But Bella's things, your mother's . . . It can't have been easy for her living in a house of . . ."

Dead women. Living in a house of dead women. And now Julia's going to join them. Will her things join Mum's and Bella's?

Will her ghost join theirs, following Dad round the house when it's empty, apart from him and me? It makes me want to run as fast as I can, back to my safe box in the city, surrounded by all those other boxes full of strangers, no trees tapping at the window, no ticking clocks, no ghosts.

But I can't leave. After Julia dies, I can't leave him to that.

CHAPTER 32

The doctor tells us Julia could go anytime now. She's been sleeping more, less lucid when she's awake as her morphine dose increases, fed into her arm with a pump. It's agonizing and, like Dad, I wish it could be easier for her. I wish it could be a slow and peaceful slip into death, instead of this struggle. We're taking turns sitting with her so she's never alone—me, Dad, Sean; Max and Lena. I don't know if Jack has been in. He comes in and out of the house, is still staying here, but I've rarely seen him come in or out of her room.

It's two in the morning and I'm sitting with her. Her breathing is so shallow I move closer and put my hand gently on her chest to check it's still moving. Dad came in with a cup of tea a while ago but I made him go to bed, promising I'd wake him if there was any change. None of us has said the word "vigil," but that's what it is.

"Tess." The whisper is so faint I don't think it comes from Julia at first; I look round expecting to see Bella behind me. But Julia's hand touches mine and I look back to see her eyes open.

"Do you want me to get Dad?" I ask.

She shakes her head. "No. You."

"Don't try to talk," I say, smoothing her hair back from her forehead. The gray has crept farther along the length of her hair. I wish I could color it for her. I don't want her to die without her hair glowing and red all over.

"Have to," she says, and the words come out slurred. "Have to tell you."

"Tell me what?"

"The wedding."

My hand pauses, lifts away from her hair.

"Sorry," she says, the word coming out on a shuddering breath.
"For what?"

"I confronted Jack at the wedding...said I had to tell the truth.
Hiding it from Leo, from everyone...it was doing so much harm."

"Tell the truth about what?"

"The accident. When Ellie died. It wasn't me driving. It was
Jack."

"Jack? But he was..."

"Too young. Yes. He was seventeen but hadn't taken his test.
His father had taken him out before. The lane was quiet and he
nagged and nagged. So I gave in, but he went so fast and the road
was icy..."

I shudder, imagining it.

"He begged me to say I was driving. He'd been drinking the
night before, could still have been over the limit. He was only
seventeen, we both would have been prosecuted. I couldn't
bear...couldn't bear to lose two children."

"Oh God," I whisper.

"I know it was wrong. But I thought I was protecting him. But
he seemed to hate me for it. I couldn't stay. I couldn't look at him
anymore. I knew if I stayed, I'd end up hating him right back."

I touch her hand. "Oh, Julia."

"I left and he went more off the rails and then, at the wedding...I saw them. Jack and Bella. Kissing. We had...we had an
argument, but he wouldn't listen."

I clench my fists and tuck them under my knees.

"I knew he was struggling—drinking and taking drugs. I didn't
want him to drag Bella down with him and I told him to leave
her alone. He said he loved her but I ignored that, told him—
told my *own son* he was a bad influence. The look on his face
when I said it...I told him to get out and he went. But..." She
takes a shallow, shaky breath. "I don't know where he went and
after...after..."

Bella died. After, Bella died. Wearing no underwear or shoes,
full of alcohol and drugs.

"I should have said something to the police when they asked all their questions, but they said it was an accident and...it was Jack, he was my *son*."

I can see the tortured guilt in the twist of her face, the tears on her cheeks.

I move my hand away from her.

"I'm sorry," she says again.

"You should have told Dad—as soon as you found out. You knew what he was capable of. Christ, you left because of it. You should have told him what your son did to his daughter."

She winces and the syringe driver hisses as it administers more morphine. I can see her eyes dulling as it creeps into her bloodstream.

"No," I whisper. "Don't you dare sleep now. Tell me. Tell me what your son did to my sister."

She shakes her head. "He wouldn't have..."

Wouldn't he? I think of how Bella changed, how she started withdrawing, how she and Lena would go off together, shutting me out. Jack did that to her, turned her into someone I no longer recognized. Was he getting her hooked on drugs?

Bella is vivid in my mind when I stand up, in my face, her hair tangled, her eyes burning bright. *Don't*, she says. *Don't get distracted. Remember, remember...*

But I push past her, shoving at empty air as I leave this room full of death. I don't need to remember. I know now. Julia has told me. However Bella died, accidentally or deliberately, Jack is the cause.

CHAPTER 33

I leave Julia's room and go directly across the landing to the room Sean and Jack are sharing, throwing the door open with a bang.

Sean sits up with a gasp, but Jack's bed is empty.

"Where's your brother? Where the fuck is he?" I shout, pulling the quilt off Jack's bed like he might be hiding under there.

"I don't know. What's wrong?"

"He..." I pause, remembering Julia's words. Were they in on it together? Some kind of twisted plan to fuck with their mother's new stepdaughters? If I hadn't kissed Sean first at the wedding, would he have come looking for me? And yes, I kissed him, but he did come looking for me, didn't he? It wasn't me who sought him out.

"I found out," I say, sinking onto Jack's bed. "I found out about him and Bella."

Sean rubs a hand across his face. "But you already knew that, didn't you? They were together on and off for ages before the wedding."

I shake my head. "But the drinking...the *drugs*. She died and it was his fucking fault."

"Tess..." His voice is gentle. "Listen, they might have been...experimenting. But if you're trying to say Jack was in any way responsible—"

"I'm not saying he killed her. God, the whole world has drummed it into me that it was a bloody accident. But she changed. She stopped taking photographs, stopped working hard at school. You know your brother, you know how manipulative he can be. Whatever happened, it was his fault, I know it was."

"But..." Sean gets up, comes to sit next to me. "Even if all this is true, it still doesn't make him responsible for her death."

But I want him to be. I *want* someone to be responsible. Because...because I stopped listening to her. I didn't know any of this was going on because we stopped talking. When I close my eyes, Bella is in front of me and she's crying, standing there in her tank top, jeans half-undone, barefoot. She tried to talk to me and I didn't listen. She was going into the woods alone or not alone. She was walking to Dean House and visiting Greg, who I thought was *my* friend, and, instead of listening to my sister, instead of trying to get her to talk, I recoiled and pushed her away. This admission pulls all the rage out of me and I sag, so tired all of a sudden, tired enough to sink onto the bed that smells of Jack, tired enough to sleep. But I'm close. I sense it. Close to remembering.

My mind skitters away from the nagging memories in panic. I don't need to remember this now. I need to confront Jack, I need to make him admit what he did, make it all his fault, none of mine for not listening. I could have talked to her about Greg and Dean House, but I never knew about Jack, so I couldn't have helped her there, it can't have been my fault if it was Jack's.

"I thought it was him," I whisper—confess. The first time I've spoken these thoughts out loud. Thoughts I've buried for ten years along with the argument we had about it. "I thought it was your father who hurt her and I knew about him, but I never said anything. She told me they were friends," I say. "I reacted like a child, like we were five and she'd stolen my best friend. We argued about it." My breath catches and I pause.

"I didn't understand it. I didn't understand her anymore. I was angry with her for messing everything up—she had it all. She was so bloody beautiful and popular and brilliant. She could have done everything. Then she dropped all her friends and started hanging out with Jack and you and Lena, who wanted nothing more than to get drunk or high, and she fucked up her exams. No one knows that. We got her test results after she died and she failed them all. She was never going to college, even if she'd lived. She was never going to be a teacher, or a photographer, or anything. I was so...so *angry* with her." I take another trembling breath. "I didn't know about Jack and the drugs. I didn't know about Max."

I open my mouth to say something else, but there's a sound from Julia's room and we both freeze. Sean pulls on his jeans and walks across the landing, me following.

He crouches next to Julia and touches her face. "Tess," he says, looking up at me. "Go and get your dad."

My legs are shaking as I go to Dad's room, shaking his shoulder. He opens his eyes and looks at me, but he doesn't ask anything. I think he knows.

Dad sits in the chair next to her bed, Sean on the other side, me standing behind Dad. Her breathing has become shallower and there seems to be an endless gap between breaths.

"Shall I call the doctor?" I whisper.

Dad shakes his head. "There's nothing he can do. We just have to..."

Wait.

Julia opens her eyes and looks at Dad. The morphine glaze seems to have gone, she looks at him and she's fully there, the Julia who moved into this house more than twelve years ago, with her bright red hair and her loud, loud laugh.

God, she had a good laugh. She woke the house up. She woke us all up. I wish I hadn't wasted so much time resenting her at the beginning. I wish I hadn't left her room angry just now. There's no more time to apologize, to explain, to ask. Dad is holding her hand; he leans forward to kiss it, to kiss her cheek and smooth back her hair.

We wait.

The gaps between breaths become longer. There's a lump in my throat, a growing quiet panic in my stomach. No, not yet, not yet, not again. But I can't will her to breathe harder, to breathe faster, I can't will her heart to keep beating, and at three twenty-six in the morning Julia dies.

Sean buries his head in his hands, Dad keeps stroking her hair and whispering things I can't hear, and, behind him, I swallow down the lump in my throat but I can't stop the tears from falling, hot and fast down my cheeks and I'm so sorry I wasn't here more, I'm so sorry I didn't get to hear that bloody great laugh of hers more.

CHAPTER 34

Lena brings the vodka. We sit in a row on the fallen tree in the clearing in the woods where Bella and I were found and she passes the bottle along from her to Max, to Jack to Sean to me. Julia's funeral is tomorrow. I came out here alone. I came here looking for Bella but she wasn't here. I don't know how long I sat on this tree before the others arrived. Not together. Sean first, sitting next to me without a word. Max and Lena then, Lena swinging her bottle, and finally Jack, who wasn't there when his mother died, who's barely said a word since.

We did this before the wedding, but Bella was with us then. It was two or three days before, I can't remember exactly. Bella and I had come here, and the others drifted along, one by one. Who was it that first mentioned the murders of Nicole and the other girl the previous summer? I can't remember, but I remember we passed stories along, like campfire ghost tales, stories that painted a serial killer stalking the village, some twisted perverted monster. It was mostly Lena talking, the rest of us quiet. Bella kept looking at me. It was the next day that we had our fight about Greg.

I take another swig of vodka, feeling the burn right down to my feet. The world keeps doubling, blurring. When I look at the others, sometimes they're as they are now, sometimes they're the teenagers we were ten years ago and Bella is sitting with us. Ghost Bella takes the bottle Lena passes down and tilts it to drink. Tonight's conversation overlaps with our horror stories from then. My hands are shaking when the bottle comes back to me; vodka spills down my chin as I take a drink. It wasn't vodka last time, I remember, it was rum stolen from our kitchen; sweeter, darker, a warmer glow going down.

Jack lights a cigarette, offers the packet to the rest of us. We all take one, like we did that night. I didn't smoke then, not properly, don't smoke now, but I take one and light it anyway and the harsh smoke makes me cough, hurts my chest as I try again, inhaling deeply. I was sick last time—not in front of everyone, but when I got back to the house. It was the last time I smoked until now, first and only time drinking rum.

I wonder if Sean's told them about the camera he found. I think, as we all sit here again, I want to find who we were back then. Maybe we're all captured on that film of Bella's and the nostalgic ache I feel as time slips in and out as the vodka level gets lower makes me long to be back there, Bella safe and alive next to me. I'd talk to her if she were really here. I'd make her tell me what was worrying her, I'd make it all better and, in doing so, I could stop what happened, reverse it, wipe it out.

But maybe I won't find this—togetherness, a group bonded in grief and reminiscence. I'll find instead a secret Bella, proof that I really didn't know her. The Bella who took Max from me, who was taking drugs with Jack. It's taken on too great a significance, a half-full film on an ancient camera that might not even work. I might collect the photos and get an envelope full of blank paper. I don't think so, though. I think I'm going to find my sister again on that film. Something steered Sean to find the camera in the chaos of Dean House—what else but the ghost of Bella, still trying to talk to me?

"We need more booze," Jack says, getting up off the log.

"I'll come with you," I say, jumping up, ignoring Lena's raised eyebrows, Max's startled look. Max stands up as well.

"Do you want me to come?" he asks, and I have to look away from the frown on his face, the one that says he's worried about me. The one that says he's worried what I'll do. It's half concern, half wariness and it's been there since that night in my flat.

"No, it's fine," I say, voice stiff. "I'll be fine."

"I knew you were waiting for a chance to get me alone," Jack says as I follow him along the path, feeling the avid attention of the others burning into my back. "Bit tasteless, though, Tess—the night before my mother's funeral. At least wait until the day after, when I'll be all weak and susceptible from grief."

He says this too loud, still playing the bad-guy role, because he knows the others are still in earshot. A role I know is not an act. I don't answer. What I have to say I don't want the others to hear.

He carries on the teasing at normal volume as we get far enough away not to be overheard. He keeps slipping away—one minute he's three feet in front, his voice almost in my ear, the next he's a hundred feet away. I know it can't be real, so I keep my gaze focused on the path in front of me. I keep seeing flashes of white in the trees, Bella flitting her way between the trees. Also not real, I tell myself.

"You're right," I call. "I did want to get you on your own."

My words stop him dead and he spins round on the path to face me, no longer retreating and advancing, but staying put, planted tall like a tree.

"Julia told me," I say. "Before she died—she told me about you and Bella. About the drugs."

He smiles, laughs. "Seriously? That was my mother's deathbed confession that's had you in such a spin? What—I suppose she made out I was this shady figure tempting precious Bella to the dark side. It's a joke—half of what we took came from Bella, not me." He shakes his head. "Have you any idea how weird you've been acting? Lena's convinced you're the one on drugs."

I wince. I've barely spoken to anyone but Dad in the five days since Julia died. I left a message for Sophie when I knew she'd be at work and haven't taken any of her calls since. I've thrown everything into helping Dad arrange the funeral and avoiding everyone else. I thought I had it together, concentrating hard enough on the little tasks to mask my exhaustion. I thought maybe I'd sleep after Julia died, but instead the insomnia is getting worse and I still haven't found the missing sleeping pills. There's too much happening in my head—every time I close my eyes, all the bad things go skittering through my mind, like monsters released from cages. In the day, I can keep those cages locked, but at night...

"Stop trying to make out that it was nothing—you were Bella's boyfriend when she died. Her bloody *drug dealer*. You were with her that night. She kept you secret. Don't try to make out that it's not significant."

"I wasn't her boyfriend," he says, smile all gone, taking a step closer to me. "We were having sex, that's all. And I wasn't the only one. Come on, Tess, you are not that naïve, not that obsessed still with pretending she was some perfect princess. I was not the only one she was sleeping with. I wasn't even the only one at the bloody wedding she'd slept with. Do not try to turn this into something the day before my mother's funeral."

I step away from him, poised to run. "Scared I'll go to the police and they'll start looking a bit harder at you?"

He smiles again, faintly. "No, just warning you. What do you think I'll tell the police if you send them my way? I'll tell them all the stories about Bella they won't have heard before. And they'll pass those stories on to Leo. Do you think your father wants to hear the police telling him what a little druggy slut his dead daughter was?"

My hand flies back to slap him, but he catches my wrist, squeezes it until I gasp.

"Leave it alone. Leave your dead sister to sleep." He lets go of my wrist and marches away.

"And what about *your* dead sister?" I call after him. "The one you killed?"

He turns back and stares at me, white-faced.

"Julia told me," I say, standing on the balls of my feet, ready to run.

He shakes his head. I expected anger, I expected him to come roaring at me, all rage and denial, but he looks calm, defeated as he stands facing me, shoulders sagging. It's me full of anger, trembling with it. At Jack, who killed his baby sister on an icy road, then came into our lives and took Bella away.

"Look at you," he says. "All righteous anger and disgust. Just like when we were kids, thinking you're so much better than the rest of us."

"You were driving. You caused Ellie's death."

"I was a *kid*. It was an accident. You think because Julia wasn't driving it absolves her of all responsibility? She knew how dangerous the roads were, she was the adult. She chose to take me and Ellie out with her."

"But you were driving," I say again, taking a step closer to him. I want him to admit to what he did. I want him to acknowledge it.

"You think I wasn't fucked up by it? Of course I was—Ellie was my sister. But it was an accident. It destroyed me but it was an accident. And in the aftermath of that, my mother left—walked out on us, couldn't look at me, wouldn't speak to me." He laughs, a wild, bitter sound. "And you think I should have forgiven her? Yes, she said she was driving, but I wish now she hadn't. Maybe if I'd told them the truth, my own mother wouldn't have left us. I went to see her a few nights ago and do you know what her last words to me were? *I forgive you, Jack.* Well, that's bollocks. That's just a slap in the face, isn't it? That's her admitting she couldn't stand the sight of me for ten years, that the reason she left all of us was because of me. And I was a kid, Tess—not much older than you when you lost your sister. Look how much it fucked you up, and you didn't have your parent blaming you for it, did you? So before you come roaring at me about Julia and Ellie, think about that."

I don't want to think about that. I don't want to think of my own guilt, remembering the terrible fight Bella and I had before the wedding. I've told myself the same as Jack is telling me—I was a kid, I can't blame myself for the awful things I said, I was a kid. Jack was seventeen when his sister died. I can't imagine it—can't imagine how he could have dealt with the guilt, the awful, awful memories.

"You didn't have to take it out on us," I say, voice barely more than a whisper. "You didn't have to take it out on Bella."

"Is that what you think?"

"I think you know what happened. I think you know how— why—she died."

He steps closer to me and I force myself not to back away.

"Is this why you're here with me? You think I'm going to confess to something? Well, sorry, Tess, but I don't know what happened to your sister. To me, it was just another person I cared about taken away." He pauses and when he speaks again, his tone is almost gentle. "Truth is, I cared about your sister. I liked her. She got me, we were the same. She was the only person I could talk to and then she died as well."

He reaches out and pushes a lock of hair out of my face. I flinch and pull away.

"I'm not the bad guy this time. I do not have your sister's blood on my hands. Can you say the same?"

"What are you talking about?"

"You and Leo...you're the ones the police keep talking to. They obviously believe you know something about Dad's death. So perhaps you should own up to your own crimes; don't come after me for something I had nothing to do with."

He turns and walks away, leaving me frozen and alone in the woods.

Jack's gone from the house by the time I get there and Dad's out, a note on the table telling me he's gone to pick up Max and Lena's parents from the airport. The house still feels full, though, and it squeezes something tight inside me, the presences I can feel in Dad's house of dead women. No sound but the ticking of Dad's clocks, all out of sync, but beyond it, I swear I can hear breathing. It raises all the hairs on the back of my neck, and my hands are shaking as I step back outside and lock the door. How am I ever going to be able to live here again if I can't even stand to be alone in the house for two minutes without being chased off by ghosts?

I head for the village to collect the film I dropped off. They hand the photos over in a sealed envelope and I resist the urge to tear it open there and then. I put it in my bag and force myself to wait until I'm away from the shops and people, stopping at a bench in the lane back to the house.

My hands are shaking as I open the envelope and my shoulders sag as I look at the first black-and-white photograph. It's a squirrel on a wall, close up and beautifully detailed and shadowed, but it's just a squirrel, not an answer to anything. The next couple are the same—a shot of the woods, moodily shadowed, one of the river, light playing on the water's surface. I pause as I get to the next photograph. It's me, standing in the garden at home, head bowed, curls covering my face. I never noticed her taking this. My heart thumps as I flick through the next ones. They're of Dean House, taken at night. Darkness, dust, the creepiness of those empty rooms captured by Bella in stark black and white.

When did she take these? Did she visit Greg at night? Or did she go there alone—before she took me there? There's the living room, the hallway, the stairs. I stop at the next one and then flick back through the others. What did I see? Something different. There, in the corner of that one. A shadow that when I squint takes on the shape of a figure. Whenever she took these photos, she didn't go there alone.

There's another photo, near the end, that shows the figure with more clarity. It's a boy, facing away from her, dark clothes, head in shadow. I can't tell who it is, but I can guess. I stare harder at the photo, willing it to come to life, willing him to turn and face me so I can be sure. It has to be Jack, who haunted her last months, who took her back to Dean House at night, who's present in these photos, but hiding in the background. Hidden. Secret. Guilty.

The last photo, though, that's the one that steals my breath.

CHAPTER 35

The morning of Julia's funeral, I give up on sleep at six o'clock and tiptoe out of my room. Dad's room is open and empty, so I'm not the only one struggling to sleep. He's nowhere downstairs, and I worry until I catch sight of him in the garden. I fill two mugs with tea and go outside. He's sitting on a peeling wooden chair on the terrace, staring at the daffodils that have just come into flower. Winter has turned to spring in the time I've been here. He doesn't look up or seem to notice my approach and it makes me wonder if this is what he's been doing when no one else was here and his wife was slowly dying upstairs.

"You're up early," I say.

"Couldn't sleep," Dad says. He's staring at the garden, looking so lost and alone in the space that used to be beautiful when Mum tended it. He's huddled in his chair, looking smaller, older. He's only sixty-three, but he doesn't look it today. He looks decades older.

I sit next to him. "Are you thinking of working in the garden again?"

"I was thinking..." His voice drifts off and he sighs. "I don't know if I can do it again, Tess. I looked out and saw the daffodils and..." His voice breaks and he covers his eyes with his hand. I take his other hand, clutching it tight with both of mine.

"The seasons are still going to pass," he says. "Time's going to rush by and I'm going to be alone. I don't think I can keep doing it. I don't think I can go through it again."

My throat closes up, aching with unshed tears. He had me and Bella after Mum died and he had Julia with him after Bella died. But this time...there's only me left. I can feel it all closing in, the dark of the woods creeping closer, trees taller and tighter together. I want to run back to the city, to the safe box I live in, the safe teaching job where every day is the same and no one goes into the woods.

But Dad's alone. He's been alone for months, even when Julia was still breathing upstairs. And I don't have a safe teaching job anymore, do I?

"I'll be here," I say. "I'm not going anywhere."

He looks up and gives me a tired smile. "You have your job—your life in town. I won't let you give it up for me."

"But I don't," I say, the words coming out in a rush. "I have Bella's life, not my own. I never wanted to be a teacher—that was what she wanted. I hate living in a city, I hate the grayness, the claustrophobia, the way I sometimes think I can't breathe, surrounded by so many people. I hate teaching."

"Oh, Tess," Dad says. "I always wondered, when you said you wanted to teach instead of applying for that landscape gardening course you always talked about. But you were so sure, so insistent."

"I'm not going back to teaching. I actually lost my job...no, don't, it's fine," I add when I see Dad react to my words. And actually, it is fine. I feel lighter again as I say the words, like they held weight. "I've already decided. I'm going to apply for a landscape gardening course. I'm going to stay here and commute." I lean over and pull out a weed that's choking a budding rosebush. "This garden can be my homework. We can work on it together like we used to when Mum and Bella were alive. Yes, time will pass. Yes, the seasons will keep turning, but we'll get through it together, as long as it takes."

He shakes his head. "I don't want you to..."

"I won't be giving up anything," I say. "I'll be gaining something. I'll be finding *my* life. We could make it beautiful again," I say. "The two of us working together—me teaching you which are flowers and which are weeds."

"Are you sure, Tess?" he asks. "Sure you want to give up your life to come back here? I've always understood why you've stayed away."

I pull up a few dandelions. "I've been running from it for ten years," I say. "It's no wonder I can't remember what happened— I've been running from everything that reminds me of that summer, living a life that isn't mine, that I never wanted." I pause and sink down to sit on the damp grass. "If I'd stayed, if things had been how they should have been and Bella was still alive, I'd have stayed home and gone to the local college, taken the landscape gardening courses I wanted to take. Bella would have done her teaching course—she'd be the one living in the city. I'd be here or close by, maybe with my own business. That was what I always wanted. Like I said before, Dad, I'm not giving anything up by staying. I'm getting my life back on the track it was meant to be on the whole time."

The vicar clears his throat. "I believe Jack will now come up and speak about Julia."

We look at Jack, sitting farther along the front row. He gets up and goes to the front, standing behind the lectern. He stares straight ahead, then glances at me and smiles. I shiver and have to resist the urge to jump up and stop him from speaking. Wouldn't this be the perfect opportunity to get a final revenge on his mother for leaving him? To devastate us all as a final punishment with twisted lies and accusations?

"What I remember most about my mother," he begins, looking at me and Dad as he says it, "is her coming in when my brother or I had a nightmare. She'd come in and sit by our beds and tell us stories—nice, safe, gentle stories, to help us go to sleep again. She'd say that her stories were magic. That her stories could chase nightmares away, so we only had good dreams. She took her magic stories to another house when I was seventeen." He pauses and takes a deep breath. "I like to think the magic worked there too on her new family."

There's a lump in my throat that aches as he continues talking about a woman I don't know and don't recognize. Dad's squeezing my hand so hard it hurts and I can feel him shaking next to me. I should have offered to speak. I should have done this for him, like I should have been there for him since Bella died, like I should have been there when Julia first got ill.

"I regret not seeing more of her since her wedding to Leo," Jack's saying now, and Dad lets out a shuddering sigh next to me. "I was angry—we were angry, but Mum was happy with her new family, like she was never happy with us. I don't know why, maybe I'll never know now that she's... but I regret it because if I'd got to know Leo and Bella and Tess, I could have had a second family too—this second family who must have been so *special*, so *amazing*, she could walk away from us and not look back." He stops and I think maybe he's getting upset. He looks down and when he looks up, I expect there to be tears, but instead of tears, there's that smile again, bigger, aimed right at me and Dad, who's now openly sobbing.

"Still," he says after a pause that lasts a decade. "It's not too late, is it? Perhaps now that my wife has kicked me out and both my parents are dead, I can move in with Tess and Leo. Play happy families like Julia did."

I stand up as Jack sits down, arms folded, still smiling. It's not fair. Not fair for those to be the only words spoken at her funeral—not fair to Julia, not fair to Dad, who's in no fit state to speak. I move past Dad and walk up to the front, stand next to the vicar.

"I haven't prepared anything," I say. My voice wavers, so I stop and take a breath. I close my eyes, but I feel myself swaying, so I open them again, grip the lectern with both hands. "But as Julia was all about the impromptu, it seems fitting. Impromptu parties, picnics, and barbecues on sunny days, she had the best and finest impulses."

I look away from Jack and his punchable smirk to Dad, gray-faced and red-eyed, and Sean, unsmiling, sitting tall. Max, Lena, and their parents make up the rest of the front row—Julia's family.

"Julia gave my father a second chance at love, and Bella and me a second mother. We didn't think we needed her, but she fit into our lives and filled a gap. She made our family whole again and I wish I'd said that to her more. I wish I'd spent more time telling her how grateful I was for all the love she brought back into our lives. When Bella died..." I pause and swallow. "When Bella died, she held us together, stopped Dad falling apart completely. And she's done it again now. She knew for a long time this day was coming and I think...I think she wanted Jack and Sean to be here, and Max and Lena and their parents—I think she wanted us all together, not for her own sake, but for ours."

I feel Bella's presence next to me and it gives me strength.

"We were splintered and broken for a long time. Too much death, too much loss. I hadn't realized how broken we are, but Julia has laid the framework to fix things. I hope...I hope Jack and Sean want to stay in my dad's life. This is a gift, Julia's final gift, so that's what I'm up here to say. Thank you, Julia. Thanks for everything."

Maybe my words aren't entirely true—do I really trust any of them? I was beginning to—Max and Sean anyway—but everything I've found out...how can I trust any of them when I believe they all have their own agendas for being here? Those photos...so no, my words aren't true but I wish they could be. I wish things were that simple, and I can see from Dad's face what he feels. He squeezes my hand as I sit back down and his eyes shine with tears as the music plays and Joan Baez starts singing "Farewell, Angelina" and we say a last goodbye to Julia.

Sean comes over to me as we all stand outside, Dad accepting condolences from friends and neighbors.

"Did you mean it? About fixing things? Us staying in your lives?"

I can't meet his eye. "Dad needed to hear it. Especially after your brother's words."

"I see. So that was all bullshit." His voice is stiff, expression back to the scowl I remember. It's defensive, that look of his—I've got to know him enough in the last few weeks to realize that. A part of me wants to smooth his ruffled feathers, tell him I do mean what I said, but... I don't know him. The enforced intimacy between all of us, it's not real. We've been thrown together, stripped bare by Julia's illness and death, Greg's body being found, but none of it is real.

Max is watching us from where he stands with Lena and his parents, immaculate in his black suit, hair swept back, handsome and perfect. But the tingle, the thrill I used to feel whenever I saw him, is completely gone. We've all changed, we've all grown up except Bella, who hovers invisible on the periphery, permanently eighteen, stuck in her skinny jeans and tank top, unable to stop bleeding, unable to stop being dead.

"Have you had that film developed?" Sean asks in a low voice.

"Not yet," I say, trying to keep my tone casual. Is it him in the photograph? No, that doesn't make sense. He was the one who gave me the camera in the first place.

It's not finished, Bella says.

I bite my lip. She's standing right next to Sean, her arm touching his. I don't even have to close my eyes to see her anymore. She's crept into my waking world. It makes me think of her sleeping with Max when I dreamed of him being mine. It brings coils of jealousy rising to the surface. My dead sister stands next to Sean and I'm jealous. Of course it's not finished. But I don't know how to end it.

Bella leans forward. *Wake up*.

Wake up? I am awake, I am. I'm always awake.

I walk back to the house ahead of the others to take plastic wrap off the plates of sandwiches, make sure the kettle is full and the wine chilled. I'm glad I do because Detective Levinson is waiting outside the house.

I frown. "You do realize it's my stepmother's funeral today?"

"I'm sorry. I won't be a moment—it was you I wanted to speak to."

He follows me into the house, hovers as I put sandwiches and sausage rolls out on the table.

"We've spoken to people who told us about the relationship Greg Lewis had with Nicole Wallace." He pauses. "Your sister was named as well. As someone who was close to him."

I stop, freezing halfway to the table with a plate of cheese sandwiches in my hand. "They weren't *close*. Not like that—not like you're insinuating. She was going out with Jack, with Greg's *son*, for God's sake." I stop and shake my head. "These are all just rumors, though, aren't they? Even if Bella was hanging out with Greg—Mr. Lewis—that doesn't mean..."

"Of course. I just wanted to make you aware. Also...there's something else."

"What?" I glance toward the window. The first people from the funeral are making their way up the lane.

"You told us you barely knew Greg Lewis, that you'd stopped working in the garden of Dean House. But you were seen. In the gardens with Mr. Lewis. Several people have told us you were there on many occasions right up to when he...disappeared."

I'm flooded with memories of dirt under my nails, weak tea and ginger nut biscuits in a half-finished garden, muscles aching from digging. Old books about gardening, lessons about Latin names, lessons about plants and flowers.

"It was a long time ago," I say. "I...I don't remember exact times. But I *had* stopped. All your witnesses, they're the ones who are mistaken. Telling you about my visits would have muddied things. It would have stopped you from seeing—"

"Tess, it's not your sister's death that's concerning us right now. It's Greg Lewis's, who was murdered. We know your state of mind is fragile right now. The incident at your school, the insomnia. You have to appreciate it looks..."

Suspicious. It looks suspicious. If I were on the outside looking in, I'd have the handcuffs out. I'd be arresting the crazy woman who attacks her students and sees her dead sister.

"Who told you, anyway? Was it Jack or Lena? You know he's trying to stir things up, trying to implicate me or Dad..."

"I'm aware of the lingering hostilities. But you need to come into the station to answer some more questions. Tell us more about this... *friendship* between you, Greg Lewis, and your sister. There may be things you remember that can help us."

"You need to go," I say through numb lips. "I have fifty people coming back here from my stepmother's funeral. You need to go."

"I will. But don't go anywhere, Tess. And you need to come to the station. I'll expect you in the morning."

What will I say when he asks those questions? Will I tell him about the last photo that was on the film in Bella's camera? The photo that's making me wonder... oh, it's making me wonder the most awful things. Or will I tell him about the final argument I had with Bella and the terrible lie I told?

When did you stop sleeping, Tess? Bella whispers.

Was it after I died? Or was it before? What is it that's waking you up every night? What do you need to remember?

THEN

CHAPTER 36

AUGUST 2008

It's four days before the wedding and we're trying on the brides-maid's dresses. I no longer have dirt under my nails. Bella is trying to do up the zipper on my dress. I've been sneaking downstairs at night and eating, unable to sleep until Bella gets in from wherever she's been sneaking off to. She's struggling to pull the zipper and I'm hot from humiliation, a scenario playing in my mind of having to go downstairs and tell Dad and Julia that I no longer fit into the dress.

There's a tug and a whoop and the zipper is pulled up. It's so tight I can barely breathe but it's on.

"You look gorgeous," Bella says as she steps next to me, but I turn away from the mirror. Her dress, two sizes smaller than mine, is loose around her waist. I frown. Julia already had to have it taken in on the last fitting and now it's too big on her again. But the mint green goes beautifully with her blond hair and, even too skinny and pale, she looks like a princess. The jealousy is like hot needles pricking my skin. All I can imagine is Max, Sean, Jack—all of them—watching Bella walk up the aisle behind Julia. Then I picture them looking from her to me. My wicked imagination even puts Greg in the picture, watching from the entrance of the hall.

I want to take off the dress and take off my sixteen-year-old skin, peel off all the misery and aching want.

Bella's face grows somber. Does she feel it too? Despite her beauty and the fact that everyone wants her, does she feel any of that misery? Of course she does.

"Tess, did Dad say anything to you about—?"

A car door slams and Bella spins around, her lace skirts

swirling, her question forgotten, a smile growing on her face that chases away the sadness that was there only a few seconds before. "They're here."

The next day, the chaos of pre-wedding planning and the relentless heat has chased us into the woods. It's only supposed to be a small wedding—the ceremony at the town hall, followed by a reception at home. But it keeps getting bigger and bigger, ten people becoming twenty becoming forty. Now there are four crates of champagne filling the kitchen and the plan for sandwiches and homemade sausage rolls has become a formally catered buffet. None of our moods are helped by the onset of a heatwave. Instead of lying around in the shade, the four of us were sweating as we carried hired chairs and glasses in and out of rooms, Jack and Sean nowhere to be bloody found. After Bella lost her temper over a dropped glass, Dad told us to take a break.

We haven't come to the woods, just the two of us, for such a long time. The sun filters through the trees, making the light stripes of green and gold. It's warm on my skin and I'm only wearing a T-shirt and shorts, my freckled knees dappled with bruises from banging them on the stacks of chairs we've been ferrying about. Bella sits next to me on a log, throwing stones into the almost dried-up stream. Her own legs in cut-off denim shorts are long and brown, smooth and freckle-free. But she's gotten too thin. When did she get so thin and drawn-looking?

The stream smells stagnant, mud and rotting leaves and God knows what else sluggishly floating downstream. The smell coats the inside of my nose like something corporeal and I know it'll linger there long after we get up and go home. Bella has the old camera next to her, the one Greg gave her.

"You have to stop going there," I say.

"Going where?"

"To see him. Greg."

Bella laughs. "What—are you my mother now, giving me orders?"

"You told *me* not to go there."

She glances at me, a frown on her face. "That's different. I can look after myself."

"What—and you think I can't? I'm sixteen, not six."

There's a long pause and I watch Bella dropping stones, a far-away look on her face.

"Tess? Did he ever touch you?"

My face goes hot. I can feel the sweat leaking through my T-shirt. "Touch me?"

"Touch you—hurt you?"

"Bloody hell, Bella—shut up!"

The squirming distaste her words elicit is as stagnant and rotten as the stream. Her words put that ugliness inside me. What I'm remembering is me lurching toward him, trying to kiss him. God. Greg Lewis. It's her fault—her fault for telling me Max only saw me as a sister, making me humiliate myself trying to prove her wrong.

"God, of course not. Ugh, I can't believe you'd—"

"He tried to kiss me."

Stop. Stop. Her words are a slap in the face. He pushed me away, rejected me, was embarrassed by my stupid, clumsy pass. I remember the things he said about Bella and her friends, the squirm of fear I felt.

She keeps talking. "And I keep thinking about Nic, how she used to go on about him, about how sexy he was for an older man. I knew she had a secret boyfriend, someone besides Jack, but she refused to tell me about him. And now she's dead and Greg grabbed me and kissed me and it was awful, it was like he was a stranger and..."

It feels like worms are crawling under my skin. The worst part of it is not the horror I feel, the jitter of fear, but the thread of something like jealousy, of something like hurt, because, once again, it's her, always her who gets chosen. It's not *fair*, I want to cry.

"Well, he didn't just kiss me," I shout at her. All a lie, stupid fat lies that come hurtling out. "He took me up to his bedroom and he did more than just touch me."

He didn't. He never did. He listened to me when I told him about Max, the crush I had. I told him, as we pruned roses and dug in the dirt. I told him about boys at school I had feelings for who never liked me back because they always saw Bella and liked her. Mugs of tea and soft ginger biscuits and sympathy and knowledge, that was what he gave me. Until I tried to kiss him and ran off and hadn't been able to go back since.

I don't want to believe it. Bella...Nicole...he wouldn't have. Why would he? But if he didn't, then Bella is lying to me, and why would she lie about that?

But I lie right back, such ugly, rotten, stagnant lies. "I went round there because I felt sorry for him because of the wedding and he gave me whisky and he...he started touching me." I watch her face twist with revulsion, I watch her recoil and I'm glad to have shocked her, glad to have taken something from her.

"What did he do, Tess?" I hear the warning in her voice, but I can't stop.

"He had sex with me." The lie bursts out and my cheeks flood with color.

Bella's hands squeeze mine too tight and tears spring into her eyes. "Oh God. Oh, Tess..."

The horror on her face makes me scrabble for other words, something to undo what I just said. I wanted to make her jealous. I thought...I thought she liked him, but she's looking at me in a way that makes me feel dirty. "I tried to stop him like you did but he wouldn't stop. I didn't want to, but he made me..." I want to scrub at my own skin, sew my mouth shut. I'm saying this, spilling lies, none of it true. Greg never once looked at me in that way. Why did I say it? Because I wanted to punish him for pushing me away? Punish Bella because he wanted to kiss her?

Bella is breathing fast. She jumps up, starts pacing around. "We have to go to the police, tell them what he did to you. We have to—"

"No!" I get up and grab her arm. "I can't. I can't go to the police. Everyone would find out. I can't do it."

"Tess—we can't let him get away with this. He's a rapist, a pedophile..."

I shake my head, my lies blooming, building into something awful as Bella paces around. "What if it's him?" Bella says. "What if he was Nic's secret boyfriend? He tried to kiss me too and...the way he was, it was inappropriate. And Lena says he was the same with her. She thinks that's why Julia left him, not because of Ellie." She stops pacing and stares at me, her eyes huge. "What if he killed those girls? What if you're next?"

Her words turn my stomach and I push past her to lean over the stream, only just making it before adding a splatter of vomit to the rotting trickle of brown water. Oh God, oh fucking hell, what have I done? I've started something and I don't know how to stop it. I can't tell her I was lying. Why would someone lie about that? I start crying and sink down onto the bank as she sits next to me and strokes my hair.

"No—stop it. It's not...he's not a bloody murderer. He's Julia's ex, Jack and Sean's dad."

"He raped you," she says, her voice so damned cold.

"It wasn't like that! You have to promise me you won't say a word. To anyone. The wedding's in three days—if you say anything, it would kill Dad and Julia. And I can't...I won't say anything. God, you know what this village is like." My panic grows as my lie takes root and spreads. I can see it in her face, filling her up, eating her up. "Please, Bella—promise me you won't say a word."

She pulls me toward her and I bury my head in her T-shirt.

"Okay, little sis," she whispers. "It'll be our secret."

It's been two days since that awful confrontation with Bella in the woods. I've been out looking for her because the thread of fear that she'll say something keeps growing bigger.

Dad and Julia are in the kitchen, talking in low voices. They're

surrounded by stacks of plates and boxes of glasses, and Julia's
dress is hanging in a zipped-up carrier on the back of the door.

My heart flutters. "What's up?" I say, trying to keep my voice
steady. Maybe Bella has said something and that's what Julia and
Dad are talking about. I feel sick and wish I hadn't come in and
interrupted them.

I'm sorry, I'll say. *It's not true, Bella got it wrong. She*—

"It's Greg," Julia says. "He's gone."

"Gone? Gone where?"

"We don't know. The boys have been away with friends and
when they got back to the house, it was locked up and he was
gone. Suitcase, passport . . . all gone."

I sit down. Oh God, is this because of me? My stupid mistake
trying to kiss him, the horrible things I said? Has Bella been round
there, accusing him with all my lies?

"Did he leave a message?"

"Apparently he texted Jack to say he was going away for a
while." Julia glances at Dad. "He couldn't cope with the wedding,
he said."

That isn't right. He wasn't bothered about the wedding, I could
see that when I went round there.

"So Jack and Sean are . . ."

"They're here," Dad says. "We've told them they can stay as
long as they like. Until Greg comes back."

"But—"

"I don't want them staying in that house alone, Tess. Jack might
be over eighteen, but Sean isn't. And it's my wedding—I want
them here, they *should* be here with me. With us."

Julia frowns and squeezes Dad's hand. "This will make it easier,
Leo. If Greg stays away, there's no risk of . . ."

"Risk of what?" I blurt out.

"Tension," Julia says. "Greg's been making things difficult."

"Difficult how?" My mind is swirling. He told me he wasn't
bothered, he sounded so casual about it.

"Coming over, threatening Leo."

"Threatening? When did this happen?"

"It doesn't matter now," Dad says, but he doesn't look at me as he says it. "He's gone—the wedding will be perfect now." He leans over and kisses Julia and I turn away.

None of this seems right. I can't imagine Greg threatening Dad. He genuinely didn't seem bothered about the wedding. But... but what if the threats had nothing to do with the wedding? What if he came round after I tried to kiss him and said those terrible things? A picture grows in my mind of Greg telling Dad to keep me away from him; of Greg telling Dad I had some stupid stalker crush on him, telling him about the kiss. Was that why Dad couldn't look at me?

All these awful thoughts and more, they won't go away. My dad is so mild and gentle, but what would he do if Julia's ex told him his baby daughter had been round his house drinking and kissing him? What would it take to make my quiet father snap?

And where has Greg gone? What about his business? What about his sons? Did I do this with the angry threats I screamed at him when I went there? I think about the lies I told Bella and the trickle of fear becomes a full-on flood. What if she went round there and confronted him with what I said to her? If she did, then this is my fault. I made him run. How am I supposed to even look at Jack and Sean now? They're going to know— they're going to see guilt in my face.

The wedding is tomorrow. I have to speak to Bella. I have to tell her the truth before my lies get out and blow this whole thing apart.

AUGUST 2008: THE DAY OF THE WEDDING

I wince as a hairpin jabs into my head but don't say anything be- cause Julia is working miracles. I watch in the mirror as she tames my frizz into a sleek coiled updo that makes my face look thinner and more...grown up. Her own hair is a mass of curlers and she's still in her bathrobe. She shouldn't be wasting her time on me on her own wedding day but she insisted.

She catches my eye in the mirror and smiles. "What do you think?"

"I love it," I say, smiling back. "Can you get up at six and do my hair like this every day?"

She laughs and steps back. "There, you're done." She pauses. "Thank you, Tess."

"For what?" I say, getting up and unzipping the dress carrier hanging on the front of my wardrobe.

"For everything."

"It's going to be brilliant," I say. "The weather is perfect and we have enough champagne to get the whole world drunk."

"Well then," she says. "I'd better go and get ready, hadn't I?"

Bella comes in as Julia leaves and my smile fades. We haven't spoken since the weird trip to Dean House last night, but in the light of day, I can see how thin and tired she looks. She's been acting weird for days and the look she shoots me now is angry, like I've done something wrong. It makes my stomach turn over—does she know? Has she guessed I lied to her? I feel sick. Why did I say it? Why, why, why? I've tried to tell her the truth, so many times. Even last night, when she took me to Dean House, I wanted to tell her but the words wouldn't come out.

I sip champagne and stand in the shadows watching Dad and Julia dance to the live jazz band they've hired for the reception. It's such a beautiful day. The forecast has been threatening a break in the heatwave, promising storms, but there's no sign of it yet, other than a single dark cloud in the sky. The day has been perfect—bittersweet for me, watching Dad marry someone else. Bella disappeared with Max and Lena as soon as the ceremony was over and I've been wandering round like a spare part ever since, pinching too many glasses of champagne.

I blink as I see someone come in through the side gate. It's Max.

Where has he been? He's frowning and staring down at his phone as he walks toward the house and I impulsively follow him.

I find him in the kitchen filling a glass from an open bottle of champagne.

"Is there enough in there for me?" I ask, keeping my voice light. I stand next to him as he fills my glass and his arm brushes against mine. My heart is pounding. I've hardly seen him in the buildup to the wedding and this is the first time we've been alone in forever.

He fills the glass too fast and the champagne fizzes over the top and down my arm.

"Shit," he says, reaching for a cloth. "Fuck's sake. Sorry, Tess."

"It's fine," I say, laughing. "Are you okay? You seem distracted."

"What? Oh no—I'm fine."

I lean down to lick a drop of champagne off my wrist and when I glance up, he's looking at me. This has to be it, the moment. I reach up and brush my lips against his.

He jerks back so hard his arm hits mine and champagne spills all down the front of my dress.

"Christ, Hardy-girl," he says. "What was that?"

My face floods with color while his pales and there's a tic going in his cheek.

"Look, Tess, you didn't think..." His voice trails off and I rush to interrupt.

"Ha, sorry! Too much champagne, I think. Ignore me. Forget this ever happened." I turn to go so he can't see my eyes filling with stupid tears and my back stays rigidly straight as I walk away, wanting him to call me back, wanting him to bloody kiss me back.

But he doesn't and I speed up, walking through the garden, right to the back where I can hide my humiliation in the shadows of the overgrown fruit trees, still clutching my empty glass, the front of my dress sopping wet.

"Need a top-up?"

I glance back to see Sean behind me, a full bottle of champagne in his hand.

"Oh no, not *you*. Seriously, why don't you just fuck off?"

He stiffens and turns away but I grab his arm. "Wait—I'm sorry. Ignore me. And yes, actually, I *do* want a drink." I hold my glass out.

He stares at me with a frown on his face and I think he's going to walk off, but then he shakes his head and half smiles. "I don't get you sometimes."

"Yeah? Well, I don't get me, either."

"I never thought they'd actually go through with it," he says as he fills my glass to the brim. "Cheers." He clinks the bottle against my glass and tilts it back to drink.

"Neither did I," I admit. "But...they look happy, don't they?"

"Do you think so? I think they're fooling themselves."

I frown. "Do you have to be so bloody bitter all the time?"

He looks at me and laughs. "Says the girl who just told me to fuck off."

He sighs and takes another swig of champagne. "Everything's just so weird—Dad's gone, Julia's got a new family. I haven't...it doesn't feel like I've got a home anymore."

"Aren't you back at boarding school next month?"

"Doesn't mean I don't want a home to come back to."

I don't tell him he could come back here. I don't want him coming back here. Right now, with humiliation filling my veins instead of blood, I don't want any of them coming back here.

"I guess it's like that for you as well. Bella will be off to college. It'll just be you left."

My glass is empty again and the world is starting to look fuzzy. "It's felt like it's just me left for a while now," I say. "Bella's been acting so weird, spending all her time with Max and Lena and Jack."

"You could always visit me at school—I'm not that far from here," Sean says after a pause, filling my glass again, watching as I take a massive swig.

"Visit you? Why would I want to visit you?" It's the champagne that makes these blunt words come out and I regret them as I see his cheeks go red.

"Yeah well, I...it doesn't matter."

I can see Bella talking to Max at the top of the garden, leaning in really close, a glass of champagne in her hand, Jack hovering near the band, watching them. I turn to look at Sean at the same time as he turns to me and I don't know if it's him or me who leans in first, but then we are kissing. But when I close my eyes, the world started to spin and I have to pull away.

I open my eyes and, for a second, he isn't Sean, he's Greg, and my stomach somersaults remembering the lies I told Bella.

"Sorry," I say. "Too much. Too much champagne. But I like you too." I sink down onto the grass, my eyes closing. Too much. All too much.

NOW

CHAPTER 37

I wake with vomit in my mouth, sour and bitter. I swallow it down and gag. My head feels groggy, my eyes are gritty. Just a dream, I tell myself. Just my brain warping memories. It's not real, not the truth. But the memory, not one that's been lost, but one I've tried so hard to forget, is ugly enough and my cheeks grow hot thinking about it.

She raged like fire when I said it, my lies about Greg Lewis. Raged and talked about the police and revenge and proof. She raged that it was true, all true, the rumors. Him and teenage girls—I was her proof. My lies were her proof. He was a pedophile. He was the one who killed Nicole Wallace and that other girl. She was convinced because of what I told her. What did she do? What did my sister do with the lies I fed her?

And Dad...Dad, who's been down to the police station twice now, who had a fight with Greg, who never asks me what I remember about the night of the wedding. I always thought he was trying to protect me from remembered trauma. But what if Bella went to him, told him the lies I told her? I shudder. If Bella told him, did he go raging after Greg? No, he couldn't have. My dad is not a murderer. But what about Bella? She was so angry. Oh God, oh God.

I look down at the photograph I went to sleep clutching, the last photo from Bella's camera. It's him, Greg, standing at the top of his stairs, bare-chested, looking confused and frightened, night sky in the window behind him, shielding his face from the glare of the flash.

Did she go there for me, whatever night this was captured on her camera? Did she go there for her proof, for her revenge?

I'll have to tell all this to the detective. Tell him everything about my relationship with Greg, about Bella's, about all the fears his own sons had about him and those two murdered girls. I'll have to tell him the lies I told my sister and how she took me back there the night before the wedding and how she looked out into the woods and cried. How the house was empty, how he'd already gone. Oh God, I *can't*. How will it look? I'm due down there this morning to answer more questions. How can I tell them all this and not have me, Dad, even Bella look guilty?

If it was Bella, if it was her who...it was my fault. I made her do it. But. But there was someone else with her, half revealed in the photographs. Who was it? Someone else knows what happened to Greg, someone else was with my sister when she went there looking for her *proof*.

Dad drives me to the police station and I'm silent the whole way, jittery with nerves. He parks outside and reaches to squeeze my hand.

"Did Bella tell you?" The words burst out of me.

"What?"

"Before the wedding—did she tell you about Greg and...what she believed he did?"

I look at him but there's nothing but confusion on his face. And worry. There's worry there too.

"Tess, sweetheart, I don't know what you're asking. What did Greg do?"

I shake my head. "Nothing. Sorry. Ignore me."

"I'm scared, Tess," he says in a low voice. "Why do the police keep questioning you? Is there anything...? You know you can tell me anything, don't you?"

"I didn't do anything," I say, and he squeezes harder.

There are tears in his eyes and he looks so much older and I hate that this is happening now, the day after his wife's funeral. I hate Greg Lewis for doing this to him.

"I know," he says, his voice breaking. "It's just routine, isn't it? It'll be okay, Tess."

But will it? I can't remember what happened, which means I can't remember anything to clear my name, either. What if they arrest me? Fear squeezes me tighter than Dad's hand clutching mine and I can't breathe. Oh God, how can this be happening? I want to run away, run and hide somewhere with my hands over my ears and my eyes tight shut.

I take a shaky breath and pull my hand away from Dad. I force a smile. "Okay, here we go. I'll be home soon, okay?"

"I'll wait."

"You don't have to—I don't know how long I'll be."

"I'll wait," he says again.

They take me to a different room this time, a gray room with a table and two hard chairs. They ask me if I want a lawyer present and I shake my head. I haven't done anything—I won't let any of them scare me. I don't need a lawyer; I just need them to believe me. Bella takes the seat next to me, solemn-eyed and quiet.

"Okay, Tess—you're not under arrest and you can leave at any time," Detective Levinson says after setting up the tape recorder. "This is a voluntary interview but you are under caution—you do not have to say anything, but it may harm your defense if you do not mention when questioned something which you later rely on in court. Anything you do say may be given in evidence. Do you understand?"

"Yes." Despite my determination not to be scared, my voice is wobbly.

"Tell me about your relationship with Greg Lewis."

"I told you before—we didn't have a *relationship*. I helped out in his garden. We met all of them when they moved to the village."

"So the relationship was never sexual?"

I flinch; can't help it. Of course, they notice. "I was fourteen when I met him—no, it wasn't sexual."

"But you were sixteen when he disappeared."

"And he was forty."

"We have witnesses who claim he had several relationships with girls under eighteen."

I clear my throat. "Well, I wasn't one of them."

"Helena Rees has told us she believes he was in a relationship with Nicole Wallace, and Nicole's father has confirmed she had a boyfriend at the time of her disappearance."

"He knew she was with Greg? No. That can't be right . . . when she went missing—he'd have told you if he knew. It was *Jack* she was going out with."

"Unfortunately, he was unaware of the identity of the boyfriend. Our initial lines of inquiry at the time were that she ran away with someone. Jack Lewis had an alibi." He pauses. "And no one came forward to suggest Greg Lewis even knew her."

The criticism is implicit. What—does he think we all closed ranks to protect . . . who? Nicole or Greg? Or . . . I go cold. Does he think ranks closed to protect *me*?

"Helena also told us about a couple of incidents with her and with your sister. Inappropriate behavior."

I clench my teeth but don't say anything.

"Let's talk about Rebecca Martin."

"What? What on earth does Rebecca Martin have to do with anything?"

"We know about the recent assault, but your head teacher has also told us you have a history with Rebecca."

I shake my head. "No, there was a misunderstanding, that's all. I tried to help her."

"They've told us you were so convinced she was being abused that you reported it to the police when you had no evidence. Why were you so convinced, Tess?"

"There were photos on her phone—that's the only reason I took it. And I saw . . . I saw fear on her face. I did, I didn't imagine it."

Detective Levinson leans forward. "Is it because it happened to you? Or your sister?"

I lean back and fold my arms. "None of this has anything to do with—"

"Tess. We know Greg Lewis raped you."

My hands curl into fists. "No. No, he didn't."

"If it's true, if he did that, then it's understandable if you fought back. If it was an accident, or self-defense..."

I shake my head. "No. I didn't do anything. He didn't do anything. I told you—I hadn't seen him for weeks before the wedding."

Detective Levinson exchanges a glance with the second detective in the room.

"Tess—we found his phone in your room."

"What? You've been in my flat?"

He shakes his head. "In your father's house. We had a warrant to search it."

"But you can't have!"

"Can you think of any reason his phone would be there?"

I shake my head. "No. Stop. Stop this. It wasn't me." I fumble in my pocket and pull out the photograph, crumpled and creased. "This was on my sister's camera. There's someone else there—my sister was in his house at night with someone else."

There's a pause as Detective Levinson looks at the photograph. "What does this prove?" he asks me. "You could have taken this photograph."

I shake my head. "It was Bella's camera. Ask Sean—he found the camera. He found it in Dean House when he was clearing out his dad's stuff. I can barely manage to take a decent shot on my phone. Bella was the photographer."

"Do you know who the other person in the photograph is?"

"No, but if you can find out, you'll know..."

I stop. He's right. The photo proves nothing.

"We were at the house the night before the wedding," I say, and I see the detective's shoulders stiffen. "Bella took me there. The house was empty and she was crying and looking into the woods."

"What are you saying? Do you think it was your sister? Your dead sister who isn't here to answer any of our questions?"

I don't know. The way he says it—it makes it sound like I'm

trying to blame Bella to get myself out of trouble. I have nothing concrete. I've never mentioned any of this before, not even when they questioned me after the wedding, a decade before anyone knew Greg Lewis was dead.

I listen back to my own words as a hallucination of my dead sister sits bleeding next to me and I sound despicable. I hate myself as Bella's blood flows faster and pools around my feet.

"I want to go now," I say, pushing my chair back. "Can I? You said I could leave anytime. Or am I under arrest?"

Detective Levinson shakes his head. "You're free to go at the moment. But Tess?" he says as I stand to leave.

"Don't go anywhere, okay? We'll be talking to you again."

CHAPTER 38

Dad looks as though he hasn't moved the whole time I've been away when I slide into the passenger seat next to him. I see him visibly relax and it only frightens me more. He was expecting me not to come out, he was afraid I'd be arrested. The thought is huge and ridiculous but terrifyingly real. They just interviewed me under caution, so they might. They might actually arrest me for this. For murder. But I didn't. I *didn't*. I couldn't have. But the panic keeps growing because of the little voice that keeps saying maybe I *did*. Maybe I *could* have.

"Was it..." he begins, his voice trailing off.

"When did they search the house?" My voice is raised. I can't help it.

"The day before yesterday. You were out and..."

"And you didn't think to tell me?"

"I'm sorry, but the last few days, the funeral—everything's been so traumatic, I didn't want to worry you more." He pauses. "And there was nothing to find, was there? Nothing to worry about."

"Of course. It's fine, Dad. Today was just routine, like you said. Let's go home." I look out of the window as I speak. I don't want him to see the fear on my face. Who put that phone there? And where was it found? Those gaps in my memory from the night of the wedding and before. I'm so fucking scared of what's in them.

Max is waiting when we get back to the house, his face somber. "I'll make you both some tea," he says. "And then why don't you both get some rest? It's been a tough few days."

It's only early afternoon, but both Dad and I take the tea Max gives us upstairs. I'm so exhausted I really do think I can sleep the rest of this awful day away. The tea is too strong but I'm so thirsty

I drink it. My legs feel like lead weights and the simple task of going to the bathroom to get water seems like an impossible task right at this moment. All I want to do is sink into bed and sleep...

"Tess? Tess! Wake up."

Max is shaking my shoulder and I struggle to open my eyes. The room is dark and it takes a moment for my eyes to adjust. He's sitting on the edge of the bed and I frown. He's holding Bella's camera.

"Where did you get that?" My words come out slurred. What time is it? How long have I been asleep?

He looks at the camera in his hand. "I found it downstairs—it was on the table."

No, it wasn't. Unless Sean left it there...

"You had it all along?" he says.

I shake my head to try to clear it. My box of sleeping pills is open on the cabinet next to the bed, but I don't remember taking one. I haven't seen the pills since they went missing last week.

Once upon a time...Bella's voice whispers in my head.

"So where's the film?" Max asks.

I think of the photo of Greg, the last one on the film, the shadowy unidentified figure.

"There was no film in it."

He looks at me. "Really?"

I nod, swallowing down the dryness in my throat.

He laughs and it sounds so odd in the stillness of the night, so *wrong*.

"I was so worried about that bloody camera. Bella wouldn't tell us where she'd hidden it, told us she was going to take it to the police to prove..."

"To prove what?"

He smiles at me, but it's Max the stranger, the one I met in my flat.

"Why did you do it, Tess?"

"What? Why did I do *what*?"

"You didn't have to kill him. We would have helped you. Bella…all she wanted to do was help you. You didn't have to kill him." Max strokes my hair and I feel my eyes drifting shut, my mind drifting.

No.

That's not right.

I need to stay awake and *think*.

It wasn't me…

I didn't…

I…

Wake up, Tess.

The words are hissed in my ear in Bella's voice and it pulls me awake. I don't…I'm not in bed anymore. I'm in a car and Max is driving. What? Where are we going? I can feel myself drifting again and I swear I feel Bella's hand on my shoulder, squeezing, keeping me awake, pushing me along toward the truth. Problem is, I'm no longer sure I *want* to remember. Once upon a time, two girls went into the woods and only one came out. I'm less scared about getting to the end of the story than I am of finding out the beginning—why the two girls went into the woods in the first place. Did one of them do something awful, something that merits a whole story in its own right, something so terrible it never made it into the storybook, because it was too grim even for a Grimm's fairy tale?

The car slows and we pull up outside Dean House. Of course. Of course it would be here.

Max comes round and opens the car door. He looks hollowed out, as tired as me. What's keeping him awake at night? Does he hear his own beating heart under the floorboards? It feels like months since I got the phone call from Dad to tell me Julia was dying, not weeks. Months since Max called, me still holding him in my heart then as some tender thing. What is he now? Now that we've slept together and I've seen his stranger's face?

"What are we doing here?"

He grips my arm as I stumble getting out. My legs feel numb. "We need to talk. Away from your house."

"It's you, isn't it?" I say, as he half drags me into the house. "It was you in the house with Bella. You in the photograph."

He looks puzzled, but the look is fake. I saw the skittering look of fear first. "What are you talking about?"

"You were at the house when Greg disappeared. When he died."

"There was film in the camera, then," he says flatly.

I nod.

"Where is it?"

"Safe. I don't have it with me."

"This is all Jack and Sean's fault. Why did they have to sell the house?"

God, I thought I loved him when I was fourteen. "What did you do?" I say, and my voice breaks on the last word.

He turns to look at me. "Me? I didn't do anything. It was you, Tess. It was you. We all...we all went along with your fake memory loss. We stuck together like friends should."

"You were looking for the camera in my flat, weren't you? I thought..."

"You thought what? That I was overcome with desire?" He smiles. "Poor Tess."

"Shut up."

"Your sister made us cover it up. Hide what you did."

"I didn't do anything. It wasn't me. It was..."

"Who? *Me*? Your *sister*? Your sister was the one who made us go there. Telling us stories. Telling us he was a sick old pedo, telling us what he did."

"Does she have the photos?"

I turn as Lena steps out of the living room.

"I should have known."

Lena laughs. "Should have known what?"

"Should have known you'd be involved."

"Of course you assume the worst, don't you? Still in denial. You with your superior sneer. It has to be Lena, doesn't it? Lena the troublemaker. Of course I have to be a murderer as well."

"I know you were at the house with Bella."

"I told her about him watching you, you know," Lena says. "The dirty bastard watching you digging about in his garden."

I shake my head.

"Bella told us. She told us he'd groomed you. She told us he got you there in the house and—"

"*No.*"

"What did he do, Tess? Did he fuck you? Did he rape you in his dusty old torture chamber? Did he whisper what he did to those other girls as he slipped his hand under your shorts?"

My hand flies out to slap her and she grabs my wrist, squeezing it until I cry out.

"We were there to defend you, you little bitch. We were there to find evidence that he was a kiddy-fiddling serial killer." She laughs. "You think it was just you? He tried it with me, he tried it with Bella. If he'd had the opportunity, all of us would have been dead, more of his victims. You did the right thing, killing him."

"But I *didn't*..." I step back, stumble over a chair.

"I told the police. I told them everything. You'll be okay. Even with the phone they found, you can tell them it was self-defense."

The whole world is spinning. Her words, her relentless words...did I? Was it me? Was it? I don't understand...she won't shut up. Keeps saying it over and over—it was you, Tess, you did it. But I didn't, I wouldn't...

Wait. How does she know about the phone?

No. It was Bella. It was my sister, with Max and Lena. I saw the look on her face when I told her my lies. That awful burning anger, the recoil of disgust. She told me he tried to kiss her and I was jealous. Not concerned, *jealous.* She came home that night, she got into my bed, and I *knew* something was wrong. I should have kept asking, should have made her tell me, but all I did was add fuel to the fire. Was it more than a kiss? Her clothes were torn and she was shaking and...He'd already tried something with her and I let her think he'd been abusing me. She went round there full of rage and I might as well have been there with her because it was me that sent her there.

Lena steps closer and my heart is pounding. We both freeze as car headlights brighten the room. I shove past her and run down the hallway. Jack and Sean are getting out of Jack's car.

"Where's Dad?" I say, stopping short and turning to look at Max and Lena.

"He's fine. He's at home, sleeping like a baby," Max says. "We called Jack and Sean. They deserve to know the truth about what happened to their father. Isn't that why you've asked us all to come here?"

I shake my head. "But I didn't. You brought me here. I was sleeping and I woke up in your car."

Max frowns. "No, you asked to come here, Tess. We thought you wanted to confess—to tell us the truth before you told the police."

But...

"Come on," Max says, his voice gentle. "Come with me. Just tell us what happened with Greg and we can make it all better. Everyone's worried about you. You need help. Some time somewhere safe, with doctors to sort out your...problems."

"No, you don't understand. I know what you did. You..."

He reaches over and strokes my hair. I close my eyes and sway.

"Come on," he whispers, leading me to the sofa. "It'll all be fine."

I sit down and my eyes drift shut. This is better. He's right. I'll rest my eyes for a moment before Jack and Sean come in. Rest my eyes and clear my head of all this confusion. Then I'll go home and tell Dad everything and we can go to the police together.

Bella is next to me, shouting *wake up wake up wake up*, but I can't. I'm drifting back into sleep, the taste of rotten leaves in my mouth and Max's hand is warm on my head as he strokes my hair. I don't know why he brought me to the house, but he's rescuing me, whether from Jack or myself I don't know and I don't know what he and Lena were talking about trying to say it was me who killed Greg but...

I try to open my eyes. This isn't right and Bella is still shouting.

"What are you doing?" The words come out slurred.

His hand moves away from my hair as he stands up. "I'm sorry, Tess."

Wake up, Bella screams, but I can't...

CHAPTER 39

"I'm sorry, Tess," a voice whispers.

I open my eyes. I'm in bed—not my bed. The room is dark, smells musty and damp. It's a smell both familiar and unfamiliar—dust and damp, old books, old wood. The smell of an old house. It doesn't induce fear, it ignites a nostalgia deep in my gut. Max is sitting next to me, his head in his hands.

"I never wanted this," he says. "It was all going to come out and Lena said..." He shakes his head. "She thinks this is one of our games, like when we'd manipulate our parents into undoing a punishment, or break up some couple so she could go out with the boy."

My eyes adjust to the darkness and I see where they've put me—in one of the bedrooms at Dean House. My box of sleeping pills stands next to the bed, a glass of water beside it and there's a bitter taste in my mouth. It's just me and Max in the room. Where's Lena? And Jack and Sean?

I blink, trying to think, trying to unscramble what's going on. Why are we here? Why has Max brought me here?

"Dad," I whisper. "What did you do to him? Where is he?"

"He's fine, don't worry. I left a note to tell him you're with me," Max says.

For a moment, I'm reassured by the soothing tone in his voice. It reminds me of the Max I fell in love with when I was fourteen, who always used to notice me and take the time to talk to me. I thought we had something so special, right up until the wedding. I thought we were destined to be together, the great happy-ever-after. Didn't I tell Greg all about it? Didn't I make him laugh, planning to use his garden for our wedding one day? Didn't he smile and pat my hand and tell me I could grow my own wedding bouquet? Silly, fanciful dreams that bloomed and grew right alongside the roses. I stopped watering those dreams after the wedding, after Bella died. I let them die too.

How silly. Bella was telling me all along. *Wake up*, she kept saying, but I didn't want to. I still don't want to, not if this is what I'm waking up to.

"Why am I here?"

Max sighs. "It could have all been fine. Even after Jack and Sean sold the house and the land surrounding it and they found the body. There was no evidence, no proof any of us were involved. You didn't even remember what you'd done. We worked so hard sowing the seeds about Greg and those murdered girls, to widen the circle of people who could have killed him. You kept muttering about remembering things, but you were easy to distract—the shoes, the texts. But it meant you were behaving so oddly, they couldn't help but look at you with suspicion. Even then, though, there was no evidence against you. We all would have been fine. Then, before they dug up the body, Sean let slip, oh so casually, that you had the camera. He had no idea how freaked out me and Lena were."

Bella's camera, hidden in Dean House the whole time.

"I looked for it at your dad's house and at your flat. I looked everywhere. I thought...if I found it before you developed the film, I could stop all this."

I remember the things out of place in my flat after Max stayed. I remember the awkward sex and it stings as I realize it was more than a mistake, it was—what? Distraction? A way to get into my home, nothing more. Oh, how very silly I was.

"It was you, wasn't it? On the camera?"

"We were all there. With you."

No. Not right. I wasn't there. I wasn't.

"Bella went nuts as soon as Greg appeared. Lena was holding her back. She went berserk, she was screaming at him. Greg launched himself at her and I thought he was going to hit her..."

I hold my breath as he pauses. The chair next to me creaks. Max is white-faced.

"And then you jumped in front of her and you had your gardening clippers," he says. "I know you didn't mean to kill him, I know it was an accident."

"No..."

"Bella made you go home. She made me and Lena leave. Do you really not remember any of this?" He shakes his head. "The next day I didn't sleep. I wanted to tell the police but Bella begged us not to. She said she'd get rid of the film, said she'd sort it. She made us swear we'd all protect you. I waited for the police to come. But they didn't. I knew you'd gotten away with it. I just wanted it to go away and it did. Bella died and no one even looked for Greg."

"But he contacted Jack—after the wedding."

"That was Lena. She kept his phone. Sent a few texts to Jack to stop anyone from looking or reporting him missing. It was easy— Jack was already worried his dad had something to do with the murders. He thought he'd run off to avoid getting caught and he wasn't going to drop his own dad in it by reporting him missing right away, was he? So, quite unwittingly, Jack helped us cover it up. He pretended he'd had more calls and texts than we actually sent."

"And then Jack and Sean sold the house..."

"Even when they found the bones, there was nothing to connect us to it. But you...your behavior. It was only a matter of time."

"We tried so hard to protect you," he says. "We never knew if your memory loss was real or faked. But when you came back, saying you were starting to remember..." He shakes his head.

"But why am I here? Why haven't you just told the police all this? Or why not carry on lying? Because I don't remember. I swear to you I don't remember."

"Because of that fucking camera," Max bursts out. "All we had to do was keep quiet, but I knew Bella was taking photos, gathering her evidence. I asked her at the wedding if she'd gotten rid of the film and she said not yet. She said she was going to, but then she died. We didn't know what she'd captured on that damned film, if it was enough to implicate us. We didn't do anything but we were there. I thought you had it. I knew you hadn't seen the photos, but I thought you had the camera and it was only a matter of time before you tried developing the film. You were so desperate to remember what happened to your sister."

"Max...Max, please...I don't. I can't have. I would never... Please. Think what it'll do to my dad, he's just lost Julia."

"Max?" It's Lena's voice, raised sharply in warning. She steps into the room, followed by Jack and Sean.

"What the hell is going on?" Jack says. "Why is she here?"

"What's wrong with her?" I hear Sean say as I struggle to wake up fully.

Someone pulls me up to a sitting position.

"She took too many of her bloody sleeping pills," Lena says. "She told Max she wanted to tell us all the truth but by the time we got here, she was barely conscious."

"She said she wanted to confess," Max says.

"She said it was her," Lena says. "Her that killed Greg. Max heard her say it, didn't you, Max?"

No—this isn't right.

"What the hell are you talking about?" Sean says.

"She called us, I told you," Lena says. "But she passed out from taking too many bloody sleeping pills." She turns to me. "I've called the police, Tess—told them what you told me. I'm sorry, but they have to know the truth."

"No—no, it's not the truth. Max—tell them." I've gone cold, ice through and through.

Max is crying. "I can't," he says.

"Your dad raped her," Lena says to Jack and Sean. "It was him the whole time—Nic Wallace, the other girl. Then he took Tess. Three days before the wedding. She came here to help him in the garden. You know she'd been doing that for months? He was grooming her. I'm sorry, but he attacked her and she...it was self-defense, but she stabbed him with something and he died. Bella helped her bury him and cover it up."

"How do you know all this?" Sean says quietly, stepping up and looking from me to Lena.

"She told Max. The guilt got too much and she confessed to him. We've been trying to convince her to go to the police by herself, trying to convince her it would be better for her."

"I knew it," Jack says, and he comes over and hauls me forward by my hair. "I fucking knew it."

I scream, reaching up to try to get his hands out of my hair.

"Jack, stop. This is too far...too much," Max says, pulling on his arm. But I see hesitation on his face. He's not trying that hard to pull Jack away. He's trying to convince himself that he's not part of this. But it was him who brought me here.

Jack shakes Max's hand off. "Why don't you run on home, Maxie-boy? Pretend you weren't even here." He turns back to me, squeezing my jaw with one hand. "Everything is your fault. All down to you and your family fucking up my life. You killed him. You killed my father, you and your bitch sister. And all these years, you've *known*."

"Get off her, Jack."

Sean.

He doesn't shout, but Jack freezes anyway, hand still squeezing my jaw, so hard that tears come to my eyes.

"Fuck off, Sean," he says, voice breathless. "This little bitch murdered our father."

"Do you believe that? Really?"

The hand relaxes slightly, the clenching pain becomes a deep ache, but he doesn't let go.

"Three days before the wedding, we were all here. How was she acting? How did she behave? Like she'd been raped and then killed someone? Who was acting strangely, Jack? Think about it. Who was freaking out and drinking and huddled in a little group every time we turned round? Was it her? Was it?"

Jack lets go of me and shoves me away, standing upright and

turning to Max and Lena, who are hovering, caught between Jack
and Sean in the doorway.

Sean looks at me. "You kissed me at the wedding," he says.
"We talked. About my mum and dad, about your sister. Do you
remember?"

Some. I remember some. I feel a surge of giddy relief. Sean
doesn't believe it's me and that belief helps clear my head. Oh
God—of course it wasn't me. It's not the memory of the days
before the wedding that are lost, is it? There are holes, yes, but
who remembers everything about a time ten years ago? Christ,
I'd remember—if not the deed, then my emotions. I remember
enough. I shake my head again. Everything's so muddled. I didn't
take those pills, Max must have put them in my tea.

"It wasn't me," I say. As I say it out loud, I realize—if it wasn't
me, then...

Sean is pleading with his brother. "Jack, come on," he says.
"Remember what you were like after the accident when Ellie died.
Do you think I didn't know? Did you think I wouldn't figure it out
from your behavior, what it did to you?"

He steps away from the doorway, closer to his brother, and
I see Lena tugging on Max's arm, pulling him out of the room.
I lurch toward them—if it wasn't me, then it had to have been
them.

"You were never the same," Sean is saying in a softer voice.
"Mum told me, but I already knew. She told me you were driving
the day Ellie died."

"She was fucking *lying*," Jack roars, launching himself at his
brother.

They both go down in a crash as I stagger toward the door,
stumbling, falling, continuing at a crawl.

"Run, Tess," Sean calls. "*Run*."

I half fall down the stairs and I'm scrabbling for the front door
when I hear the sirens. I run out as the first uniformed officer
reaches the house. Max's car is gone.

"They're upstairs," I shout. "Stop them. Stop them—they're

killing each other." My legs give way and I collapse on the gravel. I lay my face against the hard, sharp stones and I cry.

Detective Levinson gets out of another car. He comes over and helps me up, his grip gentle, but he doesn't let me go when I'm standing.

"Tess Cooper—I'm arresting you for the murder of Greg Lewis..." As he talks and puts me in handcuffs, I keep muttering the same thing over and over again.

It wasn't me.

It wasn't me.

Black spots float before my eyes and Bella is with me, whispering for me to *wake up*, but I am. I'm finally awake but no one sees. No one will listen.

CHAPTER 40

They take me to the hospital even though I insist I'm fine. But even as I say it, I'm shaking, unable to stand without help. I can hear the slur in my words and in the end I stop protesting as they help me into the ambulance, still handcuffed, a uniformed officer in the ambulance with me.

Dad arrives before the police, but the uniformed officer standing outside my door won't let him in. I hear him arguing and it makes me cry because it's the same hospital they brought me to after Bella died.

Detective Levinson comes in, looking grave.

"It wasn't me," I say. "I swear—whatever Max and Lena have been saying—it wasn't me. It must have been them." I stop, swallow. "Or Bella."

This time, I tell him everything. About the secret garden, about Bella and Greg and me. About the lies I told that set her off.

My voice is hoarse by the end of it and when Detective Levinson starts going over the same questions again, I lay my head on the pillow and cry. Dad comes in with a doctor and they all start arguing.

"You have Sean and Jack at the station," Dad shouts. "And Tess is going nowhere. Let her recover."

Detective Levinson glances at me and whatever he sees makes him relent. "Okay, I'll leave. But I'll be back in the morning."

Dad sits in the chair next to the bed after Detective Levinson leaves. He holds my hand and there are tears in his eyes.

"Have they found Max and Lena yet?" I whisper.

Dad shakes his head. "They will."

"I didn't do it, Dad—I swear to you. It was Max and..." I pause and swallow. I don't want to tell him the rest, but I have to. "It has to have been them. And Bella. She was with them. I'm sorry, I'm so, so sorry."

Dad closes his eyes. It hurts so much having to tell him this, but it's been hidden for too long.

"I've told them—when they find Max and Lena, they have to question them about Bella as well. About what happened out in the woods. I think...I think she was going to go to the police and they stopped her and that's how she..."

My voice trails off. How she died, that's what I was going to say. I think Max and Lena killed Bella as well. That's why Bella came back to me. This is the truth she wanted me to uncover. My stomach turns over in slow, lazy waves and there's a bitter taste in my throat. Bella is still here, hidden in the shadows in the corner of the room. I don't understand...I thought she'd disappear. Now that I've found out the truth, I thought she'd disappear.

"But they still think it's me," I say, hot tears spilling. "They've arrested me. Oh God, oh God, they don't believe me. What if they don't find Max and Lena? What if they keep insisting it's me even if they do?"

"Don't talk anymore," Dad says. "Try to rest. The doctor said you're suffering from severe exhaustion. You need to rest before you answer any more questions; you have to make sure everything is clear in your mind."

It doesn't sound like he believes me, and the bitter bile in my throat surges higher.

"I should have...when Steve Wallace told me about Nicole and her secret boyfriend, I suspected Greg even then. Some of the things Julia told me about him. But I had no proof. I should have told the police then, but I didn't want to hurt Julia. They told me what that bastard did to you. I never knew. I swear I never knew or I'd have...If you did do it, I'm glad. I'm glad." He says it so fiercely I have to look away. But when I look away, I see Bella, her gaze as fierce as his.

Dad glances at the closed door and leans forward, dropping his voice to a whisper. "All this time, I've been so worried, Tess. I never told. Never told anyone."

"Told anyone what?" I say, stomach turning over faster.

"About what you said in the hospital. After they found you and Bella in the woods. I knew it wasn't true. Couldn't be true. If what you're telling me about Max and Lena is what happened...It's awful but I'm so relieved." He drops his head and I feel his tears drip onto my hand.

The waves in my stomach have frozen to ice.

I close my eyes after he leaves but I can't sleep. The night passes with every second lasting an hour in my quiet hospital room, my brain replaying everything that's happened. I hear footsteps and open my eyes to find Detective Levinson standing next to my bed.

"We've found Max and Helena Rees," he says.

I sit up. I look at the door and realize I can't see the shadow of my police guard outside.

"Helena is still insisting it was you, but Max has said enough to corroborate your story." He pauses. "After a lot of questioning."

Why? After all their elaborate plans, why did Max confess?

"We looked again at the evidence. They couldn't explain why they left Dean House last night. Your fingerprints weren't on Greg Lewis's phone. But Max Rees's were. There were calls and texts from his phone that corroborate your story. He broke down." He pauses and sighs. "I'm sorry, Tess, but he's saying it was Bella. That all he and his sister did was help cover it up. That his sister sent the texts after Mr. Lewis's death to help Bella. He was able to quote the messages."

"Then..."

"You're free to go once the doctor has been in. But we still need you to come in and answer some more questions. As a witness, not a suspect. Your father is waiting outside."

"And Bella? Did they say what happened to Bella?"

He shakes his head. "Both of them deny any involvement in your sister's death. There's still no evidence to suggest that Bella's death was anything but an accident."

"But..." But what? Do I tell him that Bella is still here, still insisting it wasn't an accident?

"What about the murdered girls? Was it Greg Lewis?" I say this as the detective turns to leave.

"It's something we're investigating." He glances back at me. "We're gathering evidence that...if it was him, then by killing him, your sister and her friends may well have saved you. If you'd continued visiting him..."

I go cold. It could have been my body out there in the woods, not Greg's.

I sink my head back against the pillow after he leaves. That's it, then. All the ghosts laid to rest. I look to the corner of the room where Bella still hovers.

All except one.

We sit around the table, Dad, Sean, and me. I've spent all day at the police station, answering questions, telling them again everything about Greg, Max, Bella, and Lena. I told them everything Max told me, all the strange happenings that I put down to paranoia that I now think were down to Lena. Sean, after he'd been treated for cuts and bruises, sat in a room down the hall, answering the same questions. Jack's gone home to his wife and son. Whether they'll let him back, I don't know.

I didn't tell them about Bella coming back.

And I didn't mention what Dad said at the hospital—it makes no sense. His words went over and over in my head all night in the hospital, but I don't remember saying anything to him after Bella died.

I'm numb now. I have no more words. We sit in silence at the table, staring into mugs of cold tea. I think I'm going to sleep tonight and I hope there'll be no more bad dreams. I guess at some point soon, Sean is going to go home, but he hasn't mentioned it and Dad hasn't asked him to go. I don't know how long we've been sitting there before I notice Bella is sitting in the fourth chair.

My eyes fill with tears and I blink them away. I think she's here to say goodbye. I think when I sleep she'll disappear for good. I found out the truth like she wanted. I found out the truth and now we can both sleep. She leans forward and looks at me, tears in her own eyes.

Remember, Tess.

I shake my head. I still don't remember that night. But I found out what happened, I don't need to remember it—Max confessed.

Remember.

I scrape my chair back. "I'm going to bed."

Dad glances up, eyes blinking back into focus. "Sleep well, Tess."

Sean follows me out of the room. "I'm sorry for what my dad did to you," he says in a low voice.

I clench my hands into fists. "Sean—stop."

The look on his face is tortured. "I suspected, didn't I? All that time, I wondered and so did Jack. Could we have saved those girls if we'd said something? Could we have saved you?" He pauses. "We might even have been able to save him. That's what's eating Jack up—if we'd gone to the police, Dad might have ended up in prison but he'd be alive."

"Stop," I say again.

Sean looks at me, his eyes gleaming with unshed tears.

"He didn't...he didn't do anything to me. I don't know if he killed those other girls, but he didn't do anything to me."

"But..."

I open my mouth to tell him I lied, but the words won't come out. "Max and Lena made it up. Bella was mistaken, she saw something she misinterpreted and Max and Lena used it to try and make people believe I did it."

I'm still lying. Is that why Bella hasn't disappeared?

*   *   *

I do sleep. Not right away, but I do sleep.

When I open my eyes, I'm walking through the lane with Bella. It's night and she's talking, mid-conversation.

"You never would listen when I told you," she's saying.

"Am I awake or is this a dream?" I say.

"What do you think?"

I look down. I'm wearing the jersey pajama trousers and T-shirt I went to bed in, I'm barefoot like her. I can feel the sharp stones under my feet and the cold breeze on my arms. I don't know. I don't know if I'm awake. I don't know if this is real.

"Where are we going?" I ask.

"You know where we're going. You've always known where we were going."

Time drifts and we keep walking in silence, broken every now and then by Bella speaking. "I tried to tell you, tried to explain."

"What?"

"What happened. Why we did it. Why you..."

"Are you talking about Greg? I know what you all did. I know..."

She shakes her head. "Not Greg."

"Then..."

"You need to remember, Tess," she says. She stops walking and I see we're outside Dean House and I'm shaking my head, because I don't *want* to. I don't *have* to.

"Yes, you do," she says with a smile and then we're inside, we're upstairs on the landing and I can see the woods out of the window, I can see the trees looming up and the moon is shining through the window and lighting the stairs and there's shouting and there's a...there's a...

Oh.

Once upon a time, two girls went into the woods...

"I remember," I whisper, and Bella steps back, fading a little.

"I remember what I did."

CHAPTER 41

Once upon a time, two girls went into the woods and only one came out...

That's how the fairy tale starts but I couldn't remember how it ended or what happened to the two little girls in the woods. It's been so long since my mum read it to us. It always scared me, even then, so Mum started skipping it, reading the happier stories instead.

I remember the little girls—they were silly, sneaking out of their safe, warm homes to run into the woods. And I remember there was some sort of monster, some macabre lesson for the two naughty girls who sneaked out at night.

Am I remembering right, though?

"I tried to tell you before that night," Bella says.

"I didn't want to hear it."

"You were scared. I get that."

"You were screaming at me, yelling. We'd both drunk too much."

The world slips and we're back there, in the woods, the night of the wedding. Bella is in her tank top and jeans, barefoot. Still clean, still whole. She's crying and so am I.

"You kept sneaking off, Tess, and I knew you were still seeing him. I had to stop it. Stop him before he raped you again."

"He never did anything to me."

"That's not what you told me—you told me he was the monster. You told me what he did to you and I—"

"I lied."

"What?"

"I lied. I fucking *lied*. He never touched me, never even looked at me after you came along."

She recoils and shakes her head. "You lied? What...why would you lie about that? No, you're in denial. I get that, what he did to you..."

"I lied. He never touched me." I scream it at her, the words ringing out over the approaching storm. "It was me—I kissed him and he pushed me away. And he was kind but he never touched me."

"You fucking *lied*?"

"Yes—I lied and then the words were out there and I didn't know how to take them back."

"Oh God, Tess, what have you done?"

I can't answer her. The enormity of my lie increases the distance between us. She was so loving and fierce and protective after I told that lie. She was my Bella again.

All the color has gone from her face. "Oh God, Tess...you don't know what you've done. You told me he was the monster. You told me and I thought if he did that to you, he must have killed Nic."

No. *No.*

"That time he tried to kiss me, Tess, I got away, but what if I hadn't?" She's crying harder. "I couldn't get clean after, I couldn't scrub his hands off me. Then you told me he raped you and...it's why I can't sleep, because in my dreams he rapes and kills both of us over and over again."

I put my hands over my ears and I can hear a roar, a monster broken loose. *No.* He was my friend. He would never, never— look how embarrassed he was after I tried to kiss him. If he was what Bella is saying he was, he wouldn't have pushed me away, would he? But...I was a *good girl*, he said. Not like the others. I got so angry when Bella said he tried to kiss her, like I was jealous of him perving on my sister. I wouldn't, I won't let it be true, because that stupid flash of jealousy makes me sick, makes me as bad as him for even for one second wanting him to have attacked me not her because why is it always her, center of attention, always Bella, never me.

So I lied, made up that awful, horrible story and now Bella has...

No.

It starts to rain, heavy drops that get faster and faster and soak us in seconds.

"I went to confront him. I was going to make him confess."

No. I scream it out loud. "No—stop it, *stop it.* You're lying."

"I'm not fucking lying," she screams back. "*You're* the liar. You told me he raped you. I thought he was the killer and he was going to kill you too. I had to stop him. I had to—"

Lightning hits a tree and we both scream and jump away, too close to the edge of the embankment. The rain is a deluge, hitting us hard enough to hurt.

"What did you do?" I shout over the roaring in my ears, the howling wind, the crash of thunder.

"We killed him."

The roaring stills for a moment and there's silence. Then it's back in a rush, worse, bigger. Terrible.

"We killed him and I'm scared, Tess. We have to tell the police. Tell them what you told me, tell them what he did to me and..."

"No!" I scream again, voice breaking on the word, and I push her away. "I'm not telling the police *anything.* It was your fault, you—flirting with Max, flirting with everyone. Leaving me behind. You knew how much I liked Max but you wouldn't stop flirting with him so he wouldn't look anywhere but at you. And then...Greg was *mine.* My friend and you stole him as well. It's your bloody fault I lied."

"You stupid girl," she yells back, shoving me hard. I stagger back and stumble over a rock. "You made up that monstrous lie because you were *jealous*? You stupid little *child.*" She shoves me harder, her hands almost punching my chest.

"Stop it," I shout, and I shove her back, as hard as I can, all my anger behind that *shove.*

I push her again and she lets me and I'm mad and I want her to fight back and again I come at her and I *push*—

Oh God, wake up wake up wake up

I remember. I remember how many times she tried to tell me. How often she tried to warn me without telling me what he'd done to her.

"There's something wrong with him," she'd say, and I'd shake my head.

"He's just a lonely man."

"A lonely man who befriended young girls? Haven't you ever wondered why? Wondered why Julia really left him?"

"I was lost. He found me in his garden one day. He didn't call the police. He talked to me. And he listened."

"He was grooming you."

I laughed. "Grooming me? Is that what you think?"

"It's what I believe. All those stories about Nic and the other murdered girl. All the speculation about the person they believed responsible. The profiles... they all fit."

"There are probably hundreds—thousands—of men living alone, living reclusively in the area. Why him?"

"Because none of those other men have stolen my sister."

I close my eyes and the door opens again, like it did back then. He steps into view, out of the shadows, and my mind turns handsome, charismatic Greg Lewis into a monster, stretching him taller, painting malevolence onto his face. He's right there, his hands around Nicole Wallace's neck, raping and killing her. Nicole's face turns into mine, into Bella's...

That's the moment I'm trying to push away, that awful, awful truth.

I try to catch her. The moment I see her slip, arms thrown out to try to keep her balance, I reach out and try to catch her. I almost catch her hand, I feel my fingertips touch hers, but she's gone, tumbling down in a landslide of mud and rock. I see her fall; I see her head smash on the rock. I see it and I know she's dead. Her eyes are open and there's all this blood. Mud and blood and Bella. Lying there with her eyes open and . . .

I stumble down after her, slipping and sliding, grabbing roots and jutting rocks to try to slow my descent, but the mud under my feet is a river and I'm going faster and faster. Falling, no longer climbing. I'm getting closer and I can see she's dead and as my foot hits a rock and I go somersaulting, I'm thinking no, no, no, not real. Wake up, Tess. *Wake up.*

I open my eyes and I'm alone.

I remember.

We killed him.

Bella's words in the woods. Her confession. The roar of the wind and rain sweeping through the trees. Bella's voice as I stood there shaking, the roar of the wind sweeping through me, the roar and the rage. It swept through me and I pushed her, all the strength of the storm in my arms as I shoved . . .

As the whole awful memory stands before me, the words of the fairy tale come back. The final lines I've been hiding from for ten years: *As the girl stood there alone, she realized she was the monster and not a little girl at all . . .*

I thought Lena was the monster. And Max. And Greg Lewis. I thought they were the monsters Bella sent me to find.

But the monster is me. It's always been me.

Dad is still downstairs, sitting in the dark kitchen, staring at nothing. I sit opposite him and take his hands.

"I remember," I whisper.

He squeezes my hands. "Tess . . . don't."

"It was me, Dad. I did it. I was angry—we were arguing and I . . . pushed her and she fell. It was me. I killed Bella."

It's what I said to Dad at the hospital after Bella died. Not so coherent, confused enough that he could make himself dismiss it as nonsense muttered by a daughter with a head injury, a daughter drifting on morphine.

I did it but I never meant to...

Those words could have meant anything, couldn't they? Muttered by sixteen-year-old me, lying in a hospital bed. It was nothing, that's what Dad told himself because he couldn't stand to think anything else.

"I'll have to tell the police," I say, tears pouring hot down my cheeks.

"No," Dad says softly.

"Dad—I have to. Didn't you hear me? It was *me*. I..."

"It was an accident. An accident. Just like they said it was. You didn't mean to do it, did you?"

I shake my head.

"Tess...God, Tess." Dad's crying as well and I can't bear it. Can't bear what I've done to him. "I can't lose you as well. I can't. You're all I have left. Please don't leave me on my own. Please."

I lay my head down and cry, painful sobs pulled from my chest, crying so hard it hurts. Dad cradles my head in his hands and strokes my hair and says it over and over. *Please. Please don't. Don't leave me on my own.*

I don't know what to do.

I close my eyes and Bella is there, next to Dad, her eyes bright with tears.

"I'm sorry. I'm so sorry."

"I know. It's okay, Tess," she says. "You needed to remember but you can sleep now."

Forgive me, my mind whispers.

Always, baby sis. Bella's voice is fainter now. *Now sleep...*

I don't know what to do. I have to tell the police, don't I? But Dad is still crying and saying please don't, please don't leave me...

Stay. Bella's voice again. Echoed by Julia's, asking me to look after him. *Stay. Live your new life and stay. Let it remain an accident.*

"I can't." I say it out loud. "I'll never sleep again if I hold this secret inside."

Oh, Tess. Oh, baby sis...

I get Detective Levinson's card out of my pocket, pick up my phone. I leave a short message before putting the phone down and turning to Dad.

"I'm sorry."

For a second it feels like Bella's squeezing my hand and then she's gone.

I drift...

...the woods and the house that always wait for me when I close my eyes fade...

...and I sleep.

From the *Western Vale News*, August 2020:

TRAGIC TALE OF ARABELLA COOPER
REACHES ITS SAD CONCLUSION

When eighteen-year-old Arabella Cooper was found dead in the woods surrounding West Dean in 2008, her death was ruled an accident. But ten years later, in a series of shocking discoveries, the truth was uncovered. Greg Lewis, posthumously proved to be the "Babes in the Woods" murderer of Annie Weston and Nicole Wallace, was found to have been killed himself, by Arabella Cooper, aided by Helena and Max Rees, who were convicted of perverting the course of justice and withholding evidence of a crime. Lewis is also believed to have murdered missing teenager Rachel Wells, whose body has never been found. The final twist in the Lewis/Cooper case was when Tess Cooper came forward and confessed to pushing her sister during an argument, which resulted in her falling to her death.

This tragic tale reached its strange conclusion this week when Tess Cooper was quietly released from prison and was met by Sean Lewis, youngest son of Greg Lewis. It is believed she joined her father, who left West Dean soon after his daughter was arrested.

ACKNOWLEDGMENTS

Once again, I'm hugely grateful to so many people for all the help and support with this book.

Special thanks to Lucy Dauman and Rosanna Forte, my editors at Sphere, and to Millicent Bennett at Grand Central for your wonderful support. I also want to acknowledge the sheer brilliance of all of the team at Sphere and Little, Brown, especially Thalia, Gemma, and Stephanie.

Of course, none of this would have happened if it weren't for my super-agent Juliet Mushens. I will be forever grateful for everything the team at Caskie Mushens has done.

Thanks to former DCI Stuart Gibbon of GIB Consultancy for the advice on police procedure—his book, *The Crime Writer's Casebook*, was also invaluable. Thanks once again to Savage and Gray Design Ltd for the wonderful website and book trailers.

All the thanks, as always, to all my writing friends, especially the Romaniacs and the Cowbridge Cursors.

And, of course, to all my family and friends for their continued and fantastic support, in particular Tim, Jess, and Georgie—my very special bunch of Savages.

ABOUT THE AUTHOR

Vanessa Savage is a graphic designer and illustrator. She has twice been awarded a Writers' Bursary by Literature Wales, most recently for *The Woman in the Dark*. She won the Myriad Editions First Crimes competition in 2016 and her work has been highly commended in the Yeovil International Fiction Prize, shortlisted for the Harry Bowling Prize, and the Caledonia Novel Award. She was longlisted for the Bath Novel Award.

Vanessa lives by the sea in South Wales with her husband and two daughters.